THE EDGE OF THE FALL

The
EDGE *of*
the FALL

KATE WILLIAMS

PEGASUS BOOKS

NEW YORK LONDON

THE EDGE OF THE FALL

Pegasus Books Ltd
80 Broad Street, 5th Floor
New York, NY 10004

Copyright © by Kate Williams

First Pegasus Books hardcover edition June 2016

ISBN: 978-1-68177-138-0

10 9 8 7 6 5 4 3 2 1

Printed in the United States of America
Distributed by W. W. Norton & Company, Inc.

The de Witt Family and their Circle

Rudolf de Witt – father of the de Witt family and owner of Stoneythorpe

Verena de Witt – Rudolf's wife, daughter of the late Lord and Lady Deerhurst

Arthur de Witt – their oldest child, returned from Paris

Michael de Witt *(deceased)* – youngest son of the de Witts'

Emmeline de Witt – eldest daughter of Rudolph and Verena, married to Samuel Janus

Celia de Witt – the de Witt's youngest daughter

Samuel Janus – Emmeline's husband, former summer tutor to Celia

Tom Cotton – former assistant groom to the de Witts, soldier during the Great War

Mrs Cotton – his mother, a former servant of the family

Mary and Missy Cotton – Tom's sisters

Jonathan Corrigan – Michael's university friend, from New York

Stanley Smithson – footman

John Thompson – footman

Jennie Christmas – parlourmaid

Rufus Sparks – university friend of Mr Janus

Jemima Webb – university friend of Mr Janus and political campaigner

Lady Deerhurst – sister to Verena, mother to Matthew and Louisa

Matthew Deerhurst – Verena's nephew and Celia's cousin, in India

Louisa Deerhurst – Verena's niece and Celia's cousin

Heinrich de Witt – Rudolf's cousin

Lotte de Witt – Heinrich's wife

Johann and Hilde de Witt – children of Heinrich and Lotte de Witt

'It really is beautiful,' she said, raising her voice over the wind.

They were walking along the cliffs, not too far from their guest house in Margate, and they had the place almost to themselves, a stretch of surprising green, then hundreds of daisies tipping right to the edge. The air was exhilarating, whipping her hair out from its style, throwing her skirt against her legs. 'I do love it here.' She squeezed his arm. 'How clever of you to find it.' It was astonishing, really, to remember how during the war they'd thought places like the cliffs dangerous. The sea in front of them stretched out for miles, so bright it hurt her eyes.

She linked her arm in through his, leant her head on his shoulder, reaching a little since he was so much taller than her. She felt him tense, nestled her head closer. Things were so difficult for him. He'd suffered greatly before he'd met her. His family had been cruel. Yet she knew that, with patience and her generosity, he'd come through. In a sense it was actually rather easy, there was so much advice in magazines for women like her on how to help damaged men, even though the advice was about war and Arthur had been in Paris the whole time. You listened with quiet, sympathetic understanding and if he spoke, you were to repeat back precisely the same words, reflect, empathise, love. You didn't have to have been at the Somme to suffer, she wanted to say to him. She felt the warmth of his arm on hers, wished she could fold herself into the whole of him. The families behind them with their ice cream, the old people arm in arm, all seemed miles away.

They walked together, more slowly now because her head was on his shoulder. The sky was the colour of a paint she'd once had as a child, the blue of a baby's eyes. She heard the word in her mind. *Baby*. She hugged the idea tight to herself, like a present. She would think about that later; right now her every thought was about *him*, so that even though they weren't speaking, he would be able to sense it, feel her affection, her devoted kindness. His shoulder was softening.

'You can't see anything but sea for miles,' she said. After all that time of hiding away, of having to pretend not to walk together, of stowing themselves in the dark corners of restaurants, those nights that she spent alone, sitting at her window, dressed in the gowns she'd bought, wondering whether he might come. Now they were together, walking openly. She couldn't believe, really, how generous he'd been to her over the past few days.

Yesterday, at a flower stall, right in the centre of town, he'd suddenly turned to her and said, 'Which ones would you like?' She had been confused, blushed – it was so unfamiliar – pointed at a few pink sweet peas. He'd smiled, demanded four bunches of them, then gardenias, daisies, dahlias and some beautiful flowers that were dozens of pale pink ruffles with darker pink at the edges. 'Any amount,' he said. 'Whatever you'd like. Have whatever you want, my love. My dear.' By the end of her choosing – for every time she stopped, he encouraged her to go on, take more – they had a bunch of flowers almost bigger than her torso.

The woman had arranged them, gathering up the stems, holding them together as she tied the whole thing up with skein, then a pink ribbon she chose. He handed over dozens of notes (the flowers must have been terribly costly, sent from other countries, surely), then popped the flowers in her hands. 'For you, my darling,' he said. A small crowd had gathered by then and at that one of them began applauding. Another man whooped. She heard two women sigh. 'Lucky girl,' one said. And she was. She was a *lucky* girl. For the rest of that day, her face had been as pink as the flowers. The colour of happiness; pleasure. That night, in the hotel restaurant, he wouldn't let the waiter pull out her chair. 'That's my job,' he said. 'I must look after my wife.'

Wife! she thought. The word he never used, the word he said they never should use. 'Our relationship isn't to be defined by words,' he'd said. 'It is too special.' *Never mention me.* Keep us free of words, for words *sully*, make us of the world, and we are *free.*

'Those flowers were so lovely,' she said to him. 'No one's ever done something like that for me. Thank you.'

He let her squeeze his arm. That's how she knew he was agreeing with her, that inside his head he was saying: *I love you. I will always love you.*

'I'm so fortunate to have you.' The women in her head talked to her. *Lucky girl!*

'It was nothing,' he said, his voice quick and low. She smiled, wanted to hold him. He was like a little boy, embarrassed by the great gift he had given.

'What would you like to do tonight, Arthur?' She almost said the word *husband*, then shied away. 'Shall we go to the hotel restaurant once more?'

He shrugged. 'Perhaps.' Then he manoeuvred her with her arm, towards the sea. 'You're right,' he said. 'It *is* beautiful. Why don't we go closer?'

'Closer?'

'To the sea. It's very handsome, as you say. You can see how the romantics thought this kind of place was the most beautiful.'

'I wouldn't want to go too close.' His passion for touching close to the edge of things.

He patted her arm. 'Dear girl! Don't worry yourself. I'm here to look after you.'

She held on to his arm. 'Of course you are. You're always here for me.'

He steered her closer. The grass was crisp, untouched, she thought. 'Look at it from here,' he said, a half foot or so from the edge. 'Don't you feel free, looking out like this?'

She clutched his arm. Directly below them the sea wasn't calm at all but slashing at the cliffs. The spray surged up towards them. The rocks were uneven, jagged. *Don't look.* She closed her eyes, but all she could see were fragments of stone tumbling down into the water. Once upon a time, the cliffs must have been miles further out to sea, but they had receded, collapsed into nothing and taken everything down with them. She held tight to him, forced herself to open her eyes.

'Such wild beauty,' he said.

'Oh yes.' She didn't want him to see that she was afraid. She'd told him she'd never liked being high up, right from being a little girl. He must have forgotten. She felt she was swaying a little. Think of something else, she told herself. Her great, magnificent bunch of flowers, spread out between three vases (as there was no single one big enough) in their bedroom. She fixed her mind on their delicate pinks, tried to hold her body still. She turned back, saw a man and a woman, arm in arm, sauntering towards them. They reminded her: this was all normal. A perfectly nice summer's day. This was what couples *did*. Then she looked down again and her stomach lurched.

He shuffled closer to the edge – *only an inch from the side*! She held back, the space between their arms greater. 'I love the sea air in my face,' he said. 'Can you feel the spray?'

'Oh yes!'

'Are you quite sure?'

'Oh yes, my dear.'

He brought up a finger, touched her cheek. 'It's quite dry. Let me help you step forward.'

'Oh, I'm fine here.' She wanted to pull him back to her.

He turned to face her, making her spin, forcing her to push her feet hard into the grass to stay still. 'Don't tell me you're *afraid*. I won't believe it.'

'I'm never afraid with you!'

'Well, let me hold you then. Come along. I will hold you, keeping your waist, and you can move forward.'

She shook her head. The couple she'd seen were coming closer. The woman wore a stylish hat. The man looked familiar somehow. She couldn't quite see his face, but there was something about his outline, his walk.

'Come now.' His eyes were darkening. 'Don't be foolish.'

She looked at him. She had to do as he said, she could see. She had to move the way he wanted to, prove it to him. He wanted to play the game again, like that time before. She had to let him. *It won't be long*, she told herself. *You just have to stand where he wants you to, let him hold you. In a minute, maybe less, it will be over.* All those things she did with her minutes, let them drift by as she gazed out of the window, tried and failed to read or embroider. This minute here would be nothing more than that. She had to trust him. She did trust him. He was her husband. She loved him!

'Are you coming?'

'Yes!' She gathered together all her strength, all her love, all her need for him, and stepped forward. In a moment, he was behind her, holding her tight at the waist. She was right on the edge. The water was churning below her, dizzying, sickly. *Stop.* She tried to stare out at the wide expanse of blue that had pleased her so much, could not.

'See, my dear!' he said, content now. 'You can admire the beauty of nature from here. Nothing brings you closer, does it?'

She looked up and the other man was coming closer. Who *was* he? She felt sure she knew him.

'This is the way to see the grandeur of nature, its purity.' He was shouting now, voice into the wind.

She nodded weakly, trying to charge her mind, her every thought, into the soft, safe pressure of his hands on her waist. She closed her eyes again, thought of his fingers, their slightly dry flesh, the whorls on his thumbs, the delicate moons of his nails, the strength of his palms, holding her tight, safe.

But then, as she did so, the pressure of his palms began to change. It started to loosen, move away. She felt her body tremble. 'Darling,' she began, but the words themselves seemed to shake her, move her closer to the edge.

'See,' he said in her ear, his voice low. 'Regard the beauties of nature.'

'But—'

'The world is ours,' he said, as muffled as the sound of a shell held against her ear. 'We could hold it in our hands.'

She imagined, then, how it would be if she was falling, clutching at the air, begging. And – in a moment – she was. Falling. She cried out. The air caught the sound.

PART ONE

ONE

Stoneythorpe, May 1919

Celia

Stoneythorpe looked nothing like it used to. Walking in, the house wound around Celia, threw its dust into her face, everything in it a mockery – *we aren't the same!* She tried to see it as someone new might, not remembering the house full of people for a party, her mother presiding, immaculate in one of her pale blue gowns. She came into the hall, reached out her hand for the Chinese vase in the entrance. They'd packed it up before they'd turned the place into a hospital in the last years of the war, she'd bundled it in newspaper full of reports from the front and advertisements for false teeth. Jennie and Thompson had wrapped up vases, boxes, portraits, silver frames, stacking them into crates and then dragging them out to the garden, hauling them into the ground by the rose bushes, throwing soil over the top, promising themselves they wouldn't forget where they were.

When peace was declared, Celia thought they'd seize the vases out of the soil as quickly as they could. But they didn't, not for ages. They left them languishing there for nearly four months. *We never get round to it*, Verena said. *We don't really think of them.* It wasn't true, not for Celia anyway. She'd dreaded the beautiful things coming out, how they'd throw into sharp relief the broken house, its shabby walls, how everything was lost, how they'd let it fall into such disrepair even before her mother had turned it into a hospital – and when did the harried nurses or soldiers have time to care for a house? And yet, when she and the servants finally did open up the soil, tugging the crates, unpacking the layers of paper, pulling them off carefully – the vases, the boxes, the frames were not the same. She'd remembered them glittering, expensive – as a child she'd thought the vases the stuff of palaces. But the frames were tarnished, the boxes worn and the Chinese vase was not white but grey, tiny hairline cracks running down from the lip. Thompson had stared at everything, lifted the frames, turned the vase around. 'But they were so well packed up,' he said. 'I don't understand it.' It was as if the war had aged everything, dirtied it all, however much you hid things away.

Celia sat on the lowest step of the stair, the wood hard and cold on her legs. Her father Rudolf had longed for the house, said Elizabeth I had once visited. The de Witts would be Tudor highborns, Celia supposed he thought, not German meatmakers. And perhaps they were for a while, hosting great parties for the village, sitting in their pew in church, her sister Emmeline engaged to marry the local aristocrat, Sir Hugh Bradshaw. Celia looked back at them, almost laughing. *Didn't you know?* she wanted to cry. *It was all just make-believe, we were actors in some masque playing for Elizabeth, and then the war came and exposed the truth of what England felt: you are Germans and we hate you.* 'Little Celia,' Rudolf had said, when he was finally sent home from the internment camp, the place he'd never talk about save the fact that they hadn't even had their own mattresses. 'The war stole your childhood.'

But it hadn't, not really. She'd been fifteen when the war had broken out, adult enough for everything that came afterwards, all the things she did, the mistakes she made. She, the family, all of them, had kept going, looking ahead.

Now, when they'd got to the years they'd all been hoping for, she didn't want them. She didn't know what to do with peace. She didn't even want to be here any more, but there was no room for her at Emmeline and Mr Janus's flat now Emmeline was pregnant. Celia was like the vase: cracked, not the same, perched on her spot, still painted.

'Louisa?' she called. There was no answer. She supposed they should have covered the place in bunting to welcome her. They would have done, before the war. But then, before the war her cousin would have been staying because they were having a ball or going for some sort of holiday. She wouldn't be coming to live with them because her mother had died and she was alone. What was she going to say to her? Celia didn't know. Louisa, almost five years younger than her, was always the baby left out of their games. Now she was sixteen, parentless, nearly an adult, and she was come to be in their family, another sister.

The whole thing had got off on the wrong foot. They'd gone into town to collect some things for Louisa, some welcoming cakes for tea and the like (well, such was the plan; in the event the only whole cake in the baker's was a tired-looking plum sponge), and had meant to be back just before she'd arrived. But they were late starting out and Verena had to stop to talk to a woman she knew and then they saw Mr Pemberton, the solicitor, and you had to talk to him – and so they were late back even though, all the while, Celia felt the panic as if she was back in a dream about school and late for a lesson, wanting them to hurry along, go faster. Verena had talked on and on about being kind to Louisa, treating her delicately. *The poor child*, she said.

'Can't you go faster?' Celia pleaded with Thompson, who was driving the cart in a flurry of mud (they'd had to give up the car in the war, and how could they ever afford another one?). But they were still late, and when they arrived, Jennie had come out to meet them, said that Louisa had been there for an hour or so, gone up to her room, hadn't wanted to talk.

So Verena sent Celia to find her. 'You girls,' she said. 'You'll know what to say to her.' Celia felt her frustration rising, angry with her mother for escaping any conversation that might be trying. And now here she was, sitting at the bottom of the stairs, shouting for Louisa, her voice echoing across the hall. Over the last month since they'd had the news that Louisa was coming, she'd imagined all the ways she'd be kind to her cousin, how she'd take her to places and they'd talk, play music together, discuss books. The poor girl was only sixteen! Celia would comfort Louisa – and in the process, feel better herself, less alone. Helping others, that was the way to feel better, so the teachers at Winterbourne had told them.

She hadn't thought much of Louisa when she was young, always the little girl trying to join in, run after them when she was too slow and fell over her feet. Then, during the war, Celia hadn't seen her. As soon as the British newspapers started filling up with the Kaiser and his evils, Aunt Deerhurst said that it would be better if they really didn't meet. They'd come for Michael's funeral in that freezing winter, but Louisa had hardly spoken. Cousin Matthew had talked on, attracting all the light. Celia was ashamed of herself; she'd been so caught up in her own grief, she'd hardly seen Louisa at all. Now she would make it up to her. They'd welcome Louisa into Stoneythorpe and then it would begin.

She started up the stairs. Verena had arranged one of the spare rooms for Louisa, one previously used for storing bits of furniture. It was two doors along from Michael's room, which was still locked up, preserved as it had been – dozens of wooden aeroplanes hanging from the ceiling, his books and clothes piled up on the shelves and cupboards – waiting for him to come back from the war.

But instead they'd got the letter saying the body was buried in France after his brave act in battle.

She remembered walking past the dark window that late summer night in 1914, hearing voices, thinking nothing of it – but it had been Michael planning to run away to war with Tom, her best friend. It was all Tom's idea, she knew, he had no longer wanted to be their servant, assisting the groom, having to look after her. If she'd realised, if she'd gone out there, then perhaps Michael wouldn't have run off to join up.

Then, of course, she reminded herself, he'd have had to join up anyway by 1916, and probably the same would have happened.

'Died bravely', the letter said. She was the only one in the house who knew that it wasn't true, who knew what had really happened. Michael's door, closed, still waiting for him, the one room in the house that had never changed.

She walked up the stairs, hands trailing the banister. 'Louisa?' she called again. Surely her cousin could hear her. She passed her own door, wide open, the books strewn over the unmade bed. Louisa could have peered in, she thought, looked anywhere really. She'd had the house to herself.

She walked up to the next staircase. She never came here, up to the top of the house. Her brother Arthur's room was at the end of the corridor and she had no reason to visit him.

It was strange having Arthur around the house again, after he'd been away for so long. He'd spent many years in Paris – first hiding from Rudolf, then from the fighting. Sometimes she hated him; he'd been kept safe when Michael had died. Spending Rudolf's money, doing as he pleased, not even coming to Michael's funeral, never caring about any of them.

At other times she thought it had been nothing but slaughter, and at least someone had escaped. He'd always be the eldest brother, would grow older than his current age of twenty-six, while Michael couldn't move, stuck forever at twenty-two.

She knocked on Louisa's door. 'Hello, cousin?' There was no reply. She pushed it open. The empty room looked unchanged, apart from Louisa's trunk in the middle of it. She'd made a half-hearted attempt at pulling a shawl out. Celia moved into the room, stood at the window. She couldn't imagine what Louisa would make of the garden, overgrown, untidy, stones missing from the walls, weeds sprawling across anything that was once a flower. Lady Deerhurst, Louisa's mother, would have thought it terrible – if she'd been alive. After the war, they'd promised they would improve it, make the beds and the gardens handsome, create Verena's Versailles garden again. But they'd let them collapse, really. She turned away, hurried out of the room.

'Louisa?' she shouted, out in the corridor. Her words echoed back to her. She hurried down the stairs. She called again, with no reply. She felt a thin creep of fear slide up her body, wrap around her heart. Where was she? Celia hurried down into the hall, rushing now, throwing open the door of the parlour, the dining room, the study, the second receiving room. Broken furniture, legs snapped and piled up in the corners, paintings still dusty on the walls. She hurtled to the kitchen. Jennie, Thompson and Mrs Bright said they hadn't seen Louisa.

'Try the garden,' said Jennie. 'She'll be somewhere.'

But what if she's not? Celia thought, heart pounding, pulling open the back door and running into the garden. *The poor child*, Verena had said, *she is so delicate*. Celia ran, feet catching on the damp grass. There were spring flowers poking up from the soil; she ignored them. 'Louisa!' she shouted. 'Where are you?'

The words swung around the sky, flew. She called again. 'Louisa!'

There was no sign of her. Perhaps, she thought, she'd walked into the village. She gazed around the deserted garden. She must have done. She could be anywhere now. Celia wanted to scream at her mother. Why didn't we go faster?

'Louisa?' she shouted.

Then a sound. She heard a laugh – high, silvery. A woman's, definitely. Or a girl's. Then a man's voice, a laugh too. Celia edged forward. It was coming from her dell at the back of the garden. She stilled, listened. The laugh again. It was definitely coming from there. She ran to the back of the garden, cut through the gap in the wall, into the dell.

She saw her cousin sitting, just where Celia liked to, on the mossy stone next to the pond, the willow tree hanging over her. Louisa had always tried to follow Celia and Tom here when she was a child. 'Wait for me!' she'd cry. They'd hurry on without her. Celia remembered, ashamed, how she'd sent Louisa away, shouted at her to leave.

'Cousin,' Celia said, hurrying forward. 'We were looking for you.' Louisa looked at her, her face serene. 'We were worried about you! We didn't know where you were.'

Louisa shook her head. 'I'm sorry. I didn't realise. I wanted to walk.' She was three years older than the last time they'd met – at Michael's funeral – Celia reminded herself. She'd been a child then. Now she was handsome, her pale blue eyes light pools in her face, her thick golden hair fluffed around her cheeks. It had been stylishly cut, not so long ago, just past the chin, but the style was already growing out, strands straggling free. She was tall, just as tall as Celia, but wore it better, graceful where Celia was like a stalking heron, legs poking out of her skirt, stooping to avoid being seen.

Her face was thinner. Celia knew it was misery, loneliness in the curves of her cheeks, shadows under her eyes, but she couldn't stop a flash of jealousy. Louisa had become beautiful. She was wearing a black dress, but it was fashionably short. Louisa, Celia realised, had the looks, the contrast between bright hair and pale skin, to wear the newly stylish colours: yellow, mint, pale blue, delicate and pretty. She felt suddenly conscious of her scruffy jumper, the old fawn skirt, not even her good belt.

'I'm so sorry about your mother. We thought she was going to get better.'

Louisa shrugged. 'We all did.' They should have been to visit Aunt Deerhurst. But Louisa's letters had said she was recovering. She'd been lying, of course, Celia knew that. All those stories about the flu had flooded their minds, so that it was the only disease that killed – as long as you didn't have *that*, you'd be fine. Aunt Deerhurst couldn't die of a stomach poisoning. But she did.

Celia resisted the urge to stare at Louisa's beautiful face. She looked like the photographs of Verena as a young girl, before she'd become broken and sad, the days when she had wanted to be a ballerina. Except Louisa had the look of a modern girl, everything but the short hair.

She also tried to push down a creeping sense of possession. The dell was hers, the place she used to guard from others. Louisa would never have been allowed here in the old days. Celia wouldn't have let her.

'Who else is here?'

Louisa shook her head. 'No one.'

'I heard someone here.'

'Well, there wasn't.'

Celia gazed around. Once, she'd thought of the dell as a magical place, where you could hear voices from lands you'd never see. But all that shimmering stuff was gone now; she was too old for it.

Perhaps, instead, she'd imagined voices, Michael or Tom shouting for her to play with them across the grass. The garden was full of ghosts.

Louisa bowed her eyes. Celia softened. 'Why don't you come out with me, Louisa? Mama is outside. We have things for tea for you.'

Louisa stared at her.

Celia crouched down, near her. 'I'm sorry I said that there was someone here. I must have been mistaken. Come out. Mama and Papa are so eager to see you.'

Louisa shook her head. 'Please. I'll come out later.' She looked down, covering her face with her hair. The light of the willows fell on to the dark mass of it, making patches of red.

Celia's legs were hurting. She'd got it all wrong. Poor Louisa, so unhappy, and she'd started off inventing other voices, only speaking sharply because she felt the dell was hers. And now their guest wouldn't come out.

'We'll have the tea waiting.' The words sounded weak. Louisa didn't answer. Celia walked out of the dell and into the garden. She looked back and Louisa was still staring into the pond.

She walked slowly to the back of the house, not looking up at it. When she was younger, she'd liked to pick out the windows, admire the light glinting out of them, wonder what was happening in each one. She didn't any more; so many were deserted. Even their old telephone lay untouched, dust piling up over the numbers you might dial. Rudolf used to like new things, order them in from London. She turned up towards the kitchen – then looked again. Her brother was leaning against the kitchen wall, smoking.

'Arthur! I didn't realise you were back from work.'

He blew out a ring. 'I just arrived. Finished early. What are you doing out here?' He looked smart in his suit. He was working hard, Celia knew, earning money for his businesses at his office in Winchester, some sort of property investment, he said. He was even looking after what was left of de Witt Meats – although they'd renamed it Winter Meats so as not to lose any more customers. He'd got back some contracts with pie factories, and some of the big farmers who used to supply were breeding good livestock again (although at huge prices; it was a seller's market these days). Arthur said he might be able to make it successful once more. With the new world upon them, men who went anywhere to work, he said, they'd need meat.

Lots of people would tell her how lucky she was to have a brother like him (how lucky, really, to have a brother at *all*), kind, hardworking. Looking after the business, which was more than she was doing. And he was handsome – too handsome, maybe – tall and thin with his thick hair curling over his forehead, so dark it would surely never go grey. Green eyes that shone out at you, made you feel you were the only one he was speaking to.

She was the plain one in the family, the disappointment hanging behind three good-looking siblings. Michael was dead, Emmeline didn't care about looks any more and so that only left Arthur. *It means nothing*, she wanted to say. To shake the truth into them. *His beauty doesn't make him kind.* He'd left them all, stayed in Paris, not even coming back when they'd written to him about Michael's death. *Don't trust him*, she wanted to say. But instead, she smiled, stayed quiet. *It's wrong to bear grudges*, she thought.

'I was looking for Louisa. We got back so late that we missed her. And now she's run to the pond by the tree – you know – and she won't come out.' She tried to stop the tears pricking at the back of her eyes. 'I wanted to make everything nice for her.'

Arthur stubbed out his cigarette, moved forward to pat her on the shoulder. 'Poor Ceels. So she's refusing to come.'

Celia felt a tear trickle over her cheek. *Stop it*, she said to herself. It came again. 'Mama was worried about her but we were late back from town. She wouldn't even come to find her. She sent me. And I got it wrong.'

Arthur patted Celia again. 'Listen, why don't I go and try to smoke her out. I'll tell her they're making tea. I'll have a go.'

'Would you really?'

He flashed her a grin. 'Of course. Anything for my little sister. You go and get them set for tea. I'll bring her in.' He spoke, Celia thought briefly, as if Louisa was a fish. Then she told herself that she was being ungrateful. He strode off down the garden. She ran into the kitchen.

'Let's put the tea out,' she said to Jennie. 'Louisa's coming in with Arthur.' She ran out to the hall for her mother. Verena was coming in, hobbling, stooped as ever. You're not an old woman, Celia wanted to cry. She was only fifty; the Pankhursts were fifty and look at them. But Verena was like an actress playing a role, ridiculously bent over, creeping across the stage, wrapped in shawls, her face sunken in. Louisa had all her beauty now. Verena's eyes had lost their colour, seemed barely grey.

'Did you find her?'

'I did. Arthur's going to get her, though.'

Verena nodded, didn't question it as Celia thought she might. 'Louisa always adored Arthur when she was a little girl.'

Celia nodded, went back to the kitchen, Jennie and the tea tray. Jennie, Thompson and Smithson were the only servants left from the old days. Smithson had come back from Mesopotamia, sad and angry, not relieved as Celia thought he might be. He and Jennie were planning to marry in September, so they must be happy, surely.

Jennie was talking about how it was good for Celia to have someone young in the house again. Celia nodded. She couldn't remember Arthur and Louisa together. She remembered Louisa always chasing after her and Tom, not Arthur. He was never even there. She put the plate of cake on to the tray, passed it to Jennie to carry in. They walked into the parlour together, Celia behind. Over Jennie's shoulder, she saw Louisa, flushed and happy on the sofa, sitting between Arthur and Verena. She was laughing. Verena was patting her knee.

Celia was caught again by a swift jealousy. It was ridiculous, unreasonable, she knew, but she couldn't help it. It flooded around her, strengthening, growing as she passed out the plates, then the cake. Jennie served tea, offering the stuff to Arthur as he told another joke and Louisa laughed, then even Verena was giggling. Celia sat back in the chair with her cup, watched them, silently. They were all in a castle and she was on the other side.

*

Over the next few days, Celia tried again with Louisa. But whatever she said seemed always to be the wrong thing. Only Arthur could make Louisa laugh. She heard the two of them walking together, laughing as they passed her room, talking loudly in the hall while she was in the study. Laughing, always laughing. *I thought you were sad!* Celia said to herself. *I was going to make you feel better!*

But instead, it was Arthur doing everything she had planned to do – playing cards with Louisa, talking about books, walking around the gardens with her. *I came back to live here because of you*, she wanted to say. Which wasn't true at all, or at least only part true; she'd come back for Louisa, but there was nowhere else for her to go. She couldn't stay in London at Emmeline's any more, not now she was pregnant. Mr Janus, Emmeline's husband, said he had work to do, meetings, and there was no space. Celia knew his meetings well enough, turning the system upside down, making the poor rich; he'd said his work was more important than ever, now the war was over. And on leaving London Celia thought about how she would have Louisa. But she didn't.

She tried to join in. When she heard them talking in the parlour, she walked in and smiled. They fell silent, looked at her awkwardly. At the dinner table, she tried to talk to Louisa about Emmeline's pregnancy, told her about the time Stoneythorpe was a hospital. Louisa nodded, added polite words, didn't ask anything. When Arthur was deep in conversation with Rudolf about a business matter, Celia went one further, started talking a little about her time in France driving an ambulance, after running away there in the middle of the war.

She tried to tell Louisa how dreadful it had been. Louisa only nodded. *I'm telling you this!* Celia wanted to cry out. *I haven't told anyone else. Can't you see?*

She talked about the ambulance training in the girls' school in Aldershot. Louisa stared at her plate. Celia knew she wasn't interested, but she kept pressing, despite herself.

That night, after everyone had taken coffee in the parlour, after

Verena and Rudolf had yawned and gone up as they always did, talking about putting out the fire, Celia didn't follow them. She waited. Arthur lit a cigarette. He winked at Celia. 'Mama will never smell it.'

Celia ignored him. She leant across to Louisa. 'It must have been terrible to lose your mother,' she said, the words tumbling out fast. 'Poor Lady Deerhurst. So sad.'

Louisa turned and fixed her cool blue eyes on Celia. She nodded.

'I'm so sorry,' Celia kept on, emboldened. 'With you nursing her so much. It was wonderful you were there for her. It must have been very hard.'

Louisa nodded. Celia thought she saw a tear glitter in her eye.

'You can talk to me about it, you know. I'd love to, if you wanted to. Not if you didn't, of course. But we could talk about it. Go into town maybe for tea.' Celia could see Louisa's face changing, the eyes opening, her body turning towards her, just a little.

Arthur stood up, came closer. 'I'm taking Louisa to town for tea,' he said. 'Next week. Aren't I, Louisa?'

Louisa nodded. And then the opening, the ray that Celia had seen in Louisa's face, moved together, closed up. 'Yes,' she said. 'And thank you, Celia. But Arthur has told me to write it all down. He says that's the way to feel better.'

Arthur seated himself in between Celia and Louisa. 'It is. I know. Writing it down, first.' He shrugged. 'Aren't you tired, Celia? Surely you want to go to bed.'

Celia stared at the fire, burning down, sparks glinting over the wood. She nodded, rose, went out, closed the door behind her. She walked up the stairs and heard Arthur laugh.

TWO

London, Peace Day, 19 July 1919

Celia

'Well, you would have thought they could have put on a better show than this,' Emmeline said, hands folded across her great stomach. 'We won, after all.'

'Maybe they don't want to seem too victorious,' said Rudolf, doubtfully. 'Who knows?'

'I expect it will come alive when the Queen appears,' said Verena. She adjusted her hat against the white glare of the July sun, hopeless, though, for it was painfully strong, shining off the buttons on the men's coats, showing off every imperfection, dropped thread, break of colour in the clothes of those spectators in front. 'Then things will really begin.'

They were sitting in the wooden stands on the Mall. Five rows of soldiers were marching in front of them. The stands were covered in banners, flowers, flags. They'd paid three times the normal price for their tickets to get a better spot, but they were still ten rows back and the road was obscured by the people in front. Verena's back was straight as a die, her hat like a sun on her head. All the rich people, every girl Verena had grown up with, Celia supposed, were in special boxes with an excellent view of the park. Then, tonight, they'd go to one of the Victory Balls in Spencer House, Clarence House or even Buckingham Palace. But there was no space for the de Witts, not even at one of the lesser balls in a Kensington townhouse. Who'd want a German there? They should have changed their name at the beginning of it all.

Celia sometimes wondered if people could tell. When you

looked at her family, they appeared so very respectable. Rudolf with his short beard, his great dark eyes and smart suit, Verena in public as upright as a dancer, her hair marshalled into the tightest bun imaginable, and Emmeline, the family beauty, blonde and so delicate, with her big blue eyes and face shape that was part heart, part angles. And she, Celia, the youngest, twenty now, which didn't seem young any more. They'd teased her for being lanky, an overgrown bird in the nest, thinning hair, brown eyes too big for her face. She'd grown into her looks, she supposed, her thin hips and body were in fashion now, her hair looked better since she'd had it cut shorter last month. From a small distance, she could even be attractive enough, brown skin, round cheeks and her heavy-lidded eyes.

If she knew what to do with make-up, she might be able to make herself look pretty, but she had no idea. She wondered how other girls just seemed to know what to do with the stuff, bright red mouths, pale pink cheeks. That was for girls like Louisa, not her.

When the war broke out, they'd been rich, even powerful, perhaps. The de Witt family. London painted with 'de Witt, de Witt, keeps you fit' adverts for their canned meat. Celia had turned fifteen in 1914, a child still, expecting nothing, but sure that it would all be happy riches to come.

Then the war broke out – and everybody began to leave Stoney-thorpe. Michael was first, running away to war almost as soon as it had been announced. Tom, her best friend, went with him. Sir Hugh broke off his engagement with Emmeline and she eloped to London with Mr Janus, Celia's tutor at the time.

Rudolf, with his German name and background, was interned in the Isle of Wight along with hundreds of other men. And so there was only Verena and Celia left, her mother letting the house crumble around her, weeping her time away. Celia dreaming of Tom, her childhood companion for as long as she could remember.

And eventually Celia had left Verena, too, borrowing Emmeline's birth certificate and signing up for the war effort, driving ambulances full of terrified, half-dead men in Etaples. It was there she heard that Michael had died. *Died bravely*, said the letters from his superiors. They'd come back in a sea of darkness.

She'd thought of Tom, clung to the idea of him. And when they were both back at Stoneythorpe she'd told him she loved him. It pained her to remember it. He said he'd never love her, never want to – he had just spent time with her because he had to, as a servant. He told her to find a new world, new people. Everything went grey.

In 1917, walking though Leicester Square, Celia had met Michael's university friend, Jonathan, whom she hadn't seen since before the war. They'd gone out together, eaten and danced. She'd had too much to drink, offered herself to him, thinking that might dull the pain of war and rejection. But he'd said no, said she wasn't like other girls, talked instead of marriage.

And it was that night, outside in the snow, when Jonathan had told her the truth about Michael's death. Her brother hadn't died in battle, he'd been shot by his own men for failing to go over the top.

She remembered falling, feeling nothing but falling, holding on to one thought: that what really happened to Michael must be her secret and her family could never know. She clutched it close to her now, her heart sick with the truth.

'I'll have to stand to see anything,' said Emmeline, crossly, still fretting over their position. 'Surely the authorities could have arranged the seats better.'

Celia was drawn back to the present.

Looking at Emmeline now, Celia could hardly believe that she was once going to be Lady Bradshaw, the wife of the local aristocrat, presiding over hunt balls and fetes.

Now she and Mr Janus lived in a tiny flat in Bloomsbury, Mr Janus always plotting revolution, the pulling down of the upper classes, Emmeline nodding along, the supportive wife. He was away for a few days – an important meeting, he said. He'd never have come anyway. 'It's mass performance to keep you obedient,' he said.

'It looks much like it did for the Diamond Jubilee,' said Rudolf.

'I could barely see a thing then either. And the hotels cost a fortune too.' He'd almost perfected his English accent now. As Verena said, it was important.

They'd booked places in the Savoy, quite in advance, but when they arrived, the manager had told them it would be twice the original price. Even though they were two less than they'd said. Louisa was supposed to be sharing with Celia but she'd come down with a terrible headache yesterday afternoon and had decided to stay behind at Stoneythorpe. Then Arthur had received a letter about an urgent business matter that he had to go to Winchester for. Still, the manager said, the price was the same and it didn't matter if the party was smaller. These were exceptional circumstances.

The restaurant was crammed so tightly you could barely walk between tables and it was so short staffed that Emmeline had stood up and declared, 'I shall serve myself!' Even walking to the Mall this morning had taken them almost an hour, the crowds were so thick. People were in holiday mood, men in uniform, arm in arm with girls. Surely, Celia wanted to say to them, surely you're just pretending to smile. Yes, we won the war. But look at us.

She gazed at the men, marching in red jackets, black trousers, their swords sparkling, as neat and rigid as toys, glossy horses to either side, the white wedding cake of the Palace at the end, like a pot of gold on the rainbow. Thousands and thousands of people cheering them just for walking down the street. 'Look at how they've just got the healthy ones out,' she said. 'You'd think they hadn't even fought.' The first lot of plans had been for four days of celebrations. But who could have faced that?

'Stop it, Celia. Don't talk so loudly,' said Emmeline, pinching her. She was so large that you thought she might have the baby now, but it most likely wouldn't be for another six weeks, the doctors said. Emmeline said she was so full of energy she felt like a schoolgirl, so they shouldn't fret. She said she didn't even need her husband; Mr Janus had gone off to one of his secretive meetings with the Workers. Probably best he wasn't here, anyway, Celia thought. He'd never be able to contain his feelings. He'd be shouting about the ruling classes, claiming that the soldiers parading down the street were traitors to the people. She almost found herself agreeing with him.

'These are soldiers used for show,' she said.

'Ssshh,' said Emmeline again. 'People can hear you.'

'But it's true.' Where were they, the men that she had taken in her ambulance? They had been bleeding, missing limbs with lungs full of gas, jaws broken, eyes burned beyond repair, broken faces, hands shot to pieces. One she remembered, screaming all the way, had no face, none at all, just a mass of red. These men, marching in formation, looked like pictures in a magazine, not even a limp or a withered-looking hand, smart, upright, rosy-cheeked. She wondered, bitterly, if people wanted the other type to hide away. The government maybe did, because they were a reminder – horrible, wounded, sickly – of how they couldn't protect their people.

But those broken men were everywhere: sitting on their heels outside pubs, rocking back and forth with their hands over their ears, hearing the bombs still; leaning on wooden legs as they put their caps out for money on corners; in the long queues outside shops and office doors that she supposed were in response to advertisements for positions vacant, none of them with a hope, because they had half-burned faces, or a missing ear, hair singed off or an eye that never closed. Or the most hopeless of all, the ones who wore those white porcelain masks, painted with bright blue eyes, almost obscenely red lips. 'Thank you, sir,' she imagined the proprietors saying. 'We will let you know.' Or the more truthful ones who would say, 'I'm sorry, sir. You'd put the customers off with a face like that.'

'We're not celebrating the past, Celia,' said Rudolf, talking over Emmeline. 'It's the future. It has been the War to End All Wars. We will never have war again. Always peace.'

She gazed at the next line of men, marching smartly in unison. What about those thousands who were still stuck out there? France – and those ones in the desert. When were they coming back? Another line of men came past. She'd forgotten to keep up with the list on her programme and now she had no idea which regiment was passing. How much time they must have spent rehearsing such a performance. How much *money*.

If Tom were beside her, she could tell him this. But he didn't want to see her.

Tom had only sent two letters since he'd left the hospital. He said he'd met up with his captain in the army, who'd found him a job in his business. But she hadn't heard any more from him, and he hadn't left an address. She knew that she'd been silly in thinking that she might see him when they came to London – this city of millions, swelled by even more who'd come to watch the parades. Still, she'd looked out for him, strained to see through groups of men in case he might be there.

'Celia!' said Emmeline. 'You're gazing into space. What are you *doing*?'

'I was thinking.'

'We should try and join in,' said Emmeline, standing up, shifting uncomfortably as she did so. 'Everyone's singing.' She waved her flag, bought for nearly a shilling. 'Come on, Celia. Put in some effort. Aren't you supposed to be the war heroine?'

'No, I'm not!' But she gave in, joined arms with her sister, sang along as she waved her flag. God Save the King. *Victorious*. She thought of Stoneythorpe, ramshackle, fallen-down, the garden overgrown with ivy, Verena's Versailles canals stagnant. So ruined and worn down that the work needed to bring it back to some sort of order was unimaginable, entirely so. And yet, how lucky they were to have a home and so much space. They should, she knew, really divide it up and let other people live there, change the whole thing entirely, so it wasn't Stoneythorpe at all.

At the end, after hundreds and hundreds of men had marched past them, thousands of people had cheered and waved their flags and the makeshift Cenotaph had been endlessly saluted, they queued in their lines under the boiling sun to leave their seats and were immediately jostled by the huge crowd. There were men, women, children on shoulders, and sellers bearing trays of everything: fried fish, cakes, flags, a whole set of plaster models of Field Marshal Haig, standing to attention on a lining of newsprint.

Rudolf looked around vainly. There was no one who might help them, no porters or servants for hire. And by the time they got on to the road for cabs, they'd be nearly at the Savoy.

'If we get separated, let's meet back at our room,' said Rudolf. 'Celia, look after your sister. Take her back to the hotel and keep close to her. Dear Emmeline is the priority.'

Emmeline sighed. 'There's no need. I'm fine. I told you.'

Celia nodded, took tight hold of her sister's arm. 'Come along, sister. Let's go quickly.'

She put her elbows up and started pushing through the crowds, past the children thrusting out hands for sweets, the men who'd already been drinking, women laughing arm in arm. 'My sister is with child,' she shouted loudly. 'Let her through!'

'I don't know why we even came here,' said Emmeline, as she collapsed into a chair in the Savoy reception, dropping her flag. 'We must be mad.' It wasn't even calm in the hotel's black and white tiled interior, dozens of men in uniform and women in hats going back and forth, laughing, talking, shouting to someone or other. They only had a chair because one man had seen Emmeline approach and jumped up.

'We all told you not to come, sister,' said Celia. 'You remember.'

Emmeline put her head in her hands. 'I'm exhausted. I can't get up. I literally can't get up.' Pins fell from her hair, clattered to the floor.

'We'll have to at some point. Papa said we should meet him at their room.'

'I can't possibly go up the *stairs*.' Two women dressed in evening gowns glided past. Had the parties started already?

'Well, why don't we go through to the tea room and get some tea?'

'All I want is tea. All I can think of is tea. But I can't move.'

'You'll have to.'

Her head was still in her hands. 'Sit by me. Please.'

Celia perched, uncomfortably, on the leather arm of the chair. She reached down and tried to right her sister's hat. Her hair was damp, matted – it felt like illness, smelt of it too. Emmeline was breathing heavily, now. She raised her head. 'I feel,' she said, then closed her eyes again, as if even that was too much effort.

'Sister?' Celia said. Emmeline didn't answer. *What if she had the baby now, in the middle of the Savoy?* She squeezed Emmeline's hand. *Don't be silly*, she told herself sternly. Still, her heart was surging. 'That's it, sister,' she said, trying to sound calm. 'Breathe.'

She looked up and a man in a suit was approaching. 'May I help you, ladies?'

'Are our family above? We were separated at the parades and my sister is a little unwell. As you can see.'

Emmeline raised her face, pale and sweating, dropped it again.

'Ah yes,' said the man, 'quite so. Where is your room, ladies? Let me take you up there.' He clicked his fingers and called over two porters. 'Get a couple of maids, would you?'

'Now, you said your family was with you?'

'My parents. But we are not sure if they're upstairs or not.'

'And do you have a doctor with you?'

The panic came rushing into Celia's chest, hard now. She shook her head.

'A nurse, then?'

'No. My sister is not due to have her baby for at least six weeks.' She held Emmeline's head, slumped on her chest now. 'Her husband's at work.'

He raised an eyebrow. 'Indeed. I think we shall have to get you someone right away. We have an excellent doctor, Dr Freedlove. Whether he can get here, I don't know. I will send a man for him. We must get your sister upstairs as quickly as we can.'

'Thank you,' she whispered. Her voice was drowning. The whole of her was drowning. In the rush of people, the echo of heels, the chatter, the laughter, soldiers and women, parents and children, she was falling and none of her was left.

Within a few hours, the fireworks started. They were in Celia's room and Emmeline was in bed, trying to breathe slowly, as they told her to, groaning quietly. Rudolf had sent a man to the flat to leave a message for Mr Janus. Verena had fretted and wept so much that Dr Freedlove had told her to stay in her room. 'The sister can stay instead,' he said. 'You sit there, dear,' one of the nurses, a girl called Burns, had said at the beginning. 'You can help count later.' A second nurse, Gregg, an older woman, thickset, strong-faced, was holding Emmeline's hand. A man from the hotel stood outside for anything they might need. The manager had promised new bowls of hot water every ten minutes. They would have to run up and down the stairs with it, Celia thought, not spilling it.

Celia stood by the dark window, trying not to listen to her sister. She watched shots of gold, silver, bursts of red, heard distant screams of delight. She'd loved fireworks as a child, watching Rudolf and the footmen assemble them outside the house, laughing as they exploded. She'd been looking forward to seeing the fireworks today. But now, they didn't need a great wheel of red and white fire in London, perched on the Palace over the King and Queen. Instead, they had one in their room, Emmeline, possessed by a whirling, terrible thing, a fire inside her that made her twist and scream and beg for it to stop.

'Can't you help her?' Celia cried at the doctor. 'Please!' She wished Mr Janus was here to shout and demand.

'She's fine, getting along. Now, miss, you need to count for us.' He was a small, bustling man with glasses, sleeves rolled up. His movements were slow, deliberate. Celia wondered, desperately, if he'd even be quick running from a bomb.

They told Celia to count through the minutes, starting when Emmeline quietened, stopping when she began to scream again. But even when they said she was quiet, she was still writhing, moaning. 'I can't!' Celia said, when she'd muddled the numbers too many times, put eighteen in front of thirteen, forgotten whether she was on twenty-one or thirty-one. 'Please, can you do it?'

'We're occupied,' said Nurse Burns. She was rather a pretty girl, Celia thought, dark hair, red lips, probably half the age of Nurse Gregg. She was crouching at Emmeline's legs, trying to hold them still. 'You have to do it. Don't look at your sister if you can't.' The lamp propped over the nurse was so bright it made Celia's eyes burn.

She forced herself to count through. You learnt as a child, she told herself crossly. You can. One. Two. Three. Four. She stopped, started again. She looked down, kept going.

I drove an ambulance, she wanted to say to them. I'm strong. But she said nothing, they wouldn't listen. Emmeline screamed again.

Then, soon, the pains were so close together that she couldn't count them, and Dr Freedlove didn't even seem to need her to. She carried on trying, using her fingers now, because there hardly seemed to be a rest between Emmeline's screams. Ten, eleven, twelve. Then came the blood, so much of it. The fireworks exploded in her head, the Catherine Wheel shot round in a circle.

'There's the head!' Burns shouted and Emmeline screamed, the fireworks exploded again, and the rest of it came slithering out, like some kind of seal. 'It's a boy,' said Nurse Burns with satisfaction. 'A fine boy.'

Emmeline fell back, legs apart, nightgown covered in blood, closed her eyes. Dr Freedlove held the child up – not so rough! Celia almost cried – then clapped it on the back to hear it scream. 'Wash him, please,' he said. 'Quickly. Before the mother goes to sleep.' He rubbed his hands together. 'She's about to.'

Burns attended to Emmeline, wadding material between her legs, washing her face. Celia watched Gregg sponge the child in the corner, wrap him up in a blanket. What a strange thing it was, dark pink, covered in hair, all clenched fists. It looked nothing like a human at all. And its cry was so strange, a thin, hopeless wail, more like the croaking of a bird than a child. Burns pulled the sheets over Emmeline, then left to get more water. Celia walked over, stroked her sister's forehead. Emmeline's face was white, her forehead clammy, hair so wet and tangled you wouldn't recognise it.

'Hello, Emmy,' she whispered. She felt as if it was almost impossible to touch her. She couldn't believe a person could still be alive after losing all that blood.

'Do you think she's quite alright?' she said, turning to Dr Freedlove.

He smiled. 'Yes, quite well. A good sleep is all she needs.'

'Can we give her some water? Or tea? Emmeline, would you like some tea?'

'No drinks just yet, I'm afraid. We'd overtire her. Best the body rights itself, you know.'

Gregg came to the bed. The baby was still wailing. 'Would you like to hold him, Mother?'

Emmeline didn't open her eyes.

She turned to Celia. 'Would *you* like him, miss?'

Celia gazed at her, uncomprehending.

'Miss?'

Celia held out her hands. The child was terrifyingly light, a bundle of nothing, really. He was still wailing, eyes closed. She tried to see Emmeline or Mr Janus in him but couldn't discern either in the squalled pink face. *What if I drop him? After all that.*

'Good, healthy lungs,' said Gregg. 'Shall I take him from you, dear?'

She nodded.

'Poor thing,' she said, gathering up the baby in her arms. 'He's tired us all out.' She patted Celia's shoulder. 'Never seen blood before, miss? You forgive me, I'm used to it now. Never mind. Stay single, I would.'

'I should go and tell my parents. I wish Mr Janus – her husband was here.'

'Sit down first, dear. You look like you're about to faint. I'll call for some tea in a minute.' She jogged the baby. 'Never had a hotel birth, me. And what a day for it. I was supposed to be at a party in the street.'

'Me too,' said Nurse Burns. 'First one in ages as well. I'd bought a new dress.'

Nurse Gregg touched the child's face with a finger. 'You're my little Peace Day baby, aren't you? If he was a girl, you might be able to call her Peace. Or something.' She put him down in a nest of blankets made in a drawer. The baby began to cry. 'Naughty boy! You need to give your mama some rest.'

'Indeed,' said Dr Freedlove, cleaning his instruments at the side of the room. 'Can you ask the man for some more hot water, Gregg?'

Burns came back to Emmeline, pulled down the sheet and started sponging her legs. The water dripped. She looked up. 'Sir? Are you sure we're quite finished, sir?'

She stood up.

'Things don't seem quite right, sir.'

She glanced up, her wide eyes making her look, Celia thought, disconcertingly like a child.

'Well, the poor girl is exhausted,' Dr Freedlove said. 'Ridiculous to have come to town in her state. We'll get the afterbirth out and let her sleep.'

'I don't know, sir.' Burns put her hand on Emmeline's stomach. 'Doesn't feel right to me, sir.'

'Just a lot of fluid, still swollen.'

Emmeline was lying back on the pillow, her face waxy. Celia watched the nurse and Dr Freedlove talk, back, forth. The baby was still crying.

'Haven't you seen this before?' Burns was saying. 'I have. Exactly the same, just two months ago. We have to.'

'I agree with Dr Freedlove,' said Gregg, smugly. 'You're letting the excitement get to your head, Burns.'

'I don't think we can take the risk.'

Celia stepped forward, assumed her best imitation of Verena in the old days, when she had been grand. 'What are you talking about? Please explain.'

'I believe there's another child in there, miss,' said Nurse Burns. A strand of hair had fallen from her bun. 'I don't think it's over.'

'And I believe just as strongly that there is not,' said Freedlove. 'Nurse Burns, you simply aren't seeing correctly. See your sister's face, miss? That is the face of a mother who has birthed her baby. Nothing more.'

'So you mean,' Celia said slowly, gazing at the three of them, the doctor, Gregg and then Burns, her face alive with agitation, 'you can't know for sure if there's another baby in there or not?'

'*I* know,' he said. 'There is not.'

Celia moved over to Emmeline, put her hand on her clammy forehead. 'Emmy?' Her sister didn't open her eyes.

She looked up at the doctor. 'What if there is? What if there is another baby?'

'There is not.'

'We don't have much time if there is,' said Burns. 'In my experience, second one should come out as quickly as possible after the first.'

Celia looked back and forth to the doctor and the nurse, their faces set. She wished for Mr Janus, but there was no point. And no time to find her parents, that was clear enough from Burns's face. She reached down to her sister.

'Emmeline,' she said, touching her forehead. 'You have to try again. I think there is another baby. You need to push again.'

Emmeline didn't open her eyes.

'Sister? I'm sorry, but you must.'

Then Emmeline opened them, wide and bewildered. 'No,' she said. 'I can't.'

Celia clutched her hand. 'Just try. I will try with you.'

'I can't. I won't.'

Nurse Burns was at Emmeline's other side. 'Just give it a little go, dear. Just a small one. We'll get you something to drink, some water. Only a small few pushes, that's all.'

'Get her tea,' said Celia. 'She needs something proper to drink. And ask for a biscuit.'

Dr Freedlove bristled. 'I won't have that. Mothers must only have water.'

'She can't do it on nothing but water,' said Celia. She looked at Nurse Gregg. 'Ask the man outside for tea and three plain biscuits. And some hot water. As quick as he can.' She patted her sister's forehead. 'Good girl, Emmy. Nice tea. Then we can have one last push.'

Nurse Gregg returned and Celia held her sister's hand as she drank her tea. Emmeline was crying, big round tears falling down her face. 'I can't,' she whispered. 'Really.'

'This is very ill advised,' said Dr Freedlove. He'd rolled down his shirt sleeves, was buttoning them up.

'She's fine,' snapped Celia. 'In ten minutes she can sleep as long as she wants. Anyway, who pays your bills? I can guarantee my father won't if he finds another baby died and' – she looked down at her sister – 'goodness knows what else.'

Emmeline bit at the biscuit, fell back. Celia propped her up. 'Sorry, dear, but you have to. Do you want to eat?'

Emmeline shook her head, tears rolling. 'Why?' she said. 'Why are you doing this?'

Nurse Burns patted her legs. 'Don't waste energy talking, miss. Now, just gather it all up and push it right down. You know.'

Celia hoisted Emmeline up. 'Come on, sister. Do it hard.'

Emmeline closed her eyes, clenched her fists, her face red. She stopped, fell back against the pillow, tears pouring down her face. 'I can't,' she said. 'I really can't. Why do you make me?'

'Right, dear, try again,' said Burns.

'But I can't *feel* anything.'

'No one can at this stage, dear.'

Celia stroked Emmeline's hair, thick with sweat. Her forehead was clammy, face pale. The doctor was right. She looked about to collapse. If she died now from strain, it would be all Celia's fault. She could hear the child crying in the drawer. Someone should go to it, she thought.

She stroked her sister's forehead. It seemed as though Emmeline couldn't even feel her touch.

'She's feverish,' said Gregg. 'Look at her.'

'Right, dear, time to push again.'

Celia propped up her sister's head. 'It's the last time,' she lied. 'You can do it!'

Emmeline's head lolled but she clenched her fists again. Celia could feel her body tensing. Nurse Burns crouched down. She stood up. 'Would you look at this, Dr Freedlove.'

Grudgingly, he walked to the bottom of the bed. Celia watched him. The nurse pointed. He crouched. 'Turn the lamp,' he said. They were still. Emmeline groaned, her eyes closed, face white.

He stood up. 'You're right, miss. Now it's urgent. Mother, you need to push hard. Now!' He was rolling his sleeves up now, his face concentrated.

'Come on,' said Celia. 'You can do it.' She tried to pull Emmeline to sitting again, but her sister was heavy, leaden in her arms. 'Emmy!' Her sister groaned, didn't open her eyes.

'Nurse Gregg. Wake her up.'

Gregg came over, slapped Emmeline's face. She fell back. Celia wanted to hit Gregg too. Gregg hit her again. Emmeline's eyes fluttered, closed. 'No good, sir.'

'Try water. All of it.'

'Don't!' screamed Celia, but Gregg had already reached up and dumped the entire bowl on Emmeline's head. It caught Celia and a few drops must have hit the baby in the drawer, for he started crying again. Emmeline didn't stir.

'Pass me my bag,' the doctor said.

Celia looked at him, pinning back his sleeves. 'Aren't you going to wash your hands?'

'No time, I'm afraid. Try and wake up your sister.'

Celia shook her. 'What are you going to do?'

'You can hold her. You're going to have to keep her still.'

'But what are you going to do?'

'Is there any hot water?' he asked again. 'Send the man for some. Although probably too late.' She flurried to the door again. Celia watched him take out two knives and then a thing that looked like two big spoons joined in one. 'What's that?'

He didn't answer, rubbed it with his flannel.

'Aren't you going to wash it?' Even on the front, they'd washed the knives in hot water and disinfectant.

'If the water gets here in time. Otherwise no. She'll die. As will the baby. We'll have to take the risk. Please assist me, Nurse Burns.'

'But what about Emmeline? You can't do this. She'll feel it.'

He was busying himself moving the light. Nurse Burns held up the spoons. 'I doubt it. She can't feel anything. Look at her. But if she does, it will be over soon. And you're here to hold her down. Now take down her pillow, so she's flat. That's it.' Celia touched her sister's forehead. 'It will be over soon. I promise!'

He crouched down. 'No sign of the water? Hold up her legs please, Nurse Gregg.'

Celia hated the woman as she pulled up Emmeline's legs, bent them back at the knee. She felt sure she saw her sister wince.

He picked up the knife. 'Ready to hold her?'

Celia nodded, hands on her sister's chest. He brought the knife down and Emmeline screamed. The baby screamed from the drawer too. Celia fell on her sister, pressing down. 'Good girl,' he said. 'Not long.' He did it again and Emmeline jolted again. The baby was weeping now, hysterically. Celia could hear – suddenly – all the other noises of the hotel. She heard people walking past, someone in the room above testing the bed. People were downstairs dining and talking, others were going out of the hotel for the evening. And she could hear the man bearing the water knocking on the door, growing more desperate. 'Can I come in?'

No one heard but her. Dr Freedlove was using the spoons now and Emmeline was screaming, her torso bucking, begging them to stop. The baby was shrieking. Celia was holding tight to Emmeline, but she couldn't stop her moving. 'Keep her still!' shouted Nurse Gregg.

'Why didn't you give her something?' Celia shouted. 'Why?'

The spoons were flashing in the light. The baby was still weeping. Dr Freedlove delved in again and Emmeline screamed once more. Then there was another scream, a new one. A child. Freedlove held up the child, spanked it and it wailed even harder.

'A girl,' said Nurse Burns, words spilling out of her in her relief. 'You could call her Peace. You could get both of them in the papers, you know. Peace Day babies.'

Emmeline fell back, eyes wide, staring. Celia averted her gaze from the terrible blood all over the sheets. She walked to the drawer full of blankets and the weeping baby.

'Don't pick him up!' said Nurse Gregg. 'You can't go to babies the minute they cry. He's settled over there, perfectly fine. They need to learn.' Celia ignored her, hoisted the baby into her arms. He was tiny, pink like a baby cat. She went to the door to open it for the man with the water. Nurse Burns was fussing over the second baby.

'You did it, Emmy,' she said, coming back, sponging her sister's head, still holding the baby. 'Two Peace Day babies.' Her sister looked sicker than ever.

'Will she live?' she asked Freedlove.

'Of course. This was nothing. An easy birth, if you ask me. We'll just stitch her up and she'll be fine.'

'You're going to give her something this time?'

'We'll try.'

Celia stared at her sister. Her eyes were closed, her face waxy. She'd crossed over into another world.

'Can you remember where Mr Janus is working, Emmeline? Which friend he was with?'

Emmeline didn't answer.

Nurse Burns came up behind Celia. 'Would you like to hold her?' said Burns, the little girl wide-eyed in a blanket in her arms.

Celia nodded and held out the boy baby. Burns did a little juggling, handed her the blanket. Celia gazed into the baby's eyes, looked at the tiny fist next to her red, screwed-up face. 'I'll look after you,' she said. *I found you.*

THREE

Peace Day, 1919

Celia

Two hours later, Celia walked down the stairs. She'd tried to settle in her room, but her mind was spinning, overwhelmed. She'd written to Mr Janus but they had no idea where to send the letter as Emmeline didn't seem to know where he was. She'd have to wait until his return. He was probably awake, calling for justice, rousing his audience. Everybody else was asleep; her parents, Emmeline – quiet now, given a sleeping draught by Dr Freedlove, his final present – the babies, probably even Nurse Gregg, in her chair by the bed. Nurse Burns had finally gone to her party, Rudolf pressing twice her usual fee into her hand.

Celia knew she should sleep too. But when she lay down, her eyes sprang open, her head pounding, face on fire. She told herself that the more she lay in the darkness, the more upset she'd get and the more she would resist sleep. The answer would be to walk a little, settle her mind, then try again. She dressed herself hurriedly and wandered out of her room. She supposed, at this late hour, she'd have the hotel to herself. Hopefully, she thought, the hotel manager had gone to bed. She rather dreaded his kind solicitousness, the concern, and underneath all of it (she felt quite sure), his gently insistent wish that they leave, as soon as possible.

But downstairs the reception area was still bustling. Men and women were arm in arm, groups were chattering. You'd think, Celia thought, that it was the middle of the day, not past midnight. The throngs comforted her, made her feel as if she were

38

hidden, that she could slink in between them and no one would see her face, say, 'Are you quite alright, miss?'

She fell into a chair, near the bar area. 'May I have some tea?' she said to the waiter who came to her. He looked exhausted, his moustache limp.

'Only drinks with meals, miss,' he said. She looked to the side. The group of laughing young men on the next table were eating piles of ham, drinking great glasses of wine.

'I'll have a sandwich, then. Anything.'

'Cheese?'

'Fine.'

'Sherry, miss?'

She shook her head. 'Tea is fine.'

She watched him retreat into the flurry of bodies around the bar area. If she were outside in the sun, she'd close her eyes. Here she had to sit upright, look *normal*. She gazed down at her white dress, patted it on to her knees. Actually, she thought, she *was* hungry, she really couldn't think when she'd last eaten. The cakes sent up by the manager after the birth hardly counted. A cheese sandwich would be most welcome, really. Maybe, she thought, she should call him back and ask for ham.

She looked up and caught a man's eye by mistake. He was standing against the wall. Tallish, wearing uniform, tanned by the sun, short hair, an expression of satisfaction on his face. She looked down immediately, instinctively, then found herself gazing back again.

This time, he raised his eyebrows at her and she felt her face grow hot. Did she *know* him? Perhaps she did, one of the men in the ambulance station, one of the MOs? If so, she should surely smile. Then she thought not. She was a lady alone, eating a sandwich, and who minded if she'd known him in Etaples? All that was three years ago.

Where was the waiter with her tea? That would give her something to look at. Her gaze was swinging, nearly pulling back to him. What was she *doing*? She blushed and looked down at her lap.

When she lifted her head, hoping for the waiter, the man was standing in front of her.

'Good evening, madam,' he said. He *was* tall, she was right, wearing the uniform of a junior officer, handsome tanned face, an Eton kind of voice cut with something regional. Kent, maybe?

She gave him a vague smile. Where *was* the waiter?

'Are you alone on Peace Day evening, miss? Seems a shame.'

She shook her head. 'My family are upstairs.'

'May I join you, miss?'

She shook her head. 'I'm just going to eat my sandwich, then return. My family will be wondering where I am.'

He bowed his head, a strange mock-courteous action. 'Sorry to bother you, miss. Good evening.'

He turned. Then, as he did so, she looked past him and all of the people in front of her suddenly changed into a group, a large group of them all holding hands, it seemed. They were like a cocktail party, a band of friends. They all knew each other, except for her.

'Wait,' she said, to his back. 'I—'

He turned around, saw her face. In a minute, he was sitting next to her.

'Name's Gilligan,' he said. 'Stephen Gilligan. Nice to meet you, miss.'

She was almost surprised by how close he was to her.

'Celia,' she said. 'Celia Smith.' She was ashamed of herself for lying, still, about their name, when the Germans weren't enemies any more, not strictly, things were all about peace and the Kaiser was beaten down, paying money for forgiveness. But still, she wanted to be someone else, anyone.

'Have you come up just for the parade?'

'Yes. You too?' She didn't want to talk about herself. *Tell me about you*, she wanted to say. *Just keep talking.*

'I know it's quite a cheek, me coming over. But I saw your face and I thought – there's someone who's seen war. You know. Not all this *let's get over it quickly* business. You know, smile, move on, don't talk of it.'

She nodded. 'I didn't see the war, though. I was at home the whole time.' She'd make herself into someone else, just by saying it. She wouldn't be the woman who'd told the recruiting office she knew how to drive when she'd only once been behind the wheel of Rudolf's car. She wouldn't be the woman who held tight to Shep, her closest friend in those days, in the training school in Aldershot and then at the station in France.

She wouldn't be the girl who watched an ambulance, chased by a bomber, swerve off the road – and then saw that the driver was Shep. She would forget crying so much that she thought it would never stop hurting. She would forget hearing the news that Michael had died, forget the pain. That wouldn't be her, she was someone else, far from the war, above it.

He nodded. 'Too young, I suppose. Of course.' He paused. The waiter arrived, put down the sandwich and some tea. 'Sir?' he asked.

'A sherry, please.'

'Thank you, sir.'

She poured her tea, the sound of the milk and water in the cup echoing against the voices.

'I was watching you while I was standing there. Hope you don't mind me saying, but you seem lonely, miss.' He flashed regular white teeth. She supposed he was the sort of man who women wanted to speak to, who knew he had them in his hand.

'I'm not. Well, a little. Surrounded by crowds, one feels it, you know. My sister's just had twins, upstairs.'

He raised his hand, as if a glass was in it. 'Congratulations, Miss Smith. I hope they're all doing well.'

'Were you in France?' she said, cutting him off. The birth was so hot and new in her head. She wanted to talk about something else. 'Tell me about France.' He could have been anywhere, of course, Belgium, Mesopotamia like Smithson, Greece, but all the men she met had always been in France. She was a pull for them, she thought, even though they didn't know it, they saw the same thing in her.

'I don't know where to start.'

'Start anywhere. Before the war, if you like.'

And he did, began talking about his life before, a student at London University (failed to get into Cambridge, father still disappointed), joined up in early 1915, long days of training, then out to France, to wait, sit there, counting the rats, and it was for such long stretches of time between waiting and something happening, then it was all rush and shouting and blood and violence.

'Too dreadful to talk about to a lady like you,' he said.

'I don't know much about it,' she said.

She did. She thought about the letter the family had received after Michael's death, about the lie it told, written because an officer higher up knew Michael from Cambridge and felt sorry for him, didn't want to tell his family that they'd taken Michael out and shot him.

Celia remembered screaming when she was told. She remembered Jonathan trying to calm her, taking her home. He'd written three times since the end of the war and she hadn't answered.

Come to New York, he said in his last one. *My father could help you with the fare. My sisters would like to meet you.* She couldn't bear it, she didn't want the story of Michael's death to be true. Her parents' proud, perfect boy, the Cambridge student, army officer – shot like a dog because he'd stayed back in the trenches, afraid, weeping, hiding.

Gilligan looked nothing like Jonathan, who had been blond and wide-faced. But still, he reminded Celia of him. He exuded the same confidence, an expectation he'd always be listened to as he talked on about the weather, the mud, losing the men beside him. She smiled, nodded. He broke off, sometimes, to tell her how grateful he was that she listened to him, that she understood. Because now that they were back, people didn't want to talk about it, said *get over it, we have!* But it was easy enough to get over things if you just had to read the news, wasn't it? People like him had actually seen it. And you can't forget that, anyone who said they had was lying. They were lying to fit in. But why should anyone do that?

He leant across, grasped her hand. 'You understand, don't you, Miss Smith?'

She nodded. 'People haven't really forgotten,' she said. 'They're just pretending.'

He raised his head. 'That's what makes me angriest, the pretending. Why not tell the truth? We'll never recover!'

She nodded. The crowd was thinning out. A rowdy group of men stood up, laughing, slapped each other on the back, threw her and Gilligan sideways looks.

'I should go upstairs. Thank you, Mr Gilligan.'

'I shall escort you.'

'No need, sir, I insist.'

He clasped her hand. 'I'll pay for it.'

She shook her head. 'It can go on my room.' She blushed at the thought of her father seeing the account for sherry.

'Please let me escort you.'

'I really am fine, Mr Gilligan.'

'Please. It's Peace Night, Miss Smith. You shouldn't be alone.'

The waiter was coming towards them.

She seized her hand back. 'I can't. Maybe I'll be here with my family tomorrow.' She dashed towards the stairs, her heart beating hard.

She rushed up, two steps at a time, face burning. How stupid of her. She thought she could just listen to him talk, and then what? She should have guessed; that he'd feel the same black hole too and think that spending time with her, any girl, might stop it.

Upstairs, she unlocked the door to her room, went in, flung herself against the bed. Her head was still pacing. Outside, on the Strand, she could hear the shouts of people celebrating, men singing 'Tipperary', women shouting. Everywhere, she thought, everywhere there must be men looking for women, company on Peace Night.

She lay on her bed, head turning, staring at the ceiling. 'We're alive!' they might as well be saying outside, as they laughed. 'We've survived.' They were together, hands clasped, arms around each other, *alive*.

She was alone.

FOUR

Celia

Celia tried everything to stay in London. She told Emmeline that she'd surely need help with the twins, talked about what she could do for them. But Mr Janus was insistent: Celia had to leave again.

The hotel manager had hurried them out of the Savoy two days after the birth. 'It's not a place for children,' he said. 'So many people.' They'd packed up their things and struggled into two cabs to the flat in Bloomsbury. It wasn't ready for the babies at all.

Verena and Celia busied themselves with the washing and the tidying. Then Mr Janus burst in, back from his secretive work. Celia made him some tea and he held the twins, fast asleep. After an hour, he asked when they were going to leave.

Celia begged to stay. 'Emmeline needs the help.'

'Sorry, Celia,' Mr Janus said, 'but we have meetings. You'd be in the way.'

'I could help with the meetings,' she said. 'I could take notes.' She had done, once or twice, in the old days, when she'd stayed with Mr Janus and Emmeline during the war. His friends Mr Sparks and Jemima had been there regularly, talking about how they'd bring in the revolution, change the world, see men and women equal, wealth shared, poor people living as long as the rich.

But Mr Sparks didn't come any more and Jemima was living with her elderly parents in Norfolk.

'It's different this time,' Emmeline told her quietly. 'There's more anger. People were promised things if they fought. So what Samuel is doing is really important. And more dangerous.'

'I know that's what they say! I've heard them.' Celia knew she was too easily annoyed by Emmeline playing the older sister, but she still rose to it. 'I just think it is as pointless as it always is. All talk. People don't want a revolution.'

Emmeline had shrugged. 'We'll see. And you have to listen to Samuel. You can't stay. At the end of the week, you'll go back to Stoneythorpe.'

Emmeline was right about Mr Janus – things were different this time. It wasn't the old talk of plans, the stuff that Celia sometimes thought was pie-in-the-sky. It was discussions of demonstrations, fighting. In the three nights she stayed before Emmeline finally sent her away, Mr Janus went out two nights, and the third he had the men over. Emmeline was asleep, but Celia listened at the door. They were talking about an armed demonstration, how they might have to fight the police.

'Aren't you worried?' she said to Emmeline, the day before she left. 'Aren't you worried about him? They're talking of fighting.'

Emmeline was feeding Albert. It was amazing, thought Celia, how they had tiny characters already. Albert, bigger and stronger, cried out for food all the time. 'He's a fighter,' said Mr Janus, holding him up. And he was, a strong child, trying to lift his head already, and he fought everything, the mat you put him down on, the bed, even Emmeline when she took him to feed – and he'd need to empty both sides of her before he'd stop crying for more. 'He doesn't trust the world,' said Mr Janus. 'Quite right.' But when the mat or the napkin or the towel had been brought to obey him, he was all smiles again. He made noises at things. 'He's trying to talk,' said Emmeline. 'Clever boy.' Mr Janus said he was going to be a leader. Celia supposed he was right. Albert slept on his back, open to the world, ready for its blows.

Lily was entirely different. She was small, puny really, never took enough milk. Albert was always ravenous, hard to satisfy. She'd only take a little, then fall away, fretful. She cried and she didn't make noises like her brother. She was shy, hid away from anyone looking at her, slept curled tight, and when Celia held her, she felt fear. 'I'll look after you, little one,' she said. 'I promise.' She knew it was wrong, but Lily was her favourite. It wasn't only because Celia had known she was there, looked into her eyes on that first night, said *I found you*. She also saw herself in her niece, shy, ill at ease, afraid.

'Please let me stay,' she begged Emmeline again. 'You need me to help.' She held Lily close. 'You know I'm good with them.'

Emmeline's face was pale, blue-purple smudges under her eyes. Albert slept well – sometimes five hours at a stretch – but Lily was always awake. Celia thought she hated the dark. 'Samuel says we need the place to ourselves.'

'Or how about if I found rooms – Father would pay – and came in every day? I wouldn't have to stay here.' Albert was lying on Emmeline's lap now, arm waving at the air.

Emmeline shook her head. 'Not for the moment. Samuel needs the flat for himself. He has things he must do. I'm sorry.'

'You mustn't let him! They're dangerous. And how can you look after two babies yourself? You're still exhausted!'

Emmeline shrugged. 'That's the way it has to be. Maybe you can come later. But not now. I'm sorry. He says other things are more important.'

'He doesn't care about you.' Lily was nestled against Celia, not sleeping but quiet.

Emmeline straightened up, pulling her wrapper around her. 'You're wrong to say things like that. And if you say it again, you'll never come back here!'

Celia clasped Lily closer. 'I'm sorry. I didn't mean it, sister. I was wrong. I'll just miss you, that's all.'

Emmeline touched her hand, lightly, a fairy touch. 'I'll miss you too, sister. But it won't be for long. Anyway, Mama and Papa need you at home.'

So Celia took the train back, got home, watched Arthur and Louisa talking endlessly, ignoring her. They walked in the garden together, deep in conversation. Sometimes Celia would come through the door into the parlour and find Louisa, alone, writing.

She'd push whatever it was under her papers and look up, gazing through Celia.

'Were you writing something?' Celia said.

Louisa shrugged. At dinner, she stared at Arthur, listened only to what he said.

One night, the events of Peace Night still burning hard into her mind, she thought she'd attempt to talk to Louisa. Arthur was outside, smoking.

'The war must have been quiet at home,' she said. 'It was quiet here for me too. Mama wanted me to stay. But I had to leave, I really had to. I wanted to go and help. Was it the same for you?'

Louisa shrugged and Celia took it as an encouragement – she started talking about being in the house with Verena, feeling alone, her desire to help. And then she wasn't stopping, the words tumbling out, talking on about France and her life there, confiding, describing. She talked of the men screaming for help, how she recited Shakespeare to them so the pain would stop, the relief when she arrived at the hospital, the white cloth doors ghostly against the dark sky. She talked about Shep, how she hadn't realised she was driving the ambulance in front of her and so when the bombs rained down, she'd thought it was someone else. It was only when she got out to help that she'd seen Shep's poor face. 'Then I heard the news that Michael had died and I didn't go back,' she said. 'The others wrote to me, but I didn't go back. I was too much of a coward. I just stayed in London.'

By the end, she'd been looking at her hands, staring at them as she talked. She knew her cousin was listening hard, that she'd clasp her hands, tell her how she could never imagine such horrors. They'd have a sympathy, so close you didn't need words. Louisa would understand. Celia looked up. But Louisa was staring out of the window. Her cousin wasn't looking at her at all. Celia watched her raise her hand, pick at her fingernail.

'Cousin?' she said softly.

Louisa dropped her hand, looked at her, gave a smile. 'It must have been very awful, Celia,' she said, quietly. She stared at the door. Celia knew: she was waiting for Arthur to come. They sat in silence until he did, striding through the door, demanding Louisa, sweeping her off to look at something or other. After that, Celia stopped trying.

The year slipped by, into September. The leaves turned the colour of burnt honey on the trees. Emmeline wrote to the family that Albert was trying to sit up, Lily was still quiet. She didn't invite them to stay. There were demonstrations about work on the streets of London, near Parliament and the palace, but if Mr Janus was involved, Emmeline didn't tell them.

Celia wandered around the house, sat on her mossy stone under the tree. Rudolf had begun to tell her she needed a purpose. He talked about how, when he was her age, he was already setting up the business – and that Verena was married and learning to run the home. 'You must do something, Celia,' he said. 'Those school reports of yours from Winterbourne always said you had excellent potential. Now look!'

On the day Rudolf told her she needed an occupation, Celia threw herself on to her bed and wept. Then there had been a knock at the door.

'Come in,' said Celia. She was hoping it was her father, meaning to apologise. 'Oh, it's you,'

Louisa stood there, holding a flower. 'I'm sorry you're sad, cousin. I came to see if I could help.'

Celia shook her head. 'I don't think anyone can help. I just have to get out of here.'

Louisa stood, uncertain at the door. 'I can try. Why don't you talk to me?'

Celia sat up. And then, to her shame and horror, all the anger came flooding out. 'How can you help me? You're only a child. There's nothing you can do! Why do you think you can?'

She was shouting at all of them, the whole world, everyone and everything that had been taken from her. But her anger was directed at Louisa. Her cousin stood there, and her lip wobbled. She put the flower on the table by the door, backed out and closed it behind her. Celia turned to cry, thinking, she saw now, about herself and not Louisa.

Celia meant to apologise to her cousin. Really she did. But instead, that night she told them she had a headache and would eat her meal in her room – and so she wrote a letter to Tom. Even though she knew that she shouldn't. It was all over now. She said to herself sometimes that she hadn't really been in love with him while he was away fighting. She had just *told* herself that she was in love with him. It was just her old life she missed.

Then she listened to the words inside her head and they said, *You love him!* She *was* in love with him. She'd thought once the war was over they could be together, but then he'd told her that Rudolf was his father – that his mother and Rudolf had had an affair when she'd worked at Stoneythorpe – and her heart was filled with anger. Her father would never have done that. Tom was wrong.

He'd been shocked by her horror. *You don't think I'm good enough for your family, is that it?* And then the war ended, and they'd been swept up in the excitement. He'd put his arm around her. They didn't speak of it, but the figure of Rudolf hung between them. The night had been cold, glittering. And yet, in the months afterwards, she thought he went back to how he had been before. He hadn't really forgiven her for being so angry when he said Rudolf was his father.

After the war, he'd left the hospital for a convalescent home by the coast. He wrote to say he was going to London to work, gave no address. She'd written letters to his home, but got no reply.

Finally, a few weeks before, she'd received a letter. Thompson brought it up to her. 'I don't know who it's from, miss.'

She tore it open. Tom's handwriting.

Meet me by the church at three tomorrow, he wrote. It looked scrawled, quick. Her heart thumped with anticipation, with the feelings she had spent years trying to control.

The next day, she'd hurried out after prettifying herself. He was standing outside the church, looking up at the sky.

'Hello, Tom,' she said. He turned around to her, not quite

smiling, she thought, but perhaps the sun was in his eyes. 'Thanks for asking to meet me. I thought you weren't getting my letters.'

'My mother sends them on.'

'It's – nice to see you.' The scars on his face were fading already. His eyes were less bloodshot too. She gazed at his arm. He could probably move that fully as well now, the injuries leaving his body. He looked taller, wider, as if he was making money and lived well. His hair had thickened and grown longer over his ears. The war hung heavy on her, she felt it dragged her around. Not him.

'And you.'

'Are you here for long?'

He shook his head. 'No, not really. Look, Celia, I'm sorry. But, you know, things are different. You mustn't write to me as much as you do. We should be friends, of course. But you need to find other friends. Who are your friends?'

She shook her head, blushing.

'You need to find some. Celia, you have to leave Stoneythorpe and find friends.'

'I thought *we* were friends!'

'We were. But we were children then. You can't rely on me.'

'You're still angry with me.' She remembered that awful night, Tom saying he knew Rudolf was his father, Celia refusing to believe him.

'I'm not angry with you. I just think that you need to see that things have changed. I should go. They're waiting for me.'

'Won't you give me your address in London?' She knew she was begging, asking a man for something he didn't want to give. But she couldn't stop herself. It was her only chance.

He turned away. 'I'll send it to you. Goodbye, Celia.'

She hadn't heard from Tom since then and she'd resisted writing to him. But here she was now, sitting down with pen in hand for him, trying to forget all her childish dreams about the two of them falling in love and marrying.

Father says I need an occupation. I know it's true. But I don't know what to do.

She heard his response. *Who are your friends?*

And then she wrote to Jonathan Corrigan in New York, even though she knew she shouldn't, that he'd write back, wonder how she was, ask her to come and see him, that she'd be giving him some sort of small hope when she was only in love with Tom. She felt ashamed of herself, sealing it up to send.

Next morning, she put the letters to Tom and Jonathan on the table to be sent, came down to breakfast and Louisa was there with Verena and Rudolf. Arthur had left early, they said, business. She gave Louisa a smile and her cousin smiled back, shyly. She must have forgiven her, Celia thought. She'd apologise properly later.

'Now, you two,' Rudolf said. 'I've got an idea. I have been look-ing into finishing schools. I think it would benefit both of you to go.'

'No!' said Celia, just as Louisa said, 'Yes!'

Rudolf raised his eyebrow. Verena started talking about flower-arranging and learning to be a lady. 'There are a few excellent ones I have read of in London,' she said. 'But Miss Trammell's is the best.'

'Those places teach you how to get a husband,' Celia said hotly. 'I don't want a husband.'

'I'd love to go,' said Louisa. 'Some of the girls at school were talking about going to that sort of thing. But Mama didn't believe in too much education, you know.'

Celia looked sideways at Louisa. Perhaps this would be the way to speak to her cousin, they could really talk on the train back and forth. She looked at Rudolf. 'What does this school involve? Do we have to go every day?'

'Not every day, no. Two days a week. You'd stay in London. And as for Lady Deerhurst's thoughts, things have changed,' said Rudolf. 'Girls need education.'

'Is table-arranging education?' Celia knew: she was too clumsy for it, too lanky.

Rudolf picked up his knife. 'They are about teaching you to be *rounded*. It would be good for you, Celia.'

'I don't want to go,' said Celia. Everything anyone said made her jumpy, she wanted to shift places and move, not sit still. How could they, she thought, sit still, talk of scones or flowers or the rest of it? People had been dying. 'I wish I could travel instead.'

Louisa gazed at her, wide-eyed. 'Where will you go?'

Celia shook her head. And then, speaking before she even realised what she was saying, the words were out. 'Germany.

'Germany,' she repeated, and sat up, looking at Rudolf. 'I would like to go to the Black Forest.' Those childhood days with her cousins Johann and Hilde, swimming in the streams, eating bread and cheese at Aunt Lotte's heavy table, Uncle Heinrich, Rudolf's cousin, carving trinkets out of wood. The house had been her father's family summer home, when he'd been a boy, when he and Heinrich had played there together.

Rudolf dropped his knife to his plate. It clattered. 'It's hardly a place for a holiday.'

'I mean it, Papa. Like we used to do, before the war. You always said we could visit our cousins, once everything was over.'

Verena coughed. Rudolf straightened up. 'Yes, well, you were a child then. I hardly think they're in a fit state to receive you. There's no money.' They'd received three letters since the end of the war. Johann had come back injured and they'd lost half their money in a war investment scheme.

'Your cousin was on the *other side*,' said Louisa.

'Maybe they'd feel better if I went. I could take them things from here. I want to go. Then, on the way back, I might go to the battlefields of France. I've read a lot about the tours they run there.'

'Why anyone would want to go to the battlefields, I don't know,' said Rudolf. 'Why can't they leave the past in the past?'

'I don't think it's wise,' said Verena. 'I don't think anyone is travelling to Germany these days. Is it even possible, husband?'

'I believe people are travelling on business. So she could… But no. It might be dangerous.'

'They'd think I was German.'

Rudolf shook his head. 'You can barely speak it.'

'I can. Well enough. Anyway, I'd be with Hilde and Johann. So no one would know about me.'

Rudolf shook his head again. 'Impossible.'

Celia stood up. 'You know, I'm nearly twenty-one now. I can go if I want to. You can't prevent me.'

She looked down at her mother and father. They seemed – suddenly – very small.

'No,' said Rudolf. 'We can't. But we don't have to pay for you. Celia, your cousin needs you to stay with her. The Black Forest we can think about later. When the political situation is settled.'

'Louisa can go to finishing school alone,' said Celia.

'No, she can't. She's too young. You must go too.'

Celia looked at them both, her cousin and her father. Perhaps it was the answer, her possibility of reaching Louisa, befriending her. 'Alright,' she said. 'I'll go.' She snaked her hand across to Louisa's. 'We can go together.'

Verena passed over the prospectus for Miss Trammell's Finishing College. Flower-arranging. Dancing. Dining. Etiquette. Embroidery. Louisa put out a finger, traced the outline of a picture of a girl holding a flower.

But then Arthur came home. Verena told him the plan over dinner that night.

Arthur snorted, threw down his knife. 'Ridiculous. Have you asked Louisa if this is what she wants?'

'Of course she wants to,' said Rudolf, drinking quickly from his glass. 'Verena's poor sister would have wanted us to do our best for Louisa. And Miss Trammell's is an excellent establishment.'

'She doesn't want to. Can't you see?'

Louisa was looking at her plate.

'She does!' said Celia. 'You think no one would want to be with anyone but you.'

Arthur stood up, threw back his chair. 'Get up, Louisa!' He walked around the table, stood behind her. 'Tell them! You don't want to go to this stupid school.'

She looked up at him, her eyes fluttering rapidly. 'I'd like to go to London. I told you.'

'Then you should go to London proper. Not flower-arranging in some place full of silly girls.'

'Now—' Verena began.

But Celia had already stood up. 'Why can't you stop it? Why can't you let her make up her own mind? Why have you got to be in charge?'

Arthur turned on her. 'Rather than you? Is that what you mean? You just want to have everyone to yourself. And you do it by getting your claws in and hanging on tight. No one wants you otherwise.'

Celia fell back. The cold water of his words hit her face. Verena leapt up. Rudolf was saying something. And then Louisa was standing. They all stopped, stared at her. She gazed back – for a moment. Then she turned, ran from the room.

Arthur slammed out of the door after her.

'Don't let him *follow* her,' Celia said.

Verena shook her head. 'I'll go. I'll go and find her.'

Celia stared at the door. 'What happened?' she said to Rudolf.

He shook his head. 'Who knows? Anyway, you can start as soon as I pay the fees, I think.' He was going to do it, she realised. He was going to ignore the awful words Arthur had said to her. Just like her parents always did.

'I'm too old for finishing school.'

'You will be company for Louisa. And that's what she needs.' He turned away, walking slowly to his study.

Celia turned to look out at the garden. A match shone against the darkness. Arthur was smoking out there. She wanted to go to Louisa's bedroom, knock on the door. She could apologise for being unfair and shouting last night. But Verena was in there. She'd wait.

She sat down at her desk. She barely used it these days, the thing was so small and rickety. Rudolf had bought it for her thirteenth birthday; pink and white, painted with flowers. She'd written at it, dreaming about her future, all the things she might do, the potential the teachers said she had. She wondered what any of the girls from Winterbourne were doing now. What was there to do? Maybe they were dreaming of their fiancés, stuck at home too.

She picked up her pen and began writing to Hilde. *It is some time since I last wrote*, she started, then stopped. How was that an explanation? I can't write, she wanted to say, I don't want to write to anybody.

She tried again. And then again, once again, until she had a full sentence. *Things have changed. I wish I could come to see you. Papa said I might. Is there anything you'd like from England?*

She thought of Tom, couldn't help her mind reeling back. Don't write to him again, she said to herself. Don't! The house creaked around her, floorboards shaking. Surely it was noisier than normal? She put it down to her guilty heart.

Celia couldn't sleep at first and then woke repeatedly all night, jolted out of sleep as if there had been a loud noise – but the house was silent.

She woke to shouts. The light was bright through the curtains. She buried her head in the pillow, but the noises were too loud. She pulled on her shawl, poked her head out. Arthur was shouting something. She heard Verena's voice begging him to stop. She ran down the stairs, hearing the voices rise.

They were all at the front door. She hurried forward. 'What's going on?' she shouted. No one turned. Someone was crying. The sun was already bright, flaming out. She pushed between Rudolf and Verena. Arthur and Louisa were arm in arm, standing on the driveway. Louisa was wearing her best white gown, her hat awry, huddling her shawl around her.

Arthur looked as if he'd thrown on his clothes.

'I'm going then!' he said. 'We're going now. You can come and visit us if you like.'

'Where are they going?' said Celia, knowing he might chastise her, shout back. 'Where are you going?' Smithson was sitting on a cart full of boxes. Were those Louisa's *things*? Was that what the noises were last night, them packing up the clothes in boxes?

Arthur looked at her. 'We're going to London.'

Verena coughed, almost a sob.

Celia stepped forward. 'What do you mean, you're going to London?'

'Louisa's always wanted to go to London. So we are.'

'I have,' Louisa said, so quietly you could barely hear.

The marble was cool on Celia's feet as she moved on to the driveway. 'Well, then, I'll come too.'

Arthur shook his head. 'You won't. We're leaving now. We've waited long enough.'

Verena started to cry. Celia put out her hand, reached for Louisa. Her cousin edged back. 'Stay. Please.'

Arthur seized her arm. 'We're going. Don't take on so, Mother. We'll come back.' He was moving towards the cart now, laden with boxes. 'Louisa's young. She needs to see the world, live a little. Not stay cooped up here until she's carted off to some dreary finishing school.'

'Where will you stay? What about your reputation? You're far too young to go to London! Please, dear, it's not safe there. Stay here, we can make visits there if you like. Go with Celia to the finishing school,' pleaded Verena. She held out her hand. 'Come inside. Let's discuss it. We can think of a way.'

Louisa drew back.

'Please don't worry, Aunt. Arthur knows a respectable family with two daughters. I will stay with them,' she said. 'I'll bring presents when I come back. I promise.' Her lip was quivering. She was wavering now, Celia thought, on the brink of changing her mind, if they prompted her hard enough.

'Don't go,' said Celia. 'Come with me instead, to the school that Papa was talking about.'

Arthur reached for Louisa's hand. 'I'm looking after her. She's safe with me. It's time for her to go out and meet people. You all did.' He turned to Rudolf. 'You'll send money, won't you? London's expensive.'

'What about your work, Arthur?' said Rudolf.

'That will take care of itself.'

'But Louisa's so young,' Celia broke in.

'Not much more than you when you ran away to France.'

Celia shook her head. 'It's not the same.' And it wasn't, not anything like her fleeing into the war, lying about her age.

'It's more than the same. That's always what you're like, dear sister. One rule for you, another for everybody else.'

'Please,' said Celia, hearing the begging tone in her voice. 'When will you come back?'

'Maybe a month or two. A few weeks. I'll write with our address. Now, we should go.' He pulled Louisa's arm, gently. 'Let's say goodbye, Louisa.'

Louisa lifted her face. Celia thought she saw a tear, but then in a second it was gone, and her face was flushed, excited. 'Goodbye, Aunt Verena, Uncle Rudolf.' She looked at Celia. 'Will you come soon?'

'Write to me. Please write to me.'

Arthur chivvied Louisa away, almost pulling her in his hurry, helping her up on to the cart. Up there, she turned back, Celia could see, but her face was tiny over the pile of boxes. Celia and her parents stood there, watched them go. Verena held up her hand, waved as Smithson bumped the cart down the driveway.

Rudolf stood at the door and stared after them.

Celia turned to him. 'You always let him do whatever he wants. Why do you do that?'

Verena wiped her eye with her handkerchief. 'Who could stop him? Anyway, he will look after Louisa. He's very fond of her, anyone can see that. As soon as they send the address, we can go and see them. You'd like to go out with them, wouldn't you? Have some fun.'

'Arthur won't let me.'

'He'll come back,' said Verena, speaking quickly because Rudolf wasn't responding, instead staring out at the empty driveway, the sun burning up the horizon. 'They both will. I'm sure of it.'

FIVE

London, August 1920

Celia

'Come along now, ladies, pay attention.' Miss Trammell was holding up an iris. 'Remember the rule. Long-stemmed flowers first. They must form the *centrepiece* of the arrangement.'

Celia gazed at her flower. It was nothing like Miss Trammell's, thin and formless, the stalk so weak it looked about to break. It didn't look like the kind of thing that would stay upright if you placed it in a vase. Miss Trammell was as stiff as a board, she looked like she never even lay down. She would always be upright, her hair in a bun, not a single escaped strand, the blue suit without a crease, her eyes missing nothing behind her glasses. Well, Celia thought to herself, who are you to judge her? You've ended up here, two days a week at the finishing school you said you wouldn't go to.

After class, she walked to the school boarding house in Hammersmith, alone. Emmeline usually said they were too busy for a visit. Celia sat in her room, looked at her notes from the class and thought about Louisa.

After that awful morning in Stoneythorpe, they hadn't heard from Louisa or Arthur for weeks. Finally, Arthur wrote to say that they were living with a woman called Mrs Merling, who had two daughters and had bought Louisa a kitten. He said they'd been to parties. Rudolf sent money. Arthur didn't ask about Celia, she supposed that they didn't want her, thought she was too dull.

Finally, just before Christmas, over three months after they'd left, Arthur agreed that he and Louisa could meet them all in

London. It had been a terrible day, lunch in a grey, chilly restaurant, Louisa quiet and unsmiling, Arthur talking too fast. Rudolf and Verena pretending everything was normal.

Louisa was beautifully dressed in a pale-green gown with a lace layer over the top, a bow around her waist. She had tiny heels on her green shoes, a lace wrap over her shoulders. Her hair was the same but her face was perfectly made-up, bright lipstick on her mouth, her eyes darkened with stuff. She'd got the hang of the new make-up, unlike Celia. She looked so pretty, Celia wanted to reach out and touch her, as if she was art in a museum. But she couldn't say anything, avoided her eyes. Afterwards Mrs Merling had given them tea, showed off her parlour, talked of how well she looked after Louisa.

On Christmas Day, Verena wept, gazing out of the window. She'd bought presents for Louisa, piled them up under their tree. Celia had told her she'd been making a mistake but she too had bought a silver necklace for Louisa in Winchester, wrapped it in tissue paper, kept it in her room, just in case.

Then five months later, as spring was breaking, they'd had a letter from Mrs Merling. Celia had arrived downstairs at Stoneythorpe. Verena was sitting in the breakfast chair, her face white. She was holding a letter.

'What's wrong, Mama?'

Verena stared up at her.

'Louisa's gone. Arthur and Louisa have gone. Mrs Merling has written. She said they've gone, there was some sort of incident with the cat. And now they've gone and she doesn't know where.'

Celia patted her hand. 'I'm sure they've just moved places. They'll write and say where they are.'

Rudolf came to the door. 'They'll write for money. Or Arthur will.'

'She's my sister's child,' Verena said. 'I said I'd look after her, care for her if anything happened. And now I've lost her.'

'She's with Arthur,' said Rudolph. 'They can't stay away for ever. Arthur will look after her; he's a good boy.'

'But what if she goes off on her own? We don't know where

they are. Do you really think Arthur will look after her?' Celia asked. She was beginning to worry, images of Louisa, alone, swirling up in her mind. What if Arthur had left her and she was wandering the streets, no idea where she was?

'Oh, you know Arthur, Celia. He only *pretends* to be bad. She'll be fine if she's with him,' said Rudolf. 'It's if she's gone elsewhere, off on her own, that's what Mama is worried about.'

'I am too!'

Louisa, so young, Arthur gripping her arm on the drive as they prepared to drive away. 'She's only sixteen!'

'She won't go anywhere without him. And he's so fond of her. They'll come back. We'll hear from them next week,' said Rudolf. 'They'll need money. They can't just disappear.'

But they waited for word – and no letter came. Arthur sent no demand for money, Louisa didn't write. After a week of Verena weeping, writing letters to anyone she could think of, Rudolf went to speak to Mr Pemberton, the solicitor. He came back, told them that Mr Pemberton knew a company of agents who could look into Louisa's whereabouts. The Merlings said they hadn't been in touch, didn't know where they'd gone. One of the tracers from the agency thought Arthur and Louisa might have gone abroad.

Every day they waited for news, hoping that some information would come through, that one of the tracers would find a clue. Rudolf kept paying the agency, through Mr Pemberton. Verena wept and Celia found herself obsessed with missing persons – how could you just disappear? How could you? But they had. Celia went up to stay with Emmeline and to visit the Merlings, but Mrs Merling maintained she knew nothing.

Rudolf said he felt sure that they weren't in London – the agency would have found them if they were. 'Mr Pemberton said they must be somewhere else,' he said. 'Perhaps abroad. We have to wait now until they contact us. We can't do more. It would be a scandal if it got out. We'll have to wait. She's safe with him, after all.'

It had only been a week, they told themselves. Then two. Then three, now six. At night, Celia lay awake and thought of Louisa.

Perhaps she was wearing colours, dancing in Arthur's arms, admired by dozens of men, happy, laughing. She would have forgotten all about them. If she ever gave a thought to Stoneythorpe, it was as somewhere where she'd been unhappy, a dusty house full of memories. Arthur had taken her away, set her free. Celia knew, in her heart, that she'd gone.

Then there was the news in June that Louisa's brother, Cousin Matthew, had died of a fever in Calcutta. The news came to the Deerhurst estate and then to Mr Pemberton. Celia looked at the sofa in the parlour. Matthew had sat there after Michael's funeral, talking about painting. He blurred in her mind, a serious child, then a young man. Dead in India, the firm had written, did not suffer. *He loved the country, worked very hard for us.*

'We need to tell Louisa,' Celia said. Rudolf redoubled the efforts to find her again. 'Mr Pemberton thinks some of the money is hers, after all.'

Nothing came back. They couldn't find her. A representative from the company came to meet with Rudolf to talk about the death. He visited Stoneythorpe, stern and upright in black. The company man was very unhappy that Louisa couldn't be found. There was nothing that could be done, Rudolph said. They were trying.

'You will simply have to wait for her,' Mr Pemberton said.

In July, they travelled to London to meet Emmeline in a hotel and take tea on the day after the twins' first birthday. Mr Janus was away, said Emmeline. She was looking more tired than ever. Albert was huge, the same size as a three-year-old Celia had been smiling at on the train. He was walking, determinedly heading off into the hotel dining room, his strong torso wobbling on two squat legs. 'I can't believe how quickly the year has gone,' Verena said to Emmeline. 'He's a little boy now.'

Lily was still tiny but she bounced into Celia's arms as if she knew her, when of course she couldn't really, said Emmeline. 'You do,' whispered Celia, looking into her eyes. 'You really do. You know me.' When she held the child close, she still felt her fear.

'I don't suppose you've heard from Louisa?' Verena said to Emmeline, when she knew, of course, that if Emmeline had she would have said, and anyway, Emmeline hardly went out.

Emmeline leapt up to retrieve Albert, who was crawling under a neighbouring table. He, out of all of them, was the only one who was really at home in the hotel. 'No, Mama. I wish I had.'

That night, Celia dreamt of Arthur and Louisa, wandering through forests together, hand in hand. She chased after them, shouting for them to wait. Louisa turned, looked at her and laughed. She turned back, walked on.

'Yes, that's it,' Miss Trammell was saying to the girl at the front. 'Just there. So the rest of the flowers can bloom out like the sun.'

It was August now, and still no word from Arthur or Louisa. Celia hoped it was because they were happy, forgetting Stoney-thorpe and everything about it. They were celebrating, dancing at parties, somewhere in France, perhaps. They were laughing. If they ever thought of Celia, they'd only think she was an old spinster joke, which she was, twenty-one and arranging flowers at Miss Trammell's.

'Chance would be a fine thing,' said the girl next to her. 'To get any sun, I mean.'

Celia smiled, vaguely. The girl, Miss Brown, had been making friendly overtures ever since she'd started at the beginning of term. She'd sigh under her breath – so that only Celia could hear – when Miss Trammell started talking, sorted out Celia's flowers when she couldn't get them to stand, came up and wished her good morning when they were on separate tables.

Miss Brown was young, would have been pretty if it hadn't been for her large nose. She had sparkling eyes and shiny brown hair. She'd probably make someone an excellent wife, they'd be very happy. *I'm not like you!* Celia wanted to say. *You don't understand.*

Miss Brown had been at home during the war, as Celia should have been. She talked of sewing circles and first-aid classes. I've had a friend, Celia thought, just as you want one. I had Shepherd, in the ambulance station, until she died and none of us could save her.

She fiddled with the flowers for the rest of the afternoon, ignored Miss Brown trying to smile at her. At the end of the day, she gathered her coat and hat.

'I wondered if you'd like to take tea with me?' Miss Brown asked. She blushed. 'If you weren't doing anything else, that is.'

Celia shook her head. 'I can't, I'm afraid. Not today. Sorry.'

'Tomorrow, then? I'm free then too.'

Celia shrugged, seized her coat and hurried past her, knew she was being unkind. She knew the look in Miss Brown's eyes. She wanted someone to make all this silly occupation worthwhile, a friend to share it with. But Celia had known Shep and had lost her – and had lost Louisa too. She walked out, angrily arguing with herself. She hurried past the park, through the heat, past mothers with prams and workmen carrying ladders and bricks, towards her room in Hammersmith.

'Celia!' She turned and saw Tom emerging from behind a glossy parked car. He was smartly dressed in a suit, hair shining, expensive coat. He looked like an actor who'd popped up in the wrong play.

For a few seconds she was too surprised to speak. 'What are you doing here?' she said at last.

'I came to find you. Have you finished for today at the school?'

'No one would call it a school. But yes.' She paused. 'How did you know how to find me?'

'You wrote to me about it, remember?'

'Oh, yes.'

'So I found out the address. I thought you'd be finished about now. Are you going home?'

'I'm going to Hammersmith.' She could hardly speak, her heart on fire. This was what she'd wanted, for months. Tom walking beside her, talking.

'May I come with you?'

She shrugged. 'Of course.' *Why? Why now, after ignoring me all these months, after saying I had to find other friends?* There was a beat in her heart: *what do you want?* She threw it away, ignoring the voice.

He fell into step beside her, dodging the prams. 'A lot of babies around here,' he said.

'I suppose so.' She turned to him. 'You look well. Nice suit.'

'I have my job with Captain Dalton now. I was under him in France. He went back to his family firm, exporting to Europe. I've joined him. I've learnt a lot.'

'Good.'

She paused.

'I haven't seen you for over a year.'

He turned, briefly, looked forward again. 'Has it been that long?'

'Yes. You remember, my cousin Louisa has come and gone since. She came to live with us and then she and Arthur left. We haven't heard from them.'

'Yes. Didn't you say they were living with a family called the Merlings?' So he'd read her letters.

'They've left the Merlings' now. Who knows where they are? Papa says they're abroad.'

'They've gone?'

She shrugged. 'Papa says Arthur is keeping her safe.'

'I'm sure he is.'

They'd reached the Hammersmith tube by now and he held the rail outside the station. 'Let's go to Covent Garden from here. Are you free?'

'I suppose so.' She followed him down into the station. Her heart beating hard.

'Is your office here?' she asked, as they were coming out of the Underground into Covent Garden twenty minutes later. The street by the station was thronged with people. She wished she'd put on her nicer hat (or even cared about hats at all, since she never normally did).

'No. It's near Monument.'

'So why here then?'

'The chaps at work said it's the place to take a girl.'

'What do you mean, *the place to take a girl*?'

He shrugged. 'You know.'

But she didn't know. He'd ignored her letters, told her to make new friends. And now here he was, taking her somewhere his friends thought a girl would like.

'How are you finding finishing school? In your letter you said you feared it would be dull.'

'It is dull. Louisa was going to come too. I only said yes because she wanted to go. Now she's somewhere with Arthur. And I'm here.' She followed him around the corner, past a large restaurant where groups of people were sitting outside, talking and drinking. Three men brushed past them, chatting. The buildings, she thought, looked old and tired. The paint was peeling. But the people were like ornaments on a Christmas tree, shiny, full of sugar. The girls were very fashionable, bright, small hats like the tops of bluebells, shoes with heels. Rudolf would never let her wear skirts like that.

'You know, Celia, you should be doing something better. You used to want to go to college.'

'I know. But Papa wants me to be at home. He says I have lots of time in the future.'

He strode ahead, then turned back. 'Celia, it's not your fault that Michael died. It isn't. Emmeline and Arthur do what they want. Why shouldn't you? Try for college, or get a job. Something. Girls work in offices these days. Go to Paris. Didn't you want to go to Paris?'

'Papa needs me.' And he did. Who was she to be selfish and rush off to Paris or somewhere, after everything he'd suffered? The memories of the dark days of the war surfaced, Verena hardly getting out of bed. If Celia left, it might go back to how it was. She was holding it together.

'You can't stay there for ever. How long is this finishing course, anyway?'

'A year. But you can do another if you do well in the exams.'

'Which of course you will.'

'No! I'm terrible.' She was. Flowers fell apart in her hands, she forgot the table arrangements, failed at the curtseys, couldn't plan the menus, came bottom of the dinner-party test for asking the girl to her left about religion. When she'd come home with her report, Verena had almost cried.

'Then you should leave.'

'I'm just doing this to please Papa. Then I can do what I want.'

'But what if you spend the whole time pleasing your father? You're twenty-one. You should be free!'

She stopped. A pretty girl in a smart hat almost bumped into her and then went crossly on her way.

'Tom, why are you asking me—' Celia stopped.

The girl in the hat. She knew her.

'Louisa!' she cried, turning back towards the girl. 'Stop!'

The woman was walking away, but turned when Celia shouted.

'It's me, Celia!' She ran closer, touched her arm. 'Louisa! We've been looking for you!' She gazed at Louisa's eyes, saw the flecks of green in the blue around the pupil. She'd cut her hair into the shingled style, like all the girls in the magazines. It edged her face under her hat. She was fashionably dressed, looked older than Celia, even.

'It is you!' Celia almost flung herself into her cousin's arms. 'I knew it! What on earth are you doing here? Why haven't you written?'

'Hello, cousin.' Louisa bit her lip. She looked nervous, unsure. She disentangled herself, stood away.

'How are you? We've been worried about you!' Celia was gabbling now, she knew, talking, talking, trying to stop Louisa from walking away. She felt her cousin pulling her hand from her grasp. 'We've been looking everywhere for you.'

'Well, I'm fine.' Her eyes shifted to the side and she turned away again. 'I should go.' Celia thought she looked afraid.

'What about Arthur?' Tom was standing close, but she wasn't going to introduce him. She hadn't got time. She held tight to Louisa's hand.

'What about him?'

'He's not with you? We thought he was.'

'I should go.' She pulled away.

Celia seized her cousin's hand back. 'Don't go! How are you? Tell me how you are. We could meet. Are you staying nearby? What hotel are you in?'

Louisa shook her head. 'Goodbye, cousin.'

'Don't go. Please.'

Louisa tugged her hand back, but more gently this time. 'You can tell them I'm fine, if you like. I am. You don't need to look for me.'

'We miss you. We thought you were in Europe.'

Then she thought. 'Cousin, we have news of Matthew—'

Louisa turned away. Celia grasped her again.

Louisa waved her hand, gently, as if flapping away a small fly. 'Good afternoon, cousin. I have your address. If I want to, I'll write.' Celia stood there, watched her walk away. The white dress danced in the sun. She turned a corner, was gone.

'She doesn't want to see you.' Tom was watching too.

'You don't understand. Something's wrong. She looked afraid. I should go after her. We've been looking for her for so long.'

He took her arm. 'You shouldn't. You'll make it worse. You have to wait for her to come to you. She will, I'm sure. People always do.'

'What if she never does?'

He shrugged. 'Then you have to accept it.'

'This way,' Tom said, pointing to a door with peeling gold paint. 'Let's go in here.'

The doorman ushered them through to a rather grand lobby with cream seats and tiny trees and flowers in pots dotted around. They stepped through a doorway of iron and glass to a great dining room, filled with smart-looking people talking over silver plates of cakes and tea.

She couldn't help herself. 'Is this where your friends said you should take a girl?'

'Don't you like it?'

'Of course I like it. That's not what I meant.' But he wasn't really listening as he skipped ahead after the waiter and sat down at a good table by the window. He must, she thought, look rich to them. Perhaps he was.

The waiter pushed her chair in and she shook out her napkin. She felt hot looking directly into Tom's face; she wanted to look away. She needed time to think about her meeting with Louisa.

She watched the men scurrying around. It seemed strange to see places where all the workers were men once more.

'Business is going well,' Tom said. 'I'm rather enjoying it. Captain Dalton said he'd need me to take over the travelling soon.'

'Must be interesting.'

He smiled, slightly, and beckoned for a waiter.

'How is your mother?' she managed to say, after he'd ordered tea.

'Oh, quite well.'

'And Mary?' Rudolf had offered to take Tom's younger sister into service while Tom had been in hospital. Mary had refused, said she would go to a hospital to train as a nurse instead.

'Doing well, I think.'

She gazed around them. The waiter came with the tea and a plate of scones. Louisa's face flashed in her mind. *If I want to, I'll write.*

'Thank you.' Celia took a scone.

Then Tom leant forward. 'Celia, I've been thinking. I've got an idea.' He grinned, his eyes bright.

'What is it?'

'I want to find out about my father.'

Her heart sank, but then off he went, talking nonstop. 'Celia, I'm determined. I know there's something there.'

She breathed. 'I know your mother said that my father is also your father. But he can't be. I'd *know*. He wouldn't have done that.'

Tom split his scone with his hands, picked up the knife for the butter. She watched his movements, deliberate and slow, his long fingers, neatly pared nails. Then he looked up. 'How do you know? He wouldn't tell you. Why else would he have paid for my education? I think Rudolf really is my father.' He gripped her hand. 'Celia, you can help me.'

She stared at him, felt his hand tight on hers. 'Tom—'

But he wouldn't stop, he was talking again, his hands picking wildly at the scone. 'There's something there,' he repeated. 'I know it. I have to find out. You can help me. You can ask them at Stoneythorpe. You could find the records from then, the household records. There would be a clue in there! And a diary. Did your father ever write a diary?'

That was it. She pushed back her chair. 'Is that all you wanted? I told you, no! He's not your father, he never could be. You wish for it, but it's not true!'

'You don't want to help me?'

She shook her head violently. 'No! Of course not!'

'Celia,' he said, putting his hand out. 'Sit down. Let me explain.'

'I don't want to hear any more!' There were tears coming, she could feel them at the sides of her eyes. She fought to push them down. 'Is this the only reason you came for me? Why can't you stop with this?'

He was reaching for her hand. 'Celia. Don't talk so loudly.' People were turning around. She could see a waiter coming for them.

'I'm going to leave.'

His chair scraped as he stood up too. 'Celia. Don't.' The people around them were openly staring now, as if Tom and Celia were putting on a play for them.

'Your mother lied. Why can't you face it?' She turned, hurried to the exit. A waiter, wordlessly, disapprovingly, passed over her coat and hat. She flung them on, ran into the street, turned and hurried away, barely knowing where she was going, but going fast, so that he couldn't catch her.

As she walked out towards the theatres of Shaftesbury Avenue, she saw a cab approaching and ran to catch it. 'Waterloo, please,' she told the driver. It would eat up practically the rest of her allowance for that week, but she didn't care. She sat back in the coolness of the taxi, stared out of the window, felt hot, red thoughts dash across her mind.

On the next day, she travelled up to London as normal. But at

Waterloo she took another train, didn't head west to Hammer-smith, but up again to Covent Garden. She got out at the same station, and walked the same route that she and Tom had taken the night before. At the door to the hotel, she leant against the peeling gold paint and put her hands over her face, let the tears fall.

'Miss Witt.' Celia looked up into Miss Trammell's face. 'What exactly is this?'

Celia looked down. The flowers were broken. She'd been shred-ding them with her hands, not realising. Her mind had been full of Tom and Rudolf and Louisa – it was only a few weeks since she'd seen her cousin. She had forgotten she was even at Miss Trammell's class. She gazed up at the woman's thick glasses, the powder gathering in the creases of her face, the bun at the back of her head that never let a hair go free. 'I'm sorry, Miss Trammell,' she said. 'I wasn't thinking.'

'But this is a whole bunch of flowers that you've spoiled, Miss Witt. Do you not care for beauty?'

'Of course I do. I just...'

'Miss Witt, perhaps you might come with me,' she said. 'Let's go to my office. Class, continue. Miss Evans will come in a few moments.'

Celia followed Miss Trammell out of the classroom, head down. Miss Trammell opened the door to her office. 'Sit down, Celia,' she said, gesturing at a threadbare chair.

Miss Trammell perched behind her desk, steepled her fingers and looked over them like an owl.

'Miss Witt, is our world really the right fit for you?'

Celia gazed at the mottled wood of the desk.

'Miss Witt, we would never ask anyone to leave, exactly. But you are hardly happy here, don't you agree?'

Celia nodded.

'Our strengths are not yours.' Miss Trammell shuffled through a pile of papers. 'Your results were very poor, half fails and the rest you barely scraped through. This does surprise me. Your reports from Winterbourne School were really very good. But more importantly, Miss Witt, you do not seem to like it here. I cannot see you've made any friends. And our academy is all about making friends.'

Celia shook her head.

'You don't stay for any of the social events and I never see you walking with the other girls.'

'I know. But my father wants me to be here.'

'Yes, dear. But you don't want to be here, do you?'

'No.'

'Well, then, dear, you must work out what you do want. It's very clear that the answer is not studying at our academy.'

'I could try again!' She couldn't go home and tell Rudolf and Verena that Miss Trammell had sent her home. Rudolf would be so ashamed. If Celia couldn't even make it through a course of flower-arranging and menu-planning, what *could* she do? Verena would weep, she'd have to tell Lady Redroad and people might laugh at them.

Miss Trammell shook her head. 'Miss Witt. I said to your father when you began – the academy never gives up on a girl. Every girl can be coaxed to bloom. And I've had some challenges over the years! But I'm not in the business of making our ladies actively unhappy. And that's what we seem to make you, Miss Witt.'

'I'm not.'

Miss Trammell stood up. 'Miss Witt, I will write to your father about the fees.' She stood up, smiled. 'I'm sure we can come to some arrangement.'

And then it struck Celia, as Miss Trammell picked up her papers and smiled for her to stand too – she was free. Yes, Rudolf would be angry, but she'd never have to come back.

Celia hurried through Waterloo station, her heart light with her own liberty. She would never have to read notes about flower-arranging on the way home *ever again*. She felt so free, she considered buying chocolate and a newspaper at the stand. The papers were covered with news about someone who'd fallen off a cliff in Margate. Poor thing. A suicide, she supposed.

She hurried to the train, her mind reeling. She'd travel, see the country, the world! She'd travel the Black Forest and then the rest of Europe. She'd do what she wanted.

At Stoneythorpe, Jennie pulled open the door. Her hair was disarrayed, her face red. 'Oh, Celia. Your mother's been waiting for you.'

Celia looked at Jennie's face, her swollen eyes.

'What is it?'

Jennie waved her hand. 'She's in there.'

Celia ran to the parlour. Verena had her back turned, looking out of the window. 'I've got to tell you—' Celia began. 'There's something I must tell you.'

Verena turned and her face was white. 'She fell.'

'Who?' asked Celia. 'Who fell?' But her heart flung itself to the bottom of her body and a voice called out: *Don't listen! Don't hear!*

Verena put her hand to Celia's face, but didn't quite touch her skin. Her fingers drifted. 'It's Louisa, Celia. Louisa's dead.'

SIX

Stoneythorpe, September 1920

Celia

Celia gazed at her mother. 'What do you mean, dead?' Verena's words seemed like a magic spell, something flying up into the sky. 'How can she be dead?'

Verena put her hands over her face.

'I saw her in London just a few weeks ago.' The door of the restaurant, gold paint peeling off the wood.

Verena didn't move. 'They were in Margate. And she's dead.'

Celia gazed at her. 'How did it happen?'

'She fell from a cliff. Arthur was with her.'

'Where is he?'

'I don't know. The police are looking for him. Your father's gone with them. They've been here all day, asking about him. Treating me like a criminal. They're coming back tomorrow. Asking so many questions.'

'I saw stories at the station about a girl who fell from a cliff. Was that Louisa?' The flurry of details screaming out about the death. *Poor thing*, she'd thought. *Poor girl. A suicide.* Louisa, her long fair hair strewn about her as she lay crumpled on the rocks. Louisa in her pale-green tea dress before Christmas, her shoes with the heel.

'She killed herself?'

'We don't know. They need to speak to Arthur.'

'Is he still in Margate?'

Verena shrugged. 'I don't know. I can't …'

'I saw her. I saw her in London. I told you. I ran after her and tried to talk to her. She wouldn't talk to me. She said she was fine. She *looked* fine.'

Verena put her head in her hands. 'Celia. Please stop.'

'I should have made her come. I should have forced her.' She could have made Tom help her, pull her into a car.

Verena turned away. 'Rudolf is coming back later. Emmeline is arriving tomorrow. You can ask them. I can't think. I'm going to bed.'

Celia sat in the parlour, staring out of the window. Then she roused herself. She went to find Thompson. 'I have to go to Margate. She can't be on her own.'

'Margate? You can't go alone. And there's nothing you can do for her now anyway, miss. I'm sorry.'

'I have to go. Will you take me to the station?'

He shook his head. 'They'd never allow it. Wait until Mr de Witt comes home, at least.'

'I have to go now.'

'Let's wait until he comes home. He won't be long now.'

She waited in the hall until Rudolf returned, half an hour later. He put down his hat, exhausted, dropped it on the hall table. She begged him to let her leave. 'You can go tomorrow, Celia,' he said. 'Stay here for the moment. Your mother needs you.'

'Louisa needs us. She's there. Alone.'

'Tomorrow.'

While she waited that night, Celia's mind spooled and shot. She tried to distract it, to force herself to stay calm. She tried to remember happy things. The birth of the twins on Peace Day.

The next morning, she woke to a hammering on the front door. She heard Thompson walk to it across the marble floor. There was a shout of voices, questions. He slammed the door again. But then they were still shouting. 'Where's Arthur de Witt? Why are you hiding him? Bring him out here!'

She put the pillow over her head, tried not to weep.

'How could this have happened?' Emmeline was staring at them. She and Mr Janus had hired a driver, hurried down first thing in the morning. 'Louisa's dead, Arthur's nowhere to be found and there's all those people from the papers screaming outside. What are we going to do?'

'Nothing,' said Verena. 'Arthur will come back. It was a terrible accident.'

'That lot outside will find new blood,' said Mr Janus.

The police were due to come back again in an hour.

'How could Arthur have disappeared? How could he have disappeared in the confusion of the fall? That's what the police said, yes?'

'Do you think he fell too? When nobody was looking?' Celia said.

Rudolf shook his head.

'Of course not. He's just gone somewhere, stricken with grief,' said Verena.

'That's quite what happened. He's been driven out of his mind with grief. He loved Louisa.'

'Maybe he panicked,' said Emmeline, joggling Albert. 'He always did as a small boy, don't you remember? He'd run away for anything. If anything even got spilt, he'd run away. Even if it wasn't his fault. That's what has happened now. He's run away in a panic.'

They all pondered it: Arthur running away, afraid of being told off for spilt milk.

'He needs to come back,' said Celia. 'If he just came back then everything could be sorted out.'

Jennie came into the room. She looked overwhelmed. 'The men from the papers say if you'll speak to them just once then they'll go.'

Rudolf shook his head. 'Mr Pemberton said not to speak to them. Tell them to go away.'

Celia watched them, listened to the words, let them run over her head.

They kept running over the next days, when the detective from the police came to talk to her, asked her questions about Louisa, her state of mind, if she'd received any letters from her. They asked her about Arthur, if she knew where he was, over and over. She described six times, always to different people, her meeting with Louisa in London. *Why didn't you stop her? Why didn't you follow her?*

They said they'd write to Tom to find out what he had been doing. They went over and over where she had been on the day Louisa died. Why did she leave the school? She listened, nodded, shook her head. No. I don't know.

'They think we're hiding him,' said Emmeline, flatly, that evening. 'They think we know where he is.'

'Well, do you?' asked Celia, weary after a day of being questioned. 'Maybe you do. Just tell them.'

'Don't be stupid.'

Verena was crying. 'They said terrible things. They asked about Louisa's money, over and over. And what benefit came to Arthur. Awful. I said she was his cousin. He was looking *after* her. That's all.'

'All the money would have gone to Matthew, we told them that,' said Emmeline, wearily. 'And then, who knows, probably a cousin on their father's side. The father comes first, doesn't he? But they're obsessed with it.' Mr Pemberton was trying to work out what would happen to the money now. Or even where it was. They needed to see if Louisa had left a will. But the police had said they found nothing in her belongings.

'Why are you talking about money?'

'Celia,' said Mr Janus patiently. 'If the money comes to us, we might be suspects. Don't you see?'

'What?'

'That we might be involved in her death. Didn't you say they asked you where you were on the day she died?'

'Well, I was at the school.'

'You're the only one of us who was seen in public. Emmeline was at home, so were your mother and father. But still, don't you see? Arthur had nothing to gain from killing her. The money wouldn't come to him – it comes to your parents, if it comes to anybody. So why would he do it?'

She gazed at her parents. 'No.'

'I think we're out of suspicion. They know that your father didn't hurry down there to push her off. That would be ridiculous. But watch what you say.'

The reporters were still outside, but Celia ordered a taxi into Winchester. She needed a black coat to wear, something more suitable than her shabby grey thing. She came out of the back door, met the car at the side and they drove through the reporters. The driver talked, but she gazed out of the window.

At Winchester, she asked him to stop at a department store. She was about to enter when she saw a newsstand. She edged closer. Arthur was on the front of every page. *Blood in the Aristocracy!* one paper cried. *Mysterious death!* shrieked another. She bought all the papers. She told the man on the stall that she was learning to be a reporter herself. He said he could offer her some old papers.

Celia took all the papers, then bought a bag from the department store. She bundled them up into it. Then she wandered the floors for the next two hours, not really looking at the clothes. The staff probably thought she was there to steal things.

That evening, back at Stoneythorpe, she opened the bag and stared at the papers. Pages and pages about the decline of the aristocracy. Their country houses were crumbling and now their morals were disintegrating too. The fathers had led society in fighting the enemy and upholding the values of Empire – but now the sons were lost, dilettantes, spending their time at parties with cocktails and committing dreadful murders. The more recent stories were all about Germans.

One editorial said all the Germans should have been expelled after the war, that if Asquith had listened, people would be safer. Now, here they were, throwing English roses over cliffs because of their own selfish greed. Louisa's fortune was variously estimated. *The Times* said £25,000, the *Express* twice that, another declared it was nearly a million. Celia had to admit to herself that she had no idea how much it was. There was talk about the German mind – mean, cruel, murderous.

There was little real news, she supposed – politicians infighting, more arguments about inflation. So it was hardly surprising that the papers seized on Arthur and Louisa.

Haven't they killed enough of our flower of youth? cried the *Mercury*. *Now they kill young girls as well!* Celia read long descriptions of Rudolf's internment camp at Knockaloe and sentimental tableaus of Lady Deerhurst's death at the hands of the Spanish flu – even though it hadn't been the flu at all. The Deerhursts were strong, upstanding, honourable – dragged by marriage into the horror and cruelty of Germans. She read portraits of them – Rudolf, interned and criminalised, Verena the innocent, tricked into marriage by Rudolf and then unable to escape. Arthur was evil. Emmeline wayward for marrying her tutor. She read that Michael had only gone to war to undermine the effort and support the enemy and she screamed so loudly that she thought she'd woken the whole house. Under it all was Louisa, lost, alone, dead at the bottom of a cliff.

SEVEN

Celia

'I want to go to Margate,' Celia said again a few days later. 'She's on her own.'

'You can't go alone,' said Rudolf. 'But someone does need to identify her.'

'I'll come with you,' said Mr Janus. 'I'll identify her. I've seen more violence than you two. They'll only want someone who saw her recently anyway, they won't mind who.'

'I saw her. I saw her a week ago. I could go. I was in the ambulances.' Celia said it faintly, though, for it was not the same, driving a man with injuries, seeing him being pushed into the back of her ambulance. They had been shot at, gassed, blown up – but they weren't Louisa. 'You haven't seen her for a long time,' she tried.

'I can remember. I think this one is my job,' Mr Janus said.

Two days later, Emmeline, Mr Janus and Celia travelled down, listened to the policeman, and then went to the morgue. Mr Janus came out, his face quite white, holding tight to the arm of the policeman. 'You wouldn't know her,' he said faintly. 'You really wouldn't know her.'

'I never thought I'd see myself rely on a policeman for support,' he said that evening, in the hotel. 'But I couldn't stop. I held him. I couldn't let go.'

Emmeline put out her hand. 'Tell us, husband. If it would help. Tell us what you saw. We can be strong.'

He shook his head. 'No words to describe it. They don't exist.'

Celia nodded. He was right. You might say you could be strong, you might think you could bear to see the human body mangled, torn, the soul flung out, the face blooded. You couldn't. She couldn't. Not Louisa, the pretty doll, made to decorate the world. She held her sister's hand and felt gratitude to Mr Janus surging in her heart.

Then, on the way home, she wondered – should she have gone in? Perhaps then she would have seen something. There might have been some clue that told her the truth. She imagined Arthur's handsome face reflected in Louisa's big pale blue eyes. His horror as she fell.

The police told Mr Janus they were keeping Louisa's belongings for the moment. 'We should go to the guest house where they were staying,' Celia said. 'We should go to look.'

Mr Janus shook his head. 'They'll see us. What would it look like?'

'Please.'

'Well, perhaps we could try. Quickly.' They walked to the seafront and towards the hotel Louisa and Arthur had stayed in. The White Cliffs Hotel was a shabby-looking place, once grand, she supposed, but now with peeling paint around the windows, muggy glass in the main door. 'We can't go in,' said Mr Janus. 'They'll tell the police. It will look strange.'

Celia jumped forward. 'We have to. We have to see it.'

Mr Janus shook his head. 'Come on, Celia, don't you see it's impossible? There will probably be police in there as well. Let's go.'

She nodded, followed him.

A dark-haired little man caught up with them. 'Mr and Mrs Janus?' he said. 'Miss Witt?' Mr Janus grasped Celia's arm. 'I wondered if I might ask you a few questions.'

'No!'

'You could put forward your side of the story. Name is Pete Sanders. I'll take an exclusive from you.'

'No!' Mr Janus hurried her forward. But Mr Sanders followed them, talking all the way.

'Don't follow us in here!' Mr Janus shouted at the door of their hotel. Mr Sanders hung back.

Celia wished her sister and Mr Janus goodnight, then went up to her room. Next morning, at eight (Mr Janus and Emmeline weren't getting up until nine), she pulled on her gown and shawl, grabbed her shoes and hurried out of the door. Downstairs, the maids were dusting the hall. She ran out into the quiet street, hurried back to the White Cliffs Hotel. Mr Sanders wasn't there.

The hall was busy with guests coming in and out. She walked quickly up the stairs – it might be, she supposed, as if she was secretly going to the ladies' lavatory. She ran up to the second floor and cut past the rooms. Room 24 was at the end. This, according to the police report, had been where Louisa had stayed. The door was open – and a pile of brushes and dusters outside. She edged around them. There was no maid in the room. The joy of luck struck her heart and she stepped in. The room looked like all the others, clothes draped over the chairs. Emmeline and Mr Janus had been wrong. There weren't police here – and they hadn't even kept the room as it was when Louisa had died. They were offering it to other people already.

She put her hand on the bedspread. It had probably been washed five more times since Louisa had slept there. She moved to the window. It looked out on to the road, towards the cliffs. She could have seen them from here, Celia realised. Louisa must have stood there, gazed out at the cliffs – and so saw the place where she'd one day die.

'Can I help you?' A maid was standing behind her, her face set.

'I was just – looking for my room.'

'What room is that?'

'Fourteen!' Celia cried, and then made a dash for the door. She heard the woman call after her, but she picked up her skirts and ran, hurtling down the stairs, out into the road. She walked slowly back to her hotel and into breakfast with Emmeline and Mr Janus. 'I took a sea walk,' she said. They looked at her blankly.

'We have to go to the police station today,' said Mr Janus. 'I know we spoke to them at Stoneythorpe, but they want more now. In case anything jolts our memory, being here.'

They went to the police station, sat in separate rooms, talked about Arthur and Louisa. When they came out, reporters followed them to the hotel, shouting questions. Mr Sanders was there, coming up close. He slipped his card into Celia's hand. 'Talk to me,' he whispered into her ear. 'I'll listen.'

The stories whirled around. The detectives said they'd opened an inquest. Without Arthur, they said, they couldn't know what had happened. Celia, Mr Janus and Emmeline sat through three days of it. Celia listened to the evidence, dizzied. *Talk to me*, she heard Mr Sanders saying. *Me.*

And then finally, they were free.

'Death by misadventure,' pronounced the coroner.

Death by misadventure.

The newspaper men gathered at the door for a comment but Mr Janus refused. He shook his head at Mr Sanders.

'No one implicated Arthur,' said Mr Janus, when they'd got through the men and reached their room. 'They said he was near. But she tripped and fell. That's what they say.'

'See,' said Emmeline. 'Arthur just panicked. He shouldn't have done. He should have stayed here and it would have all been sorted out.'

An accident. A terrible accident.

After the suspicion, the stories, the cruel words, here was the truth. An accident. But still the newspapers wrote long comments about how, even though Arthur didn't kill Louisa, he was unkind to her – a poor girl sacrificed to German evil. Mr Janus told Celia not to look at them, but she couldn't help it. 'The stories will die down,' he said. 'There's nothing to write about now. No news. They're all just annoyed that they didn't get the bloodthirsty outcome they wanted.' He snorted. 'One in the eye for them.'

On the next day, they passed Mr Sanders walking to the police station. Mr Janus turned around and shrugged at him. 'An accident,' he said, smiling slyly. 'Bet you're annoyed by that.'

'Stop it!' hissed Emmeline. She pulled him away.

Celia hurried after them. When she turned back, Mr Sanders was still watching them. He had an odd twisted smile on his face.

'You can take the body,' the detective had told Mr Janus. 'She's been investigated for the post mortem.'

The funeral man told them that they would put a mask over Louisa's face. Like a soldier's mask, Celia thought miserably. The body wore a blonde wig that curled over her eyes. It was how she might look had she been on stage playing a big expressive role, even pantomime. Celia thought of Louisa as she had seen her last, the thin girl who wouldn't speak to her. She put orange blossoms on the coffin lid, even though she knew they were for brides.

On the way out of the parlour, the funeral man put something into Celia's hand. 'The family ring, madam. No other jewellery.' Celia clasped it, then pushed it on to her own finger, her right ring finger, not left. It was too small. She didn't care. She wouldn't take it off.

Two days later, Celia was sitting outside in the cold, head in her hands. Her mother was still in bed; who knew where her father was. It was late afternoon. She was hating herself, reviling her weakness. She'd gone up to Louisa's room, laid on her bed, put her head on Louisa's pillow, trying to find her. It had been washed, of course. Louisa hadn't even *slept* there for ages, but still, she couldn't help it. She found herself lying on Louisa's carpet, trying to find the spot where her feet had fallen as she climbed out of bed, trying to catch some of her soul. She'd lain there, head on the rug, until she'd come to herself, realised how ridiculous she was being and got to her feet. Then she started crying.

Later she was sitting in the garden, head in her hands, when a shadow fell over her – and she looked up to see Jennie.

'There's someone to see you, Celia.'

She shook her head. 'I'd rather not. Whoever it is, can you tell them to come back tomorrow?'

Jennie stood, too long. 'I don't think so.'

Celia looked up and there was Tom, walking out through the

door and coming towards her. She stood up. 'What are you doing here?'

'I wanted to see you.'

Jennie raised her eyebrows, walked away.

'I suppose you read all about it in the papers.'

'The police came to see me. Not that I had anything to say. I'm sorry, Celia. I really am. Your face – it breaks my heart.'

'Poor Louisa.'

And then he was sitting beside her, clasping her hands, looking at her. 'Oh, Celia, I'm so sorry.'

'She fell off a cliff. I've been looking for some trace of her here. I can't find her anywhere.'

He was gripping her hands harder. The late autumn sun burnt his face. 'Tell me about it. What happened? I want to help.'

She gazed back, looking at the flecks of hazel in his irises, the curve around the pupil, his hands around hers, the wrinkles on his hands becoming part of hers, the whorls on his thumbs touching her skin. She was about to speak, tell him. And then she stopped.

He was only there because he felt bad. Otherwise, he'd never see her, never want her. He hated her, was angry with the whole family. She shook her head. 'It was kind of you to come. Really it was. But you can't help us.'

'I could listen.'

'You said you didn't want anything to do with us.'

'This is different.'

So you only want to see me when my cousin is dead. She shook her head. He'd listen to her talking about Louisa, be kind, and then what? He'd go again, she'd write to him and he'd ignore her letters. She took her hands back to her lap. 'Thank you for coming, Tom. Thank you for thinking of us. But I can't. You probably should go.'

She watched him amble off, his tall body silhouetted against the dying sky. He walked towards the door of the parlour – she thought of calling him back, but he went into the house and the moment was gone.

EIGHT

Germany, August 1921

Celia

'Celia!' shouted a voice. 'This way! We're over here!' She looked around the dockyard. The boat pumped steam over their heads. Throngs of people in black were pushing towards her. She felt a hand seize hers and tried to shake it off. The voices around her were babbling words that sounded nothing like the German she knew from school.

'Celia,' the voice said. 'It's me!'

She looked at the dowdy woman holding her arm and realised it was cousin Hilde. She looked exhausted, brow furrowed, hair even paler than before.

What happened? Celia wanted to ask. Instead, she grasped her cousin's hand. 'Thank you for coming to meet me.'

Rudolf had finally allowed it. In the aftermath of Louisa's death, she'd begged him again to let her visit the Black Forest.

'You're needed here,' he said. 'Your mother needs you. Think what it's like for her, with Arthur gone, with Louisa...'

Celia shook her head. 'It's just a few weeks. Please.'

And so Rudolf did, his face sad and old. Verena wept, but, thought Celia, she always wept.

Death by misadventure. Louisa, dead at the bottom of the cliffs, her pretty hair ruined. The body in the ground. If Celia left, then maybe Arthur would come back. He'd return and the police would speak to him and everyone would know it was only an accident.

The newspapers had, for the most part, left them alone after

85

the coroner's verdict and Verena said people were speaking to her in the street once more. But still, the taint remained.

And then she reminded herself: what did it matter that the newspapers got it wrong? They were alive. Louisa was dead.

'Thank you for visiting. We could never come to you in England.' Hilde's English was slower and more accented than it had been before. Of course, she wouldn't have been speaking much English over the years of the war.

'You could now. They've changed the rules.'

Hilde shrugged. 'No money. Come. My mother and father are waiting.' She took Celia's hand and led her through the crowds of people. Halfway through, she gave it a squeeze. 'I'm glad I found you.' The porter hauled Celia's trunk behind them.

They finally pushed their way through to the far side of the crowd. There huddled Heinrich and Lotte, looking tiny, as if they'd shrunk. 'You'll see Johann later,' Hilde said.

Celia wanted to hang back, keep hold of Hilde, but she knew she could not.

'Hello, Celia,' said Heinrich, stepping forward. He held out his hand. 'You have become an adult, a woman.' His back was bent, hair barely covering the top of his head. Lotte had been plump in the old days, floury cheeks, thick arms, hands always busy, cooking, baking, sewing, writing. Now her body was thin, and it looked as if her fair eyebrows had almost fallen out. She'd painted over them, carefully, with thick make-up, the black smudging into the surrounding skin.

'I'm so sorry about Louisa,' she said. 'What a shock for you.'

Celia nodded. 'Yes.'

You've grown old. But then, so had Rudolf, who now looked eighty when he was not even fifty, and Verena shuffled around Stoneythorpe, too tired to lift her feet. 'You can talk to me in German,' she said instead. 'I'll understand.'

'Very well,' said Heinrich. 'You can tell us if we're speaking too fast. Anyway, let us go. We must catch the train.' He did not make a movement toward the porter. Celia reached for her purse. She understood that she was looking after herself here; no father to pay for a porter. Lotte patted Celia's arm. 'Best not to speak too much, dear. Not on the train. Let us do the talking. You speak nicely – but still *foreign*.'

How was it, she asked herself, once they were finally bundled into the train, that she had thought Hilde and Johann and the family could stay the same? At home, at Stoneythorpe, they had all changed a hundredfold, everything altered or lost, but she had thought of her cousins in the Black Forest as unchanged, preserved like dried flowers and kept in a paperweight globe. But all of them were different and Celia wanted time to stop. If it ceased, if the clock face held still, then Louisa would be alive. She'd push back the hands and seize her that day in Covent Garden.

Hilde was talking about the scenery from the train window, praising the beauty of a river. Lotte was murmuring too, about the horizon. Celia tried to listen, forcing herself to smile.

She felt dark with shame: she could tell from the grey faces, the shabby, sick-looking people in the train, the ruined houses from the window; this country had suffered. It looked nothing like it had the last time she had visited, six years ago, when it had been all pretty cottages, flowered gardens, tall churches. And here she was, coming as if it were a holiday by the sea – as if this was the way to escape the hopelessness of home.

'What is it, Celia?' said Heinrich. 'Do you feel ill from the train?'

Celia shook her head. 'Sorry.'

'Well, we're nearly there. Johann will be pleased to see you.'

The thought of Johan threw her into confusion. He was her cousin, he was part of her, and yet he had been that most terrible thing: a German soldier. They had thrown gas at Tom, burnt Belgian babies. *No sense of fair play*, the newspapers had said. She thought of one story from *The Times*. A British company had laid down their weapons at precisely the moment of ceasefire, about to retreat. Instead, the Germans held out their weapons and fired, killing all twenty of the men, even though the war was over. Such cruelty.

The train was juddering to a halt. They clambered off, Hilde helping to carry Celia's bag. The station, too, was nothing like it had been, the roof broken and the platform spattered with puddles. They piled on to a cart dragged by an exhausted-looking horse and set forth. Celia furrowed her brow, trying to stop the tears from falling. This was the enemy? This broken, ruined, grey place, dark roads full of people trudging, heads bent, stalls with a few sparse loaves of bread.

They passed through the village on an empty road. People stared up at them as they passed. The old church on the green was missing the top of its steeple.

'The village is changed,' she said.

'That's true,' replied Heinrich. 'Much changed. Many of our friends have gone, moved to the city.'

'I thought you worked in the city,' she said. He and Lotte had chosen the area when they got married. He'd longed to return to the village after growing up here and Lotte – despite being a Berlin girl – had always loved the country. He'd worked a few days a week in the city, and as soon as they'd had children, they'd never wanted to leave the village.

'Not so much any more. I am like your father, a gentleman of leisure, thanks to my advanced age.'

They turned out of the village and along the road that led to the house. Celia felt the trees grow thicker and closer. Perhaps her mind was playing tricks on her, but she felt sure that there were fewer houses than there had been. There had been hotels along here, a few shops. Now the places looked like broken farmsteads, large cottages rather than the wide, expensive family houses she remembered. Hilde saw her eyes scanning around. 'Sadly altered, I know. Luckily, dear, we have enough to get by. We don't have what we did – who does – but Heinrich saved carefully before the war. For that, we are thankful.'

They turned up the long drive leading to her uncle's home. She breathed a sigh of relief. Yes, it was shabbier, the door splintered and the sides of the roof broken. But it was still the same place, the dark wooden front, the tall windows, the flowers around the door.

'Here we are!' said Heinrich. They climbed down from the cart, Heinrich holding her hand.

'Johann!' he called. 'We're here.'

The door pushed open and a thin, pale-haired man in a wheelchair struggled out. Celia clutched Hilde's hand.

'What's happened?' she whispered. 'What's happened to him?'

Hilde shrugged. 'He lost his legs in the fighting. He was in France. Come, he'll be pleased to see you. He talks about you so much.'

They stepped towards him.

'Hello,' she said to Johann, looking him straight in the eye but blushing to do it. Why did it hurt so to look at him? She smiled, shakily. Should she say: I'm sorry you lost your legs?

'I'm a bit different,' he said, saying the word 'different' in German. He gave her a shy smile. That hurt her; she knew he felt he had to make these jokes, to put people at their ease, so they wouldn't blush, feel bad. Hundreds of soldiers, she supposed, must be doing the same.

'It's nice to see you,' she said. 'It's been a long time. You've been fighting.'

He nodded. 'I lost them near Etaples. I got sent there after recovering from injuries at Passchendaele, but I didn't last long!'

Tom had been in Passchendaele, she thought, gassed again there, come to them at Stoneythorpe coughing and sick. When she'd given any thought to Johann during the war she'd done her best to imagine that he must be in Russia or somewhere. Not France, not Etaples. Not there. He'd been maybe a mile from the ambulance station. Every night she had gone to sleep thinking about Michael – but it had been Johann who was nearer. He had been waiting in his trench, watching for the surges of men, listening to the guns.

'We're very proud of our handsome young man,' said Lotte, clutching his shoulders.

Celia blushed awkwardly. 'I'm sorry.' What was she apologising for – the battle, his death, the fact that she still had her legs?

He shrugged, gave her a bright smile that struck through to her heart. 'I'm alive. We've all lost something.'

'Now, now,' said Heinrich. 'No dwelling on the past. We have our guest to stay. Let us go inside.' She followed him into the house, her heart beating hard.

'We heard about your cousin,' said Johann. 'I'm sorry you had to go through that.'

A thought struck her heart. 'Did it reach the newspapers here?'

Heinrich shrugged. 'Not really. Only a little because all the newspapers were writing about Arthur being German.'

Her heart sank again. Well, the papers had all been wrong! Lotte asked her questions about Louisa, Celia nodded, tried to explain clearly without letting the words pierce her heart.

After a drink of tea, Lotte showed Celia to her room, the same one Celia used to have, all those years ago. Now, since the roof was leaking above Hilde's own room, the two would be sharing.

'I'm sorry about poor Michael,' Lotte said, laying covers on the bed. 'Poor boy. So very sad.'

Celia nodded. She wanted to talk about Louisa again, but the words wouldn't come. 'How is dear Verena?' Lotte continued. 'How I wish we could see her.'

They talked for a while about Verena, the house, Arthur and Emmeline and the twins. The twins were the safest – Lotte launched into a long description of how to care for little ones.

Celia longed to go outside, run free towards the trees and the little stream that meandered in between them. But Hilde and Lotte were talking enthusiastically about babies and she didn't dare leave.

'Mama wants grandchildren,' said Hilde, after Lotte finally wandered off to the kitchen. 'She loves babies. She's not going to get them from either of us. Who'd have me?'

'Lots of people,' said Celia, but lamely. There weren't any men for anyone in England – unless you happened to be rich and beautiful like Elizabeth Bowes Lyon, always in the society pages. 'You're very pretty, Hilde. You shouldn't say things like that.'

'I'm not pretty any more. It's all gone. And no one saw it either. I was just locked up here, waiting for news about Johann.'

'That must have been hard.'

'Mama isn't so thin because we had nothing to eat. We didn't do too badly out in the country – and we had money, like she said. She just wouldn't eat. I heard her talking to herself. She said she wouldn't eat until he came back. And then he did, and – you see what he's like – she still wouldn't eat, not properly. I suppose she thinks he's not really back.'

'But he is. He was injured, that's all.'

Hilde shook her head, smiled. 'It's not just that. You'll see. Anyway, I should go and see where he is.'

Hilde wandered out of the room and Celia seized her chance. She hauled herself up on to the window sill and eased herself through the window. Her skirt caught in the damp grass as she jumped forward. She breathed deeply, delighted. Just within a few feet of the house, and she could have been back in the Black Forest of six years ago. The air tasted of fir trees, woody rain, spring flowers. She hurried on, knowing she had only half an hour or so before the sun came down and Aunt Lotte would expect her in to eat. She was nearly at the forest when she heard the sound of a twig cracking behind her. She turned – and two women were standing there, middle-aged, their arms folded over their aprons. Their faces were still, angry, and it struck her that maybe she was trespassing. Maybe this wasn't village land any more.

'I'm—' she began, and then couldn't find the German to say 'I thought it was free land'. She fumbled for her words.

'What are you doing here?' said one woman. She spoke slowly, her heavy accent obscuring her words. 'Who are you?'

'I'm – visiting,' she said. 'My uncle.'

'Where are you from?' the other asked.

Celia felt her thoughts tumbling. 'Sweden.'

She shrugged. 'You should go home.'

Celia took a step to the side. Maybe they were slightly mad. Confused ladies who took a pre-dinner stroll and thought strangers were dangerous. Heinrich had always said they were deep in the countryside here – and country people were more suspicious. The women watched her take two more steps. Then she began heading forward, smiling, but not too widely, in case they might think she was laughing at them. She walked past them and still they watched her, did not reach out. Once she was a metre or so past them, she began walking more quickly – and then she ran to the house. The window was closed.

'Hilde!' She banged on the window.

Hilde pulled it open. 'What on earth are you doing there? I thought you were in the bathroom.'

'I went out for a walk. Can you help me in?'

Hilde reached out her hand and Celia grasped on to it, lodged her feet in the wall and then began to scramble in. Hilde gave her a tug and she was over the window ledge. She held Hilde's hand as she stepped down.

'You got heavier, cousin.'

'It's true,' said Celia. What was the point of being tiny, fashionably thin? Louisa had been thin and now she was dead.

'Well, it's dinner time here in a few minutes. You need to change your dress, there's mud on it.'

Hilde helped her pull the gown over her head.

'I met some strange people while I was out,' said Celia. 'Two women who weren't very friendly. I think they were a bit touched.'

Hilde shrugged. 'Maybe they were. We have more like that now. Come for dinner. Why don't you sit next to Johann? You two must have so much to talk about.'

That night, she lay in her bed. Her blanket was rough, as if it was made out of straw. She wondered what had happened to the thick eiderdowns that the house had once had. They'd dined on good meat and vegetables, badly made gritty bread. Lotte had barely eaten and had slipped more food on to Celia's plate. Heinrich talked of how he hoped the whole family would come to see them next time, Hilde clasped her hand under the table – and Johann smiled at her, shyly.

'We're so happy you came,' he said. 'Tell us again about Stoneythorpe.'

Celia had tried to swallow more of the bread. 'You can come next year. Papa would be very pleased.'

'Such a shame about Michael,' said Heinrich, shaking his head.

'Poor Verena,' Lotte said. 'To lose her son, and now her sister and her niece. The flu came here too, killed all four of the Waldes, in the farm along the road.'

Celia nodded, feeling her heart twist with guilt, no point correcting and saying that Aunt Deerhurst didn't have the flu. People had lost so much, and she had been fretting at home, heavy with misery, because Tom didn't want to see her and she could think of no occupation. She was selfish.

'We still don't know where Arthur is.' Celia dreamt that he'd returned while she was in Germany, now it had been proved there was no reason to run away.

'Yes, Verena wrote about that. We can only hope he returns soon,' said Lotte. 'Let us find our dessert.' She stood and began clearing the plates. 'No, Celia, not tonight. You are our guest. Hilde will help me.' They carried the plates to the kitchen.

Johann was looking down at the table. His shoulders were twitching, his hands fiddling with each other, his eyes blinking. Celia recognised it, what she had seen in so many of the men at Stoneythorpe, and others too – men she saw on the train to London, one serving her in an umbrella shop who tried to take her money and instead twitched so much that another man had to stand in for him. They were thinking about the bombs. She tried to catch his eye, smile. He only saw the wood of the table, the bombs within it.

'Here we are,' said Lotte, bustling in. 'Berries and cream. Hilde picked them herself. Here you go, Celia. You first.'

After dinner, they played a little cards and Lotte sang an old German song. Heinrich talked at length of Johann, his excellent mind, gentle disposition, how he had excelled at school. He said again how pleased he was to see Celia, his eyes misting over. He talked of the beauty of the Hampstead house, how he longed to see Stoneythorpe, how they had lost so much. Celia wanted to say: *it isn't anything now. We've lost our money too! At least you still have Johann.*

Johann hurt her heart. He sat apart from them while they

played cards, making a windmill out of old matchsticks, sticking them on top of each other, one by one. Celia felt her heart crack as she watched him, utterly absorbed, fixing the sticks, his eyes alive with concentration. The bombs could not touch him there, while he patiently, carefully put one stick on top of the other.

As they got ready for bed, there was a bumping on the walls. 'Oh, don't mind that,' said Hilde. 'It's only Johann. He does that every night.'

Lying in bed, Celia thought of the melody of Lotte's song, letting it run through her head, the swooping scales sounding out. Her aunt's voice was still pretty, only cracking a little on the high notes.

Some time later, she woke to the sound of hard knocking on the front door. She looked around her; pitch black still. It must be the middle of the night. She saw the lights from candles shining under her door. She heard Lotte opening the front door, shushing the people who were crowding through. 'They're sleeping,' Celia heard her say. Then there was a rush of voices, all in German, mostly men, some high-pitched women. They sounded upset, as if someone was hurt. Celia could hear her aunt agreeing with them, softly, trying to talk to them. Heinrich talked loudly until finally they all quietened.

When Celia woke the next morning, Hilde had already left and made her bed. Celia climbed out of bed, splashed water on her face, dressed quickly. She walked into the dining room for breakfast and the babble of voices stopped. The faces turned towards her.

'What is it?' she said. The German words sounded wrong as they came from her.

'Nothing, dear,' said Lotte. 'Come, sit down. Have an egg.'

She let herself be manoeuvred to the table.

'Dear,' said Heinrich, clearing his throat. 'We've been talking. It is too dull here for a young person of your lively disposition! There is nothing to do – and you're used to London.'

'I'm weary of London.'

Heinrich waved his hand. 'No one could be weary of London. I myself have not been there for almost twenty years. And yet I remember now the pleasures I had. Such nice cafes!'

Lotte cleared her throat. 'Heinrich, dear,' she prompted.

'Oh yes. Well, anyway, London is a great city. And the Black Forest is simply dull in comparison. Thus we are going to take you to Baden Baden. We can take the waters. There is much to do there. Tourists come from all over the world. Queen Victoria even visited. Aunt Lotte and I went once, when we were first married. A most interesting place.'

Celia blushed. 'I like it here.' She knew she was ungrateful to say it. Johann was smiling at her. The waters might give him strength, she knew. But she had wanted to come *here*, to the forest, full of the fairies of her childhood. 'Wouldn't it be terribly expensive?'

'Baden Baden is expensive. But it would do us all good,' said Heinrich, waving his hand, looking rather like Rudolf as he did so. 'We haven't had a holiday, well, since before the war. What's the use of money if you can't spend it?'

Celia saw a little of the old Heinrich here, the man who loved late-night cafes, restaurants, making Lotte cross talking about his youth with Rudolf in London. She toyed with her bread.

'Anyway, my little Hilde is growing older. I may like to stay in the country, like a hermit, but she needs to meet some young people. Find a—' He stopped and blushed, looked towards Johann. He was intent on his yoghurt and didn't look like he was listening.

'When do we leave?' asked Celia, resigned. So that was it. They were spending all their money on a last-ditch holiday to find Hilde a husband.

'Straight away! Straight after breakfast.'

'Now?'

'That's right. We'll all go and pack.'

'But why so quickly?'

Heinrich grinned and stood up sharply. 'When I make a decision, I like to stick to it.'

She looked up at him. 'How long will we stay?'

'Two and a half weeks. Just in time to take you to the boat

for home. So get all your things with you. We'll go straight from Baden to your train.'

'I wish we weren't going,' said Celia, as she followed Hilde to their room. 'I wish we were staying here.'

Hilde closed the door behind them. 'I'm pleased to go!' Her eyes were dark, surprising Celia with their anger. 'It's fine for you, going to London all the time. But what about me? I am stuck here and there is no one here for me to meet. I've been asking to go to Baden since the war ended. No one is going to stop me.'

Celia flushed. Hilde wouldn't be prettier next year, perhaps much more plain. She needed to make herself as appealing as she could, eat more, take the waters. 'Sorry, Hilde. I just like it here.'

The other girl crouched down under her bed and pulled out a trunk. 'That's because it is a holiday for you! Not for me. I'm stuck here, like Johann, except I have my legs.' She pulled open the wardrobe and began throwing clothes into the case. Celia watched them fall, dresses, cardigans, jumpers, blouses, no order to them.

'Johann could meet someone too, you know. Wounded soldiers are very popular at home.'

Hilde pushed down on her gowns and pulled in some more from the wardrobe. 'The same here. Because there aren't enough men to go round. So we have to have the blind ones, the lame.' She lowered her voice. 'I want a proper man, one with all his limbs, who can see, who doesn't shriek when you drop a saucepan. I want one who wasn't in the war.'

Me too, Celia wanted to say. Because the only one she wanted from the war had been Tom – and she couldn't have him. 'I'm sorry, Hilde. Maybe you should all go. I'll stay.' She could wander out to the river on her own, come back for bread and cheese like the old days.

Hilde stood up, shook her head. 'What are you talking about?' she asked, her lip curling. 'You know we can't. We are leaving because of you.'

'What do you mean?'

Hilde's eyes were like a fire, blazing. She put her hands on her hips. 'What I said. They don't want you here. You're a stranger and they can guess you're the enemy. They came last night and demanded Father get you up to speak to them. He said you were French – that got you off the hook. Mother said you were asleep. But they're coming back soon, which is why we have to go.'

'Me? The enemy? But we're at peace now!' Celia felt her legs falling away from under her. The women in the forest, the people banging on the door last night. 'How can it be so?'

'No, you English are at peace! You won. You're still the enemy for them, one of the people who makes them poor.'

The room was spinning. 'I've put you in danger. I've put you in danger by coming here.'

Hilde closed her trunk carefully. 'You did.' Her voice softened. 'But you weren't to know. Father should have said no. I told him to. I said, the people around here aren't how they used to be. All the rich people have left, and now it is only the poor who suffer and blame others. But he was insistent. He said you were his cousin's child and you needed us.'

'I'm sorry.' Celia's heart was banging hard in her chest. 'I didn't mean – I didn't think.'

'No. You didn't. And you know what Father really wanted you here for? Have you guessed his plan?'

Celia shook her head. Hilde's face was all pain. Celia wanted to say to her cousin, *no, don't tell me any more.* 'I don't know.'

'So naïve of him. Ridiculous, really. He thought—'

There was a knock at the door. 'Hilde, Celia.' Aunt Lotte's voice. 'Are you ready to go? The cart is here.'

'Nearly, Mama.' Hilde gripped her arm, hissed. 'This is my chance to get out of here. And maybe Johann's. Don't spoil it for us.'

'What was it?' said Celia. 'What was Uncle Heinrich's plan?'

'I'll tell you later. We have to go.' She pushed Celia out of the room, closed the door behind them.

NINE

Baden Baden, August 1921

Celia

'Ice cream, miss?'

Celia shook her head and waved her hand at the man holding out the array of cones: pink, yellow, green. There were dozens of ice-cream sellers in Baden – all fighting for the tourists' coins.

She walked on, ignoring the toffee seller, the cake seller, the biscuit seller and the three stalls offering sweet pies. The sun beat down on her hat. Ahead of her was a great party of tourists, rich Germans from Berlin, she supposed, heading up to dine at a restaurant. It was astonishing to be here, really it was. You thought that Germany was poor and suffering, the Black Forest had certainly seemed so, and instead here was flooded with money. Heinrich said that some people had grown very wealthy from the war – and Baden was where they spent their money because no one wanted Germans abroad. Plenty of the people in Baden weren't even German, of course, when you got close, they were speaking something else entirely. This was what they wanted to find for Hilde, a rich man who would keep her – and give to her family.

Celia continued wandering, rather aimlessly, in her best lace dress. Rudolf had bought it for her before she'd started at Miss Trammell's – he'd been hoping she would be invited to many balls. It had been expensive, but hadn't lasted well – it looked pretty shabby next to all the fine day gowns in Baden and the skirt was threadbare around the hem. Still, she told herself, it was vain to worry about dresses. She was alive.

They'd hurried away from the house, throwing their things into the hired cart as quickly as they could before the neighbours noticed, then hurtled to the train station. Hilde's face was fearful, her father snapping at her not to look back. On the train, Hilde had left with Heinrich to take a short walk to the restaurant car. Aunt Lotte had leant over, patted Celia's leg. 'Hilde shouldn't have told you, dear. It's really nothing to worry about. Just a little bit of upset, that is all. She's young, she's easily afraid.' Johann was deep in his book, a description of nineteenth-century microscopes.

'I was wrong to come.'

'No, dear, not at all. They are never very friendly. We will just take a short break and return.'

When Hilde had come back, Aunt Lotte gave her a hard stare. 'Come outside and talk to me, dear,' she said. 'Johann, why don't you tell Celia about the book you're reading.' She shut the door. Celia smiled over at her cousin.

'What are you doing?' she asked.

'The book is interesting.' He shook his head. 'I'll tell you about it when I've finished.'

She left him alone, looked out of the window.

'Have you two been having a nice chat?' said Lotte as she burst back in.

Celia nodded. 'About microscopes.' She could barely say the word in German. Johann was still gripped.

Lotte smiled beatifically. 'That's good.'

Along the way to Baden, the train got busier as they dipped through the thick flocks of black trees, past jagged mountains and a river that was so shiny Celia felt sure that, if she looked into it, it would reflect only the clear blue sky. As they drew closer to Baden, more houses appeared, all built from dark wood, the sloping roofs sharp against the hills. They drew into a station crammed with women in hats and smart men. Celia gazed at them, shiny people, like dolls. Louisa would have liked it here. She should be here, not Celia, who was selfish and not humble and had all her other faults. It should be Louisa.

'Look at them,' breathed Hilde, out of the window. 'Where have they all come from?'

'First time in Baden?' said the cab driver, after they'd clambered in, manoeuvred Johann into the middle.

'Not for us,' said Heinrich. 'My wife and I came when we were young. But for the children – it is all new.'

'Good time to come, sir, I would say. If you ask me, since the war, Baden is the best it has ever been. I'm told the rest of the country is too afraid to enjoy itself. Not here.'

On the drive, they peered out of the window to look at the resort. The towns and villages before had been full of women, old ones, young ones – seemingly none in between. But Baden was full of men. Young men, strolling with ladies, chatting in large groups, dressed in pale suits and straw hats, smart shoes. They looked in shop windows, walked out of cafes, read books on benches, stared out of the back of cabs. Celia gazed at them all, hot and confused by their presence. They were young, happy.

But these men must have fought. They'd surely battled against Tom and Michael, and all the others, had taken Shep's brother into the prisoner camp, shot and thrown gas at all the other men she had driven in her ambulance. Men like them flew the aeroplane that had soared above them at Etaples, rained down its bombs, killed Shep. A tear welled up in her eye. And yet, she was half German. Englishmen had maimed Johann so he could never walk. She didn't brush the tear away, she let it fall. Her aunt and uncle were craning out of the window, Hilde too. Celia looked up and Johann was gazing at her. She tried to smile at him. I'm not crying, she was about to say. Just happy. Then he looked away and the chance to speak was gone.

Their hotel was near the edge of town. It had once been a mon-astery. The dining room had been the monks' refectory, the library the cloister. 'Look at this!' Heinrich said, when they arrived. 'Isn't this beautiful? Our driver was correct. Baden is even more beauti-ful now, after the war.'

Celia still couldn't understand it. 'Where have all these people come from?' she said. 'Did they all avoid the war?'

Heinrich shrugged. 'Or they grew rich from it, like I said. Some borrow money.'

Upstairs, Celia and Hilde had a big room with a large window that looked on to the gardens below. Aunt Lotte came and peered out. 'Very high up,' she said. 'Put on your best dresses and come down for tea.'

'I'm tired,' said Hilde, sitting on her bed.

'No, no,' said Aunt Lotte. 'We must see who is here. It is time to go down and show off your dresses. Johann can rest, but you – we must seize every minute. Wash your faces. I shall return to set your hair, Hilde.'

The door shut behind her and Celia threw off her boots and leapt on to her thick pink quilt.

'You might break it,' said Hilde, dubious. She sat down at the dressing table and began unpinning her hair. Celia watched her fingers working. Hilde's hands were careful, pulling out and restyling the brittle strands, rubbing with her fingers, trying to thicken them out. She picked up her comb and put it in her hair, working up from her forehead. Celia heard banging around next door and knew it was Johann.

'I thought Aunt Lotte was going to style your hair.'

'I don't want her to. She only gets upset about how thin it is. I have a whole patch where it's gone, right at the back.' She ruffled it with her hand. 'She'd cry if she saw it.'

'If you got it cut, then no one could see all that,' Celia said. 'My hair is really no good anymore.'

Hilde turned, her eyes small. 'Yes, but what does it matter for you? You're independent, you always have been. You can do whatever you want. I told Papa that a million times, but he was still stuck—' She stopped, pulled out another strand of hair.

'Stuck on what?'

'Oh, never mind. I have to get married. And every day I'm getting older, my looks are fading.'

'Don't think like that.' Celia swung her legs off her bed, over the side. 'I'll help. Tell me what to do.'

'Look at that!' said Aunt Lotte, coming in twenty or so minutes later. 'That is beautifully done.' Lotte had puffed up her hair too, put earrings in – Celia knew they had to be glass, but they might look like diamonds at a distance.

'Celia helped,' said Hilde. 'Well, she tried.'

'I'm learning,' said Celia.

'I am most impressed.' Lotte reached down to pinch Hilde's cheeks. 'Let us go forth.'

They stood up straight, smoothed their skirts and followed Lotte and Heinrich down to the hall and then into the library. Celia's eyes blurred dizzily as she stepped into the room. It was like staring into the wrong end of a kaleidoscope.

Her eyes accustomed themselves and she gazed around. The room was thronged with smartly dressed people, walking, taking tea, smiling. There were over a hundred of them, all ages, some fat, some thin, but all brilliantly dressed. The women were a riot of vivid colours, deep gold, peacock blue and pale green, lace at their cuffs and throats, diamond rings on their fingers. Her eyes went to two sitting on chairs by the blue-curtained window. Their skirts were astonishingly short, barely covering their ankles when they were seated. Their hair sparkled with diamonds, as if, Celia thought, they were going to a grand ball in Russia. Not tea in a hotel. They were laughing, but Celia couldn't hear them over the thrum of voices, the high well-spoken German of the group directly in front of them. She stared at the women, laughing without sound.

'Austrians,' snorted Heinrich. 'Always too much money.'

A dark-haired woman brushed by Celia. Her gown was so beautifully embroidered, the skirt a skeined pattern of flowers and leaves, that Celia wanted to touch it – and was painfully aware of how much cheaper her and Hilde's gowns were. The men, too, looked like pictures from magazines. Heinrich, Lotte, Celia and Hilde could have been a group of cavemen wandering into the court of Henry VIII, under-dressed, lost, missing the ruffs and farthingales.

Celia grasped Lotte's hand. 'Look at them all,' she whispered. 'Aunt Lotte. Do you think we fit in here?'

'Oh, Celia,' sniffed Lotte. 'Don't be silly.'

'They're all so rich. We – look different.'

Lotte squeezed her hand. 'Our money is just as good as theirs. Now, come along.' But Celia saw the hesitation in her step as she moved forward, the wild glance of her eyes. She too was afraid.

For the rest of the afternoon, they sat together and drank tea. Hilde looked around her, eyes fearful and glassy, strands of her elaborate hairstyle dropping out already. 'Don't worry, girls,' said Lotte. 'I shall locate the gentlemen. Nothing to be done yet. I am just doing my research.'

Hilde's leg touched Celia's under the table, moved closer so their knees were almost exactly aligned, bone on bone. Celia felt her cousin's leg trembling through the thin material of her gown.

Lotte continued her research. For days, they did what would look to outsiders like seeking pleasure. They set off on morning walks to artists' studios, took tea in four different hotels, dined in the Randgast – the best tea in Baden, a driver had told them (although it was not the best hotel). They had gazed at the golden windows of the Belvedere, the restaurant for royalty, Heinrich said – only the chosen few could have a table, no matter how much money they had. Celia and Hilde had wandered through four cabinets of curiosities, eaten chocolate cake for elevenses and toured the racecourse in expectation of the race soon to be run. They were escorted everywhere, but at a discreet distance. Lotte tried to leave at least three feet between her and the two girls. Then, she said, they could be free. And they could smile. Celia didn't much want to smile. The other women stared unkindly at their gowns. Most men pushed past them – but occasional ones (who, Celia noted, were doing it to everybody) winked, smiled, tried to catch her eye. She looked down immediately at her hands, her mind confused and thrown, telling herself, *but they were sent to fight too, conscripted, they had no choice.* And, she reminded herself, she was wrong to care. This was about finding a husband for Hilde.

Often it was just the three of them. Johann only came with them for some of the outings; he usually stayed at the hotel. In the mornings, they wheeled him out on to the terrace and he turned his face up to the sun. He refused water and tea, even coffee. 'You'll shrivel up,' said Lotte.

Most mornings, they asked Celia to sit by Johann to keep him company. She asked him about his matchstick houses. Once he let her build a roof, piecing together the sticks into a slope. She thought that her Aunt Lotte wished them to talk, but he seemed happier if they didn't.

Heinrich often spent the mornings back at the hotel, attending to business. In the afternoons, he took a stroll with the women and pressed them all to take cakes at tea time.

'It is just like I remember it,' Heinrich said one evening, after they had been there for five days, sitting on the balcony of the hotel. Johann was with them, making a church out of his matchsticks, leaning it carefully against his plate. 'Baden is really quite marvellous.'

'You are quite right, husband,' said Lotte. She turned her face. Celia saw it as she did so: pale and fearful.

Hilde sat quietly, did not reply. A tear fell down her cheek, making a thick trail through the face cream Lotte insisted upon her wearing in the sun. Celia gazed out at the mountains. No people up there, no one to ignore them, no men to sail past Hilde's carefully arranged hair.

'Celia, dear,' said Lotte. 'Are you listening?'

Celia turned and all three of them were staring at her. 'Sorry, Aunt. I was looking at the mountains.'

'Better to look at the mountains than talk,' said Johann, under his breath, next to her.

'What was that, dear?'

Johann shook his head, bent to his matchsticks.

Lotte turned to Celia. 'What do you think of Baden, dear?'

Celia shrugged. 'It's beautiful, of course. Lots of people.'

'That's right. Lots of people. Lots of eligible people.'

There was a cough and the bang of a chair. Celia turned and Hilde was on her feet, hands on her hips, eyes blazing. 'What are you talking about?' The other families looked up.

'Hilde!' Heinrich's voice was too loud. Celia saw out of the corner of her eye the mothers telling the children not to stare, starting up purposeful conversations.

Hilde waved him away. 'Listen to yourselves! Can't you see? No one wants us here. They laugh at us. They can see we're poor.'

Heinrich held out his hand. 'Hilde.'

She stepped away. 'Father, you're ridiculous! We're out of place here. Like some servants in borrowed clothes. We're spending all our money – and for nothing.'

'She's right, you know.' Johann spoke. 'No one wants us here.' He picked up another matchstick for the roof.

'Now, now,' said Heinrich. 'It takes time to be part of things.' He was soothing, smiling, the way you would speak to an angry animal. It seemed wrong to Celia. Hilde wanted someone to understand, someone to say, *yes, you are quite right.* A waiter passed by with drinks for the next table.

Hilde jumped forward. 'Time! No, not time. We have nothing that they want, we need different clothes, money, hats, voices – everything. What we have is nothing. Nothing!'

She rushed towards the door into the dining room, her skirts flurrying around her feet.

Heinrich stood, straight-backed, gazing after her.

'She's not coming back,' said Johann. 'Why should she?'

'Stop talking!' Lotte was hissing. 'You two are the most ungrateful children imaginable. We bring you on a holiday that hundreds of children would give their teeth for and you complain!' She waved her hand. 'You should be more like your cousin. At least she says thank you.'

Johann looked over at Celia. He raised his eyebrow. 'Her? Well, who knows what she really thinks? We're just a holiday for her. We'll be a story she can talk about in England. Some kind of quaint adventure.'

Celia had never heard him speak so many words before, not since they were children. She wanted to take his hand, but before she could, he started wheeling himself away. 'I'm going too. Will you open the door, Mother?'

Lotte sat there, still, as if she had been carved from stone.

'Mother?'

'I will.' Celia leapt to her feet, pulled the door open. She manoeuvred him round, pushed him through the door. He didn't look at her as he propelled himself forward. She closed it softly behind him.

Next morning, Hilde, red-eyed, refused to come down to breakfast, insisted she did not feel well enough to leave their room. Over toast and tea, Lotte said Celia could do as she liked. So she was free. She wandered down the stairs, out of the lobby, past a flurry of people with bags – and out into Baden.

But what then, she thought? Where was she to go? She would have to walk somewhere – but she had no idea where. As she walked forward, her mind rambled. Why had she come here, *really*? How naïve she had been to think she could escape everything and the Black Forest would be just as it had been. She was a coward, running away from everything at home, leaving them to weep over Louisa, wait for Arthur.

She should find a job when she got back, she thought. Something in an office. Either that or she should stay full time at home and help Verena. Her hip bumped into an older woman, she apologised.

If she'd been alive, Louisa might have come here with her, they could have wandered to get ice creams together, laughing. If Celia had been kinder to her from the start, if things had gone better, she wouldn't have turned to Arthur. She'd be laughing, talking, not dead at the bottom of a cliff.

A hand touched her arm. 'Celia. Is that you?'

She turned and it was Tom, standing there on the route to the racecourse, holding out his hand, smiling.

TEN

Celia

'But what are you doing here?' she said, gripping Tom's hand. 'Why are you in Germany?' Then she couldn't speak, her mouth opening and closing like a lost fish. He looked so smart, taller somehow, in a neat black suit and hat, a silver-tipped cane in his hand, the scars on his face faded further. 'I don't understand!' She held tight to him, as the crowds thronged around them.

He smiled and shook his arm to loosen her grip. 'I came over here on business. I told you, remember. Captain Dalton is doing a lot of export business.'

She blushed, wanting to seize his arm again. 'Captain Dalton is exporting to *Germany*?'

'Lots of businesses are. But, actually, I went to see you again. When I got to Stoneythorpe your mother told me you'd gone to Baden. She said your uncle sent a telegram about it. I had to visit here anyway for business – so I thought, why not? I was hoping I might come across you. Otherwise I'd have to start asking at the hotels.'

'You came to find me?' She didn't understand him. He'd said she should find new people, not write to him any more. Now he was following her to Germany.

'But don't you mind being here? All these people who – men who ...'

'Fought too? Of course. The only reason I'm here is that plenty of chaps wouldn't come out. They hear all that stuff about *kill the*

German at home. But the way I see it is that it wasn't their war, or mine. Anyway, you're half German.'

'Not that type of German. Not the type who could throw gas, strangle Belgian refugees, burn babies.'

He frowned, looked around. 'Celia, don't speak so loudly.' He seized her arm. 'Come along, let's walk. No more politics.'

She nodded, letting him take her arm. They strolled forward to the racecourse. It seemed so strange to be walking with him, not real. Women, she noticed, were looking at him; he stood out, handsome despite his scars. They looked at her differently as well, she could see from the corner of her eye. Their gaze was curious now, even perhaps, she thought, a little envious. 'What exactly are you exporting?' she asked tentatively.

Tom waved his hand. 'Oh, you know. All types of things. Wood. Metal. Supplies.'

'Wood? But there's the Black Forest.'

He shrugged. 'Wood products. You know. Anyway, how are you?'

'Things aren't so good at home. There's still no word on Arthur. Louisa's death was an accident but he's run off in a panic. I don't even know if he's heard the police verdict.'

'I'm sure he'll come back. Once things have died down.'

'I know he will. I know he's grieving too, that's the thing. I just wish he could come to talk to us. Mama needs him.'

'It must have been terrible for him to see her fall.'

She nodded and allowed herself to lean on him, just a little. Ladies did it all the time, she told herself. Tom wouldn't mind. He wouldn't even notice. She leant even closer, feeling a little of his body through the thick material of his coat.

Tom was still talking. 'Anyway, your relations must be pretty confident of Baden to let you wander around by yourself. Aren't they worried?'

'I'm to say I'm Austrian.' She was annoyed by his look of amusement. 'I can speak German. You can't!'

'Oh, I'm learning. I picked up enough Boche talk in the trenches, hearing them singing and shouting all night.'

She didn't want to think of him in the trenches so she pushed the thought from her mind. 'Are these men who are buying your wood from you now?'

'I was meant to be with them today. But one of them wanted to be with his family, so I have to wait. Fill my time.' He paused. Perhaps he might say, *would you like to walk with me?* He didn't.

'Do you think you'll be coming here a lot, then?'

'Looks like.' He stared straight ahead, as if gazing at a bird, but the sky was a long, flat expanse of blue. 'The way to get on is to do the job no one else wants. I can make it a success, Celia. I know I can.'

'I'm sure.' She squeezed his arm tentatively.

'I have to,' he shrugged. 'More men are arriving in London all the time, finally demobbed. Cleverer than me, university degrees, better at making general conversation. I was lucky, got my position before the rush. If Dalton advertised it tomorrow, he'd get fifty thousand letters, really he would.'

She looked around, but there was no one listening. 'Even if it meant coming to Germany?'

'That's where I'm different. I'll do it, shake the hands of fat men who sent boys to war, men who are richer than they ever were. I'll compliment them in German, say that really it was all our fault and Asquith was a dolt.' He still stared straight ahead. 'I'll make it mine.'

He moved forwards and she skipped one jump, not ladylike but the only way to catch up with him. The pleasure lake glittered up in front of them, people on the shores and sitting around the cafe to the side. A few ducks flew lazily through the warm, slow air.

'Actually, we're supposed to be finding Hilde a husband,' she offered.

'Really? Is she pretty?'

Celia blushed, stumbled. '*I* think so.'

He tapped his cane. 'No, then. Hard when you're surrounded by all these flocks of girls.' He gestured out to a group of them, accompanied by four men, all giggling near the boats, teasing each other to get in first. 'Up close, they probably wouldn't be so beautiful, you know, bad teeth, flaws in the skin. But you can't see it this way. Well covered with expensive creams and make-up and the like.'

Celia looked at her feet, the dirt on her hem. She didn't like it, the bitter metal in his voice, the way he looked over at the women as if they were horrid animals locked at a distance in a zoo. 'Hilde can't help it,' she said, stoutly. 'She used to be pretty. The war took it all.'

'In London, they'd probably make a film about her for that. Serves her right, they'd say.'

'Mr Janus says the films and the government are all one, just trying to trick us into obeying them and doing their business again.'

'Sometimes, Mr Janus might be right. Anyway, didn't Hilde have a brother? Did he die?'

'No, he's still alive. But he's lost his legs now. He's not the same.' Johann wheeled through her head, assembling matchsticks, singing to himself on the train.

'Poor man. Is he drinking?'

'No!' But perhaps he was, perhaps that was why he was always bumping around next to them, late at night, why he never would take water, even though Lotte tried to make him.

They were nearly at the lake now. The girls and the men were still laughing by the shore. Two sets had got in the boats, the others were waving. One girl was splashing them from the boat. 'Get in, you cowards!' she was calling. A red-haired girl still on the shore was squealing.

'I think you're sad, Tom,' Celia said. 'You seem angry.' Only a few months ago, he'd been marching her along in Covent Garden, telling her to do something with her time.

He shrugged. 'It's all wrong.'

'What? That you fought the Germans and now you're here?'

'Something like that.' *Except you were German,* she thought, *you wanted to be German! You wanted to be Rudolf's son. You think you are.*

The red-haired girl was scrambling into the boat, her skirt

catching over the side, her friend trying to steady her from his seat. 'They fixed everything in Paris, at the conference. After that, it will all be over. We'll be Europe again.'

'With thousands and thousands dead.'

She gazed over at the couples on boats, pushing out over the water. 'You wouldn't think it though, would you? Not when you're here in Baden.'

'That means nothing. Did you know you can go on tours to the war zones now? Cars and hotels included, an officer guide. The guidebook to the Somme is a bestseller, did you know?'

'I've seen the advertisements in *The Times*.' She had, words billowing out about the beautiful panoramas of the towns near to the places of great battles, making it sound as enticing as a trip to the seaside.

'Who are those people? Picking over souvenirs, making it entertainment.'

'Oh, quite.' She had to agree with him, she thought, or with anyone saying the same, think it ghoulish, even if really, in her secret heart, she thought she might want to go. She wanted to see those places that she never saw, except in her mind, the stretches of the Front where men felt horror and pain, now turned into benign spots for tourists, weeds growing over the abandoned guns.

'What about your cousin? What does he think about the war?'

'I never ask him.' A man picked up oars, and began to paddle out. The high notes of a girl's laugh drifted up towards them. Celia stared at the lake. A braver girl might have said, *Let's go on there! Let's follow them!* But Tom would hate it, especially as he was now, brimming with anger.

'Shell-shocked?'

'No, not really. Almost, he's a bit – too quiet, I suppose. He doesn't speak much.'

'When are you due back to them?'

'I don't know, really. So I'm free.' She longed to ask him to go with her for a coffee or a cake. *Don't leave me*, she wanted to say.

'Well,' he said, thoughtfully. 'Why don't we walk together? It is a pleasant day. Did you have any plans?'

Her mind raced, desperately. Other than to sit in a cafe with coffee, look at other people enjoying themselves – none. She had to think of something. 'I wanted to go to Liszt's house,' she said. She steeled herself. 'Maybe you could come with me?'

He shrugged. 'Why not? Do you know the way?'

'I think so.' She nudged him forward and they began to walk.

For the next four hours, they were together. He asked for tickets in a rather shaky German accent. They wandered around Liszt's house. All through it, Celia kept thinking one thought. She could not think of the piano, the chair, the walls she saw. She just kept thinking, *how can I make him stay?* They came out and the sun flamed into their faces.

'Are you sure your relations aren't missing you?'

She gathered her courage to say what had been in her mind. 'Why don't you come back with me? Why don't you come and meet them? They'd be pleased to meet you.'

She watched his face, saw emotions flicker across it. She smiled, widely. 'We could take tea at the hotel.' Then she used the words she knew she should not. 'Rudolf would be so very pleased to hear it.' She stood there, next to the great clock striking three, and watched Tom's face change: from the man who'd been so far from them to the little boy who'd craved them all, wanted Rudolf's approval, the soldier who'd gone to war thinking Rudolf was his father.

'Why not?' he said. 'I'm free.'

They wandered into the saloon and she scanned the groups. No sign. She led him out on to the terrace – and saw them there. They were seated, Johann bathing his face in the sun again.

Hilde saw her. 'Celia!' she called and waved her arm. 'Over here!'

Tom steered her towards them. Lotte bolted up, her eyes twice their size, all eagerness. He reached them. 'Good afternoon,' he said in shaky German. 'I'm so pleased to meet you.'

'Sit down, young man!' Heinrich spoke slow English, his face was burning with pleasure. 'What would you like to drink? Tea?

Now, may I introduce you to my wife, Lotte, my son, Johann – and this is my daughter, Hilde.'

Hilde blushed, whispered hello.

'Why don't you sit yourself by Hilde, sir? It is the most appealing view of the lake from there. My daughter is very fond of the view. She is most sensitive to beauty, you know. She'll tell you.' Lotte stood up as Tom moved over to Hilde's side. Hilde smiled invitingly, her eyes downcast. Celia looked at her cousin and felt a spot in her heart crack open, widen.

'Are you living in Baden, sir?' Heinrich was asking.

Celia broke in. 'Tom is an old friend, Uncle. We met by chance.'

'An old friend? More is the better. Were you a university friend of Michael's, sir? You look like a college man.'

Celia felt her face flame. *He was our servant.* It hadn't occurred to her. All this time that they had been wandering the Liszt house and she had been thinking of the words, walking back here together, talking of the weather and the tidiness of German shop windows – she had not thought. Heinrich would be insulted, that she would presume to bring a servant to be seated by them, take tea.

Tom looked so different now, a man of business. She hadn't thought. She had brought him to this hotel, this expensive hotel, let him sit by Hilde. Heinrich would be furious with her. Tom would be humiliated, hate her and her family all over again. She felt a wash of hot, sharp misery. Tom was smiling, asking Hilde a question.

Heinrich was saying something about Magdalene and Tom was nodding, his face blank. Celia was sure he hadn't understood, felt a selfish wash of relief, selfish for the lie. Heinrich moved on to business, asked a question more slowly.

'Export in wood?' he was saying. 'How very interesting. We certainly ran short of wood in the war years.'

Hilde was gazing at Tom, listening. Her eyes were shining. Celia wanted to throw herself on the ground in a faint. She thought of a girl at Winterbourne, Emily Atson, who always used to have a nosebleed in exams. That was what she needed, blood coursing out of her nose, dripping all over her gown, waiters dashing to get her water, sharp intakes of breath, some kind of dramatic, hysterical fainting. But she hadn't had a nosebleed since the age of ten. All she could do, she thought, was hope no one really understood each other and then somehow get Tom away. How could she have been so *wrong*? She'd pray now, she'd pray if she knew what to pray to that when Tom gave his surname, Heinrich would hear nothing in the word, would not remember that they once had a servant called the same. Then she had a stab of recognition, of awful recollection. When she had come to the Black Forest in the old days, Heinrich had asked her about everyone in the house, even Tom. He would remember, surely he would.

Lotte was talking about the beautiful scenery. Tom was nodding, incomprehension on his face. Celia looked at him, wondered how successful his business meetings really were. She gazed miserably at Hilde, hanging on Tom's words, watching the movement of his mouth. She looked across – and met Johann's eyes. He was staring straight at her, watching her looking at his sister – and she flushed. His eyes bore an expression she had never seen before: dark, the pupils tiny in the whites of his eyes. He was *angry* with her. She gazed at him, transfixed. It was as if all the cousinly friendliness had been stripped away and under it was the truth: hate.

A waiter came up with their drinks. There was a flurry as he laid them down. Tom touched Hilde's arm as he moved his cup and Celia saw Hilde start. The crack in her heart was growing even wider. This was terrible.

'What did you say your name was, sir?' Heinrich asked. Celia couldn't tear her eyes from his face.

'Tom. Tom Cotton.'

Heinrich's face changed. It was as if it had opened, spread wide. It was immediately white, his eyes bulging. Celia gazed at him. It was worse than she'd thought. He was furious, entirely furious. The crack in her heart was gaping now, jagged at the edges, she could feel it. She looked at Lotte. Her aunt's face was bright red, as if someone had hit her and she was about to burst into tears. Hilde was looking at both of them, confused.

I'm sorry! Celia wanted to say. I'm so sorry. It was a mistake. She gazed miserably at Tom. She looked at her hands, sure that Johann was still staring at her. She could almost hear him saying: so *this* is what you think of us! She looked up and Tom was staring at Heinrich, his face confused. He doesn't understand, Celia thought. She would take him away before he did. She sprang to her feet.

'I think Mr Cotton has to be somewhere,' she said, talking as quickly as she could, hoping that Tom wouldn't understand. 'He is due to meet someone. So he should depart now!' She pushed behind Heinrich's chair, thrust out her hand to seize Tom. Then, in a single, shocking moment, Lotte reached out and slapped her hand away.

'I knew it was you!' Her tone was angry and pained, furious. She reached across the table, grasped Tom's sleeve, her nails curling into the fabric. 'What do you want from us? Money? Is that it?'

'Lotte.' Heinrich pushed back his chair, half standing. 'Don't—'

'I will say what I feel!' Her voice was like an animal's, more a growl than anything else. She turned back to Tom. 'Haven't you had enough money from us over the years? From Rudolf? We have nothing now, and still you come for it.'

People around them were looking, turning at the sound of pushed-back chairs, Lotte's slap. A waiter was coming towards them. Johann was watching, his eyes darting back and forth. Hilde was weeping quietly, slow tears dropping down her face.

'What are you doing here?' Lotte said, leaning closer over the table, louder this time. 'Answer me! Are you going to follow us around the world?' Heinrich was holding her hand now, talking fast in German. She was ignoring him, facing forward, eyes only for Tom.

Tom looked at Celia, his face covered in confusion. 'What is she saying? What's she talking about?'

'I don't know,' she hissed, hoping it would be too quick for the others to hear. 'I think she's ill. I'm sorry. Come on, let's go. I made a mistake.'

'Don't try and get away!' Lotte cried. 'You're trying to blackmail us! I should call the police.' Their waiter, now accompanied by another, was nearly upon them.

Celia pulled Tom to his feet, out of Lotte's grasp. 'Let's go,' she said. 'Come on.'

Lotte jumped up. 'You're not going anywhere!' She stepped forward, so that she was in front of Celia. 'You'll stay here.'

Celia could see her face, red and furious. She backed up against Tom. 'Aunt—' she started.

But then Heinrich was there, behind Lotte, his arms on her, pulling her back. 'Don't,' he was saying to her. 'Let him go.'

She swung around, her face twisted. 'You care more for him than your own children!' Celia saw her uncle's face blanch. And then it began to come to her. Tom's mother, telling him the night before the war that he was a de Witt. Her cry – *your family has taken everything*! How cool Verena always grew at the mention of Tom, how she'd even blamed him for Michael's death in the first days. How Verena and Rudolf would never talk of Heinrich's visit, grew shifty when it was mentioned, hated questions about it. *When had that visit been?*

She looked from Tom to Heinrich, then back again. She could tell, from the corner of her eye, that Johann was doing the same. The same curve of the nose and the eye, the ear touching the cheek in the same way. The dark blue eyes. She gripped the chair, felt her head spin. When was that visit? The date came to her, one quick word in her head: 1898. The year before she was born. She gazed at Tom's face, already, she thought, already understanding. *Why had she not seen it?* They were so alike.

Heinrich and Lotte were talking in fast, low voices. Words came: son, children, Rudolf. *Sohn.* She looked at Tom. His face was confused, incredulous. They heard the word again. He gripped her hand. He understood.

'What is happening here?' The restaurant manager was standing there, two waiters either side. 'Sir, madam, you are disturbing the tea service.'

Celia turned, saw that Lotte had moved backwards, towards Heinrich. That was her chance. 'We're just going!' She pulled

Tom away from the table and practically pushed him towards the saloon. He let her move him forwards, as if in a dream. Then, at the door, he turned. 'Celia!' he said. 'We've got to go back. That's my father. I need to speak to him.'

'Come outside with me! You can't talk now!' The violins and the voices were drowning out Heinrich and Lotte, but she knew it, they were shouting, probably arguing with the waiters.

'Celia!' he said, pushing her back. 'That's my *father*.'

'But can't you see, not *now*? You mustn't. They're too upset.'

She looked up and saw Heinrich, watching them, as Lotte was shouting at the waiters. He gave her what looked like a half smile. She looked back – and then she realised. He was saying *thank you*. He was grateful. *Of course!*

'I'll arrange it. You can meet up with him, just the two of you. Talk about it, have dinner together. Don't you see you shouldn't talk to him now? Later, when they're not here. Let them consider it.'

He looked past her. Then someone opened the door on the other side – and she took her chance. She thrust him through, it closed behind them, and they were in the hotel corridor, the saloon shut away.

'Tonight,' she said, scrambling over the words. 'I'll arrange it so that you can meet tonight, and talk, just you two. That would be better, don't you see?'

He nodded, his eyes still distracted.

A waiter passed them, looked quizzically.

'Come on,' she said. 'Let's go! The waiters won't let us back in. I promise you, I will go back and arrange for you to meet with Heinrich.' She seized his hand, and they hurried forward, towards the crowd milling around the door.

ELEVEN

Baden Baden, August 1921

Celia

'How could it be?' he was saying, wonderingly, as they pushed their way past two plump gentlemen.

'Easily,' she said, briskly, still hurrying him on. 'Heinrich came to stay with my parents in 1898, when they were living in Hampstead. Father would never talk about it, said he was out a lot, and Mama always looked angry if it was mentioned. I suppose it happened then, and they knew about it.'

'They knew about it?'

'Of course.' She started to speak, then stopped. *Why else*, she wanted to say, *do you think Papa always loved you so? Why else would Rudolf call you 'my boy'?* He said it so often that they had thought Tom his child! *Why else would your family have come from Hampstead to Mareton with us?* She thought, her mind flashing, about those terrible days at the end of the war when she had believed him, had been prepared to believe that Rudolf had been his father, the sickness in her heart that her father had chosen someone else, her hatred of him being near her. The same pain that Johann and Hilde must be feeling now.

'So I am a de Witt after all.' His voice was hushed.

'You are.' She hated herself then, burnt for how she felt relief in her heart that Heinrich was his father. Her relief, she knew, her peace of mind, came at the expense of her cousins'. She felt hot, her stomach hurt, her head throbbed. All she wanted to do was run back to her room and throw herself on the bed. But she couldn't – Hilde would be there, weeping.

He shook his head. 'I need a drink. Where can we go around here?'

That was the last thing she wanted. All these years – especially after that night drinking champagne with Jonathan – she had thought: maybe if Tom and I took a drink together, then something would happen. He would look at me and think of me differently. Now he was asking her for a drink and she didn't want it. She wanted only to be alone somewhere, let her heart join together again, stop hearing the sound of Hilde's tears, over and over in her mind.

'I suppose there must be something like a public house,' she said. 'I don't know.'

He shook his head. Then, suddenly, 'I know! I've got it. Let's go to the Kaushaus! What do you think?'

'We can't go in there, Tom.'

'What, the most famous casino in the world? I think we must! Let's play for luck. I'll throw money on the tables.'

'I haven't got any money. Anyway, I always lost when we played at school.' But he was off, and she was hurrying after him, picking up her skirts to keep them from the mud.

'Come on, Celia,' he shouted over his shoulder. 'Hurry!'

The casino was handsome inside, gold-painted, thick red carpets, a ceiling covered in cherubs and goddesses. You'd assume, Celia thought, that it was a ballroom or a palace – until you looked down and saw hundreds of people, bent over tables or crowding around them to watch. The avid concentration reminded her of her old school hall at exam time.

'What do you want to play?'

'You choose. I always lose.' They'd played cards for money quite a lot in the ambulance station. Waterton usually won. She said Celia showed everything on her face; that you could see exactly what cards she had just by looking at her. 'You need to work on your deception,' she'd said, firmly.

'Let's try roulette,' he said. 'Did you know that Dostoyevsky lost all his money at the tables?'

'Then he wrote *The Idiot*, yes.' She'd heard every tour guide reciting that fact as they shepherded people past the building.

He moved forwards, ordered wine from the waiters, handed over cash to get chips, and led her to a table. She stood behind two ladies in glittering dresses as he pushed forward to the group of men standing close to the table. A waiter brought her a glass of wine as she watched the dealer pass cards back and forth. The colours – bright red, white, black – hurt her eyes. She sipped her wine. Tom, she saw, had already drunk nearly all of his.

He pushed back to her. 'Lost that time. Let's try another one.' She followed him over to another table, watched the cards flicker back and forth under their fingers. The game ended and the croupier handed him a set of red tokens. He turned to her, smiled. 'I won. Now, again.' He ordered another drink. She shook her head. 'I still have mine,' she said, pointing at it.

'Come next to me,' he said. She stood next to him, leant on the table. It was a heavy mahogany thing topped with green. It had probably been beautiful, once.

He took a great gulp of wine. 'Right then,' he said.

'I'll try now,' she said. 'I'll play against you and the others. This table.'

'I don't like roulette much. It's all chance. I like some skill.'

She shook her head. 'I prefer only chance.' He handed her the chips and she put them on her numbers, six, four, eighteen, two. The attendant spun. The ball fell on seventeen.

'I lose.'

'Play again?'

She shook her head. 'Listen, I'm going to sit down for a minute.'

'I'll come with you.' He followed her to a set of pale gold tables arranged along the back wall.

'Tell me about your uncle,' he said.

'What do you want to know?'

'Everything. Tell me everything.'

So she did. She talked about the first time that they went to the Black Forest and met Heinrich, how he had bent down to her, said, 'And who is this little one?' He'd held her when she was homesick, tucked her up, patted her forehead. 'Soon you won't want to go home,' he said. 'I promise.' He played with her, asked her questions about home.

She talked of Hilde, Johann, attempted not to mention Lotte. She tried to remember everything her father had told her about growing up with his cousin, their lives in Berlin, their love for classical music, but Heinrich had never wanted to study it, unlike Rudolf. She tried to remember what Rudolf had said about his aunt and uncle. 'They're your *grandparents*,' she caught herself saying, wonderingly.

She talked about how kind Heinrich was, gentle, honourable, a good father. She kept talking, only stopping when he called the waiter forward, ordered more drinks. Once Tom was sat back down, she talked again. Around her, the people continued walking in and out of the casino, laying down cards, talking, collecting chips, arguing, congratulating each other. The words flowed out of her, through her; she kept talking, finding that the more she let the sounds come out, the less she had to think about the ugly scene on the terrace, the terror on Hilde's face.

Then, finally, he stopped her. 'Celia, we've been here for hours.'

She looked at the pale gold hands of his watch (expensive, she registered fleetingly. Rudolf had sold his). It was nearly six.

'One last game,' he said. 'Let's play.'

'Really? I've played enough.'

'One last. This time, I'll win.'

'I'll wait here.'

She leant back against the chair, watched him walk to the tables. Some of them were still ringed by the same men who had been there when they arrived, intent on gambling, taking in the cards. She watched Tom move to the front, smile at a woman in a long green dress as she let him pass, felt a stab of jealousy.

She closed her eyes, feeling swamped with tiredness. Her mind ran, untidy and too fast, over the day. She tried to think of something else, the face of the cards on the table. Her mind reeled.

'I did it!' She opened her eyes and Tom was in front of her. 'I told you I would!'

'How much did you win?'

'Fifty marks! You can tell my father that. It's fate.'

She stood up. 'I should go to speak to Heinrich. I'll catch him on his own, ask him to come.'

He nodded. 'Would you?' His eyes were bright with expectation, the notes crumpled in his hand.

'Of course! And I'm sure he'll come. Like I said. He's a kind man. He'll want to see you.' She was about to say: *he loves you*, but stopped herself – that was probably too much, even if it was true. In the past Heinrich had always asked about Tom, always keen to hear about how he was. Of course Lotte was hurt. But once she understood Tom wasn't coming to them for money, she'd learn to love him too. Who wouldn't? 'I'll hurry back,' she said. 'But you must find somewhere nice for him.'

Tom thought. 'The Belvedere!'

'You can't afford there!'

'I can. I don't care. I'm meeting my father for dinner.'

She shook her head. 'They won't have any tables.' She thought of Heinrich, passing its golden brilliance. 'He said it was only for royalty and people like that, it didn't matter how much money you had.'

'Ah yes, but I have English pounds. Haven't you found they've opened doors?'

'I don't know, really.'

'Well, I have.' He looked at his watch again. 'Do you think half an hour will be enough?'

'Maybe forty minutes?' Heinrich would have to say goodbye to Lotte, after all. And he wasn't the quickest of walkers. She thought of his half smile to them, over Lotte's head. He would come with her, sit down with Tom. The future after that was a bit fuzzy, but she was sure it would be a good one. Tom could visit them when he came over on business. She and Tom might even come over together.

'I'll wait there,' he said, patting her hand. 'I'll wait at the table. Choose the wine.'

'Have some water too,' she said, but he waved her off. She

hurried out of the door of the casino, the sun striking hard on her eyes.

She rushed to the hotel, pushing through the groups of men and women – why were there people *always* standing around? – and dashed into the hotel, thinking that her hair was probably out of place. Her family weren't on the terrace. Or in the dining room. The library was full of old men, dressed in old uniforms, probably a meeting of a regiment from a long-ago war. They must be in their rooms. She wanted to go to hers, brush her hair, wash her face, but she couldn't, she was tasked with finding Heinrich. She had to keep going. She knocked on his door. There was no reply. She waited – and then pushed it open. Lotte was lying in the bed, staring at the ceiling. The curtains were half closed. Light was playing over her face. Her eyes flickered at Celia, went back to the ceiling again. Celia peered around the room. No sign of Heinrich. Easier, really, to speak to him alone. She shut the door and leant against it. He had to be somewhere else. He was probably walking somewhere, perhaps around the lake. It would take her ages to find him – and Tom was sitting at a table at the Belvedere, choosing wine for Heinrich to drink.

She walked down the corridor. Voices were coming from the doors, the sound of children's laughter, someone else talking about the servants. She rounded the corner towards her room – and saw a strange figure, half bent against the wall. It was a man, slumped, his head over his knees. She walked closer to him. He must be ill.

'Sir?' She stepped closer, tried again. 'Sir?'

He lifted his head. It was Heinrich. He gazed at her, face cloud-white, his eyes bloodshot. 'What are you doing, Uncle? I thought you were ill.' His suit was creased, his trousers dirty at the bottom.

He shook his head. A tear ran down his cheek. 'I'm sorry.'

She sat beside him on the hard floor. 'Sorry for what?' She patted the hand that was nearest to her. 'Aunt Lotte will forgive you. You know she will. It was such a long time ago. Years.'

He shook her head. 'Hilde won't see me.'

'She will.'

He was crying in earnest now. She couldn't bear it.

'This was supposed to be the holiday that made things different.'

'I'm sorry I brought Tom, Uncle. I didn't know.'

He smiled at her, that half smile again. 'I know you didn't. But Lotte won't believe it.'

'She'll come round,' Celia said, patting his hand again. 'I promise.'

He put his head back on his knees.

'What about Johann?' she said.

He shrugged. 'It's different for men. And anyway, he lives in his own world. You know.' He sighed.

'But why are you sitting here?'

'I'm waiting. I'm waiting until one of them will speak to me.'

'I'll talk to them. I'll talk to Hilde.'

He looked at her. 'Would you? Thank you. She'll listen to you.'

'I'll go now. But while I am doing it, could you ...' She stopped. Her heart swelled. She thought of Tom, sitting at the table, upright, waiting. Heinrich and he talking, smiling, eating together. Heinrich would have to brush himself down, smarten himself up – best not to go into his room to find new clothes. 'Tom asked if you could meet him at the Belvedere. He's got you a table.'

Heinrich's head was still bent.

'I'll get a hairbrush. We'll sort out your clothes and you can go.' She patted his leg. 'I know, I thought the same, that Tom would never get a table, but he says he can. And you look smart. The suit is smart.'

A rich-looking couple turned around the corner, leading a child by the hand. She gave them a quick smile, hoping that would be enough to deflect them. Heinrich's head was still buried, shoulders shaking now. She put her hand on his arm, feeling the air on her face from the sway of the woman's skirts. She watched them walk to the end of the corridor, the pale blond child turning to stare.

'Tom's so excited to talk to you, Uncle.' His shoulders shook again. Then he raised his head, his eyes red, the hair astray. She patted his hand. 'Let's go.'

'I can't.'

'What?'

'I can't go.' He clutched her hand. 'You understand, don't you, Celia? Not today.'

'But Tom is waiting. He's waiting for you in the restaurant.'

'Celia, I can't leave Lotte and Hilde. You must see.'

Panic was seizing her, curving into her heart. 'But it would only be for a short time, Uncle. Two hours. Lotte is asleep. And I'll talk to Hilde. They won't know you're gone.'

'Please, Celia.' He held out his hand. 'Please. Tell him. I can't.'

'Tomorrow, then? You can go tomorrow, can't you?'

'I can't. Celia. It's not the right time. Another time.'

'When? Uncle, when will you?'

He put his head back on his knees. The answer crept around her mind, cold and hard. 'You're not going to, are you?'

He didn't reply.

'Don't you know how long he's wanted to find out about you?'

He shook his head. 'Celia, it was so long ago. Years. I was young. It was a – quick – it meant nothing.'

'With Mrs Cotton, you mean?'

'I was young. She was too. It was wrong to do it.'

Celia stood up, losing patience. 'But you can't change it. He's here. It happened.'

He shook his head. 'Celia. Please. I can't. I couldn't do it to my family. I need to protect them, don't you see? I need to protect us, the whole family. Rudolf, Verena, all of the de Witts. I am protecting you!'

'You're a coward.' The words were out before she could stop them. 'You're a coward to leave him.'

He gazed at her, eyes thick with tears. He opened his mouth, shook his head again. Then he pulled himself straighter. 'Celia, you are a child. You understand none of this. I know what is best for my family. And it is not this. I would thank you to stop meddling.'

She leapt to her feet. 'I understand now. I have to go and tell him you won't see him, or even write to him.' She turned, ran down the corridor, stumbling over her gown, tears in rivers down her face. A door opened and slammed behind her. Perhaps Heinrich was going back to his room. Then another voice.

'Celia!' She turned, and Hilde was coming after her. 'Don't go!' she said. She was covered in shawls, four or five, swathed around her, as if she'd been in bed with influenza.

Celia gazed at her. 'I'm sorry, Hilde.'

She shrugged. 'What do you have to feel sorry about? *You* didn't do anything. I always knew there was something in your house, though. Mother said things.'

'Tom's a person to be proud of.'

Her face sharpened then, mouth thinned. 'Well, you would say that, wouldn't you? You're in love with him.'

Celia gazed at her, flushing. 'I'm not.'

'Of course you are. Anyone can see that. Don't your family mind?' She pulled the shawls around herself.

'They don't know.'

'Really? It's obvious to me.' She slid down the wall, crouching against it. 'Mind you, I see things other people don't. I saw that you were coming here looking for the old days and we all disappointed you because we were so shabby.'

'That's not true!'

'Oh, I could see it. Your face when you saw me was a picture. You corrected it, of course, but it was too late. And it was then that I knew my parents' plan wouldn't work.'

Celia felt her heart sink again. She could hardly bear to ask. 'What plan?'

'The plan for you and Johann, of course. Surely you knew that?'

'No.'

'That you two would get *married*,' she said. 'You and he, you'd take him back to England, with all your money to look after him. You knew him as he was, you still saw him as a young man. You'd marry him and Uncle Rudolf had the money to look after him.'

'Oh.' The pieces were falling into place. Uncle Heinrich and Aunt Lotte's effort to make her talk to Johann, leaving them alone together, talking of his achievements.

'They thought you two were childhood sweethearts. How were they to know that you were sweethearts with the other son?'

'No.' Heinrich throwing his arms around her at the quay. How eager he had been to have her to stay. She'd thought it had been because they loved her. Instead, they wanted her to marry Johann.

'So they brought you all the way here to impress you, spent the last of their savings. They even wanted you to have my room, but Johann protested.'

Celia held her head. 'Why are you telling me all this?'

'You should know the truth. Like I did today. It hurts, doesn't it?'

'Yes,' said Celia. All the letters that Hilde had sent, stacked up in her dressing table at Stoneythorpe, curved handwriting on pale pink paper. Every one of them saying *we need you!*

'I'm sorry, Hilde,' she said. 'I can't do what you want. I really can't.' She turned on her heel, ran away down the corridor. She looked at her feet, thought of them pounding the floor, over and over, one, two, up, down. If she just looked at them, she thought, watched them, then she would get to Tom and everything would be clear.

TWELVE

Baden Baden, August 1921

Celia

Celia hurried down the stairs, through the lobby and out into the air. It was cool now, early evening. A woman in blue raised an eyebrow at her. Celia realised: she could hardly go to the Belvedere like this. She found her pocket handkerchief and scrubbed at her face, pulled her hair back and made a futile attempt to pin it straight. She should rush on to Tom. Better to tell him, quickly, so they could leave the restaurant, before he'd ordered wine, bread, planned his speech.

She pushed her way gently through the crowds. They were smiling, talking, looking forward, she supposed, to pleasant evenings dining or listening to music, playing cards. Not like her family, Heinrich weeping in a corridor, Lotte lying, not speaking, in her bed. Tom sitting straight in a grand restaurant, waiting. And she – who had come for a holiday to forget – she had blown everything apart. She thought of Johann, out on the terrace every morning, his face turned to the sun. How he stacked up the matchsticks to make buildings. She'd watched him doing that, just yesterday. Heinrich had probably been watching her as she'd gazed, thinking – *nearly there.*

She pushed through, arrived at the glinting gold windows of the Belvedere. A cool-looking waiter met her at the door. 'Can I help you, fräulein?' he asked.

'I have a friend here.'

'Name?' He was staring at her gown, transfixed, she supposed by how creased and dishevelled she'd become.

'Mr Cotton. An Englishman.'

'Ah, yes.' He ushered her through. She passed fine ladies at tables, cast her eyes down as she followed. 'Here, madam.'

She looked up. 'Hello, Tom.'

He smiled, his eyes painfully bright. 'Is he coming behind you?' He was sitting upright, as she'd guessed, his tie straightened, his hair carefully brushed, still slightly damp – he must have washed it in a bathroom. In front of him was a heavy glass, decorated in crystal diamonds, the creamy yellow wine at half mark.

The waiter was still standing by the chair. She scrambled in, untidily, shook her head. The waiter slid a menu in front of her, glided away. 'I'm sorry, Tom.' A hundred words rushed through her head. Heinrich was ill, she hadn't been able to find him, Lotte was too sick to leave. She shook her head again. 'He can't come.' The glass in front of her was full of wine. Heinrich's glass.

His face changed, paled. 'What do you mean, he can't come?'

'I'm sorry, Tom. He can't come.'

He touched the stem of his wine glass. 'You couldn't find him?'

'No. I found him. He wouldn't come.' His eyes were so dark, it was as if the pupils had swallowed them up. 'I tried.'

'You tried.' His voice was bitter now, hard as iron. 'How hard did you try? Did you even tell him?'

'Of course I did! Tom, I found him. I talked to him. I told him you were waiting.'

'And he said no?'

'He did.'

He picked up the wine out of the cooler beside him, poured more into the glass, his hand quick. 'This is just like last time. Last time, you didn't want me to be Rudolf's son. You wouldn't allow it. Now it is the same with Heinrich.'

The waiter returned, asked about the food. Tom shook him away. His voice was quick and high, his face red. Hair was falling forward over his forehead.

'I think you should eat something, Tom. Why not some bread?' She pointed at the basket on the table.

'You're trying to fob me off with *bread* now. What a joke. Why can't you just be honest? You don't want me to be a part of your family. You want me to stay a *servant*.'

He hissed out the last word. A plump woman and her husband at the next table turned to stare. Celia turned her head from them. Today the de Witts were a special show, demonstrating family misery for everyone to see. Dozens of people were probably talking about them after the lunchtime argument and Heinrich's weeping in the corridor. Now this, in the Belvedere, the most expensive restaurant in Baden, maybe even the whole of Germany.

'Honestly, I asked him. I really did. He just wouldn't come. They're upset. It's too soon. They'll come round, I promise. Tom, you should eat something. Really.'

The restaurant circled around them, fifty, maybe sixty people smiling, talking, eating. The plump woman next to them was deep in conversation. The waiters flitted about, cool-faced, carrying plates, taking orders. She looked down at the table, the knife and fork so polished it could reflect her face.

'I've got the truth,' he said. 'I don't know why I ever trusted you. Of course you wouldn't let my father see me. You're like the rest of your family. You think you can take people up, use them, but never let them ask anything of you.'

Her heart was beating, circling wildly. Her teeth were shaking. She could feel them in her mouth, jittering and chattering. The tears were starting, hard and sharp behind her eyes. 'I can't stay,' she said. 'Really, I am going to go. I'm sorry, Tom. I tried. I really did. You try yourself, if you don't trust me. You go and ask. I did everything. And now you're being cruel.' *You'll try anything, won't you?* echoed in her head. He hated her. She'd tried to help and now everybody hated her.

She moved to stand up. Her heart hurt, crying out as if it were a child's. 'You're not being fair. I'm sorry, really I am. I tried.'

She pushed her legs out of the chair, turned and walked out of the restaurant, slowly, past the waiters, holding herself straight. As soon as she was outside, she sat down, a few yards from the door, and let the tears fall. People were probably walking past her, respectable people, thinking she was ill, mad even. She didn't care.

She was going to sit here, cry until all the tears were gone – and then what? She supposed she'd have to go back, lie in the bed next to Hilde's, listen to her weep too. She let the tears fall. It was cold on the ground and she knew it must be ten or so by now. Too late. She wouldn't go back right away. She'd stay here until she was sure Hilde was asleep, until she'd cried so much she couldn't cry any more. Then, she thought, then she'd feel better.

There was a cooling of the air above her head. 'Celia.' She looked up and Tom was standing there, the edges of him shadowy in the darkness. 'Celia, I'm sorry I was so harsh with you.'

She looked up at him. 'I asked him.' She tried to breathe, but her voice hiccuped, stumbling. 'He said no. He told me to stop meddling. I tried everything I could. Really.'

He crouched by her. 'Don't cry, Celia. I know it's hard.'

'Maybe tomorrow he'll change his mind.'

He balanced himself on his hand, propped close to her leg. 'You can't imagine how it hurts. You have a father. You've always had one. He loves you. He'll do anything for you. I find mine and he doesn't want to see me. I thought he would.' His breath smelt sweet, the wine again.

He has had all this time, she wanted to say. *He knew all this time and he never tried to see you once. Why did you think it would be so different now? Why did I think it would be different?* But she said nothing, looked past him at the beginnings of night time in Baden; two maids walking back from the next hotel, cleaners coming out to scrub at the cobblestones.

'I'm sorry, Tom. He'll come round.' It felt like a lie, even before she'd said it. 'The war's been hard on them.'

'I'll wait, come back another time, talk to him.'

'At least now you know.'

'You're right. I do know. And you and I are cousins. Second cousins. Cousins' children.'

'We are.'

'What are you doing now?'

'I don't really want to go back. Not yet. They're upset.' Hilde in the corridor. *It hurts, doesn't it?*

'I suppose they are.'

She hugged her knees. The cleaners were crouching down nearby to scrub at the pavement, slopping buckets with brushes and cloths.

'I am sorry I was sharp with you. I shouldn't have said those things.'

'No. You shouldn't have. I was trying to help.'

He put his hand over hers. 'Are we still friends?' He gave her a slight smile, the smile, she thought, of a man asking for a favour when he knew he was handsome, admired by women. 'Do you forgive me?'

She nodded. 'It was the wine, wasn't it?'

'A little. But, still, it makes things hurt less.' He took his hand from behind his back. 'I've got some here.'

'That's the stuff from the restaurant. Did you *take* it?'

'Well, I paid for it, so I could.' He took a slug of it.

'I suppose so.' It seemed rather shocking to carry a bottle out of a restaurant – especially one like the Belvedere.

'They wrapped it in a napkin. Would you like some?'

She shook her head.

He handed her the bottle. 'Just try.'

She took a sip. It was thick, sharp, sweet, expensive. Her mind reeled under it, back to the night when the war ended. They'd been in the garden, near the rose bush. Tom was talking, put her arm around her. They'd been drinking then, too.

'Steady on! You'll empty it.' He took it from her. 'My turn.' He drank and then turned to her, eyes glittering. 'Listen, Celia. I know what we should do. I'm going to go in there and ask for more. Then we'll just drink the lot. We'll be as sick as dogs in the morning, but we'll feel better. Both of us.'

'I don't think I will.' She'd felt exhausted after that night in the garden, weary and sick.

'Please, Celia. Please do it with me.' He put his hand on hers. 'I need you to.'

She couldn't leave him alone. Not after this. 'I could have a little.' She'd just drink one sip for every three or four of his. He wouldn't know.

'I'll go back. Wait here.'

'We can't drink it here, Tom. Not outside the restaurant. We need to find somewhere else.'

His eyes flickered. 'You're right. We can't drink it here. Let's go down by the lake. People sit out late there.'

'We could.' She waited for him as he trundled off, watching the cleaners scrubbing hard at the cobblestones. A tall one came towards her with another bucket of water, slopped it over the steps. Celia stared at them, wondering if they might look up, but they were intent on their work.

'Success!' Tom returned, bearing two bottles, wrapped in napkins. 'Although they didn't like it much. I think they only agreed so they could get rid of me. Let's go.' He helped her to her feet and she followed him, picking her way over the damp night grass towards the road, then down to the lake. He talked on the way, bright, eager, chattering as if someone had pressed a button, about the business in London, Captain Dalton, the panelled room for meetings, the luncheon club in Piccadilly where the clients liked to go. She made noises as if she agreed, even though she thought she barely understood a word. They passed more of Baden's evening workers, women with brushes, men with buckets and bricks, sent to mend the hotels at night when the guests didn't see.

She'd thought that there might be people around the lake, looking out at it, talking as they did in the daytime. Instead it was quiet, just a man who looked like a worker rowing on the lake with a net, fishing out weed.

'This will do.' Tom pointed at a spot at the top of the grass, swept himself down. 'I wish I had a picnic blanket. You need a picnic blanket for this kind of thing.'

'But we're not having a picnic!' The thought made her laugh, so much so that she had to hold her sides. 'We're just drinking!' she managed to say, through the giggles. She sat down, still laughing. Tom was smiling at her, not quite, she thought, getting the joke.

He passed her some wine. 'Look! I've got these as well.' He pulled out two glasses – the heavy-set crystal of the Belvedere.

'You took those?'

'No, only borrowed. I'll take them back tomorrow, don't worry.'

'Did you ask them?'

'Not in so many words. They charged me so much for the wine that I think they should be included in the price!'

He poured some of the liquid into her glass. 'There you go.'

She sat back on her heels, feeling the grass soak her dress. Across the lake, the lights in the hotel rooms were beginning to dim, one after the other. People were curling under their covers, talking, reading, settling children. She wondered where the red-haired girl they'd seen at the boats was now. Dancing, maybe, or in a dining room. Not asleep. 'Do you think it will ever come back?'

'What?'

'The war. Do you think it will come back?' All those people in Baden who looked as if they'd never fought. Somewhere there must have been fighters, like Johann, left out on the terrace. The fine dresses and the laughter hid scars, just like hers did, she supposed.

'Never. Of course not, Celia. What are you thinking of? Why would it? They did all that at Versailles. We're at peace now. Have some more wine.'

'You said it would come back, when it ended.'

'I was wrong.' He drank from his glass. 'Happily wrong. Not only about that. Wrong about many things.'

'Heinrich is a good man, you know. He cares about you. He always asked me about you.'

'We'll see. He knows where I am. He can write.' He drank again.

'He can.'

'You remember you always wanted to go to Paris?'

'I did.'

'You could now.'

'Don't start again,' she said. 'Don't start telling me what to do. It's easy for you, finding a job in business. Not for me.'

'Sorry, Celia.' He took another drink. 'I don't want to see you wasting your time, that's all.'

'Perhaps I want to waste it.'

'I don't believe that.' He drank again. 'Not you.'

'We were supposed to be so happy when the war ended. I looked forward to it for ages. Now I don't feel anything at all. And then I worry it might come back.'

He put his arm around her. 'It won't come back. How can it? Look at Germany now, look around you. They don't want another war.'

'I'm sorry about Heinrich. Maybe you could write to him tomorrow. I could give him your letter.'

'I could, certainly. Have another drink.' His arm was still around her, burning her shoulders. The wine was hot and sweet in her throat.

'Celia, I'm sorry for snapping at you earlier. I know you tried to help. Sometimes I haven't been kind enough to you, I think. Since the war broke out, I was so caught up in thinking about myself, I didn't always think about you.'

'It doesn't matter.'

'I was cruel to you when you came to see me in the hospital. I just didn't want anyone to come.'

'I know.' Months after it, she'd thought of him saying sorry, how he'd apologise, take her hand and she'd forgive him. Now, finally, he was offering her what she'd hoped for and all she could feel was tiredness sliding over her. 'You didn't ask me to come, after all. I just thought you'd be pleased to see me.'

'It was kind of you to try. Anyway, I'm lucky to have recovered. Plenty of chaps didn't.'

'You feel no pain?'

'I do. Of course. My eyes can't bear the sun or the wind, my head hurts a lot. My nose is always running, from the gas, I think. But that's nothing, is it? Not compared to the rest. Anyone would say I've been lucky.'

'No one was lucky. Not really.'

'But we're alive. A chap in my regiment sent a postcard to all three of his brothers. He wrote "I'm alive, are you?" He got no reply.'

'We are.' The ghosts of the others were coming close, Michael, Shep, all the hundreds and thousands of people on the cinefilm she'd seen, the men who'd died in the back of her ambulance.

'I'm glad.' He held her close again. 'We have each other.'

She gazed at the lake, glittering in front of her.

'I wonder, sometimes, how we'd have been different if we didn't have the war. You'd be a fine lady, married to a man with a great estate for hunting. I'd still be a servant to your father.'

'You wouldn't. You'd be something better.'

He shrugged. 'Maybe. Not this. I wouldn't be here.' His arm tightened around her shoulder. 'Who knows? The war changed everything.'

She gazed at the lake. The man in the rowing boat was gliding to the side, his net heavy with plants.

Tom drank again, cleared his throat. 'Celia, I meant it. I was grateful when you came to the hospital. Even though I – well, said some things I didn't mean.'

'It doesn't matter.'

'But you understand now. I told you no, I—'

'I offered to marry you and you said no. That's what you're trying to say.'

'Yes. I did. But you understand now, don't you? It wasn't just about how ill I was. It was that I thought – you know. I thought we were brother and sister.'

'Yes. I know that.' She sat, listening to the crickets scratching around them. Her mind reeled, circling around the look of shock on his face when she'd offered herself to him. It had been almost revulsion, she thought, horror. She drank from her glass.

'You said to me "I'm too plain for you, is that it?" It hurt me to hear,' said Tom.

'That's how I felt. You find me plain, don't you? Surely it's true.'

'Of course I don't. Who could?'

'Everyone. I'm too tall, too thin, untidy hair and my nose is too long. I should have been born more like Emmeline.'

'She's busy with her babies now.'

'She's still beautiful, though.'

'So are you. Honestly.' She could tell, from the corner of her eye, that he was looking at her.

She shook her head. 'I'm not. If I ever was, I'm not now, not after all these years of war.'

He scrambled up, so he was facing her, kneeling. 'Celia, don't say such things. You still are. I promise.'

She tried to shake her head again. He caught her face, so he was holding it, looking straight at her. 'I promise you are.'

She was going to reply – and then found, looking at him, that she couldn't. Instead, she stared. His eyes were shining in the darkness. His hands were on her face. She could hear his breath, knew that if she looked down at his chest she would see it moving, up and down. She was holding the moment between her hands, like a drop of water between two fingers. If she moved either way, it would break. He breathed again. *It gives you something else to think about*, he'd said, late at night in the garden. *Makes you forget.* Cooper slipping out of the ambulance station to meet men. She heard herself breathe. Then she moved forward, bringing her face towards his. There was a pause – she felt it – as he moved backward, only a tiny space, no more than a fly's width. Then he came towards her again, his mouth was on hers – and they were back in the garden, nearly six years ago. *So this is what it's like*, she thought. *Of course! Of course it is.* She had wondered, so often. They'd talked about it at school, in the ambulance station. But now it was happening, she thought, of course it had always been so. It had to be. He was pushing her back now, down on to the grass. 'It's wet!' he said. 'Sorry!' She laughed as he took off his jacket, laid it down, then she was laughing again, couldn't stop. 'Sssh,' he said. 'Sssh.' Then he moved her back again and he was lying over her, next to her, his hands on hers. She looked past his head. The plough, her favourite constellation, dipped and shone in the sky.

*

'Celia,' he was saying. 'I didn't realise.'

She heard him, deep in her mind, as if she was coming up from the bottom of the sea. She tried to raise her head, couldn't. She didn't want to think.

'Celia?'

She put her head back on the ground. Her body was heavy with the weight of what they'd done. She wanted not to think any more. She thought he might say *I love you*. But really, surely, she knew that already, so what else was there to say? Perhaps if she'd gone back with that officer in London, she'd know what to do.

'I'm so tired.' She closed her eyes. She could hear him talking, the words coming about something. She couldn't hear them. *What have you done?* she heard other voices say: Verena, Emmeline, her father. *I don't know!* And she didn't, not really, she didn't know. This thing she was supposed to never give away, not until marriage, was now gone for ever and she'd never get it back. She was a new person, different, she'd passed through a door. When she was at school they'd talked about the idea of it, tried to work out what it was, because no one really knew. But what they did all know was that you were changed for ever – and now a new life would begin. She supposed they were all married now, doing it properly, husbands and children. Not like her, losing the precious thing somewhere near a lake in Germany. But then she thought about Cooper again, who'd always been creeping off with men. She'd liked it, she'd been happier than the rest of them.

She looked at Tom. *You're my cousin.* Queen Victoria had married her cousin, they did in the Victorian times. She'd read an article saying it was out of fashion now. But Heinrich and Lotte had wanted her to marry Johann.

She felt different, she was sure she did. Her body had changed. *She* had changed. Would people be able to see? Surely Hilde would guess. And the thing itself – it was strange, she thought. It wasn't how she had expected it would be and yet, at the same time, of course it would be like this – how could it be any different?

She wanted to talk to him – *what did you think of it, is that how it normally is, am I different?* Was she completely altered, like magic? *I love you,* she wanted to say. Because that's what you did say, and she felt it, surely she did. *I love you.*

'Do you want to come back to my room? I'll say you're my—'

'Cousin?'

He smiled in the darkness. 'Yes. As you are.'

'I don't think that would work. Not if your hotel management are anything like ours. Let's stay here a moment,' she said. 'It's so peaceful. Then let's go.'

He lay back beside her. She bent her head to his shoulder. 'Beautiful stars,' he said.

'Yes. It's very clear.' She closed her eyes. There was a hard, smooth stone just under her thigh.

'Don't go to sleep!' he said, touching her face. 'You'll freeze out here. Let's go back.' She heard him stand, pull at her arm. 'I'll take you back.' She wanted to sleep for ever, but she gathered herself up. He linked his arm through hers.

'Your hotel will fine you for being late. I'll give you the money.'

They began to walk back through the darkness. 'Watch your step on the ground,' he said. 'It's dark.'

She wanted to lean her head on his shoulder.

He cleared his throat. 'I'm so sorry, Celia. I didn't know. I thought that – in the war – maybe. I didn't think that you were...'

She thought she could hear pity in his voice, wanted to push it away. 'I'm not,' she said. 'I have had other men. I just forgot what it was like.'

'Other men?'

'Two. One after the victory celebrations, took me to a hotel. Then last year I was in a pub with a drink and an officer offered to buy me another. He found a hotel too.' She let the words hang between them in the air, bold lies she had read in newspapers about other people. She wanted to sleep, lie down, feel his warmth. She didn't want to think. It was half true. She'd offered herself to Jonathan Corrigan, in the war, even though he'd turned her down, she'd wanted to go back to his room, be like the other women.

'They took you to hotels? Celia, you shouldn't let that sort of thing happen.'

'It was the victory celebrations. Everyone was doing it.' The lie sounded flat and weak.

'I suppose so. I was working. This way,' he said, as they came up on the road towards the hotels. Now there were a few people here and there, workers going home, three men with their arms around each other, singing in German. 'Don't do it again, will you, Celia?'

'No.' I'm with you now, she started to say, then blushed. Now what? Were they supposed to get *married*? If he asked, she supposed she'd have to say yes. 'Don't tell anyone,' she said, instead.

'Of course I won't.' He squeezed her arm again. 'What are you doing tomorrow?'

'I don't know. Not much.' Lotte would be angry with her, best to keep out of her way.

'We could go out, maybe. Go for a walk. Spend the day together. I don't have to work.'

'That sounds nice.' They'd talk about it, then she'd understand it better.

'Shall I come to the hotel?'

'Maybe I should meet you outside instead.'

He nodded. 'I suppose that's better.'

They were nearly at the hotel. 'Don't come right to the door,' she said. She doubted Heinrich would be there, but even if it was just the hotel men who saw them, they might tell him.

'I'll see you tomorrow, here,' he said. 'About eleven or so?'

She nodded. The hotel doors loomed ahead, heavy and locked. 'Would you wait to see if I get in?'

'I'll stand here.'

I love you. She reached up to him and then didn't know what to do. Despite the dark, everything felt so strange, awkward. He clutched her in his arms, held her close. 'See you tomorrow,' he said. She felt his heartbeat, then turned to run. Tomorrow she'd understand, things would be clear.

She ran up to the door, rang the bell. A big man in a black suit opened the door. 'I'm in room sixty-five,' she said. 'I was out.'

'Name? You'll have to do the late sign-in.' She felt his eye on her rumpled clothes.

'I lost my family.' He wrote her name down ponderously, said she should come to see the manager in the morning to pay the fee for coming home late. She gathered her muddy skirts around her and set off up the stairs, her heart, her head, all of her, heavy with tiredness.

On the corridor, she pushed open the door. The light was blazing. Heinrich, Lotte and Hilde were sitting on Hilde's bed. Hilde was wearing her nightgown and was wrapped in a blanket, Heinrich and Lotte both wore dressing gowns.

She stood in the doorway and stared at them all. Even her hands were covered in mud, she could see that.

'Where have you—?' Heinrich began.

'I got lost.'

Heinrich nodded. 'Celia, dear,' he said, coming towards her. She blushed at the thought that she might smell of it, what she and Tom had done. She shook her head. 'I just need to sleep, Uncle. Maybe we can talk tomorrow.' She hoped not. Not really talk.

'Please, Uncle. Let's sleep.'

He nodded. 'Of course. We'll talk in the morning.' He shuffled out, smaller, back bent. Lotte was behind him. Celia pulled off her clothes, found her nightgown. 'I meant it, Hilde,' she said, as she dimmed the light. 'I don't want to talk.'

THIRTEEN

Baden Baden, August 1921

Celia

Next morning, Celia pretended to be asleep while they all trooped down for breakfast. She stayed under the covers, not looking. Hilde came back, said a few words which she didn't answer, adjusted her dress and left again, closing the door. Then Celia jumped out of bed, washed and dressed, combed her hair. She took out her favourite pale blue gown, her favourite from even before the war. Jennie had taken up the hem but still it was too tight, a little out of fashion. But she thought it made her look prettier than any of the new stuff. Tom would like it too – it might make him remember the old times. It was the last gown from the old days that she still had, she'd given away all the others because they didn't fit any more. It was probably too plain for Baden Baden, but she didn't care. Tom thought she was beautiful. She gazed in the mirror. She did look different, she was sure of it. It shone out: I have crossed over to the other side. With Tom. She pulled on her hat and boots and hurried out of the hotel.

He was there, by the tree, as he said he would be. He looked shy and when she saw him, she was flooded with awkwardness too. She held out her hand to him and he bent to kiss it. She blushed even harder.

'Shall we walk to the park?' She nodded. He didn't put his arm through hers. They walked on together, quietly. The people milled around them. She wanted to talk to him, to ask him the meaning of it all. But she couldn't find the words to start. She'd have to tell Rudolf and Verena they were getting married, if that was what he wanted. That was what you did, didn't you, after what they'd done? If they did get married, she supposed her parents would want to host the wedding at Stoneythorpe. At the back of her mind, she thought of things she'd read, that actually girls didn't always get married. Not anymore.

'Did you sleep well?' he asked.

'Quite well. Thank you.' She'd thought she wouldn't. She'd expected to lie there for hours, mind on fire. Instead, she'd fallen asleep almost as soon as she was in bed.

'I couldn't sleep.'

'Oh.' He looked tired now she considered him more closely, his eyes smudged with purple.

They walked on.

She had to say *something*. 'How is the business?' she finally asked. 'Are you just selling wood in Germany?'

'Pretty much.'

They walked on. They passed a group of schoolchildren with sketchbooks – and then, thankfully, Tom began to talk. She gazed at the men and women around her. Were they all the same? Talking to fill the space when what they really wanted to talk about was forgotten, their sentences growing upwards like tree roots, but never breaking through. She said 'yes' as he talked on about one businessman and his particularly difficult demands.

Only a few years ago, they had told each other everything, both on their horses, galloping through the farmland near Stoneythorpe. They had shared everything. Although, maybe, she thought, he'd say that he'd had to listen, agree with her, do what she wished, because he was her servant. She blushed again, dropped her face to hide it. He didn't notice.

'Shall we sit?' They sat down on a bench by the other boating lake. She watched couples and families hiring boats and clambering in. She supposed he might suggest they do the same.

'Where are your family?' he asked.

'I don't know. Probably sitting in the hotel.'

He stared out at the water.

'I'm sorry about them.'

'I know. It's not your fault. How is your mother?'

'She's fine. She gets tired a lot. Mary's training as a nurse now, as you know. Your family tried to take her into service. What a generous offer.'

'How is Missy?'

'She's well too.' He talked on. After a while, he stood up. 'Let's go for lunch.' She followed him to a restaurant near one of the big hotels. The place was white and light with bright glass windows and large tables covered in clean tablecloths, shining cutlery. Smart men and women sat and talked in low voices. The waiter pulled out her chair and she sat down. Tom picked up the menu. 'Would you like the crab, Celia? You always like the crab.'

'Thank you.' She hadn't eaten crab for years, wasn't even sure if she'd like it any more. Under the table, by her foot, was a large brick, holding the table steady. Perhaps everything was the same: grand on the surface but held together with bricks. The vase in front of her was filled with giant lilies, excessively big, their stamens like fingers. There were so many big, false-looking flowers in Baden, horrid things. How stupid she'd been, wearing her favourite pale blue gown, thinking he would like it, that he'd even notice.

The waiter poured them both wine and water. She drank a lot of hers, then again. The wine made her feel better, her thinking clearer. He didn't touch his. She started telling him about Emmeline and the twins, even though he didn't ask.

'She's feeling tired, says she's never felt so tired. She has a girl come in to help her but that's not much good with twins. But Mr Janus won't have more people. And he's no good because he's always at meetings.'

'Oh yes. Is he still going to change society?'

'He wants fair wages for the workers, especially the miners. You know, he said they did all the work and get no benefit now, that the rich got richer through the war.' She drank again.

Tom shrugged. 'Always been that way. How can you change it?'

'Well, you're getting richer. That's change.'

'That's how those miners should do it. Pull themselves up as I did. I did it myself. No one helped me. People can do it if they try. No point demonstrating and demanding money, sitting around complaining when you don't get it. They should go out and make it happen, like I did.'

She drank again. She didn't know what Mr Janus would say to that. 'He's out all the time, working on the plans for revolution.'

'Your sister has to do it alone. Like most women. Like my mother.'

Their food came. He picked up his knife and fork and she watched them flashing in the light. She started on her crab. It tasted cold and slimy. She didn't think she'd ever told him she liked it.

She drank again from her glass. It gave her courage. He wanted to talk about Heinrich, of course he did. She had to encourage him. 'What's wrong, Tom? You seem so unhappy.'

He looked at her, then down at his place. 'I'm not unhappy.'

'Yes, you are. I can see.'

He ate again, then drank heavily from his glass. 'I can't tell you.'

She put her hand a little closer to his, not on it, though, she was too shy. 'You can tell me anything. Really you can.' She rested her foot against the brick. He was going to say *I wish I hadn't done that with you. I don't love you. I don't like you.* But at least if he said it, then it would be done and he'd feel free.

'You don't have to like me, you know,' she said. 'If that's it.' She felt brave saying the words.

He shook his head. 'It's not that.'

'Is it Heinrich? I'm sorry.' She tried and failed to imagine what it must be like not to know your father.

He cleared his throat again. 'Celia. You've always been so honest with me. About your feelings. Even last night, about the officers in the hotels. And I haven't been honest with you.'

She felt a wash of relief, warm over her heart. 'You mean when you thought we were brother and sister? That doesn't matter now.'

He shook his head. 'Other things. Things in the war. I haven't told you.'

She put her hand on his, then. That was it. Of course it was.

Like all of them, France was still with him, rolling through his mind, waking him up at night. 'You should forget them. Everyone did things they – you know. It was different then.' Men fighting with each other in the back of her van, nurses shouting, Cooper putting a bit of rotten leg on Waterton's seat in the car to make her jump. 'I know you killed men. You had to.' No story that he told her could be as bad as those she'd heard: men strangling each other in the trenches, throwing rats at each other. You couldn't judge, that was the way, it was a different world and there was no point trying to make it connect with this world, this place full of expensive dresses and ice creams and false perfumed flowers.

'I can't help it.'

The waiters fluttered behind them, the lights cracking off the glasses. 'Listen, Tom, everything is forgiven now the war is over. It's forgotten. Try to forget.' She was grateful, so relieved. It was the war that had been filling his mind, nothing else.

'I can't.'

'I know what went on. I heard the men talk. They had to kill Germans hand to hand. You did nothing bad, really you didn't. I'll tell you now, it's forgiven.'

'You would forgive me?'

'Everyone would.' She looked at the soft curve of his cheek. He'd tell her now the stories she'd heard a hundred times before – attacking German bodies, strangling them, kicking corpses. 'I'd forgive you anything.' She shifted her leg on the stone.

'Anything?'

'Of course.' *I love you.*

A tear welled up, rolled down his cheek. 'I didn't know,' he said. 'They brought him back and I didn't know.' He looked down, then up again.

'What do you mean? Was it someone who was ill?'

'I didn't really know what was happening. I couldn't see. How was I to know?' He wasn't talking to her, but gazing ahead, looking at the window. He was like someone talking through his sleep, lost in darkness.

'I thought he was—' He broke off, buried his head in his hands.

She took his hand again. 'Why don't you tell me from the beginning? Start there.'

He still wasn't looking at her. He started talking. 'It was pretty slow. After the Somme, not much happened. We joked they didn't want us to lose any more men, so they just kept us polishing guns. We were sitting about, really. I thought it was the same for the others. But other regiments were out there, fighting, going over. Michael was.'

She nodded.

'He had a hard time. I found that out later. They sent him and his men to check an enemy trench that they thought was dead, all the men gone in it. But they weren't. They rose up and killed half his men, did you know that?'

'No.' She tried to wrap her head around it. 'But not him.'

'No, not him. But it threw him. He had a – friend, there, that's what they told me, a best friend, Wheeler. And he died. Michael was very affected. He couldn't get over it.'

'You saw him?'

He shook his head, buried his face in his hands.

'I know he was shot,' she said. 'Is that what you're trying to tell me? I already know. The others don't. A man in London told me by mistake.'

Tom stared at her. 'You know?'

'I can never tell them.' She put her hand over his. 'But if you're trying to tell me about it, you don't need to. I understand. I don't think he was a coward. I never have. I saw so many men suffer from what they'd seen.' Men screaming in the back of her ambulance, the pain in their heads stronger than that in their bodies.

'I can't believe someone told you by mistake.'

'He didn't realise. He thought we knew. It's just that Michael's officer lied and said he died bravely.' She remembered the night at the Ritz with Jonathan, when another man, drunk, came up to them and started talking about Michael. 'It's my secret. Mama must never know.' She squeezed his hand. 'It's so kind of you, Tom, to try and break it to me like this. I'm grateful. I supposed it was shell shock, that sort of thing. Now you've told me so I understand.'

He was gazing at the flowers, hot-coloured, flaming things. He wasn't looking at her. She tried again. 'I'm glad you know too. I've someone else to talk with, since I can't tell them at home. I'm not ashamed of him. I'm so proud of him. He fought hard.'

Tom was still gazing at the flowers. He shook his head. 'It's not all. There's more.'

Then he looked ahead, started talking. The words were pouring out, fast. 'It was sometime after the Somme, those days when really nothing was happening, we were all just waiting, reading the newspaper reports, in shock, really. They said we had a German spy. They *told* me it was a German spy. They lined us up and said – here comes a German spy, men, do your duty. They meant us to— You know. He was a German spy, so we had to.'

She looked around, quickly, afraid someone might hear. Everyone else looked absorbed in their food. 'It was a German spy,' she said. 'You had to.' And yet the words didn't sound as sure as they had before. She heard them and they were wrong as they came from her, confused, pulled out of shape.

'You know. Like I said. Michael was affected by the death of his men, his friend. He couldn't get over it. It . . . hurt his brain.'

'He should have been in hospital. That's where he belonged.' If he'd come to Stoneythorpe, they'd have made him better, ensured he recovered.

'We just weren't *doing* anything. We were cleaning guns. So one day, the General told us – he said he needed us to do something. We had to walk out to a hut some way back from the front. We had to get our guns.'

He put his hands over his face, talked through his fingers.

'They said, "He's a spy." They made us stand so far away that none of us would know. We didn't know. None of the men back at the line would even be able to hear the shot. We stood there, guns waiting. We made a half circle.' The tears were pouring down his face. He didn't stop them.

There was a cold metal sliding around her heart, dark and hard.

'Then they unmasked him. I said, "You can't! Stop!" But the Captain said to me "What do you think you're doing? Hold your gun up. The other men will take fright." He said, "The man will hear you and he'll know it is you. Do you want to be in his place?"'

'Whose place?' she tried to say. But the words whispered out and lay in the air.

'I tried,' he said, his voice raised, hiccuping, tears on his face. 'I said, "No! Please!" But they wouldn't let me, said I had to. And I thought, I'm a better shot than half these men. I can shoot straight, fast, so he doesn't suffer. He didn't see me. He didn't know it was me.'

'In whose place?' she tried again. 'Who didn't know?' But the words wouldn't come.

He sat up, clasped her hands. 'Celia, you have to understand. I didn't want to. I *had* to. If I'd have stopped it then, raised a fuss, he would only have heard and it would have been done the next day. It would have been worse for him.' He clutched her again. 'I had to. I begged them and begged them, but I had to.'

She wanted it to stop. She wanted to stand up and turn the stars around, so she was in a different place, a different time, so she'd never come here, found Tom, lain down next to him in the grass.

'Please,' he was saying. 'You have to understand. You do. You said in wartime people have to do things that are terrible. Like killing. They made me do it.' His hands were on his face now, the tears wetting them, he was coughing and hiccuping, his voice cracking.

'Do what?' she said. The pain was stretching over her, down into her chest. The metal around her heart was spreading over her, covering her eyes, suffocating her mouth.

'He didn't suffer, Celia. He did die quickly. I promise you. He didn't suffer.' He grasped her hands. 'Please. You forgive me, don't you? I had to.'

The shock was making her slow. She couldn't hear him.

'Who?' she asked again. 'Who died quickly?' This time the words came out, clear. They rose over the flowers, hung between them. 'Who didn't suffer?'

He buried his face in her hands, his tears soaking her fingers. 'Michael,' he said.

Her heart stopped. Looking back later, that was what she would always say to herself. *My heart stopped.* Simply, it stopped beating. For two seconds, nearly three, the blood didn't course around her body, her heart didn't beat in and out; nothing worked. She sat there, feeling her heart fail.

'You shot Michael,' she said slowly.

'Yes.' He was weeping, not looking up.

'They told you he was a German spy and you shot him.'

'I had no choice.'

She felt her heart start again. It started up with more strength than it had ever had before. It was speaking to her, clear in her head. *Do it!* it said. She shook off his hands. *Do it!* She could reach out for the flower vase, pull it out, use every remnant of pain and horror and bring it down on his head. It might kill him. It might. Her hand flickered, touched the glass. She looked at him, saw the fear in his eyes.

In one movement, she pulled herself upright. *I won't do it*, she said, speaking to her heart. *I won't.*

'I will never see you again,' she said, standing up. 'Never.' *I could have killed you then.* He knew it too. 'I can't.'

'I'm sorry.'

She pulled out the chair, threw it back. She turned, hurried out of the restaurant, past the waiters and the people staring, and out into the air. Then she began really running, her skirt tangling in her legs. The material was tumbling, falling around her, like her thoughts. Michael dead, shot to the ground, Tom holding the gun, aiming at him. It was unthinkable. And yet she had to think it, let it fire through her mind, dragging every thought down with it into darkness.

'I think I should go,' she said to Hilde, that evening. 'I should go home. Sorry.'

Hilde shrugged. 'Papa's been saying we should all go.' Celia bowed her head.

They all packed together. At the station, Heinrich gave Celia the tickets to Hamburg. 'I'll escort you,' he said. She wished a stiff goodbye to Lotte, thanked her awkwardly. Hilde hugged her, crying. She kissed Johann but he was staring at the sky. Heinrich sat beside her, not speaking on the train. She looked out of the window.

'Goodbye, Celia,' he said, at the Ladies' Room at the station.

'Thank you, Uncle.' They could be any uncle and niece wishing each other goodbye. Not a man waving off the girl who had torn their family apart.

She climbed on to the train. As it was moving, she stepped out into the corridor and threw the blue gown she'd worn with Tom out into a field. A man was sauntering by the door, smoking. He raised his eyebrows at her. She looked away, imagined her favourite pale blue gown tumbled into the mud, trampled on by cows and sheep.

FOURTEEN

France, August 1921

Celia

'Here you will see the position of the second trench.' Captain Evans limped over to the screw of brambles. 'This was where C Position fell. That changed the whole course of the battle.'

Celia stared at her Baedeker guide to the Somme, trying to match the squiggles on the page with the sparse land in front of her. The trench was shallower than she'd expected, shored up with coloured bags and sacks at the side. She couldn't imagine Michael sitting in a place like this, crouching, waiting for the order. The duckboards at the bottom were splintered, spattered with weeds. Here and there, dandelions grew through the gaps. She wanted to grab them, take them for herself, flowers grown on the soil where men fell.

It wasn't too hard to find a tour in the Somme. Celia had thought that one would have to book months in advance – at least that's what the Thomas Cook advertisements said. But, she found, there were dozens of them, booths in the railway station and three in her hotel alone. When she went out for a walk into the town on her first night, two officers approached her and asked if she was looking for a tour. She booked one through her hotel, not too cheap, not too expensive, a guidebook included in the price. The woman told her that Captain Evans would take them out the next day. That night, she lay in her bed, still afraid. She'd ruined everything. She buried her head in the pillow, hating her actions, all of them.

'It looks like nothing much to me,' the woman behind her, Mrs

Wadden, was saying. 'When do you think we're going to stop for tea?' Other people were shuffling their feet. Celia felt for Captain Evans. He was no good as a guide, not really. His voice didn't carry, he was too easily swayed from the itinerary, gave in to Mrs Wadden and Mr Elms, when resisting them would have won him more respect. Even after just an hour, Mrs Wadden had asked to move, tried to join another group at one of the hotels, a tour led by a dashingly handsome officer who Celia supposed must be getting big tips – there had to be some reason for him working here; he was the type who could surely find a job at home. But Captain Evans still kept trying with them, smiling tentatively when he made his speeches about the layout of the Somme, looking at them for approval. Lame, missing an eye, plain-faced, he wouldn't find much work at home.

Just tell us what to do, Celia wanted to whisper to him. *Don't ask if we'd mind. Tell.* But every time she was about to say it, she thought of Michael, shy, unsure of himself, probably not able to tell anyone what to do either. She'd seen Captain Evans look at her, eagerly, hunting for a friend. The others were older and in groups – Mrs Wadden with her sister, Mr Elms with his wife and sister-in-law, the six others in couples. She was the odd one out, the lone woman. Or at least, she was the odd one out in this group. The other tours were full of lone women, same age as Celia or a little older, weeping in the hotel restaurants, clutching the hands of others while walking around the trenches. Fiancé hunters, Mrs Wadden called them. 'I expect you're one too,' she'd said to Celia, on the first night, during a painful group meal organised by Captain Evans. 'They're the only ones who can afford to come out.' That was the general idea, Celia came to understand: the mothers were too old, wives too busy with children, only the girls who'd been engaged could do it, come out to see where their men had fallen. Mrs Wadden's eyes said it all: *indulgent*.

Celia shook her head. 'No. I've never been engaged. I'm just interested.'

Mrs Wadden raised her eyebrows. 'Dear me. I thought things were so desperate for the young, these days. I am glad you all have the time to come out on holiday.' She patted Celia's hand. 'Still, I think you're quite right, dear. Find interests, things to talk about with young men. That's the way to find a husband.'

Celia nodded, looked back at the scant lamb chop and potato on her plate. She didn't say: *I was an ambulance driver, my friends were here.* Or what really drove her: *my brother was killed for cowardice, somewhere near the Somme.* Tom's words echoed in her mind. *He shouldn't have been there. He was ill.* Mrs Wadden was still talking, turning to Mr Elms now. She'd been wrong to come, Celia thought, as she paid up her pounds to the agent, hoping to find Michael and understand.

Now, four days later, she wished she was with the fiancé hunters. There was a group of them, just a few metres away from where she was standing with Captain Evans. They were weeping, all four of them. The captain in charge, a plump man, was trying, ineffectually, to pull one up who had fallen to the ground. She was dark-haired, pretty, scrabbling at the earth. 'I know he's here!' she was crying. 'He fell here!'

None of the men had come home, so their bodies must be buried around the battlefield. Of course, they were supposed to be in graves, but everyone knew it hadn't always been like that – some were just thrown under the earth on which they fell. That was what they were all looking for, bodies, bones and if not that, belt buckles, buttons, badges. Most soldiers had their uniform sent home, covered in trench mud. But not Michael. She should have suspected something then.

Michael's probably here. Somewhere in a field, away from the other men. He fell and then they left him there, threw soil over his face. The group of women had their backs to her. She crouched down on the soil, touched it with her hands. The grass on it was green and thick, strengthened by blood.

'Come along!' Captain Evans said, his voice casting reedily on the wind. 'Next trench. This one has a mock-up of the men's water-warming machine.'

Celia watched her group rouse themselves, drag their heels after him.

*

Celia stayed for another week. She couldn't go home. If she arrived in Stoneythorpe, she thought, they'd be able to guess everything she'd seen, it would be written on her face. She wandered around the same places again and again, looked around the town. She waited in cafes, restaurants. She walked the same trail, over and over the trenches and the nearby hill. She saw the same groups of people, women, men, fiancé chasers, a school trip, a group of old women – mothers, maybe. Different people, but they were all the same.

'What are you doing here still, miss?' Captain Evans sat next to her. She was in a bar, staring at a cup of coffee.

She looked back at him, trying not to notice his scarred eye. She'd seen him leading tour after tour, maybe twenty, always saying the same thing. He hadn't got any better at being a leader.

'I'm looking for someone.'

He pulled up the chair, awkwardly dragging his lame leg. 'May I join you?'

She shrugged.

He sat down. 'Did he die here?'

She shook her head. 'Yes. My brother.'

He touched the cup and saucer. 'I see the people who won't leave, you know. You're not the only one. Girls who can't go, want something more than what this pile of grass can give. They're like ghosts. You're turning into one of them. You should go home,' he said. 'You have a home?'

She nodded. 'I do.'

'I'm sure they're missing you.' He smiled a little, a hopeful smile she recognised. 'Can I buy you a drink, miss? Something stronger than coffee?'

She blushed, knew she shouldn't, knew she should say no to his large plain face. His hope. 'Yes,' she said. 'Why not?'

He took her to a door around the side of a restaurant. They climbed the stairs, listening to the noises from below. It sounded like a student trip; they were always the rowdiest.

She followed him up to a tiny room in the attic, only just big enough for a bed, a table and a box for clothes. He had books piled up next to the table. German poetry, she saw. She felt cracked at the thought of him sitting up here at night, listening to students laughing downstairs, readying himself for more women like Mrs Wadden, who saw his weakness immediately. The room smelt musty and cold.

'I should get some wine,' he said. 'I forgot about that.'

She sat down on the rickety chair next to the table. 'There's no need. Really.'

But he was determined, he set off downstairs, leaving her in his room, gazing at the pile of books. When he came back, with an old-looking bottle and two glasses, she smiled at him and thought – that's what I will do, I'll smile. I'll keep smiling when he passes it to me, then I'll drink it and then listen to him talk, I'll keep smiling and listening, ignoring the shouts of the students downstairs, I'll lie back with him, let him talk, his face furrowed with worry as if I were a lost tourist, wandering around the wrong trench, then I'll lie on his bed and we'll both try to forget.

He would replace Tom in her mind, remove his imprint from her soul.

She gathered up her shawl. He was still asleep. It seemed, at the last minute, too unkind to leave before saying goodbye. She patted his hand.

He stirred. 'You're dressed,' he said.

'I have to go.'

'Let's go and eat something,' he said. 'You must be hungry. They do good eggs in the cafe downstairs, they've learnt the English taste.' He was talking too quickly.

The hope in his face was too much. She shook her head. 'I shouldn't stay. I should go back.'

'You could stay a while. Sounds like you need a holiday.'

'Probably not.'

He flushed awkwardly. 'I'm—'

'Don't worry,' she said, her face more flushed than his. The

fumbling in the dark, the pressing forwards, and then him finally
– *I'm sorry, miss – Celia. It just won't—*

'Please don't think about it,' she said. 'It happens to everyone.
Means nothing.'

He shook his head. 'With a girl like you.'

Don't. 'Aren't you doing a tour today?'

'Yes, but not until two. So we can spend the morning together.
I doubt you've ever seen the view from the Lelac hill? It is very
beautiful. We could go after taking something to eat.'

She looked away so she didn't have to see the light in his eyes.
It wasn't as easy to forget as you thought, even in the midst of
the physical thing. 'I should go. I really think I should. My family
need me.'

'Not straight away?'

She looked at the floor. It was scratched, thin. What had a room
like this even been, before the war? 'Yes. I'll go to the hotel and
collect my things.' She felt ashamed of herself for even thinking
the words, but she couldn't bear him, couldn't bear the thought
of gazing at him over an egg, trailing up a hill with him, trying
to admire a view through the clouds.

He nodded. 'I wouldn't like you to be alone. I will accompany
you. Wait one minute.' She sat down on the single chair, averting
her gaze as she heard him thumping around, pulling on clothes,
splashing water. She hadn't washed.

When he was dressed, they set off down the staircase, still noisy
with the voices from the cafe. He walked with her to the hotel,
talking all the way. His deep voice, always trying to laugh, drove
into her mind. He waited downstairs – not outside, even though
she asked him to – while she packed up her trunk. She thought
the manager on reception was smiling. Then Captain Evans waited
with her while the hotel car came.

At the station, he shuffled his feet and talked about how the
weather was improving. Then he began talking about when he
might return to his family. He might come up to London, he
thought. She couldn't bear to answer. There were three women

staring at them, she felt sure, listening. She knew she shouldn't care, but she did.

'I'm fine here, really I am. You don't need to stay.'

'I can't leave you here. It's at least twenty minutes until the train.'

She turned to him. 'Please. I'm quite well here. You can go.'

'I wouldn't hear of it.'

She touched his hand. 'Really. I would prefer it.'

She saw it, watched his face sag. His big, plain, hopeful face. 'You'd prefer it?'

She nodded, blushing. 'I'm sorry,' she said.

Then his face darkened. 'Sorry?'

She nodded again.

'I don't need anyone to be sorry. Not for me. Least of all you.'

She stared at him, his scarred eye, lame leg, a few hours away from taking another group of fiancé chasers round the battlefields. She meant to say something, couldn't. She dropped her eyes.

'Goodbye then.' She looked up, and he was turning, dragging his lame leg after him. He walked slowly, not looking back. She resisted the urge to run after him, say she was sorry. There would be no point. He'd crumple up her address, throw it away.

It took her nearly four days to get back from France. The trains had been full, then she'd been delayed at Dover – delayed by herself. She couldn't bear to go home. So she stayed there, afraid, two nights in a grimy hotel by the coast, adorned with pictures of boats and seascapes. She avoided all the glances of the men in the cafes and the hotel. She walked past the newspaper sellers, ignoring them, all the stories they'd run about Louisa still burning in her mind.

PART TWO

FIFTEEN

Stoneythorpe, May 1919

Louisa

'We weren't expecting you yet.' The pale-haired girl hung by the door, hand clutching the edge. 'Mrs de Witt said you were coming later.'

'Well, here I am now.' Louisa stared back at her. She wasn't going to apologise, why should she? *I am an orphan*, she often wanted to say, to old men who pushed past her on the street, shopkeepers who turned up their noses. *You should be kind to me.* But they'd probably only turn back on her and say, *Me too!* 'Everyone's an orphan nowadays', she'd read in a ladies' magazine while waiting for one of Mrs Handley's fittings for her Stoneythorpe trousseau. 'It is positively *chic.*' Her mother's face as she died filled Louisa's mind, that horrible stuff that looked like jelly in her mouth, holding out her bent, skeletal hand, the blackened nails, begging people to touch her, kiss the cheek that smelt like rotten leaves. Louisa wanted to seize up the magazine, the photographs of the pretty ladies in hats gazing out to sea over the sides of boats, the articles about lipstick, and dash them all to the ground.

'They've all gone to town to buy presents for you. But you're here now.' The girl's accent was terribly thick – and unbearably slow. She sounded to Louisa more like a farm girl than anything else. She supposed Aunt Verena must be stuck for servants. Although Mama had often said that her sister always had a talent for hunting out the most slatternly and cheeky maids available – and appointing them. 'Verena couldn't even manage her doll's house as a child,' she'd say, crossly. 'Even that was a mess.'

'I left my boxes at the bottom of the drive,' said Louisa, deciding that the girl wasn't going to ask after them. 'The driver wouldn't bring me any further.'

The girl sighed loudly. 'I'll send Thompson for them. Come in, then.'

Mind you, Louisa admitted to herself, as the girl leant back and pushed open the door into the handsome marble hall (cleaner than it had been the last time she'd visited), Mama might have been wrong. The front of Stoneythorpe was untidy with ivy, the gardens overgrown and full of weeds, but it looked solid and beautiful, still here, not empty like their home; at least it still had a *purpose*. Mama had been wrong about quite a few things, after all – not just servants and girls, but what Matthew wanted, the war, how Britain would be stronger after it was all over. Most of all, she'd been wrong about herself; declaring she'd be fine to go to visit that hospital, where all the men were ill, saying she'd be quite well and you only got diseases if you were weak or afraid and she wasn't anything of the kind. Three weeks later, there she was, coughing, a purple tinge gathering around her mouth and the skin of her eyes, her skin hot, hot, hot, no matter how much they sponged her forehead, brushed back her hair. Louisa stared at the maid's back and realised her eyes were welling up. She lifted her hand to wipe away the tears, felt them fall harder. She leant against the wall, let the dust of it coat her hands. The image of her mother flowed up in front of her; the last time they'd been at Stoneythorpe, that dismal afternoon of Michael's funeral when Celia and Verena were barely able to speak.

'There, dear.' The maid patted her shoulder. 'I'm sorry if I was harsh, miss. You were just a little early. They wanted to make things nice for you.'

Louisa put her hands over her face. In her mind, Verena and Celia came to put their arms around her. 'Come along, dear,' they said. 'Let us help you.' Instead, the maid patted her arm again. 'Let me take you to your room, miss.'

There was nothing for it, Louisa thought. She would have to pretend to be her mother, after all. She pulled herself straight, smiled, that impersonal, cool smile her mother always used for servants. 'Thank you.'

She followed the girl upstairs, two flights, on to the second landing. Rows of neat cream doors with gold handles. Her mother said that the rooms were rather shabby, that Aunt Verena didn't have an ounce of taste – although, frankly, you could tell that from the whole business of her marriage – and the house was no better than it should be. This was the first time Louisa had been here since Michael's funeral, and they hadn't been past the parlour that day. Mama had said then that they might do more for 'poor Verena', but they hadn't visited. Her mother pretended not to have a sister, if anyone asked. 'It's for our *protection*,' she told Louisa and Matthew. It was all because of Rudolf. They needed to be as far as they could from the suggestion of a German relation. No one needs to seem German, Mama had said, by associating with them.

'I hope you like it, miss,' said the maid, opening a door to a large room with a washstand in the corner. The walls were rose and the eiderdown a darker pink, the rugs, the curtains all different shades of rose and fuchsia and carnation. At least, she thought, that meant it wasn't Michael's old room – for she had dreaded that.

The girl was hovering in the corner. 'Thank you,' said Louisa, pretending to be her mother again. 'I'll wait here for my aunt and cousin.' The girl left.

Louisa stood there a moment then pushed at the heavy door. She'd go out, explore the house, see it before they returned, see the parts they'd lock away from her. She padded, quietly, so that the nosy maid wouldn't hear, walked down the staircase, holding tight to the dusty rail. There were portraits on the wall, of who, she didn't know. They all looked a bit like Rudolf: stern. Mama had said that Uncle Rudolf just collected them, to make the place look like a country house.

She slipped downstairs and, remembering the way, through the great marble hall. She couldn't imagine what it must have looked like as a hospital, men everywhere. The place didn't look as if there'd been people in it for years. She drew a hand over the marble wall, brought it away covered in dust. She wondered if Celia ever came in here.

She pulled at the door of the parlour and it came towards her. She'd been here for Michael's funeral, just three years ago. Matthew had talked about paintings, amused everybody as he always did. He was probably amusing everybody in Delhi now, telling them stories, everyone saying how brave he was. Surely people said to him, *why not invite your sister out here? Especially as she has no one else.* When he'd first talked of going to India to work with Jardines, import-export or whatever it was they did, he'd said it wouldn't be for long. But that had been almost three years ago, and he still wouldn't come back. Or invite her to go there. She'd like it, really she would – hot weather, elephants, the colour pink everywhere. He didn't suggest a visit. 'Stay brave, little sister,' he wrote, after Mama's death, in a too-short letter. 'I know it was hard for you. You'll be happy with Aunt Verena.'

Of course it was hard, she wanted to write back. I sat up with Mama every night. She was always asking for you and when she grew more unwell and her mouth filled with foam, she started talking of giving birth to you, that was all she would talk about. Every time the door downstairs rang, I hoped it was you. Matthew! You'd make everything better.

She wrote to him, begging him to come, even though she knew the letter might take weeks to arrive. Perhaps he guessed she had written because the next week, he sent four lavender soaps in a box, ordered from some shop in London. She'd unwrapped the box, held the things under her mother's nose. 'From Matthew,' she said. The smell was awful, chemical. Her mother opened her eyes. 'All the way from India?'

'Yes,' said Louisa. 'And he's coming soon.'

Her mother would keep looking at the door, asking after him. 'He's coming,' Louisa said. 'He's coming.'

Instead, she received letters from him saying, 'I'm keeping my spirits up, so should you! Always smile.' She wanted to throw them into the fire. He didn't come, even when their mother died. She wrote to him, but the funeral couldn't wait, of course. Instead, the village came, her father's friends she didn't know and Aunt Verena with cousin Celia and cousin Emmeline. She told them Matthew was still in India, important work, couldn't possibly leave.

On the day after the funeral, Mr Grierson, the solicitor, called her in to look over the wills. He said that the house was Matthew's and would remain waiting for him. Mr Grierson said Matthew had asked him to send money to him in India, which he would – although he really should come home and manage the estate, occupy the title properly.

'I could look after it until he arrives,' she said. 'I know how the house works.' And she did, she could. Mama wouldn't like the house to be alone.

'A nice offer. But you're too young, my dear. Don't worry. Your parents have set aside a lot of money for you. You are a very wealthy young lady. You can have the capital when you are twenty-one or when you marry with permission of your family. Otherwise, you have the interest.'

'What family? Matthew?'

He looked at his paper. 'That would be your aunt and uncle. They are your guardians.'

'They have to give permission for me to marry?'

'That is correct.'

'I hardly know them.'

Mr Grierson tapped his desk with his pen. 'Well, you will come to know them better. As you are underage you must live with someone, and they are your nearest relatives. Your parents have set aside money for them as well, so you mustn't worry about that.'

She stared at her hands. 'Matthew isn't coming home?'

'That may change things, I admit. For the moment, you must live with them. Are you not interested in the sum your parents have set aside for you?'

She shook her head.

'It is over a hundred thousand pounds. You will never need worry about money again.' He leant forward. 'This is a very unique situation. Most families would set this money aside for the house. But this is yours.'

'I don't want it. I'll give it to Matthew.'

He nodded. 'You can do as you please, Miss Deerhurst. But I'd keep it for yourself. It is yours, after all. Life is long. You may need it. And one day you will have a husband, who might require it for his own house and family.'

'I wish I could give it back. I want my mother.'

He patted her hand. 'I know, Miss Deerhurst. But no use crying over spilt milk. Now, let us discuss the banking arrangements.'

She sat down in the Stoneythorpe parlour, looked at the portraits over the fireplace of Arthur, Michael, Emmeline, Celia. She'd always been too young to play properly with her cousins when she was smaller. Michael and Celia had sometimes let her join in with their games (Arthur and Emmeline seemed like grown-ups, so adult that they dizzied her), but after a while they'd grow weary of her, run off somewhere with Matthew. *Wait for me!* she'd shout, but they never heard.

She'd wanted to be Celia's friend most of all. She'd imagined herself telling the girls at school about her cousin Celia who was four years older than her! Celia might write to her and Louisa could show her letter around. They'd send each other little pictures and keepsakes, like toy dogs, a diary with a key.

But Celia and Michael only played with her when the other one wasn't around. When they finally did let her join in, she felt stupid, so much younger, not fast enough to run with them, not quick enough to understand the games they played. And she always had to go to bed so much earlier.

Once, she remembered, Celia had even sat on the stairs, telling their parents she would make sure Louisa didn't come down. She'd lain in bed under the summer light, listened to them laughing.

Now she was older, and she would surely be friends with Celia. She imagined Celia showing her around the house, describing how they had arranged things when it had been a hospital. They'd go on walks, just the two of them, maybe even ride. And after a while, they'd get the train to London together, look at the shops, perhaps go to the theatre. She smiled up at the portrait of Celia.

You've changed so much, she imagined Celia saying. *You're a grown-up now.*

'What shall I look at now?' she asked the Celia picture. She walked away, turned the handle of the glassy doors and let herself into the garden. The grass was wet on her boots. It didn't look like it had been cut recently. She walked towards the false river her mother had mocked so, dipped her hand into the muggy waters.

The long garden stretched in front of her, looking rather better, she thought, than it had done last time. The whole thing was divided by the long false river, topped off by a fountain at the very far end. Her mother had always laughed at Verena's ambitions to make a Versailles garden, but, Louisa had to admit, it had more life than Howe Hall's dreary hedges. At least there were flowers here. She reached a finger for a dirty spot on the window, traced it around. In only a few hours, she supposed, her aunt and cousin would return – perhaps Rudolf too. The whole lot of them would be asking her questions, talking about Mama, gazing at her with that soft look in their eyes, as everybody had at the funeral.

What was the point of it? she wondered, suddenly. Howe House had been the same. Why did you need all this land, if you only neglected it, let it overgrow? At home, there were great grounds, but no one there to see them. Surely, she thought, they could do something more useful with them. When Matthew came back, she decided, she'd speak to him and that was exactly what they'd do.

She walked along the river. It used to flow, back and forth, to the fountain. Rudolf had been very proud of it, said it rivalled the best engineering. Now it was stopped, stagnant. Dead fish lay face up, burning in the spring sun. She wondered how you'd mend it. Matthew would probably know, he'd be able to find the secret button you pressed to make it all start again. Her mother's voice billowed up in her head. *It would take more than pressing a button to make this place start again! My sister was always terrible with money.*

Louisa put her hand on the fountain, mossy, the carving worn down by rain. 'Well, at least she's alive!' she said. 'You were the one who died.' She felt the tears in her eyes, tried to brush them away. She walked on. At the end of the garden, there was an entrance into a mossy dell, a place where Celia had always gone to think. Louisa had tried to follow her in, but Celia sent her away, once even standing in front of her so she had to turn back. She edged towards it. She knew, really, that she should wait for Celia to take her in. They'd link arms and laugh together about how Celia would never let her before. Celia would say how she was sorry for always sending Louisa away and Louisa would squeeze her arm, say it didn't matter, really, it didn't.

She cut into the dell. It was just as she'd remembered it, the willow tree overhanging the pond, the stones dotted with flowers. When Celia had sent her away, Louisa used to hide behind the wall and listen. So she knew that Celia thought it a place where fairies lived, she even talked to them, closing her eyes and pretending she saw them. Louisa edged around and went to sit on the stone that was Celia's favourite, gathering up her skirts out of the way of the damp grass. The willow edged so low that she could touch it; she pulled it towards her, rubbed her face on the leaves.

'Well, hello, stranger,' said a voice.

She jerked her head up and saw a tall man, standing against the sun near the wall. 'You don't look like anyone I know. Are you a friend of Celia's? You'd be the first friend of hers ever here, frankly, if you were.'

She shook her head.

'Well, you don't look much like a maid. Or a neighbour. You're far too pretty.' He jumped down and swung himself under the tree, so he was standing right next to her. Now he was so close, she could see he was actually extraordinarily good-looking, with thick dark hair and dark eyes, a chiselled face. He looked like something out of a magazine, advertising a holiday to France or new coats.

'I shall have to guess again.' He held up his hand. 'I've got it! You're a foreign princess, just arrived from overseas and paying a visit to our garden. But you need to *prove* yourself a princess.' He raised an eyebrow. 'We could put you to bed with a pea, if you liked.' He threw back his head, laughed. The sound rang out across the trees.

Then she realised – she'd heard that laugh before. 'You're Arthur!' she said, delightedly. 'I didn't recognise you.'

He was still craning over her. 'I certainly am. I am most hon-oured to be recognised by a foreign princess. My fame has clearly spread.' He held out his hand.

She grinned. 'I'm Louisa. Your cousin. Don't you remember?'

He stopped, shook his head a little, like a dog shaking off water after being in the sea. 'Why, of course! Of course you are!'

She smiled. 'I am come to live with you.'

He nodded. 'So my mother said. I had forgotten.' He looked, she thought, quite honest. And yet she felt sure that he'd known; all that princess stuff had just been a joke. The shaking of the head hadn't been quite right, made up.

'Did you just arrive?' he said. 'They've all gone out. I think they were expecting you later.'

She nodded. 'That's what your maid said.'

'I'm sorry there was no one to welcome you.'

She felt the hurt welling up in her again, the memory of her mother's face.

'Look,' he said. 'Don't cry. Do you ever play balancing games, dear cousin?'

She shook her head. 'What do you mean?'

He shrugged. 'Nothing too complicated. I like to play with fate sometimes. I'll show you. I'm sure you'll enjoy it.' Everything around them was still as he moved forward, edged along to the tree. He jumped up to it, swung on the branch.

She leapt up. 'You'll fall!' The branch was creaking, thinning. 'Please, don't!' He swung out further, hands edging along. 'Arthur! You'll drown!'

He smiled at her.

'Please!' She threw her hands over her face. 'I can't look!' Time stood still. She heard a creak, looked up. Arthur had jumped down and he was walking towards her.

He gestured at the stone. 'May I sit next to you?'

She nodded. 'You made me afraid.'

'It was only fun. I like to test life.' He sat on the stone, close to her. She could almost feel the warmth of him through the cloth of his trousers. 'I'm sorry about your mother,' he said.

She shrugged. 'Me too.' She knew she should say, 'It's fine' or, 'I am feeling better'. But she couldn't. She wanted her mother back, arm around her, together, wearing the dresses of silk and wool and satin that had been strewn around her rooms as the maids packed them up; she wanted to hear her speak, fussing about the garden or the church tea party. Her soul cried out for her mother any moment she let it, so she had to force down the pain all the time, squash it by doing things. Otherwise she'd cry.

He patted her leg. 'Poor cousin. But I really must say, you have grown up. You were just a little girl. Always running after Celia, trying to be her friend.'

She blushed. 'I did.' Wait for *me!*'

'I wouldn't now. She's no fun. Always feeling sorry for herself, wandering around under a cloud. She's never been much fun, if you ask me. I'd stick with me, if I were you.'

'Thank you.' It was dizzying, really. She hadn't thought that Arthur would even want to be friendly, let alone call her a foreign princess and ask her to stick with him.

He clapped his hands. 'Now, foreign princess, what would you like to do? Shall I escort you around the grounds? Or would you prefer to stay here?'

'Maybe we could walk.' *Don't edge out again*, she wanted to say. *Please.*

He stood up. 'Well, let's walk, Princess Louisa. I shall show you my mother's prized flower beds. She doesn't plant them, of course. She has people to do that.'

'You don't need to call me princess.'

'Well, you're practically a princess, if you're the Honourable Miss Deerhurst. And I would like to call you Princess Louisa. As long as you don't mind.'

She shook her head.

'And we shall keep it between ourselves. I'll call you Princess Louisa in private. The others don't have to know.'

He held out his hand. He took her up, helped her over the stones. She clasped his palm, feeling the warmth of his skin touch hers. They stood under the willow and he asked her about her mother. She answered his questions briefly, as she'd become used to doing.

'That's not how you really feel,' he said. 'Is it? Why do you hide it?'

And then, standing by the tangle of weeds over the moss, she began to talk, the words tumbling out, telling him about her mother twisting and weeping in pain, the nurses who couldn't help, who said they couldn't give her drugs, the doctor who shrugged and said, 'It's a slow decline.' She had wanted to shout out, 'It's not slow! It's fast and she's screaming in pain. Make it stop!' The foam coming from her mother's mouth, her sick yellow look. The horrible smell in that room. Her mother begging her, 'Stay with me,' even though the smell was so awful that Louisa thought it was swamping her. Her mother saying, 'You still love me, don't you? You don't find me repulsive?' And Louisa nodding and saying, of course I love you, bending down to kiss her, but as she did so closing her eyes, so that the woman she kissed was the mother of her childhood, not the sick animal in the rumpled bed.

'It must have been terrible,' said Arthur. 'We should have come. My mother should have.'

'She did.' Verena had come one day, said she'd read to Mama, had sent Louisa downstairs. But then, that evening, she'd gone again. Rudolf needed her, she said she'd come back.

'Only one day? For her own sister?'

'She meant to come again but Mama was dead. It only took two weeks. Anyway, it was more than most. Most people wouldn't come near us. They thought they'd catch it. But it's just luck who does and who doesn't.'

'You were lucky.'

'I didn't care. I wanted to catch it. I couldn't see why I'd have to stay alive. I drank from the same glass as her, kissed her, lay next to her with my arms around her so she'd sleep. And I still didn't get it. It wasn't fair.'

Arthur squeezed her arm. 'Don't say such things. You're young and strong and beautiful.'

And then she was crying, more than she had done for weeks,

coughing, the tears slopping down her face, her heart beating hard. He put her arms around her and she clutched him, the words catching in her throat.

'It's fine,' he said. 'Don't try to talk.'

But she couldn't help it. The words had to come. They kept pouring out, in between hiccuping sobs. 'It's not fair. Why do horrible people live and Mama had to die? I hated them, all those people who were alive. I hated myself! I don't understand. Why would God leave me alone?'

He stroked her hair. 'But you're not alone, my princess. You have me.'

She was laughing at his joke about a bird when there was a woman shouting. 'Louisa?'

'That's my sister,' Arthur hissed. 'I'd better dash. See you in a bit.' He jumped down from the stone, pulled himself up over the wall and was gone.

Celia appeared around the corner. 'Cousin,' she said, picking her way over the stones. 'We were looking for you.'

Louisa flushed. Celia sounded cross. She must hate her already. Verena would be even angrier. Mama, her heart called out. She wished she was back at home.

'We were worried about you! We didn't know where you were.'

She didn't know what to say. She shook her head. 'I'm sorry. I didn't realise. I wanted to walk.' She didn't know how to answer Celia, didn't know why Celia was so angry. She wished Arthur hadn't clambered over the wall. They didn't want her to be there. She was an orphan, dumped on Stoneythorpe, and Celia was angry with her. It had been the same at school. She kept upsetting and offending people – and now she'd done it with Celia.

Three hours later, they were taking tea with Celia and Verena in the parlour. Rudolf was upstairs resting. Verena was all apologies for having missed her. 'I feel dreadful!' she said. 'You being so alone. Thank goodness Arthur was here.'

Louisa looked at Celia but she didn't seem to want to look back.

Her cousin's face was slow, exhausted, she could have been six years older, ten, even fifteen. Louisa couldn't see her as the young girl who had played with Matthew, always rushing ahead, jumping over streams, laughing and racing the boys to the end. When Verena tried to prompt Celia, she stared past them, somewhere at the portraits over the fire. The hour dragged.

'Well,' said Verena. 'Let us go and dress for dinner.' They all stood. Celia moved forward to open the door. Arthur was there. He looked past his mother and sister and smiled, straight at her. 'Princess Louisa,' he mouthed.

And then all through the dinner, that long, interminable dinner, she looked at Arthur, and knew that their legs were close under the table.

Celia was silent, stuck up, Louisa thought, and Rudolf only seemed to care that people were eating. The footmen picked on her, piled up her plate with potatoes swimming in grease, horrible things. *German food*. Even the pudding was heavy; raspberry sponge something or other. She pushed it around her plate.

Louisa thought of her leg, her foot, near to Arthur's. Even though he didn't look at her, she knew he was thinking of her. She could see it in his eyes, a light that fell towards her alone, like sun flashing on the sea.

SIXTEEN

Stoneythorpe, May 1919

Louisa

Louisa lay in bed, heart filled with fear. Every noise in the place had seemed so strange. Jennie had only departed a few minutes before, after putting out the lamp, and every scrap of Louisa wanted to cry out, ask the girl to come back. But then what if Jennie laughed at her, told her she was a silly, foolish girl? She probably would, that serving girl, the one who had rushed her forward, heels clicking, hurrying, back straight, every step complaining that Louisa had arrived at the wrong time, too early, spoiled everyone's plans.

After ten minutes, she couldn't stand it any more. She cried for the maid, her voice coming out too quiet, barely reaching through the walls. She tried again. The words only came back to her, mocking. Then there was a rustle from somewhere. She sat up, heart thumping. Something behind the curtain, the thick, pink curtain. She stared at it, the material rippling in the pale light from the night. She flung herself out of bed and ran for the door. Pulling at the handle, she opened it and burst into the corridor, slamming the door behind her.

'Cousin?' It was Arthur in the corridor, no doubt heading to his own room. 'Are you alright?'

'Yes!' Her voice came out tiny and high. She blushed at her own childishness, hated herself. 'I'm afraid,' she said. 'There are noises. I keep thinking someone's in here.'

'I know,' he said. 'The first night in a new house. Everything seems odd.' She stood for a while, gazing at him. He looked back, the whites of his eyes large. Then he stepped forward. 'Don't be afraid. Listen, why don't I stand out here. I will stand by the door, until morning, and so if anyone comes towards your room, they'll have me to deal with first.'

'Would you do that?' She knew she should say, *no, I will be fine, thank you for offering*, but she couldn't.

'For you, cousin. Now, go to sleep. I will go when the sun comes up and you probably won't even notice.'

She turned back into her room, lay down, pushed her face into her pillow, her heart pounding. In less than a minute she felt sleep overtake her, the edge of it rising up in her mind, high, so that she knew she wanted to fall.

In the morning, Jennie came to wake her at eight. Arthur wasn't at breakfast, had gone to town for business. She sat with her aunt in the parlour but her eyes were closing by mid-morning.

'Poor girl is exhausted after all that illness,' she heard Aunt Verena say. Celia didn't reply. Louisa kept her eyes closed, heard them talking, Verena praised Arthur for looking after the business. Celia said nothing. Louisa lay there, thought of Arthur standing outside her bedroom door, keeping watch while she slept.

Arthur really was a friend. In the days that followed, he talked to her, asked her about her mother, said that she mustn't try to push down her feelings but express them – because she was in pain for her mother and that was all that mattered. 'It will get better in time,' he said. 'You'll love her still, but it won't hurt. You tell me about it. It's not good to keep your sadness to yourself.'

And, even more, he seemed to like her. He said that she made him laugh, he told her that he was weary of practised girls who seemed to know everything. 'You jump at the world with innocence,' he said. 'That's so charming.'

By herself, she was sad and alone. She spent days sitting in the garden, the sun burning her hair as the hours crept by, telling herself what she'd read so many times: you'll feel better in time. *How much time?* she wanted to cry at the sky. She thought of her mother before she went to sleep, and as soon as she woke up, her mother was there, standing over her.

But to Arthur, she saw, she was fun, he said she reminded him of light. 'Everything in this house has been so heavy,' he said. 'They're so dreary here. You're far too young to be cooped up.'

'I don't feel young,' she said.

'You're so charming,' he said, ruffling her hair. 'So sweet.' Her mother had been wrong about Arthur. She'd said he was wasteful, worried his parents. But he was kind, looked after them all. He oversaw the house, dealt with the business, allowed Rudolf to say it was still him at the top, when he was old – and nervous too. At the dinner table, her uncle shook, the cutlery tapped the table, jiggling in his hands. She supposed he was remembering his time in prison. Arthur looked after everyone.

And then, one morning in July, she woke up and it wasn't until after breakfast that she realised she hadn't thought about Mama at all. She'd woken up and thought about being hungry instead. She tried to hear her mother's voice in her mind. It was far away. 'She's gone further back,' she said to Arthur.

He patted her hand. 'I told you. Grief doesn't last for ever.'

Two days later, they had the house to themselves. All the others had gone up to celebrate Peace Day in London. She'd rather hoped to go, but Arthur said they'd be better at home. He said that Rudolf would only make it dreary, dragging her round the most boring of places. And Verena would never let her out of her sight.

'Take my word for it,' he said. 'It would be dreadful. I'll take you to do something better.' So he said to Rudolf that he had business to attend to, and when she was woken, she told the maid she had a headache. She lay in bed, listening to the rest of the family bustle and bang as they headed off.

After they'd gone, she turned over and went back to sleep. She woke late, dressed herself as best as she could, came down to Arthur, who was smoking in the parlour.

'Let's enjoy it,' said Arthur. 'Let's celebrate victory together.' So they did. Verena had given the servants the day off, so they could even go into the kitchen. They ambled there, arm in arm, went through the cupboards looking for fruit cake. Louisa found an old one in the cupboard near the oven – and they took it upstairs with two of Verena's best plates from Mrs Bell's china cupboard.

'I don't think we'll even use these,' said Arthur – and so they wandered through the hall and parlour, wickedly dropping crumbs of cake as they went. They fell on Verena's pale primrose carpet and into the gaps between the marble slabs of the hall floor. The blobs of cake on the ground made Louisa laugh – so much so that Arthur started laughing too, and soon they were in the middle of the parlour, in front of all the family pictures, clutching each other, hysterical with laughter.

'Let's take the cake outside,' said Arthur. 'And I'll find something better.' She waited for him, still giggling, and he came back with a bottle of Rudolf's wine and two glasses. She wasn't fond of wine but Arthur was keen and she took the drink he poured into her glass. That made him laugh more, and soon they were both lying under the trees in the back garden, laughing at the clouds, each other, anything.

That night, they stayed up until nearly two o'clock in the morning. The servants were supposed to come in for dinner but they didn't and Arthur said it was much better that way. They drank more wine in the parlour. Then he started talking, telling her about the beautiful buildings in Paris. She was so tired she was falling asleep on the sofa.

'We should go to bed,' he said. 'Now that Peace Day is over. I imagine our dull family went to bed hours ago. They'll be back soon, droning on about all the dreary parades they've seen.' He started imitating Rudolf, listing each part of the procession in turn.

She stifled a giggle in the cushion. Then he started imitating Verena, fretting about the sun, and Celia talking about 'when I was in France'. Louisa was really laughing now, even though she knew it was wicked.

They crept up the stairs, still laughing with the freedom of having the house to themselves. She was about to go into her room when he pointed at his own, at the end of the corridor.

'Come in here, I have something to show you,' he said. She knew she should have been embarrassed, invited into a gentleman's room – Mama would not approve – but this wasn't like that. Arthur was her cousin.

She followed him in, heart full of shyness, and stared around her. The room was rather beautiful. She supposed it had once upon a time been like hers – or Celia's – a plain white square, high ceilings, large windows looking on to the garden. But he'd transformed it. The walls were black and brown, hung with red and gold, candles flickered on the surfaces. Stoneythorpe in general was a little lacking in ornaments ('Verena thinks it is elegant to keep all her belongings in the cellar,' her mother had said). But Arthur's room was crowded with things. The walls were covered with pictures of dancers, cafes, parks, some framed, some not. The shelves were piled up with wooden boxes, hung with bits of silver. She sat on the bed. He stood up, next to his shelves.

'What are all these?'

'I bought them in Paris.' He looked a little shamefaced. 'I like to spend money.'

'Me too. Or I'm sure I would if I ever did go to Paris.'

'Maybe you will, one day. You must be cold. I should offer you a blanket!' He held out a red woolly thing, deep and fluffy. When she took it from him, her hand touched his and he laughed.

'Thank you.'

'You know, I think I might have a few chocolates in here. I bought some in London! I think I still have a box.'

She watched as he reached in, took up a dark blue box and opened it. 'Ah look!' he said. 'There are so many more than I thought.' He held the box out to her and in the red and gold interior were twelve or so dark chocolates, nestled in neat white papers, tiny presents, just for her.

'Take one. Take two, if you like. All sorts of different flavours, you know, strawberry, cream, caramel.'

She held out a finger. The choice was agonising. What if she got it wrong? Two of them had pink spots on top – they might be the strawberry, she supposed. But what if they weren't?

'I can't decide. I might choose the wrong one.' The night, the darkness, the noises flooded into her mind and she wanted to cry. Arthur patted her hand. 'Don't worry, cousin. If you choose the wrong one, you can always have another.'

'Another?'

'Why of course, another. They are all yours. I ate my fill in London, had quite enough.'

She stared at the box. 'I can have *all* of them?'

'They are yours. But don't eat them all at once. Might take me a week or so to get my hands on some more.' He smiled. 'Don't look so afraid. No one is going to take them from you.'

She picked out one with a pink nib and put it carefully in her mouth. It was strawberry! She had been right! It exploded in her mouth, a bright, sweet flavour. She looked at the others as she ate it, still not exactly sure she had chosen the best one. But if she had not – it didn't matter.

'Have another?' he said. 'What about this pale one here?'

She picked it up, took a bite, her mouth still sweet from the one before. She felt its warmth spread through her. All of her grew warmer. She pulled the blanket down from her shoulders; she had no need of it now.

'You're so lucky,' she said. 'I'd love to go to London. I've read about the parties, what goes on there. I'd love to see it.'

He shrugged. 'It's so-so, I suppose. Those things can be fun but they seem a bit dull after a while.'

She fingered another chocolate, running her hand over the smooth surface. 'I wish I could see it. Sometimes I feel shut up away from everything here.'

'Well, maybe we should go one day. I'll take you.' And then he began talking about London, telling her all the things she longed to hear: parties full of girls in their best gowns; driving around the streets in cars; seeing the Royal Family; dancing in clubs in smart parts of town. She listened, nodding, barely wanting to talk in case he paused for a thought and the wonderful words ceased.

Arthur lifted up his hand. 'Do you mind if I smoke?'

She shook her head. She didn't really know if she did mind – she'd never been near anyone smoking before coming to Stoneythorpe. It was what Papa did after dinner with the men. Sometimes, as a child, she'd go into the room next morning, before the maids had a chance to start throwing open the windows and beating the rugs. The place had always smelt dark, as if it had been burning.

'Don't stop talking about London,' she said.

'I need a break. You can ask me another question in a moment, if you like.'

He took a silver holder from one box and a cigarette from another. She watched, fascinated by how quickly his fingers moved, how he held the thing to him, breathed in, lit. He blew out a long trail of smoke.

'Would you like one?'

She shook her head. Maybe ladies smoked in London.

They sat there quietly as he inhaled, exhaled smoke.

'I hate my room,' she said. It seemed much smaller, plain and shabby compared to Arthur's. She'd known it was smaller than Celia's – but seeing Arthur's made her think she'd been put in a store room.

'Hmmm. Well, we could ask for another room for you. But you know what my mother is like.'

'I'd love more space, like this. Mine's like a maid's room. It smells anyway, of medicine. I bet there was medicine stored in there.'

'You're probably right. Mind you, I'm not sure what else there is. Lots of the rooms are in a bad way, terribly damp and full of all kinds of junk after making the place into a hospital.'

He started talking about London again, the coffee houses he visited, the fine restaurants, the dancing. Louisa lay back, listening to his voice.

She woke to Arthur pulling gently at her hand. 'It's six-thirty,' he whispered. 'The maids will be here in an hour or so. You should go back to your room.'

Her eyes felt like lead weights.

'No, no, don't go back to sleep,' he said. 'You can't stay here. They'll find you.'

'I'm so tired!'

'Well, you can sleep back in your room. But you need to go there now.' He shook her. 'Come, Louisa. It's morning. Light outside. And the house is awake.'

She pushed herself up and her heart skipped at the thought that she had just spent the night in a man's room, even if he was her cousin. What would her mother have said? Aunt Verena would be furious. She gathered up her skirt, hurried out of the room, not looking at him. Her face flamed. She dashed back along the corridor and jumped into bed.

That night, she heard Arthur cough as he passed her room. She longed to go out, hear more stories of Paris and London, but she knew she must not. She slept thinking of rain on stones, pattering down on the roads in Mayfair, Piccadilly Circus.

SEVENTEEN

Stoneythorpe, August 1919

Louisa

Then came the week when everything went wrong. Not immediately. The few weeks after the family came back from Peace Day were quiet. Verena and Celia were always talking about babies, Rudolf distracted. She and Arthur spent more time out by the roses or talking in the corridors. He told her more about London, precious details that she savoured.

Then, on the Tuesday of the bad week, Rudolf began talking about the finishing school in Brook Green that Louisa and Celia could attend. Celia had hated the idea, that was easy enough to see, but Louisa had liked it. And Celia agreed and Louisa saw a rather beautiful time, where they'd catch the train together, stay in a boarding house overnight, learn about all sorts of interesting things, read books, write down notes about what they'd learned, prepare for exams. They'd travel home together, chatting and looking over their notebooks.

But Arthur fell into a rage when he heard. He was so angry with all of them – and then later that evening, when he caught her alone, he was incensed at her. 'How could you?' he said. 'I thought we made plans to go to London together.'

She hadn't realised. 'I didn't understand,' she said. 'I thought you'd be pleased.'

'What, you and Celia going off together? Why on earth would you want to spend a whole day with her? She's so dull.'

She was shocked by his anger; this was an Arthur she'd never seen before. She could think of nothing to say.

'Louisa—' he started. He seized her hand. 'Let's go away.'

She looked at him, bewildered. 'What do you mean, go where?'

'To London, of course. To all those parties and balls we talked about. I'll take you to the Savoy to dance. Now, Louisa, you have to pack. We should go tonight. Do you need me to help you? We have to do it quickly.'

Her heart was clutching. 'We're not going to sneak off in the middle of the night?'

'No, no, Louisa, of course not. You've been reading too many novels. We'll tell them, tomorrow morning, before breakfast. But we need to have everything ready, so they can't stop us.'

She thought of them, laughing together, giggling on the sofa on Peace Day with cake in their hands, running up the stairs. Her days spent in Arthur's company as he talked about Paris and London. Replaced by what – school, miles away? Her mother had sent her to boarding school, she'd hated every moment, mainly because the other girls hadn't liked her. She'd begged her mother to let her come back home – and finally, she did.

'Maybe I wouldn't like the school.'

'You wouldn't. And I'd miss you. So let's get putting things in boxes. I've spoken to Smithson. He's organised everything for us. I know a family you can stay with and I'll take lodgings upstairs.'

She'd finally agreed and the next morning came the terrible argument at the door, where she could see Celia reaching out for her, pleading with her to come back, Verena weeping, Rudolf shouting. She'd wanted to move towards them, say she was sorry – but she knew Arthur was right. It would be just like boarding school, the freezing classrooms, horrible girls. She held on to his arm. 'We'll be back soon,' she mouthed at Celia. 'We won't be long.'

Don't forget me, she wanted to say. *I'll come back*. Celia's face was so pained. Louisa remembered the child she'd been, always chasing after Celia, begging her for permission to join in their games. *Wait for me!*

Then they were on their way to London. The horses reared again and they clattered down, turned the corner – and in a minute they were out on the road. He was still holding her close. After ten minutes of the wind blowing hard in her ears, he patted her shoulder.

'I think we're free now.'

'Thank you, cousin.' She could say nothing else. Her heart was wild, her breath still short and her head would not calm.

'I'm sorry, cousin. All this must be most unsettling. But rest assured, I am here to look after you. I won't let anything happen to you.'

She sat up and stared out at the farms they were passing, fixing her eyes on them so that they didn't fill with panicked tears. She tried to breathe in the air, thinking about the trees that sped past them, each one marking their distance from Stoneythorpe.

At Boulbrook Inn they changed to a car, a private one with a padded interior that would take them all the way to London. She touched the outside, grey and shiny. 'Nice, isn't it?' Arthur said. 'Smithson organised it for me, although, of course, I didn't tell him why. I might pop in for something to eat. A man needs his breakfast, you know.'

She clutched his hand. 'Can I come too?'

He shook his head. 'You'll be fine here. I won't be a minute.' She clambered into the car, threw herself back against the leather interior. She wanted to reach out and touch each part of it, beautiful and shining, all different varieties of dark grey. But she couldn't concentrate, the darkness outside enveloped her and she wished Arthur was with her.

After half an hour or so, Arthur came back, smelling different. 'I bought you a cake,' he said. 'In case you're hungry.'

She looked at it, worriedly. 'I wish we hadn't run away so early. It seems so – wrong.'

'Oh, cousin, don't worry. They're upset now, but soon they'll be pleased for you that you're enjoying yourself. Now, what you really need to think about is this car – this beautiful car. And how you'll be arriving in London in the most splendid car imaginable! Don't you think they'll all envy you?' He started the engine with the key.

She nodded, her mind still untidy.

'Think of that! How beautiful you'll be! How sought after. The honourable Miss Deerhurst in the most fashionable car. You'll take London by storm.'

'Thank you.' She couldn't say anything else. The words were too confusing, they stuck in her throat.

He turned off the engine. 'Louisa,' he said. 'I think there's something we should think about.'

She gazed at him. Perhaps he was going to take her back.

'I think we should get married.'

'What?'

'We should get married,' he rushed on.

'You're my cousin! We can't get married!' He was joking, surely, throwing out things to make her laugh.

'Louisa, if we're married we can live together. It will keep you safe and I like spending time with you.'

'What about the family I'm meant to be staying with? We don't need to be married.' The thoughts were whirling around, dizzying her mind. 'I'm too young to get married.'

'No, you're not.'

I don't want to! she wanted to shout. She knew he was only being kind, trying to look after her. But she was about to be free, finally. London was waiting for her. She didn't want to upset him so she tried to speak softly. 'Arthur. I think I'm too young.' Mr Grierson, the solicitor, had talked on about how she should be careful of marriage. She'd thought then that she wouldn't get married for years.

'But you'd be safer that way. Anyway, I could take you to more places as my wife.'

She tried to give a gentle smile that said – *let's not say this*. She couldn't say *no*. Surely he'd understand.

Arthur turned back, looked out ahead. She'd made him angry. But what could she do? He'd been carried away by their rush from Stoneythorpe – and now he was probably even regretting the question.

Finally, he sighed. 'Let's go then,' he said. 'If that's what you want.'

They drove on. She looked forward until the light made her eyes weep, so she had to bury her face in Arthur's coat until they had settled again. 'We're passing Woking!' he shouted. He laughed, their earlier conversation seemingly forgotten. She clutched his hand, laughed too. The stems around her heart swelled and exploded. *I'm going to London, Mama.*

EIGHTEEN

London, April 1920

Louisa

There were so many parties. Every night – Monday, Wednesday, Saturday, you couldn't tell them apart because there was always a party. Silver trays bearing glasses of pale liquid, tables with piles of food that no one ate, dresses with sequins, glittering, red, blue, green, yellow, so many colours it was as if a child had picked up a dozen pots of paint, thrown them on to paper, swirled them together, and painted a hundred bodies. The gowns were gossamer thin, floating around legs, low cut, high cut, bare arms, white gloves, silver gloves, gold bags. If she gazed at them and let her eyes blur, the room was nothing but colour, bright eyes, open laughing mouths. And then the diamonds, thousands of them, fake and real, around slim necks, tiny wrists, stacked over red, blonde or brown hair, woven into curls, through plaits, curved around buns, dancing on shingled bobs, decorating tiaras. Other gems too, rubies, emeralds, sapphires; Louisa would never know if they were fake, like hers – she could have had Mama's, of course, but they were so old-fashioned. Arthur said he'd buy her some good ones when he made money through his business. If she had the choice, she thought, she'd only wear opals, like Mary Dewer. She loved their cracks of colour, the shimmering depths, she would cover her hair with them if she could, even though they were bad luck. She preferred them to diamonds. There were so many diamonds, you could grow dizzy with them. You had to make a decision not to be sucked in, to keep your mind in one place. *Look*, she said, *I can resist. I am myself.*

187

'She's doing it again,' Louisa said to the girl next to her. But the music was so loud that no one could hear.

She stared across the room, past the sea of shimmering bodies, bright faces, slicked hair in diamond headbands, painted-on smiles. Jennifer Redesdale leant against the pillar, batting those eyelashes that weren't even real while Edward Munsden talked in her ear.

Louisa knew she shouldn't be staring, knew it was gauche. She tore her eyes away but found herself staring at them again. Jennifer's mauve was very chic. Was Louisa's green gown really elegant? She'd thought it was at the dressmaker's, pale mint with silver embroidery, flat over the bosom, so short it touched her calves. Now, looking down, she wasn't sure she had the figure for these new types of gowns; you needed to be tall and wiry, like Celia, not smaller with too much bosom. She felt clumsy, too young, shy. She wished Arthur would stay with her at the balls, rather than wandering off to drink with his friends.

She'd had her hair cut, finally, to try to fit in. She'd sat in the hairdresser's as a sharp woman clipped and cut around her, fiddling, pulling her hair. She'd been too shy to ask the woman to cut off one whole skein, so that she could keep it for herself. Instead all her hair, years and years of it, lay on the floor around her feet. At first she wasn't sure about the cut, felt it too stark around her face. But she had to keep with it now, tie around jewelled headbands, play the modern girl.

Frederick le Touche was watching Jennifer. Some people shunned him. They saw an ugly little man, bent over and hunch-backed, one eye half closed by some childhood disease, a tiny mouth, pock-marked skin and dark hair greased over, which never looked quite clean. They looked at him fearfully – after all, he could hardly have been injured in the war, not with a hunched back like that. He noticed it, he saw them, and then, by the time they understood he was the chief columnist for the *Mail* and thus able entirely to direct a girl's fame – well, it didn't matter how much they made up to him, the die was set. Unless they were quite captivatingly beautiful, or did something daring like sliding down the banister wearing high heels in front of a whole party, Frederick would damn them with the worst possible fate: no mention at all, neither good nor bad. And then they would be nothing, for you were only something if you were in the newspapers. Jennifer was clever. She had always cultivated him.

Louisa wondered what he was going to write about Jennifer Redesdale. Louisa almost hated picking up the newspaper because Jennifer was always in it. Sometimes they named her, other times she was 'glamorous society beauty, R'. But either way, seeing her made Louisa's blood boil. She didn't know how Jennifer had got the time to be so glamorous. Louisa's days were so filled – parties until four in the morning or so, then stumble to bed, wake at midday in time to dress for lunch with the Merlings. Then there was tea and soon it was time to drink and dance again. She supposed she was going to have to start getting up earlier. And yet the problem was that, even if she did, she wasn't exactly sure what to order her dressmaker to do; her outfits – like this mint-green gown – never quite looked right when she came to wear them.

She gazed over at Edward, still listening intently to Jennifer, his face tipped towards her, wearing a smile that Louisa knew well: gentle, waiting to be charmed. She watched Jennifer reaching out her hand to touch his shoulder. 'I think my heart is breaking,' Louisa said, but quiet, trying out the words.

Time had passed quickly since they'd arrived in London. Too fast, she thought. Arthur had arranged her rooms in Hill Street with the Merlings, a quiet mother and two daughters who sometimes asked her to play the piano. He took the rooms upstairs, so he was still there for her – although of course they couldn't live together. Her bedroom at the Merlings' was right under his sitting room. Sometimes she'd lie in bed, hear the sound of his feet walking over the ceiling, feel reassured.

On the day after they'd arrived at the Merlings', he'd asked her to write to Aunt Verena. 'I will tell you what to write!' he said. He leant over her, speaking the words as she wrote them down, hand shaking. She told her aunt that they wouldn't be long, that they had respectable lodgings with the Merlings, that Arthur was looking after her. 'Don't worry about me. I'm perfectly safe. I'll be home soon,' he dictated.

She looked up. 'We're going back?'

He shook his head. 'Don't worry. I'm just saying that. You know, they will be so happy that you're here safely, they won't mind when you go back. They know Stoneythorpe isn't a place for a young girl.'

She signed off the letter with love and passed it to him. She hadn't realised that they would think she wasn't safe. 'Should we invite them to come and see us? I didn't give the address.'

'Well, I could invite them. I doubt they'd come. They're too busy, otherwise they'd have brought you down to London them-selves, wouldn't they?'

'Maybe we *should* invite them.' They had left so quickly. She worried about Aunt Verena.

He patted her shoulder. 'Of course. I'll write it in the letter.'

She looked at him. 'We can stay as long as we want?'

'Haven't I always said that?' He squeezed her shoulder. 'As long as we want. We can stay for ever, if we like!'

'But we'll pay them visits?'

He patted her shoulder, again. 'Anything you want.'

She'd lain in bed that second night, in her room that wasn't much bigger than her one at Stoneythorpe, listening to Arthur pacing around upstairs, wishing she could go and talk to him. The first evening, playing cards with the Merlings, had been beyond dull. But every time she wanted to complain, she reminded herself: you're in London! Soon things will begin.

The next afternoon, Arthur had gone out – he'd said he was laying the foundations of her social appearance – and she'd been alone in the rooms. She'd thrown herself, melancholy, on to her bed. She'd thought he would take her out the minute she arrived. Instead, she must go for a walk with the Merlings. They put on their hats and shawls and walked outside towards Hyde Park.

'The air will do you good, dear,' said Mrs Merling, plump-faced under her giant hat. 'Put some colour into your cheeks.'

They trailed along, Louisa feeling tired and cold, walking with the youngest Miss Merling, Lucy, only thirteen. She began to wonder if they could have talked to Verena, persuaded her to come with Celia to London. But then Arthur would say his mother would never come to London. Verena hated the bustle and the rush of people, just as Mama had. Louisa turned her face forwards. She had only just arrived. She shouldn't rush to judgements. They turned and walked towards Queensway.

'Oh, look!' cried Lucy. She pointed towards the window of a shop just outside the park. The window was full of tiny animals, little pets! They moved closer. Three puppies slept in a basket, a rabbit slumbered in a wooden hutch, two handsome Siamese cats sat in the midst of puffy cushions in the centre of the window – and to one side there was a kitten! A little tortoiseshell, sitting at the window, propped in a tiny cardboard box, right at the side, paw raised, looking out at them. Louisa walked closer, until her gloved hand was nearly on the glass. She looked at the kitten, crouched down.

'Aren't you beautiful?' she breathed. She put her finger on the glass. 'Hello, there.'

Lucy was chattering above her head. Louisa didn't hear. She gazed at the kitten, entranced. 'What's your name?' she whispered.

'Come along, girls!' called Mrs Merling. 'What are you doing?'

Louisa straightened up. 'Let's go inside!'

'We can't!' Lucy backed away.

'Oh, come now. It will only take a few minutes.'

Mrs Merling bustled up to the window. 'What is this, girls, a pet shop? Come along. We will never reach the park.'

'I'd like to go inside,' said Louisa. 'Please.'

She watched Mrs Merling's eyes stop and change, her mouth open to refuse – and then a thought passed over her face. Louisa had guessed from some of the conversation she had overheard that Arthur was paying handsomely for her to stay with them, although she didn't know how – he had said he had no money. She supposed that Mrs Merling didn't want to displease her, so early on.

'I won't take long,' she said.

'Well, just for a little while,' said Mrs Merling, smiling weakly.

Louisa pushed the door open into the shop. A hundred tiny eyes turned to look at her, yearning. But she had eyes for only one – the tiny kitten in the window.

'May I see that one, please?' she asked the small man behind the corner. He tried to direct her to the Siamese, told her the kitten had been put there by mistake during cleaning, it wasn't meant to be in the window at all. It was a poor, weak thing, he said, they'd only taken it as a job lot with some other cats that had just been sold to a lady in Belgravia. 'I doubt it will last more than a few months or so, madam,' he said. 'Not much to it.'

Everything he said made her more determined. She asked for the box and he passed it over, grudgingly. She took off her glove and poked in a finger. The kitten grasped at it, rubbed its face over her nail. 'He likes me!' she said, delightedly. She looked at the shopkeeper. 'Is it a girl or a boy?'

'It is a female cat, I believe,' he sighed.

She picked it up, felt the scratch of minuscule claws as it settled into her palm. The tiny pink nose nudged her thumb. 'I have to have her. How much does she cost?'

She heard Mrs Merling breathe sharply behind her. She turned, smiled brightly. 'You are quite happy to have my cat with you, I am sure, Mrs Merling?'

'Oh, of course,' she said, stiffly.

'But—' Lucy began. Her mother seized her arm and she stopped.

Louisa held up the little kitten. 'I don't know what to call you!' she said. Then she thought. 'I shall call you Petra.' She clutched the little tortoiseshell to her bosom.

'Can I offer you a box to carry her in?' the man asked, sourly. She supposed he'd hoped for a bigger sale. She passed over her purse to Mrs Merling to pay.

Louisa held Petra close. 'I'll look after you,' she whispered. 'My darling.' She clasped the cat to her. The man was talking to Mrs Merling about feeding it.

'I'll take her home,' Louisa said. 'I don't need to go to the park.'

*

Arthur came down that evening when Louisa was playing with the cat and a ball of Mrs Merling's wool. 'Look!' Louisa said.

'She'll take a lot of care.'

'Don't you think she's sweet?' She pulled the wool away from the cat, watched her try to paw it back. 'I called her Petra. Like Pet, you know.'

'I'm not much of an animal person.'

Louisa turned away, patted the kitten's head, dropped the skein of wool towards her paws.

Arthur said something, but she was too absorbed in the cat.

'Did you hear me?'

She looked up. 'What?'

'I said, did you want to accompany me to a ball tomorrow night? There's one you might like.'

She jumped up, the wool falling from her hands. 'Oh, Arthur! Of course!'

'Well, tomorrow, then. Mrs Merling will take you to find a gown.'

After that, it had been a whirl of parties, cocktail evenings, then even more balls. Poor Petra lay on her bed, waiting for her. When Louisa arrived home she mewed gladly, sprang into her mistress's arms. In the mornings, when she finally woke up, Petra was on her bed, already awake. Sometimes she even woke her by licking her face. 'You want food?' Louisa giggled. 'Is that why you're awake?' She hugged the cat, padded out to find her some breakfast.

She'd noticed Edward at the beginning of 1920. It had taken her a long time to recognise all the faces, a sea of them, rather like the first week at school. She'd also been – although she'd never admit it – disappointed. When she'd read the newspapers in Stoneythorpe and at home, she'd got the impression that every ball was impossibly glamorous, full of the most fabulous dresses and handsome people. So it was rather a surprise to see plain-looking people, untidy hair, dirty fingernails. Most of all, she was surprised by the sadness, how some smiles slid away when people turned, their eyes full of despair.

She and Arthur had been at a New Year party at the Savoy hotel. It was beautifully decorated, tables of food, glasses of champagne. She raised her glass, laughed, trying to seem gay so that no one would know how she had a dark hole inside her heart. Christmas and New Year made her miss her mother the most. Arthur and the Merlings had been kind, they had all celebrated together. And yet they weren't family, they weren't her father, mother or Matthew. Arthur told her that his family said they missed her, but maybe they just missed the money that came with her. They needed it to hold together that rackety old house that should have been sold long ago. She disagreed with him at first, but the idea needled at her.

She'd sent Matthew letters every month, with her address, but he hadn't replied, not even a card for Christmas. She dreaded the moment of New Year most, when everyone would cheer and hold up their glasses. *Stay here*, she wanted to say to them all. *That's all you should wish for. That no one you love should die.* She knew, of course, that most of them had lost more than she, husbands, lovers, sons. But she was weighed down by the fear of cheering in the year, the thought that they were all alive when others were dead.

She sipped at her drink, looked around the party. Everyone they knew was there. Lady Ellen, tall, impossibly slender, dark hair like a fine cap over her tiny, fairy-girl face. Her friend Gwendoline Charteris, curly hair, deep-red lips, face always vibrant and engaged. The bank of chaperones, middle-aged ladies sent to escort the younger ones. And then the men. Dozens of them, dark-haired, fair, swarthy, pale, so many she could hardly tell them apart. A woman would speak to her, tell her that they had talked the night before and Louisa would have no idea who she was. They all sounded the same as they shouted to make themselves heard.

Then she saw him. He was standing near a pillar on his own, gazing out towards the crowd. The look on his face was almost painful, she thought. It pulled her in from among all the idly laughing faces, chattering mouths. He looked as if he felt things, as if this whole whirl of people meant nothing to him. He was above it all, greater. His face looked like it had a scar across the cheek. She wondered if he'd been a soldier. If he had, he probably saw everything here as empty, without soul, she thought, after all that suffering. He was tall, dark-haired, with a heavy nose, smallish eyes. She supposed you'd say he was handsome, although much less handsome than Arthur. But it was the pain on his face that reached out for her, took her by the hand.

She started to edge towards him, unable to stop herself. Even though he wasn't looking at her, she felt sure he could feel it too; they had to be next to each other.

Then someone caught her arm. 'Louisa!' It was Arthur. 'Where are you going? You need to come this way. You have to meet Lady Bernet.'

He steered her over to meet an old lady who couldn't really hear. Then when she had a chance to look over her shoulder, the man had gone. She spent the rest of the evening sulking, yearning every time she saw the door open, always disappointed when a pack of girls burst through or a dowager came shuffling in.

For the next six weeks, she attended every party she could, scoured the walls, even the outside verandas, and he was *never there*. It was too much, she thought. It was almost as if he had been some sort of magical apparition. She danced with Arthur, dined with him, laughed when he made a joke, all the while feeling just like those spinster chaperones she had laughed at only a few weeks previously. She lay awake in her room in the Merlings' house, Petra snoozing on the pillow next to her, and wondered if she'd actually done such a silly thing as invent a man she loved at first sight. Perhaps he was nothing but a conjuring of her lonely mind. But she felt sure he was real. That almost made it worse. She'd come so close to meeting him, even speaking to him, and she'd missed her chance.

She knew, really, that she shouldn't be thinking about men. She couldn't even marry until she was twenty-one, unless she had Rudolf's approval. She hadn't thought to ask who her inheritance would go to if Rudolf didn't agree. Probably to a second cousin of her father's or something. But then, she thought, who needed money? It hadn't made the other Deerhursts happy, as far as she could see. Perhaps she and this man could live without it, in a little cottage somewhere. He could build up a farm, she could help him. She felt sure he wasn't the sort to care about money.

She couldn't talk to Arthur about him, the thought made her too shy. He said they were cousins, she could tell him anything. But the idea made her blush.

In the weeks that followed, she tried to drag her mind from the man she'd seen. She looked at other gentlemen at the balls – but they were just pointless gaggles who'd go wherever there was a party, like flotsam on the sea, washed up on a beach by the tide. Arthur was different, of course. Her mother had always talked of how dreadful Arthur was – money-grabbing, selfish, broke Verena's heart with his behaviour. After Louisa had arrived at Stoneythorpe, she'd talked back at her mother in her head. He's good and kind, she said. He's changed.

And then she saw the man again. It was at a salon evening of Amelia Gregson's, at her Marylebone townhouse, a spring party in her rooms. Louisa had only gone to please Arthur, who said Amelia's mother was someone she should know. And then, when Arthur was off talking to Alexander Desmond and those other chaps, she'd wandered off for some air. She stood on the balcony gazing out at the city below, her mind heavy. This was what she had wanted, she knew, parties and fun and laughter, and yet it felt so without heart. What else did she want? her mother's voice said. To nurse men from the trenches, covered in blood? Be a servant dragging buckets up the stairs?

There could be nothing better than this. But Louisa knew that only worked if you didn't look too closely; if you held her new life up against the light, like a sheet raised to check for stains, then all you could see were blotches and holes. She looked down at the city again, thinking of Peter Pan, flying while nobody saw.

'Hello there.' A man's voice. 'You're not cold out here?'

She looked up and it was him. She stared up. The words wouldn't come. She put her hand out, brought it back, gazed at him.

'I'm Edward Munsden. Looks pretty chilly out here. You must have been deep in thought.'

She smiled, confused, so muddled by the heat inside her, she stared suddenly at the floor. She didn't want to look at him closely because what if he was not what she thought he was, what if there were dips and shadows that made him plain, a pinched mouth, yellowing eyes? Perhaps she had not imagined him, quite, but invented him, created him out of a fleeting glimpse.

'Will you not look at me?' he asked. She brought her head up, met his eyes. There was a scar, cutting across his cheek, white as lightning. He held out his hand. She grasped it tight, felt like she was falling.

NINETEEN

London, April 1920

Louisa

In the days and weeks that followed, she thought of Edward Munsden. At night, she whispered to Petra about his face, his soft voice, the kind way he asked about her family, looked heartbroken when she told him of the death of her mother. 'He's really the kindest man,' she whispered, stroking Petra's soft hair. 'He'd love *you*, I know it.' On that first evening, they'd talked for at least half an hour before he said he had to go in. He'd sought her out since then – maybe six or seven times. Six half-hours was three hours together.

She told him about Petra, the little things she did, her habit of catching the lace at her bedclothes and playing with it. 'She's really the sweetest kitten!' she said. 'She has the kindest nature. Even Mrs Merling has come to love her.'

'One day, I shall have to call on you to meet her.'

'That would be marvellous,' she said. 'I'm always free.' That was at Mary Graham's cocktail party. She stored up his words – *one day* – gathered them to her as she travelled home. Next day, she sat all afternoon in her pink gown, and he didn't come. She wondered if she had been too keen to invite him.

Three nights later, she attended the Moss ball – and he came straight to dance with her. He didn't mention the afternoons. She supposed he must have forgotten. He whirled her around, his hands close on her back. He had to dance with other girls, of course, but every time he did, he looked over at her.

And then, the next day, Arthur came down with a cold. He

sent a message down via Mrs Merling saying he was too ill to go to the balls, so she would have to remain at home while he recovered. She replied in a letter, telling him that she could easily go herself, ask Mrs Merling to accompany her as a chaperone (even though Mrs Merling never went out, as far as Louisa could tell). He wrote back that it was impossible – she would have to wait. So she did, pacing the rooms with Petra in her arms, willing him to recover. At night, she couldn't sleep, lying there sure she could hear Arthur moving around, leaving the room, even. She held Petra close, thought of Edward clasping her in his arms. But as the week drew on, all she could think of was how other girls might be coming close to him, smiling, touching his arm.

After two weeks, finally, when Arthur deemed himself fit to attend a ball, she walked in – and saw Edward talking to Miss Redesdale. He had forgotten her.

She gazed at him, willing him to look back at her, but he was absorbed in Jennifer, smiling at her, listening. Frederick was saying something into Louisa's ear, but she could barely hear. She could see only *him* and *her*, as if they were the only three in the room.

'I have to do something!' she said to herself.

'What did you say?' said the girl next to her. 'What must you do?' She shook her head. This was a plan she would have to conjure for herself, tell only to Petra.

It took her a week to come up with her idea. She pondered what she might do late at night in bed, on lunch appointments with Arthur – and at a cocktail party, where she watched Edward and Jennifer, deep in conversation once more. 'I have it!' she told Petra. There was a fancy-dress ball planned for two weeks' time. The theme was Under the Sea. She'd been looking forward to it eagerly – she'd been rather surprised, she had to admit, about how few fancy-dress balls there really were. When she'd read about the fun young things of London, she had thought there would be fancy-dress balls every night. But even though she'd been in London for nearly six months, there had only been two – one in which everyone had to pretend to be some kind of cake (she'd worn pink) and one while Arthur had been ill, so they couldn't attend, where the theme was dressing like something to recall Africa.

She had to think of the most exciting possible costume – and Edward would notice only her, admire only her. For the next week, she plotted, demanding Mrs Merling accompany her to shops. Other girls could dress as fish or lobsters (Binky Smith said she was going to be a jellyfish). No one fell in love with a lobster, even Louisa knew that.

In one drapers' shop, she bought swathes of turquoise material, gold-tinged and edged with green and blue embroidery. She tried it against her face in the mirror in the shop, watching the light glitter off her eyes. She started practising the dress in the afternoon, Petra watching closely. She had the plans quite down to perfection, she thought. She would wear a usual gown to the party, the ordinary blue one that was already looking a little drab. Arthur would approve. He'd told her dressing up was unseemly for girls – hardly fair, since he was going as a shark. She'd tell him she agreed with him, and would merely wear a small fish brooch on the bosom of her gown. But under her shawl, she would carry the bundle of material – and slip off as early as she could to effect the transformation.

Petra licked her ear, nuzzled her cheek. 'I'll tell you all about it,' she said.

As it happened, she barely had to wait at all to put her plan into motion. Only half an hour after arriving at the party, Arthur wandered off to the bar. She gathered her shawl and hurtled up to the ladies' cloakroom. There she shut herself in the WC and pulled off her gown, quickly as she could, then the most cumbersome underthings, gathered the sea-green material and swathed it around herself, pinning it with the brooches she'd borrowed from Mrs Merling. She tugged the material up over her shoulder and waited. Finally, the voices outside her cubicle discussed moving downstairs. She heard the door slam and the hubbub fade as they walked away, back to the ball. Then she came out, fluffing her hair at the mirror. She almost laughed as she came close. She had swathed it around herself even better than she had in her own room – despite not being able to see herself in the mirror. The material was tight around her body; she was a blue-dressed girl, like a mermaid.

She crouched down to bundle up her dress and underthings in her shawl, piled them in a corner next to the sinks. Then she fluffed forward her hair, smiled one more time, and hurried through the bathroom door, holding up her costume.

She hesitated slightly at the door to the ballroom, hearing the noise of the party. Then she heard someone move towards the door. She couldn't turn back. *Hold your head high*, she said to herself. *Smile!* She waited for the person to leave the room – Billy Smiles, as it turned out, a man who had always wanted to dance with her, now dressed as a squid – and she sailed past him, walking quickly.

Keep smiling. Look up. The other costumes were a joke – cardboard fish and lobster heads. She spotted Binky, wearing a giant pink hat, tentacles dropping into her face. No competition from any of them. She couldn't see Jennifer or Edward.

No one noticed her at first, not really. Three people in orange with giant eyes perched on their heads (were they goldfish?) and two girls with large cardboard shells on their backs paid her no attention. She pushed past someone in blue puffy material – perhaps they were meant to be a wave – walked past some people in ordinary gowns who she supposed had forgotten the theme, or decided not to join in. Then she saw it: the place she wanted, a spot reasonably free of people. She thought she could see Jennifer Redesdale's head in the group nearby. Louisa jumped forward, stood there, smiled widely, shook out her long hair.

The room quietened. She could feel it almost before she heard it: the voices dimmed. They were staring at her. People were turning, looking. She heard someone gasp, felt the hiss of whispers.

'Why!' said one woman loudly. 'She's practically naked!' *No I'm not!* Louisa wanted to cry. *I'm just a mermaid!*

A group of barnacles were whispering. Binky was openly staring. Mrs Callendar, in blue, with seaweed swathed around her, was clutching the arm of the woman beside her. Arthur – thankfully

– was nowhere to be seen. She smiled again. She just had to keep smiling. They'd see that the costume was beautiful.

Then it was almost as if the sea itself parted. Edward, dressed as a sailor, was walking towards her, through the people. He pushed past Jennifer Redesdale, didn't notice her. Louisa smiled wider. He came towards her, holding out his hand. Three steps, two, one – and his hand was on hers.

'I'm from the sea,' she said. She'd meant to say *the sea loves sailors* (or squids or whales or whatever he had come as). But when it came to it, she couldn't, blushed and the words wouldn't come out, she got confused. She gazed at him.

A voice came from the crowd. 'Edward!'

It was Jennifer, red-faced in a dress decorated with sand. She was staring, mouth open.

The rest of the crowd were silent, watching. Louisa held his hand. She felt it slip down, away from her. She gazed at him. She felt him pull away, his reluctance. And then he stepped forward to her. 'Come,' he said. 'Let us dance.'

She followed after him, her hand back in his.

They stood at the dance floor waiting for the next turn to begin. She could feel his hipbone, close on hers.

Frederick le Touche came towards her. She felt his breath on her ear. 'You should watch out,' he said. 'Did you mean to make an enemy in Jennifer Redesdale?'

'I just wanted to look pretty.'

'Well, this isn't the nursery school play any more. You've just made yourself a rather powerful rival.' Then the music began and Edward whirled her away.

TWENTY

London, April 1920

Louisa

Edward left the ball after an hour or so of dancing. He clutched her hand passionately and said he had business – so by the time Arthur came back from drinking with his friends at the bar, she'd changed into her underthings and dull blue gown. But Billy Smiles had told him about it and so she had fifteen minutes of him stomping about the Merlings' parlour, complaining. 'Your antics are ridiculous!' he shouted. 'I didn't bring you here to make an exhibition of yourself!'

'It wasn't an exhibition. It was just a beautiful costume.'

'You can be such a child.'

She let Arthur's words drift over her. The important thing was that Edward had seen her, clasped her hand.

She waited for a note from him, holding Petra close. Her mind ran on the ball, how he captured her in his arms.

Three mornings after the ball, the Merlings were planning a shopping trip. She'd said she had a headache so strong that every step, sound – even a drop of dust – would only aggravate it. She'd heard them slam the door and dropped back into bed. The maids were out on their morning errands. *Solitude!* Pure solitude, where she could lie back in her bed and indulge pleasant dreams about Edward. She huddled under the covers in her nightdress, wrapped her arms around herself, pondered on how Edward's kiss might be.

She was just imagining that she had allowed him to briefly touch her neck when there was the sound of the bell. It was the time that the postman came. Edward might have sent a letter. She swung her legs out of bed, not stopping for her slippers, hurried downstairs. The Merlings' man, Jamieson, was standing by the door, holding out a package. 'It's for you, miss,' he said. 'No sender.'

She took it into her arms. It felt heavy. Perhaps, she thought, Mrs Merling had ordered something from the draper's for her. She thanked him and carried the package back to their rooms, holding it close. The handwriting on the front was strange and spiky, a long line under the word Deerhurst, a sharp triangle over the 'M' of Miss. She closed their parlour door behind her and took the thing to the sofa. Carefully, not wanting to tear the gauzy stuff inside, she began to open the paper, stripping off the layers, crinkling the cheaper wrapping that lay behind.

Then she came across newspaper. That was a surprise. She had never received material through the post wrapped in newspaper before. She doubted anyone Mrs Merling used would lack for wrapping material. She plucked at the newspaper – obviously the lowest sort. And, moreover, there was rather a strange smell coming from the package, something quite rotten. Perhaps, she thought, it was a mix-up and she'd ended up with something meant for Mr Merling, back in the Cotswolds. They'd received a box of cigars for him once. She continued to pull the newspaper off the parcel, even more layers of it, so she was practically sitting in a pool of paper.

She tugged off the last layer. Now it was a brown-paper parcel. It wasn't material, she knew that much. It was wet and cold. She knew, really, that she should put it aside now, not look at it, but she carried on tearing off paper. Then the thing fell into her hands and she screamed, threw it to the floor. It was a fish, a great fish, red slashes where eyes should have been.

She crouched on her heels, looking at the thing, wet and bloody on the carpet, gazing at the tail, the fins, anything so as not to look at the bloody eyeless face. She gazed while the horror built up in her, until she found the strength to pull open the window, tug up the thing. She tried to heave it out, but it fell back against her, bloody on her skirt. She screamed as it hit her feet.

Jamieson was beside her. 'It's a fish,' he said, holding the wrapping in his arms. 'Were you expecting a fish?' Blood dripped off the end and on to the Merlings' pale carpet.

She gazed at him. 'No,' she whispered. 'I wasn't expecting anything.'

'Well, I wonder if the kitchens might like it.' He held it up and more blood dropped on the carpet. 'It doesn't look very fresh to me, though.'

'There's blood on the carpet.' She felt sick, panicked.

He jumped back. 'There is! Oh, damn its eyes. Pass me the paper, miss, quickly.'

He seized the newspaper, bundled the thing up. 'Mrs Bills will kill me. Before Mrs Merling!'

She gazed at the spots on the carpet, blobs of the stuff. They wouldn't ever be able to get it out. No matter how much they cleaned, it would always be there. He was scrubbing at it with his handkerchief, awkwardly perched with the thing under his arm.

'Throw it away. Just throw it away.'

He held the bundle to him. 'I'll take it downstairs.'

She seized his arm. 'Throw it out of the window!'

He looked at her, dubiously. 'Now, miss, I can't do that. Someone might be walking past. I will take it downstairs. Mrs Bills' girls will dispose of it.'

She wanted to throw herself at him, clutch his hand, tell him how grateful she was.

'Thank you!' she said. 'I want it out of the house now! You'll take it away!'

He nodded, held up the parcel and walked out of the room. As he opened the door, Petra ran in. She mewed and headed straight for the spots of blood on the carpet. Louisa watched her, pawing at them, putting her nose close, licking at the blood. Then she began to cry and couldn't stop.

The tears squeezed from her eyes and she put her hands up to her face. As she did so, she retched – they smelt of rotting fish. She dashed to the toilet room and plunged them into the cold bowl of water. Then she started scrubbing, pulling at her skin and nails, seizing the nail brush and hacking at her fingers until her hands were pink and raw. Then, finally, she leant against the wall, letting the tears flow down her face. She ran to her room, threw herself on to her bed. She could smell the fish, around her, on her body, in her very skin. When the maids came back, she would beg them to wash her hair.

The next morning, Louisa woke, groggy and sick. Lucy Merling jumped up. 'She's awake, Mama.'

Louisa fell back on the pillows. Then Mrs Merling entered the room. 'How are you feeling, poor dear?' She put her hand on Louisa's forehead. 'Still hot.'

'I feel very sick.' Her voice came out weak and cracked.

'Do you remember what happened?'

She shook her head, hair brushing the hot pillow.

'You were terribly upset. We called in Dr Graham, who gave you something to help you sleep. Jamieson said you'd received something odd in the post.'

She nodded. She could feel the hotness behind her eyes that meant tears were coming. Jamieson hadn't told the whole truth, then, afraid of getting in trouble for giving it over in the first place, rather than waiting until Mrs Merling returned, as he should have done.

'Was it a note, dear, bad news?'

'No.' She breathed. 'It was some type of toy. I think it came to the wrong person. I was just feeling a little unhappy and it was a shock.' She put her hand out, towards Mrs Merling. 'Where is Petra?'

'We thought she might wake you up,' said Lucy.

'I'd like her back.'

Lucy nodded, padded off.

'Have you told Arthur?' she said to Mrs Merling.

The woman shook her head. 'We haven't seen Mr Witt. As soon as I see him, I will.'

'Oh no, I don't think so, Mrs Merling,' said Louisa. 'It would only make him worry. I don't want to think any more about it.'

The older woman nodded. 'Perhaps that would be best then.'

Louisa saw the glint of money in the woman's eyes. She wouldn't want her house to seem unsafe, wouldn't want Arthur taking Louisa away.

On the next evening, she dined with Arthur. 'What's been happening with you?' he said. She couldn't bear to say, 'Someone sent me a fish!' It sounded odd and ridiculous in her mouth, a joke, something from a funny play, not the horrible, cruel thing that it was. He might have laughed – and then she would have had to laugh too, not telling him how afraid she was. She'd have to say that ever since it happened she had been watching for someone coming to the door, how she had lain awake in bed listening to the banging of the windows, that when she had walked out with Arthur that evening, she had stared at the men on the street around them, muffled up in their coats, and felt sure that one of them was watching her. Frederick le Touche had said she'd made an enemy of Jennifer – but surely Jennifer wouldn't send her a *fish*. Just for dancing with Edward. She longed to ask Frederick, but whatever she said, she knew he might put in the newspapers.

She shook her head. 'Not much.' She smiled. He started talking – as he always did – about one of his ideas for a business. This one was importing something or other. She gazed past him at the other couples. Were they looking at her? The man at the table across from her was staring, she felt sure. If she told Arthur, he would say she was being ludicrous. But someone had sent her the fish because they hated her. She tried to direct her mind by thinking about Edward, how she would let him kiss her.

'You've been dancing a lot with Edward Munsden,' Arthur said, abruptly. She looked up from her plate. 'I wouldn't, you know. He's a bit of a cad.'

Arthur was always so protective. 'He seems respectable.'

'I don't know about respectable. He's a fortune hunter, through and through. And he's practically engaged to the honourable Miss Redesdale.'

'Who says?'

'Everybody knows. They have an understanding.'

She didn't believe it. He wouldn't kiss her hand, tell her how beautiful she was, dance with her if he had an agreement with Jennifer. Arthur was just trying to discourage her from thinking of him, of someone else.

She shook her head. 'It doesn't seem that way.'

'You should listen to me!' His face was suddenly serious. 'You're a young girl, your reputation untouched. You can't just talk to gentlemen. Especially not Munsden. You wouldn't believe what the other chaps say about him at the bar. Stick to talking to the ladies. Please?'

His face was so solemn that she nodded. 'Yes, Arthur.'

'Good,' he said. 'Chatter as much as you like with the girls. And Frederick le Touche and the rest of them. Just not Munsden. He's bad news.'

She nodded, trying to smile. Her eyes sparked with Edward, she thought of him gazing at her, touching her hand, everyone staring at him, seeing the love in his eyes.

'I'll come to collect you for the ball tomorrow,' Arthur said. 'Mrs Clarendon's, you remember.'

She'd wear her pink gown; it made her lips look rosier, plumper, ready to kiss.

On the following day, she dressed carefully for the ball, having the maids arrange and rearrange her hair, repin the gown, pull it in so tight that Millie said she wouldn't be able to breathe.

Arthur whistled when she walked down the stairs to him. 'Look at that!' he said. 'Don't you look fine.'

'Thank you, cousin. I'm glad you approve.'

She felt the skirt of her gown falling around her legs as she walked in on Arthur's arm. She smiled beatifically around the room. Arthur saw a friend – one of his gentlemen – and whipped across to the bar, promising he'd be back soon. She saw Edward – he'd been shielded by a group of women – smiled. Within minutes he was by her side, asking after her health, complimenting her gown. She let him take her arm in his soft grip and walk with her to the dance floor. Arthur's words drove through her head: *I wouldn't, you know. Fortune hunter. They have an understanding.* Perhaps her cousin was right, perhaps she shouldn't speak to him. But surely it wasn't true. Arthur must have misunderstood.

Edward held her in his arms and started to sway. She looked down at her pink, sequinned bodice, admiring it, imagining seeing herself through his eyes. She gazed up at him, blushing before she had to meet his gaze, dropping her eyes. People might be watching. She smelt his skin, the saltiness. They came away and he passed her a drink, she sipped quickly so they could be back dancing together, so she could be close to his heart.

Three dances together – and then Arthur was hurrying up to her side, seizing her arm. 'My cousin needs to come with me!'

'What are you doing?' Arthur hissed, pulling her away. 'I told you not to talk to him.'

She tried to pull back. 'Cousin, please, we're only dancing.'

Edward was coming towards her, smiling. 'Now what's this?' he said, coming closer. 'Some kind of scene?'

Arthur shook his head. 'I was just talking to my cousin,' he said sullenly.

'I must keep her for one more dance. Then I'll set her free.' The music began and Edward whirled her over the floor. 'What did Mr Witt say?' he breathed into her ear.

'He worries about me. He's protective.' *He says you're a cad and engaged to Jennifer Redesdale.*

He laughed. The noise made her uneasy.

They danced again, three more times. She knew other guests were staring, but she pretended she didn't care. She pressed closer to his arms. Arthur, she supposed, had stamped off to the bar, fuming. She'd deal with him later.

They were about to start another dance when Mrs Clarendon herself appeared at her side. 'Come, Miss Deerhurst. There is someone I desire you to meet.'

She smiled at Mrs Clarendon. 'There is another dance yet.'

Mrs Clarendon reached for her arm. 'Please, my dear. There is someone I would really like you to meet.'

Edward loosened her hands. She looked at him, and he shook his head, slightly. 'I will see you after your conversation, Miss Deerhurst.'

'Come now, dear,' said Mrs Clarendon. 'I do wish you to meet my friend.'

Louisa let herself be pulled away.

'Don't spend so long talking to men you don't know, dear. People see.'

'We're here to dance, surely. To meet.'

'Quite. Not to spend the night with one man.'

The person who Mrs Clarendon wanted her to meet was an old woman, Mrs Bell, who was escorting a daughter and could barely hear a word Louisa was saying. As soon as she could, she escaped, looked around, brushing off offers of drinks or olives. He wasn't there. She gazed around desperately, couldn't see him. She told herself to breathe, wait. He might simply have gone for air. She leant on a pillar, watching other people dance. She gazed at the dance floor, willing him to step across. He didn't.

'He's gone, you know.' Arthur was at her side. She ignored him, turning her face away. 'He had to go. You were making it so obvious.'

'Making what obvious?'

'You know. Never mind. Do you want to go? I'm tired.'

'I'd rather stay.'

'You know I can't go without you. Munsden's not coming back.'

'How do you know?'

'I saw him leave. It looked like he was going on somewhere else.'

'But—' She couldn't finish.

He seized her wrist. 'Come on, get your wrap. Time to go.'

He moved closer to her, so she could smell him, but it wasn't handsome, touching, encouraging like Edward. Arthur smelt hot and angry.

'Why?' She wanted to twist, struggle out of his grip.

'You're making a scene! People are looking.'

She gazed around quickly. Eyes darted away from her, she saw that they had been staring. She felt tears pricking her eyes.

'Can't you see? You need to come now!'

She was going to pull back. Then Mrs Clarendon was behind her, hands on her back. 'Go with him, dear,' she was saying. 'I think it is time to leave us.'

She bowed her head, followed, her heart on fire. He tugged her out of the door. She ignored the cab men and the footmen waiting in lines and flung herself away from him. 'How can you treat me like this?'

'You've had too much champagne.'

She seized her gown in her hand, ran a little way along the street. 'Why are you like this?' she cried. 'Why are you so cruel?'

'Oh, you're impossible.' He turned, called for his man, Carstairs – and then before she could speak out, he'd bundled her up into the waiting cab. 'Take us back!' Arthur commanded. The cab lurched and moved forwards. She shifted into the corner and let the tears flow.

'How could you?' she said, as Arthur pulled open the door at the Merlings'. 'How could you treat me so?'

'Cousin. You were making an exhibition of yourself.'

He held out his hand and she shook her head. 'Why do you hate Edward?'

'He's bad news, cousin. He's dangerous. Can you not see?'

She moved forwards, stepped down, shook off his hand, jumped on to the pavement. The street was quiet, a stray cat scratching at the corner of the road. 'You shouldn't have pulled me away. That was wrong.'

Arthur screwed up his mouth. 'Look, Louisa, I'm sorry. But he's a fortune hunter, like all soldiers are. He doesn't even care for you.'

'He does.'

'He pays attention to you to make Jennifer Redesdale jealous. You are nothing to him. What do you even know about him?'

'I shall find out.'

'And you propose to stay here while doing so?'

'I do! I shall.'

He laughed, hard in the empty night. 'So I pay for you to stay here and think of him?' Two cats looked up and skittered away in fear.

'What else did you bring me here for?' Something changed, clicked in her mind.

He opened the door.

'Let's go inside. Tonight has been too much already. It's not safe out here.'

'Tell me! Why did you bring me here?'

'Because you wanted to come. Because I like being with you, spending time with you. And honestly, I didn't want my family to grasp you in their clutches. I didn't expect you to go soft-eyed over a cad like Munsden. Now go inside, before you wake up the whole street.' She ran, hurried past the man, in through the Merlings' door. She slammed her own bedroom door when she got there, hoping that Arthur might hear.

TWENTY-ONE

London, May 1920

Louisa

'I think we should call the police.' Mrs Merling drew herself up to her full height.

Lucy, Mrs Merling and Louisa were in Mrs Merling's blue-papered parlour. Louisa had cried so much that there were no more tears. She slept and had woken to Mrs Merling shaking her and demanding to know who was sending her cruel things. That morning a letter had been delivered for Louisa and Mrs Merling had opened it. It was a drawing of a fish, spiky, jagged pen lines. She'd asked Jamieson who had delivered it – just a messenger boy – and then he had confessed the truth about the fish, the spots of blood on the carpet. 'I have no idea who sent it to me!' Louisa had tried to sit up. Petra, annoyed by the noise, jumped off the bed, complaining. 'Jamieson just brought it in.'

Mrs Merling had gazed at her. 'But who could have sent it? I shall write to Mr Merling immediately. And we must speak to Mr Witt. We will discuss this in the parlour.'

Louisa had crouched down, held Petra to her heart. She heard doors banging. Mary came in to dress her. She shuffled out to the parlour, holding Petra, her heart heavy.

Arthur was already there, his hair even more slicked-back than normal. Mrs Merling talked on about the police and how criminals were brazen these days. 'I cannot have this happening under my roof!'

Arthur sighed. 'It's little more than malicious prank-playing, I expect.'

'We should call the police!'

'I shouldn't think that necessary. One fish sent through the post and a single drawing on a letter? I doubt there is anything much they can do with that. I imagine they'll say it is a prank. Which I expect it is. Might have been sent to anyone in London.'

Mrs Merling turned to Louisa. 'Do you know who is doing this?'

She shook her head. 'Someone who hates me.' *What about Jennifer Redesdale?* she wanted to say. Frederick would know.

'Oh, come now,' said Arthur. 'Just pranks. I imagine it will fade away. Now, Mrs Merling, we are very grateful for your concern. But my cousin's welfare is my responsibility and she is quite safe here. If you feel she is not, then perhaps I should reconsider her position.'

Mrs Merling swallowed, shook her head. 'I see, Mr Witt. Of course, Miss Deerhurst is quite safe here. I agree, there is nothing to worry about.'

Arthur rose. 'Quite so. Now, I would like to converse with my cousin alone. I can see she's been shaken by this.'

'Oh, of course.' Mrs Merling bustled out of the room, Lucy behind her. Louisa gazed at the door. She turned, looked at Arthur as he stood and walked to the window.

'I don't understand this,' he said. 'I really don't.' He swung around. 'Do you know? Do you know, Louisa, what has been happening here?' Petra jumped off her lap, alarmed by the noise.

She shook her head. 'No. I have no idea.' She held out her hands to the cat. 'Come back,' she said.

'Really, Louisa?' In a moment, he was sitting opposite her by Mrs Merling's low table, clasping her hands. 'You must tell me. Who is doing this? Has there been anything unusual apart from the fish?'

She wanted to cry. 'I don't know who did it. There was the fish and the note. That was all. Mrs Merling thought the note was from a friend at first, she said it looked like a proper letter. Nice paper, properly addressed, that kind of thing.' Petra was still padding about at the side of the room. Louisa held out her hand to her. She didn't come.

'Louisa! Look at me, not the cat. Why didn't you tell me about these things? I think you're not safe. I think someone wants to hurt you.'

She dropped her hand. 'But – you said to Mrs Merling it was just pranks.'

'That's because the police won't help. This sort of person is dangerous. They'd be even angrier if they thought we'd contacted the police.'

'You said I was safe.'

'Well, you're not.'

She stood up, her heart on fire, blood racing, flying, scrabbling through her hands and face. 'What shall we do? What can we do?'

He shook his head. 'I don't know. Go away. Go far away.'

She grasped his hands. 'We can't leave!'

Arthur shrugged. 'We shall have to see what they'll do, then. Hope that they leave you alive.'

'Alive? What are you talking about?'

'My dear, they send a dead fish, a strange note. This isn't children playing. You're in danger.'

She couldn't speak. The words fell back into her throat. She tried again. 'But why?'

'Who knows? You're the sort of girl who inspires jealousy: beautiful, rich.'

Petra was cowering at the side of the room. Louisa couldn't reach her. 'I'm not rich!'

'Well, you will be one day. But this is a close society. Then you burst in – and, well, people get envious.'

She fell back in the chair. 'So you're saying that they want to harm me because they're jealous of me? That's impossible.'

'They want you out of the way, let's put it like that. You're taking what's theirs.'

'Frederick said I'd made an enemy of Jennifer Redesdale. Do you think it might be her?'

Arthur shook his head. 'Not her style. No, this is someone who is really serious. Someone dangerous. I think there are more people jealous of you than just her. Think of that exhibition you made of yourself at the sea party.'

She shook her head at him. 'I can't believe this.'

He leant against the back of the chair. 'Why couldn't you just stay away from him? I don't know how to protect you.'

That night, in bed with Petra, she made promises, vows. She'd forget Edward. She'd not go to parties at all, she'd get a job, be independent. She could find a way of getting at her money, even though she wasn't twenty-one, then she could live alone in Mayfair, find a kind man who would look after her, be free of all this.

'But what can I do, Petra?' she said, weeping into the sleeping cat's fur. She couldn't have her money, not really, not yet. 'You're my only friend. Tell me what to do.' The cat slept on.

TWENTY-TWO

London, May 1920

Louisa

Louisa woke to sun streaming through her windows. She sat up. They must have let her sleep; it was surely later than eight. She swung out her legs. 'Petra?' The cat must have hidden under the bed. Louisa crouched down, saw nothing. 'Petra? Where are you?'

She didn't hear anything, not even a purr. It was strange. Normally, Petra was awake before Louisa, licking her face.

She must be hungry, Louisa thought. Petra must have gone down to the kitchens to try and beg some food. She pulled on her wrapper and slippers and padded out. No one else seemed to be up, only the maids.

'Petra?' she called. 'Are you downstairs?'

She wandered into the corridor. All the doors around her were closed, it must have been earlier than she had thought. She couldn't see how Petra could have crept into one of the other bedrooms. Why would she, anyway? She loved Louisa, not Mrs Merling or Lucy. She peered into the bathroom, no sign. The poor thing must have gone downstairs, she thought, looking for scraps. She could hear the sound of the maids flurrying around in the parlour.

'Have you seen Petra?' she said, poking her head around the door of the parlour. The two girls, Mary and Millie turned round from dusting.

'The cat?'

'She's wandered somewhere and I can't find her.'

They shook their heads, promised to look out for her. Louisa closed the door and opened the dining room. No sign there, either. She tried the study (where no one ever went) and then the other bathroom. Slow tendrils of fear were gripping her heart. Had she got outside somehow? Had the maids let her out by mistake? They knew not to open the door to her. But perhaps, this morning, when they'd arrived, they hadn't been thinking, had let her run. Louisa shook the thought away and headed for the kitchens, down another flight of stairs. She could smell frying food, bacon she supposed. She stopped at the door. She hadn't been into a working kitchen since she was a little girl, a small child trying to cadge bits of biscuit or icing for the cake. Mama had told her off for trying to creep in, once dragging her out by the arm, telling her no young lady belonged in the kitchen!

She leant up close to the door, heard voices, the clank of pots. She knocked, twice. There was no answer. She tried again. Then she pushed open the door.

The cook, Mrs Taylor, turned from the stove, two kitchen maids looked up from kneading dough on the wooden table. 'What are you doing here, miss?'

It was a shabby sort of kitchen, now she saw it, the cupboards worn and the saucepans dirty. The dark-haired maid picked up her dough, threw it in between her hands as she stood, staring.

'I have lost my cat. I wondered if you'd seen her.'

'The little tortoiseshell one? No, miss.' The cook looked at the maids, who shook their heads.

'She's not here? I thought she might be here, looking for food.'

The cook shook her head. 'Haven't seen her, miss. Sorry, miss.'

'You're sure she's not here?'

The cook turned to shake the pan. 'I think we would have noticed, miss.'

'I could look? Please.'

The cook turned back to the pan. The dark-haired maid tossed her dough from hand to hand. 'I'll look for you, miss. If you tell me where.'

'See,' said the cook. 'Amy will look. But I can't see what she'd find.'

Louisa stepped forward. 'Thank you, Amy. You'd have to look really hard, because she might be far back. She can hide in the dark.'

'I'll look. Where shall I start?' The girl bent down as the other two returned to their work.

'Over there.' Louisa gestured to the farthest cupboard. 'Can you look under it?' The gap was very small, she had to admit. She couldn't imagine that Petra could crawl into it. But still, she asked the girl to look under the cupboard, across, behind, under the next one, then the next. Still nothing. The cook tutted as she fried, the other girl took over pounding the dough.

The maid fumbled in a cupboard, then underneath four more.

'I don't think the cat's here,' said the cook, shaking the pan.

The smoke was getting into Louisa's eyes, scratching at the back of them. 'She has to be! There's nowhere else she *could* be.'

'Why don't you go upstairs and try again there?' said Mrs Taylor. 'There's nowhere she could be here. Unless she slipped out of the front door. Perhaps when Mr Morris arrives he can take you out to look.'

Louisa rushed upstairs, tried all the doors, looked again. Then she scanned her own room once more. This time, she knocked on Lucy's door, hurried inside. 'I'm hunting for Petra,' she said, as Lucy struggled to sit up. 'Have you seen her?' She tried under Lucy's bed, opened the wardrobes, pulled open the drawers, tugged out the clothes, threw them on to the floor. Lucy was trying to get out of the bed. 'Stop! She's not here! I haven't seen her since you took her into your room last night.'

Louisa stood there, clothes at her feet. 'She has to be somewhere.'

'Have you tried the kitchen?'

'She wasn't there. I've been everywhere except your mother's room.'

'Well, she won't be there. Mama always locks the door and she went to bed before you last night.'

Louisa leant against the wall. 'She must have gone out. Do you think she went out? That's what Mrs Taylor in the kitchens said.

She said she must have slipped out. That I should wait for Mr Morris to take me to look for her.'

Lucy was picking up the shawls from the floor, gathering up dresses and stockings. 'He should be here soon. He's always here for breakfast.'

'That's what they said. But I don't want to wait! She might be out there, afraid.'

Lucy pushed a pile of clothes into a drawer. 'I'll come with you and Mr Morris, if you like.'

'Thank you. But I can't wait! I'm going to go now.'

'Miss Deerhurst, you can't! You're not dressed properly.'

Louisa ignored her, hurried out into the corridor. She seized some shoes – the quickest to put on – from her room and ran down towards the door. The maids had barred it after themselves. She tugged the bolts, hauled off the chain and pulled at the door. It wouldn't come. She tugged again, hard. She could hear Lucy knocking on Mrs Merling's door, telling her mother to come out. Finally the front door wrenched open and Louisa jumped out on to the top step. People were hurrying past, smartly dressed, on their way to work, she supposed. She ignored them, ran down the steps, her feet sliding in the damp. She ran around the edge of the houses to the black iron railings of the garden. Two nurses with perambulators were unlocking the gate, so she cut in behind them, hurried on into the garden.

The square gardens were smaller than they looked from her window, but the flowers were brighter, vivid against the dewy grass. She peered under a thin-looking rose bush.

'Here, Petra!' she cooed. 'Here, girl!'

She searched under more plants, a heavy purple shrub, a red flowering one that looked a bit like a tree. No sign of Petra. The nurses were walking up together along the opposite side of the garden. 'Petra!' she shouted. 'I'm here.'

She turned around, dizzily. If Petra wasn't here, where was she? She could be anywhere! She walked over to the same side as the nurses, peered under the bushes. Nothing. 'I'm looking for my cat,' she said to the nurses, trying to smile.

'Oh dear,' said one. 'What type of cat?'

'A tortoiseshell.' Louisa felt even more hopeless saying the words. 'Black paws.'

'I haven't seen it.' *Well, of course!* Louisa wanted to cry. *No one has.* She crushed her words. The woman was only trying to be helpful. She sighed, turned around. She'd go back to the house and find Mr Morris, ask him to help her. Perhaps Arthur might even be up. She began to walk back to the gate. Then she realised. Something was there. There was something on the railings, stuck on them, like she'd read heads once were, on the outskirts of London, back when people were so barbaric. It was small and dark, a strange mass of something. She drew closer, her heart hard in her chest, sickness rising. She walked forward and the garden was spinning, circling around her head, the red and purple of the petals cutting each other, exploding into fire and a thousand colours, burning through her eyes. She walked again, one foot in front of the other, forwards. The thing grew bigger as she walked towards it. *Don't!* she wanted to say. *Don't be true. Stop.*

She could hear one of the babies crying behind her. The nurse was lifting it from the perambulator, shushing it.

Don't be happening! Please! She wanted to cry out, but the words wouldn't come. *Stop!*

She was almost there. She could see it in front of her, the dark, wet fur, legs splayed. She moved forward again, reached out her hand. There was blood on the railing, dripping down into the grass.

There was a scream. It was so loud, ringing through her ears, filling the air. She dropped to the ground, clutching the railing, hearing the scream again and again.

'Miss! Stop it! Calm down.' She looked up and there was Mr Jamieson.

'Louisa!' Arthur was standing above her. 'Louisa, stop this now!' He reached down, held her shoulders. 'What are you doing?'

'It's Petra!' she gasped. 'Help her.' Mr Jamieson was looking at the black thing, holding out his hands.

'Look away, cousin,' said Arthur. 'Look at me. You need to stop crying. Stop. Tell me what happened.'

She knew, behind her, that Mr Jamieson was taking Petra down from the railings. She could hear him sighing, swearing as, she supposed, blood dripped on to his hand.

She couldn't speak, tears juddering her body, her face flooded with them, eyes so painful with salt she couldn't see. 'Help me!'

'But what happened, cousin?' Arthur had his arms around her. 'Try to breathe. Tell me.' He looked up. 'No, no, ladies, quite alright. A tragic accident.' She supposed he was talking to the nursemaids. She heard them move forwards, the gate clank as they closed it.

'Someone's killed Petra!' she said. 'They've killed her.'

'We don't know that,' he said. 'She might have fallen.'

She shook her head. 'No! She's dead! Someone did it to her.'

She buried her face in Arthur's coat, wool scratching at her skin. She was hiccuping, weeping. 'Breathe,' Arthur was saying. 'Try and breathe.'

'I can't bear it,' she said. 'I can't bear it.'

Arthur stroked her hair. 'Poor cousin. Poor Louisa. I'm so sorry.'

'I looked everywhere for her! I knew she was gone. I told them. I searched!'

He was holding her close, crouching on the ground next to her. 'Don't cry,' he said. 'Please don't cry.'

'I thought she was with me! She never leaves my room! How did she get away? I don't understand it. How could someone do this to Petra? She never hurt anyone!' She couldn't stop the words – scattering, falling, useless, hopeless words, but she said them again and again. 'Please, Arthur,' she cried. 'Please.' The tears were gluey in her eyes. She pressed her face harder into his coat. 'Petra!' Arthur stroked her hair, rocked her on the damp earth as if she were a child.

'We should move.'

She leapt up, clung to him. 'Don't! I can't go back there!'

He stood against the railing. Behind him, people were walking past, black coats, grey hats, turning to stare at them; her weeping, Arthur in his suit. 'What do you mean, you can't go back there?'

She flung herself against his chest. 'I can't! Don't you see? Someone came here after me and killed her!' She put her hand to the railing and then drew back. *Petra's blood might still be there.*

'You need to take me away. I can't stay here.' She dropped her head on his chest. 'I don't want to go to another party. Not yet. Not for ages. We need to go somewhere, far away from here.' The answer danced up in her head. 'Take me to Paris!'

He stroked her hair. 'Paris?'

'They won't find us there.'

'We could. Yes. Let me think.' He stroked her hair again. 'Let's lie low for a while, you and I. Then maybe we could set off for the coast, and then to Paris.'

'We'll be safe there.' In cafes under the Eiffel Tower, walking beside the Seine.

'I suppose we'll have to ask Mrs Merling to come with us.'

'Mrs Merling?'

'Well, of course. We can't go alone.'

Louisa stood away from him, the tears stinging her cheeks. 'I don't trust her any more. Someone let him in, the man who did this, or they let Petra out.'

'Not Mrs Merling, of course!' Arthur rubbed his head. 'Well, if she did let Petra out, I am sure it was an accident.'

'But you never know! The people who are doing this had to have help. I don't trust her.'

'So we'll have to find another companion.'

'I don't want one! How do we know we can trust whoever we find?'

Arthur shrugged. 'I suppose we don't know. We can't trust anyone, it's true. One never knows.' He ran his hand over her hair, combing a few strands with his fingers. 'At least we have each other.'

'We do.' They'd eat together in Paris, walk through cobbled streets, go to the art museums. She didn't want to think of anything else: not Petra, not the party at the Savoy when she walked through to Edward, plain as a worm, not her mermaid dress at the sea party, not dancing while others watched. *You'll put yourself in danger*, Arthur had said. If only she had listened! She would now. She'd hear what he said, understand how he had only meant to be kind.

'I don't know what to do about this, though,' he said. 'It doesn't seem fit to go alone. We need a solution.'

She leant against him, willed it. The damp grass was chill on her legs. *Paris. Take me to Paris.*

'I know!' he said. 'I have the answer! That's it.'

'What?' she said, smiling at the great grin on his face.

And then he dropped to his knees. 'Marry me!' he said. 'Then you'll be safe. Marry me!'

She gazed at him, heart racing. Her head flamed. The flowers around her burnt, the gerberas flashing into colour, shrubs turning purple, orange, yellow. Petra ran through her head, mewing, coiling her tail, chasing after the stranger, eager to please.

He was kneeling, holding out his hand. 'It's the only way to be safe! And then we can travel together, just the two of us, no one else.'

She shook her head.

'I'll look after you. Haven't I always? Don't you see?'

And then, in a moment, she did see it. Arthur was brave, kind. He'd look after her. Edward had tried to escape her, danced with someone else. Arthur would protect her. With him, no one would creep into her room late at night, *put their hand on the bed*, take Petra from her. She would be safe with him, just as he had protected her at Stoneythorpe.

'Yes,' she said, holding out her hand, letting him pull her down next to him. 'Yes, Arthur. Yes.'

PART THREE

TWENTY-THREE

London, November 1921

Celia

'Imagine if Arthur was here somewhere,' Emmeline was saying. Albert was hanging on to her dress, experimenting with his grip, even though he was too big for that now, at two and a quarter. Lily was gazing out at the ground, sucking her thumb.

Celia picked up Lily, tried not to step on the foot of the woman in front of her. 'Mama said he was in Paris. Anyway, we'd never find him in a crowd like this.' It was November 13, Third Memorial Day. They were waiting in the crowds near Trafalgar Square for the parades of men. Thousands of people were crammed into the square. Along the front, given the best places for a view, were the wounded soldiers, those who were missing legs, arms, some of them with their heads still covered with a porcelain mask. Celia was embarrassed that she had grown so used to them, their scarred faces, burnt eyes.

Emmeline clutched Albert, held him tight. 'No trying to escape, yes, little man? Arthur's going to come back, eventually.'

Arthur had hardly written, only once or twice, never giving an address. He said he was sad, missed Louisa, was waiting until things calmed down. 'I don't know what things,' Emmeline said crossly. 'Everyone knows it was just an accident. He just likes playing up the drama, as he always did.' Arthur gave an address to send to in London, an office, said that there was no point trying to find him through it. Rudolf sent him money, Emmeline sent pictures of the twins. 'I wish he'd come now.'

'You know, Celia, he was never that fond of family things, even before. I don't know why you think he should be now. He'll stay as he is, wandering somewhere. Probably even has a new girl.'

'Don't say that.' Albert sneezed, then started waving at a man walking past. Lily was still silent – as she always was. *She can talk*, Emmeline said. *She just doesn't want to.*

Things were easy for Emmeline, Celia thought. She didn't feel guilt over Louisa like Celia did. Emmeline had been busy at the time, pregnant, absorbed, then in London with the twins. If Celia had tried harder, then Louisa wouldn't have become so dependent on Arthur, thought he was her only friend, run away.

'I wish we'd paid Louisa more attention,' said Celia, looking out over the soldiers. 'I should have made more effort.'

The police had stopped paying calls. They'd said they had all the details on file, they wouldn't forget, but there was nothing more to add. Mr Pemberton had been trying to sort out Louisa's accounts – but he said that they were too complex for him to grasp, he had his best men on it. The newspapers left them alone now. They'd moved on to new stories – murders, politicians arguing, robberies. Celia turned her face away from the papers when she passed a shop. She'd believed the news in them once – now she knew it was lies.

They'd said Arthur was a murderer, made him flee. Verena still refused to leave the house, saying that Arthur might come back – and she'd hate to be out. Really she was afraid of what people would say. 'He's innocent!' Celia said to her, over and over.

But the other ladies in the area didn't like the taint of death. Verena couldn't bear their gossip. And Rudolf was struggling to balance the business without Arthur.

Please come back! Celia thought. There was no reason for him to stay away.

'I wish Arthur would come home,' Verena kept on saying. Celia knew she should stay at Stoneythorpe to help them, but she couldn't bear it. Instead, she'd gone to visit Emmeline.

'You mustn't blame yourself for Louisa, sister. I've said this so many times. She fell. It was awful, but it could happen to anyone.'

'It happened to her,' said Celia.

Emmeline pulled Albert from the railings. 'Stop that!' She put his plump hand in his pocket. 'Is that why you're eating so much? Because you miss her and feel guilty? It won't stop it hurting, you know.'

'It's just this dress.' Celia blushed. It wasn't. She was getting plumper, no two ways about it. She couldn't stop eating. Bread, especially, potatoes, meat, any fruit she could find. She'd read an article in *The Times* saying that it was a common feature, ever since the 1920s had begun, everyone ate now it was a new decade and there was finally food. Lily was wriggling. Celia put her down, held her hand.

'You ate too much cake in Germany. Now you can't stop.'

Emmeline had, rather annoyingly, returned to her old slim figure after the birth; three months of exercising and eating cabbage had done the trick. She prided herself on it rather too much, Celia thought.

'More to life than being thin,' she said.

Emmeline scooped up Albert who was trying to slide down to the floor. 'Poor Louisa. Perhaps you're right, we didn't take enough notice of her. Still, I think she didn't *want* it. She wanted to be with Arthur. And she had that, didn't she?'

Lily was whimpering and Celia patted her, gathering her close to her woolly coat.

Tom's face, his scarred face, came into her mind. He'd written to her three times since Baden. She'd thrown his letters away, torn them up before her mother might see them. Hilde had written to her, stiff words about Baden and how they had been pleased to see her. Nothing from Heinrich, Lotte or Johann. She'd meant to write to Johann, trying to tell him not to care what others thought, that he'd served his country and that was a great thing. But then she thought of him, creating his matchstick houses over and over – and she couldn't send it. At Stoneythorpe, there had been such a flurry over Louisa that Rudolf had barely asked her about her visit. She told him they had all been well and he made vague suggestions about visiting himself one day, when everything was calmer.

Celia tried, over and over, to stop herself from thinking about that night with Tom. But it rose in her mind, unannounced, like a guest you didn't want. She found herself weeping dry tears, crying out so loudly that on occasion she'd woken Lily. Once, in a moment of weakness, she'd written to him. It was late at night and Louisa had filled her mind. *I left her*, she wrote to Tom. *We should have gone back to London to find her.* She threw it away. He wrote again but she tore it up without reading, hating herself for considering writing to the man who had killed her brother.

She wanted to talk about Louisa and her parents, but Emmeline didn't want to. *You're upsetting Mama*, Emmeline said. Celia still couldn't quite believe it. She would see something, think, *I should tell Louisa about that*, then remember Louisa was dead.

'Look, Lily,' Emmeline said. 'We might see the Queen.'

'Or Daddy,' said Celia. Emmeline gave her a cross look.

'He will be off gaining equality for all somewhere,' said Celia. She barely saw Mr Janus, who was in London again, and she saw even less of his friends Mr Sparks and Jemima, who had returned to London and Mr Janus's causes. 'Before we were talking,' he said. 'Now we are doing!' They met secretly in places Celia and Emmeline weren't allowed to know about, planned meetings, demonstrations.

'Don't you care that he's never here?' Celia had said to Emmeline.

'He says he is changing the country,' Emmeline shrugged. 'I can't make him stop.'

'But changing the country would take for ever.'

'He says he's got a lifetime.'

How can you love him so much? Celia wanted to say. *Don't you ever think – I want something else?* Her sister who had once cared so much about money. Now, they all survived on the two days of teaching Mr Janus gave to private students.

She looked down at the men. Mr Janus said that the people of Britain had been conned. They had been told they were fighting for their country and the freedom of the world. And what had they actually been fighting for? Only big business, nothing more.

The freedom to sell British goods to the rest of the Empire, without the German ones or the Austrian ones coming in between. The freedom to buy big heavy arms and make money out of the misery of men. *The only winner was big business*, Mr Janus had painted on a banner.

'But the Belgians were being killed,' Celia said. 'That's nothing to do with business.'

'Yes, it is,' Mr Janus said. 'You just need to think deeper than the newspaper stories.'

'Were we supposed to leave them to die?'

Mr Janus looked up from painting the next banner. 'No, Celia. We should have an entirely different government. One for the people, not for business. If you doubt me, look at things now. Have any of the soldiers who fought been rewarded? No. Instead, they have less than they had before, they are told times are hard so they should expect no job, or less of a job, not even getting the same wage that women did in the war.'

'Can't you say that women have been rewarded? With the vote.'

'Well, not that you or your sister could vote, could you? They're afraid of young women. You understand more about the evils of this march for money.'

Celia gazed at the banner, the red paint. 'Don't you think that you want so much change that it might never happen?'

Mr Janus returned to colouring in the 'b' of business. 'It will happen. I guarantee. We just need to be ready.'

'Celia!' said Emmeline. 'Stop daydreaming. It's about to begin.'

The first soldiers came marching out, smart, buttons shiny. Even their faces looked polished. Ranks and ranks of them holding up trumpets, waving flags. They were cheering. 'Excuse me?' A man's voice came from behind her. Celia turned – and felt herself gasp. It was a soldier with a porcelain mask covering a face underneath too scarred to be shown in public. She rearranged her own face into a smile. 'Please, do go past.'

'Here they go,' Emmeline whispered. A stream of men cut across the soldiers, bearing right. They were marching slowly, holding up banners. *Soldiers need you! Look after the veterans!* 'Hypocrisy!' they were shouting. 'Unfair!'

The women behind them were shuffling and talking. 'Disgraceful. Spoiling it for everyone,' one said loudly.

'Well, I suppose they think soldiers deserve more than just a few shillings for all that bravery,' said Emmeline.

The woman gave her a furious stare. 'They should arrest them, if you ask me.'

'They deserve more than just to be wheeled out and shown off,' said Celia, to no one in particular, looking forward. The protestors were still marching towards the bands of soldiers. She thought she could just see Mr Janus at the front.

'No!' Emmeline said. Policemen were dashing towards Mr Janus and the men, holding up sticks, blowing horns. She started, but Celia held her back. She gathered Lily to her chest. 'Look at my pretty buttons,' she said. She buried her head in Lily's soft hair, heard the shouts of the men as the police pulled them away. The crowd were cheering the police on. Lily struggled against her, wanting her mother. Celia heard shouts that she thought were Mr Janus. She looked up and saw they were being dragged off, shouting and protesting.

'You need to stay still. Don't move,' she said to Emmeline, who was holding Albert and covering her face. She lowered her voice. 'Proves they were right to come here. It gets attention.' The discussions about whether to hold the demonstration in London at the Remembrance Parade had been going on for weeks, Emmeline said. Mr Sparks, the only one Celia thought talked sense, had said it would undermine their cause, lose sympathy. The others had said that if they were campaigning to improve the lives of veterans, then this was the only time to do it. 'Don't move,' she said, again, clutching Emmeline. 'We'll find them later.' If they left now, the crowd would fall on them. Emmeline grasped her hand, face still covered.

'You can look now,' Celia said. In front of them were lines of men, marching in file, proud soldiers.

They watched together, holding hands. Lily began to whimper

again and Emmeline pulled a bottle from her bag. Albert was quiet, big eyes staring. Celia looked down at the veterans below them. She thought of Michael and a tear rolled down her cheek.

She held the bottle in Lily's mouth until the child fell asleep. Her mind wandered as the regiments marched past, her thoughts drifting to her body, as they so often did these days. Ever since she'd come back from Germany, it was as if she'd lost all her strength. She was constantly weary, always hungry, and all aches and pains. She'd read how a terrible shock could do that to you, change your body. But still. She thought back to the girl she'd been, careening the ambulance over potholes, reciting Shakespeare as she went. Now she was exhausted even standing up. Emmeline had said, *yes, well, that's how it feels looking after children!* But it was surely more than that. She had been living with Emmeline, helping her with the twins, but even during her week back at Stoneythorpe, before she came to London, she'd been so tired she could hardly get out of bed. *War fatigue*, she'd read it was called. She shifted Lily on to her other hip.

'They're about to do the silence now,' said Emmeline.

'Do you think the whole place will go quiet? Really?' It seemed impossible to Celia that it would.

'It did when they bombed, didn't it?'

So it did. Ten minutes later and the whole of London was silent. There were no cars, no voices. A leaf might drop and echo. She stood there, engulfed in the silence, looking up to the sky. Then, in the quiet, she heard something from inside herself. A movement, as if something in her was shifting. She gazed up at the sky and felt it again: an almost imperceptible, unmistakable kick.

TWENTY-FOUR

London, November 1921

Celia

How could it have happened? Celia asked herself, over the weeks after the Remembrance Parade. *How, from only once?* All those girls who took men back after Peace Day! It didn't happen to them.

But now look! She'd read about the surge in babies after the war, discussed it with Mr Janus and his friends. They talked about it in the flats in the evening. Emmeline served them tea, rushed off when Lily started to fuss as she usually did at night.

Celia was grateful that Emmeline said she needed her to stay. She couldn't bear to go back to Stoneythorpe. She wanted to stay and think about her secret. Emmeline had agreed. 'I could do with the help now they're so big,' she said. 'Mind you keep out of Samuel's way, though. And don't listen to any of his conversations.'

'Of course not,' Celia said. 'I don't care about his stupid conversations.'

'Don't let him hear you saying that.'

As it happened, Celia heard a lot of Mr Janus's conversations.

'We're nearly at the stage when it will be more acceptable to have a baby outside wedlock than in,' Mr Janus was saying. 'Soon marriage won't even matter.'

'It only ever mattered for women, remember, Samuel,' said Jemima. 'No one punished an unmarried man who had a child.' Jemima and a group of ladies were pushing for a new law to make it easier to put babies up for adoption. One of her lady representatives had been to Parliament twice with it.

They had talked of abused servant girls, working-class women who didn't know, middle-class girls tricked by men who promised to marry them on the next day. All the time, they talked of girls who didn't understand, women who were baffled and tricked by wily men. Not people like Celia, who had done it with someone not really thinking that there might be a consequence. For she hadn't, she thought, she hadn't once considered that, she hadn't said, 'Stop! I might have a baby!' The idea hadn't even crossed her mind. She'd lain back with Tom on the lake bank. All she'd wanted to do was stop thinking, stop everything hurting her heart. She blushed, painfully, to think of it.

It was hard to remember how she had thought about anything before Tom had told her he'd shot Michael, but she knew she had supposed that their night was the beginning of a love affair. Marriage. And now, here she was, going to have a baby by Tom, the man who had killed Michael, killed her brother, the baby's uncle. He'd held up a gun and shot his friend, standing there, desperate, in front of him. He hadn't tried to stop it. He'd let it happen.

One evening, not long after discovering what was happening to her, she took up a pen to write to Tom. *I need to see you*, she began. She ripped the paper into pieces, threw it to the floor. He was Michael's killer.

She ignored the other voices – the ones saying that Tom had no choice, he had been forced to do it, and he wouldn't have hit Michael anyway, it was someone else's bullet. They crept up and whispered in her ear. She shook them away. But, still, surely, she knew, if she wrote to him, it would be easy: he'd marry her, the baby would be theirs. But then there were all the other times when he'd told her he didn't want to see her, that she treated him like a servant. Perhaps she was better without him.

She was growing bigger every day, grateful for winter gowns and shawls, hiding her corsets under the bed. She lay in bed at night, feeling the baby grow. 'Who are you?' she said to it. 'Who?'

She supposed, now, it must be about the size of a little doll. It might look like a little doll. 'Are you a boy or a girl?' she said to it.

'Do you know?' In her heart, she thought it was a boy. It had to be. Something so strange, so alien, making even her face grow wider, it could not be a girl. A girl would still be like her, in some way, but a boy was different, a strange body, unfurling and changing within her. 'What are you doing in there?' she whispered, late at night, once all the visitors had gone and Emmeline and Mr Janus were asleep. 'What are you thinking about?'

'What on earth is *wrong* with you?' Emmeline snapped. It was a chilly day in early December and Celia had just dropped a third flannel on the floor, meant for Lily. 'You're even clumsier than usual.'

'Sorry, Emmeline.' She was clumsy, it was true, but she felt much less ill than she had been. She wasn't sick any more, or even tired. In fact, she thought, she felt rather better than she had done before Germany. If it wasn't for the little shape growing inside her, she might think she wasn't bearing a baby at all. 'I suppose I am a bit worried about the meeting tomorrow.'

They'd kept Mr Janus in the cells for a week after that day in Trafalgar Square, then let him off with a caution – afraid of bad publicity, he'd said. But his arrest had only emboldened him. He was travelling every day now, meeting other people, talking about action. He didn't tell Celia or Emmeline much, said it was best for them not to know. He was out for long hours, leaving the children and the flat to Emmeline and Celia. Tomorrow, Mr Janus and his friends were due to have a long meeting about the next demonstration.

'Oh, that's all just talk.'

Celia gazed at Lily, who was mesmerised by the blocks on the sitting room floor. Every minute, she wanted one of them to touch her, hold her, feed her – but still she didn't want to talk. Albert only wanted his mother. He shied away from Celia, refused to let her pick him up, didn't even let Mr Janus do it much. Celia had spent hours looking at him, but she didn't see any Witt in him at all. He was almost a copy of Mr Janus, as if someone had traced around her old tutor and made him into a child, square-faced, sure of his place in the world. Lily looked to Celia like Verena, the same thin face, the same constantly nervous manner, her brow furrowed with worry. She hung back from games, shy, her tiny eyes fearful. 'Don't be afraid,' Celia whispered. 'Don't let the world know.'

'I'll have to boil that flannel again,' Emmeline was saying. 'You're hopeless today, Celia. We'll just have to hope she doesn't want to pass anything while we're waiting.'

Lily suddenly burst into tears. 'There you go. Now you've upset her!'

Celia picked Lily up, held her close, tried to jog her up and down. Still she cried. Albert was more easily pleased; Emmeline could tie him to the chair and get on with housework for an hour or so as he played with a train or even looked at a picture book. Lily cried, sometimes threw tantrums in which her whole body seemed to flame red over nothing, a cup given to her with the handle facing the wrong way, a toy bear that was too soft to be propped up. She shook and wailed, cried even harder when she was picked up.

'Do you ever wish you could escape?' Celia said, holding Lily to her as she screamed. Emmeline had worn the same gown for the last four days. She was tired, careworn, her beautiful hair tied up in a scarf. Her eyes looked smaller, Celia thought – and that meant she was getting old. No old person had large eyes.

Emmeline stared at her. 'What do you mean, escape?'

'From this.'

'From the children? Celia, what are you talking about?'

'But you're so tired all the time. You don't sleep.' Sometimes Celia wondered if Mr Janus's great surge of work wasn't rather convenient. The flat was never tidy, piles of flannels on every surface, the children's cups and plates stacked up in the sink, dirty clothes everywhere in the bedrooms, both in Emmeline's and the second box room that was now the twins'. The dirty flannels soaked in big buckets that Emmeline left by the window, but they were still horrible, so the whole place smelt nasty. Mrs Breaks came in every morning to clean, but after about an hour or so, the place was in disorder again. One twin was nearly always wanting something, and Emmeline was exhausted. Last week she had fainted and woken up with no idea where she was.

'Like everyone else with a child. Anyway, it's better than last year. Mama said Arthur only ever slept for an hour at a time until he was two. I was much better, you know. I think you were a naughty baby.'

'Probably. But do you think it's always like this?' Lily was quieter now, leant against her. Celia stroked her hair.

'What?' Emmeline bent to pet Albert, who was hitting a spoon on the floor. Celia held Lily closer as she picked up the spoon.

'Babies.'

'Yes, I should think so. Exactly the same. Worse if you have four. Easier if you have only one, maybe.'

'How does everyone stand it?'

'Could you go and get a towel to wrap her in? She'll catch cold.'

Celia carried Lily over to the sofa, wrapped her legs in a towel draped over the cushions.

'Is that clean?' asked Emmeline.

'I think so.'

'It will do. I'll boil another one, then we'll take them out for a walk.'

Celia sat back on the sofa, held Lily close to her, feeling her body soften as she began to doze. 'But how does everyone stand it?' she asked again. She pushed aside a pile of papers with her feet. Mr Janus's papers, reams and reams of reports about money and the state and the workers, scrawled handwriting covering page after page.

'Honestly, Celia. Because they love them, of course. Look, some people in life are meant to have babies and some aren't. You're not.'

'I'm not?'

Emmeline was carrying Albert to the kitchen, shouted over her shoulder. 'You've never been the motherly type, have you? Look, you always said you never wanted to get married. So you don't need to have babies.'

Celia picked up the sleeping Lily and followed her. 'But what if I had one anyway?'

'You can't just *have* one, Celia. You have to want it to happen. They don't fall from the sky.' Emmeline pulled out the ever-ready saucepan, filled it with water, turned on the gas. Celia watched the water, rising up to boil. Emmeline seized up the flannels, dropped them in, holding Albert all the time. She said she should have taken them out of flannels long ago, but she couldn't face their screams when she put them on the potty. 'I'll wait until they don't need teaching,' she said, when Verena complained. 'Best to follow nature.'

'But what about all those girls Jemima talks about who were tricked into it?'

Emmeline stirred the flannels with the wooden spoon. 'I'd say most of them were tricking the men into it, if you ask me. They think that's the way to keep them. Usually wrong.'

'Emmeline! That's so – harsh.'

'But true. You wouldn't know, sister. You don't want to catch a man. The rest of them, they're desperate. What was all that finishing school business that Papa sent you to? All the girls there were thinking of nothing but husbands. *I* escaped it.'

'But—' She made to touch Emmeline, overbalanced and almost fell against the cupboard. Lily burst into roaring tears. Celia hugged her close, shushed her.

'Now look what you've done,' said Emmeline. 'Go and try and put her down in her cot.'

Celia moved Lily up on her hip, even though she was almost too big for it now, and walked through to the twins' bed in the box room.

Had she? Had she been trying to trap Tom? Of course not. But that's what people might think. And she couldn't say he'd tricked her into it, plied her with drink, forced her. She'd drunk what he'd offered. It had happened, that was all. Inside her, she felt the child move again. She sat on the floor, held Lily close as she quieted. Then, as the infant continued crying, tears began falling from

Celia's eyes too. She rocked the baby back and forth, weeping on to her head.

'What is happening here?' Emmeline was at the doorway, holding the flannel. 'Celia?'

Celia hid her head against Lily's. Emmeline was sitting beside her, putting her arm round her shoulders. She reached over and prised Lily out of Celia's arms. 'She's nearly asleep,' she said, taking the towel off and putting the flannel on her, quickly wrapping it around her and pinning it in place. Celia watched, still crying. Emmeline lifted Lily carefully into her bed, stroked her head.

'Albert's asleep too. On the sofa. I'll move him in a minute.' She sat back. 'Now, tell me what's wrong. You know me, I always speak hastily.'

'Nothing, Emmeline. I'm just tired.' She gazed at Lily. The child stretched out an arm, smiled in her sleep.

'You must be upset about something. I didn't mean that you wouldn't be a good mother. I promise. Well, you'd be a different sort of mother. But anyway, I just don't think you're ready *yet*. You can wait another ten years or so.'

Celia opened her eyes, blurry with tears, looked down at her niece. 'But what if I have to have one now?'

Emmeline stared at her. 'What do you mean, have to have one now? Why on earth would that be?'

Celia put her hand on the wall.

'Sister? What are you talking about? What's going on?'

Celia pulled away from her. 'Nothing, Emmeline. I'm going out for a walk.' But then she realised her shawl had fallen away. She gathered it back, but it was too late. Emmeline was staring at her stomach.

'What?' her sister was saying, wonderingly. She reached out a hand to Celia's body. She touched it, flattened her hand, then gazed up at her. 'Celia, what is this?'

Celia shook her head.

Emmeline took her hand away, returned it. Celia felt its warmth. The baby moved, responding too. 'What happened?' she said. 'What have you done?' Her face was white, horrified.

Celia looked away.

'How long?' Lily turned over and sighed and Emmeline went to pat her.

'It's due in May, I suppose.'

Emmeline raised her eyebrow, hardened her voice. 'Well, you're carrying small, I'll give you that. I thought you were just getting fatter. I was a hippopotamus at your stage. Anyway, back to the point. You conceived when, August? Who was it?' She was hissing now, not to wake Lily.

'I don't know.'

'You don't know? What do you mean, you don't know?' Emmeline's face was flaming. *Oh you, playing respectable all of a sudden,* Celia wanted to say. *At least I didn't run off with my tutor.* But what she'd done was worse.

'It was a soldier when I came back from Germany.' The lie came fast to her mouth. 'I was in a cafe on the journey home. He came to me and started talking. I didn't know.' The idea of blaming it on Captain Evans flashed into her mind, trailed away. He might be easy to find, might even write to her.

'What are you talking about? A soldier? An officer?'

Celia rested her hands on her stomach. The child was still, hopefully asleep. 'I think he was an officer.'

'Well, that's a start, thank goodness. What's his name?'

'I don't know.'

'You don't know?'

'I don't. He told me. I've forgotten.'

'Well, we have to find him! What regiment?' Emmeline clutched her hand. 'Unless he's *married*?'

'I don't know that either. He wasn't wearing a ring.' He was coming up in her mind, this officer, his hair smartly slicked back, tanned skin, dark eyes, would have been good-looking if it wasn't for his rather large nose. Quiet, but a good sense of humour, she thought.

'You don't know? Did you talk to him *at all*?'

'Not much.'

'My God.' Emmeline sat back. 'Well, you've hidden it well, I'll say that. What are we going to do? It's too late to drink gin and have hot baths. There might be other things we can do. Samuel's friends might know. I'll ask tonight.'

'No! Don't.'

'You're not saying you want to *keep* it?'

'I might die doing the other thing.' The thought of the other thing had crossed her mind, late at night, but she'd thrown it away, fast. Women died of it, horrible deaths, tormented and bleeding. 'Anyway, there's been enough death, don't you think?'

Emmeline paused, thoughts slipping over her face. Then she shrugged. 'It's risky, certainly. Perhaps it would be easier if you just had it sent away. We'll work hard to hide it. I suppose it can be done. You can go to the country or something and then we'll find someone to take it.'

Celia hadn't thought as far as actually having it. She'd seen a book about 'Your New Baby' in a shop, taken a surreptitious look. Everyone looked happy in it, not like Emmeline, screaming fit to wake the Savoy as she gave birth. 'I don't think I want to do that, either. It's mine, isn't it?'

Emmeline dropped her head in her hands, groaned. 'Yours and some man you don't know the first thing about. Celia, this is ridiculous. Also, cruel. This will break Papa's heart, you know that.'

Celia's heart lurched. Emmeline was right.

'You were always his favourite, his little pet. You were the one going to make a brilliant marriage. Now here you are, about to have a baby by some soldier and you don't even know his *name*.'

Celia blushed. 'I'm sorry, Emmeline.'

'Don't apologise to me. It's Papa and Mama you'll have to beg forgiveness of. They said you were the one to make the fortunes of the family. After the rest of us made such a hash of it.' She seized Celia's arm, pulled her out of the room. 'Celia, you've been living in the clouds, I can tell. You need to think about what to do. We'll have to arrange for you to go away until it's born.' She bustled over to Albert, slumbering on the sofa. Celia followed her.

'Why should I go away? Mr Janus said it, even. He said that

a man who has a baby without being married is not excluded. That's true, isn't it?'

Emmeline patted Albert, rolled him towards the back of the sofa. 'Oh, don't be silly, Celia. This is real life. Anyway, your man doesn't know he's having a baby, does he? Probably never will.'

'No.' That was true. Tom must never know. He would never know. The child would be hers, entirely hers, and he would have no claim. 'Stoneythorpe is the country, isn't it? We could stay there.'

'But what do you imagine people would think? You'll never get married with this. With Arthur and everything.' Emmeline sat down, heavily. 'Celia, you need to think. I know you often don't, but you really need to now. You can't keep this child. It will ruin your future. Jemima will know a way we can find a family for it, someone kind.' Celia looked away. 'Sister, you have to listen to me. You can't do it.'

Celia stared at her sister. Lily was beginning to shuffle around. She'd start to wail soon. Celia closed her eyes, leant back against the wall. 'You can't!' she heard Emmeline say. 'Listen to sense.' She could, as she stood there, hear all the others saying the same. Mr Janus telling her it was ridiculous, Verena falling into hysterics, crying about their reputation, her father stoic and disappointed, all of them expecting her to do what they wished.

She opened her eyes. 'You can't tell me,' she said. 'You can't tell me what to do. It's up to me.'

'What rubbish. You need to see sense.'

'I can see sense. I am going to decide what to do later. When the time comes, that's when I'll decide.'

'You'll make the right choice.' Lily was beginning to whimper.

'I'll make my choice.'

'A baby in there has warped your mind. It did mine. You'll see sense.' Lily was crying now. Emmeline turned, marched into the children's room and closed the door. Celia looked to where Albert was stretched out, dozing on the sofa. She hurried over to him, gathered him close in her arms, felt his skin warm against hers.

TWENTY-FIVE

London, March 1922

Celia

There were an awful lot of baby manuals. Celia started with
Emmeline's, rocking Lily when she couldn't sleep or soothing
Albert as she strained her eyes in the dim light to read about feeding or rest routines. It all seemed very complicated. She bought
another one in a bookshop in Russell Square. 'My sister is very
worried about her new baby,' she announced loudly to the man,
as she handed it over. He gazed at her, baffled. She'd hurried the
paperback under her shawl and carried it back to Emmeline's
flat. There, after everyone had gone to bed, she sat up on her bed,
staring at the pages. It was like reading another language. She
simply could not comprehend it – in May, she would have a baby.
She'd lain on the ground in the darkness in Baden – and now she
was going to have a baby.

Emmeline had told Mr Janus, who'd railed at Celia about
irresponsibility – and said she might have exposed herself to
disease. She blushed, said surely not (although Tom had said
there had been others, so how could she know?). She threw the
thought from her mind. Jemima also knew, restrained herself to
hugging her and talking cryptically about how women should be
able to express themselves as well as men. They hadn't yet told
Verena or Rudolf. Celia had replied to their letters asking her to
go and visit by saying she was too busy helping Emmeline. She'd
agreed with her sister that she would go back to Stoneythorpe
when she was eight or so months along – and then everybody
would have to deal with it. Tom had written again, as had Hilde

and Johann. She'd ignored their letters. Other than that, her days had been the same. Emmeline gave her even more childcare to do, saying she had to learn. She moved around the flat, washing and dressing Lily and Albert, patting them to sleep, trying to teach them to hold a pencil. Maybe, she thought, if Lily wouldn't speak, she'd like to draw what she felt. But neither child wanted to, preferred to be read to or watch her draw.

'You need a wedding ring,' Emmeline had said, the day after Celia had told her. 'When you take the twins out, you need a wedding ring. Whenever you go out, actually. You can borrow mine.'

'I won't have a wedding ring. That's lying.' Celia shook her head. 'Surely Mr Janus would say it was hypocrisy.'

'Oh poppycock. What does he know? You must borrow my ring.' Emmeline tugged it off and held it out.

'It doesn't fit. I won't wear it anyway.'

Emmeline clutched her hand. 'I'll make you!' Celia pulled her hand back. They fought for seconds, scrabbling at each other's hands, angry and breathless. Emmeline stopped, pulled away, snatching back the ring. 'Do as you like!' she said, her face red and pained. 'Do as you like and see where that gets you!'

Celia shrugged and shook her head. 'I will!' She rushed to the kitchen, closed the door and put the kettle on to boil so the children wouldn't hear her cry.

She vowed not to wear a ring. Yet, after weeks of being stared at, people whispering behind her, men nodding, she relented, and borrowed Emmeline's. Her sister didn't say *I told you so* kindly.

'Imagine if you had your own,' said Emmeline. 'Imagine if we found that man and he gave you one.'

'I wouldn't know where to find him.'

'Well, we shall have to try.'

Mr Janus demanded detail after detail about the officer, how he spoke (she said she thought he was from Devon, slow vowels), long descriptions of his appearance, his uniform, even his shoes. After the first interrogation, she sat up late at night and wrote a description of the man, so she wouldn't trip up. He had dark, slicked-back hair, small eyes, a large nose and a good chin line, a wide smile, thin body, small of stature and smartly dressed. She said he didn't say much – 'I bet he didn't!' said Emmeline – and that he'd seemed kind.

'He was probably demobbed around when you met him, August, if he was still in uniform,' said Mr Janus, during one of the conversations. 'We might start from there.'

'Or perhaps,' Celia perked up, rather quickly, 'perhaps he just didn't want to take it off. I've heard of soldiers like that.' *Tom*, she thought. It would be easy if she just told them the truth. Emmeline would start on her – *you and the servant!* – but at least he would be a husband. Or at least *there*. She could just write to him. And say what? *You slaughtered my brother. I'm having your baby.*

She entertained strange thoughts, denying the truth, telling herself that she couldn't really be having a baby because of what they did that night, it must have come some other way. The truth laughed at her in her head.

Sometimes, late at night, she even thought about Captain Evans. She could pin it on him, say somehow that something worked in the right way. He was such a gentleman, he'd probably allow it. *Such a wicked lie*, she told herself. But what if the baby came out and looked like Tom? Then everybody would know.

'Hmm, true,' said Mr Janus, still pondering the uniform. 'But I'll look into it, all the same.' He sent Mr Sparks off for a list of all the regiments demobbed around the time: the 6th Norfolk, 7th London, 2nd Scotland, 3rd North Wales, four from the West Midlands. 'No one from Devon,' he said, wonderingly.

'Maybe he was in that London one,' said Emmeline, peering over his shoulder. 'Can you get that list?'

'I don't think he was in a London one,' Celia said, hastily.

'Well, we can try,' said Mr Janus. 'I'll ask for the names. I'll say that he promised to marry you. Not the rest.'

'Well, he didn't promise to marry her, did he?' said Emmeline.

'I didn't ask,' shot back Celia.

'Your mistake.'

The search carried on through the weeks, as Celia grew bigger, slower on her feet, too tired to play with the twins, her ankles doubled in size. She went to the doctor, with her wedding ring. He told her to rest, talked on about eating well. She told him that all she wanted to do was eat. Mr Sparks brought them a list of the London regiment and they scoured over it, hoping she might recognise a name. He even got more details on the men by bribing the official. Celia shook her head at all of it. 'No,' she said. 'I don't recognise anything.' Emmeline was furious. 'You were supposed to be clever!' she said.

'I've forgotten everything,' she said. 'Sorry.' She pulled the voluminous gown and shawl around her. She was looking like the statue of Queen Victoria now – the lower half of her like the wide plinth. She wanted to sleep all day, dozed late in the morning, slept after lunch. Then at night, she lay awake, gazing at the ceiling in the darkness. That was when she felt closest to him – she still felt sure he was a boy. 'What name would you like?' she said. One rang back in her mind: *Tom.* She pushed it away, everything, even the days together as children, riding over the fields, laughing, catching tadpoles in the pond. None of it was true any more, all ruined by what had happened in France.

Michael, she said to the baby. *Your name is Michael.*

One newspaper article she'd read suggested women should sing to the babies inside them. She'd tried, but only felt silly, singing out at the wall, and she couldn't sing the baby songs, like 'Twinkle Twinkle'. Instead, she read to him from her works of Shakespeare, beginning with the earlier plays.

'It might have a double effect,' she said to her baby. 'I might learn some more Shakespeare. I've forgotten everything I knew at Winterbourne.' Last time she'd recited Shakespeare had been in the ambulance – and she'd forgotten that, forced it out of her mind, as she had done with everything from then.

Romeo and Juliet was the first one. 'This means you can disobey your parents if you like,' she said. 'Sometimes, it's best to. I disobeyed mine. If I'm ever really wrong, you can too.'

Ay me! Sad hours seem long.
Was that my father that went hence so fast?

She lay there in the darkness, reciting the lines. Outside, she thought, the city was silent, all darkness, everyone asleep. Only a few were awake: the night workers fixing the Underground, rebuilding London's roads. They and she, lying awake in the flat in Bedford Square, talking of love in Venice. 'I won't read you the bits about death,' she whispered.

Emmeline wrote a letter to Verena telling her that Celia wasn't very well with a cold.

'It's not much of a preparation,' she said. 'But it might be a start to tell her you're indisposed.'

'Celia!' Emmeline was shouting. Celia tried to rouse herself. She could hear her sister crying out, but she couldn't raise her head.

Emmeline ran to her bed. 'Celia!' She sat on the bed. It sagged heavily. 'A letter from Mama. Papa isn't well.'

Celia tried to pull herself up.

'Look!' She shook the letter at her. 'Look at this. She said he's in bed, got pneumonia. He's asking for us. She wants us to visit.'

Celia rubbed her eyes. 'Well, we have to go. We must go.'

'But if we go and you're like this, it might shock him so much that it makes him worse. He might die.'

'He won't die.'

'He might.'

'But what if we never go and he dies?'

'You'll kill him.'

'We have to see him, Emmeline. Mama needs us too. Come on, let's pack up the twins' things.' Celia hauled herself up. 'Emmeline! Let's go.'

TWENTY-SIX

Stoneythorpe, April 1922

Celia

Stoneythorpe loomed up in front of them. The great, ivy-clad front looked smaller than Celia remembered. She gazed up at the windows, now cracked, the schoolroom looking out on to the drive, the parlour, her mother's bedroom. The front garden and lawn were looking overgrown, the yew tree so heavy with leaves that it could almost topple into the grass.

The car came to a stop and Emmeline and Mr Janus helped her out. 'Try to walk quickly,' said Emmeline. 'Then they won't guess.' Celia doubted it. She was a great size now, and although she was swathed in scarves and a large coat, she felt that everything betrayed her, the tipped-forward way of walking, her swollen ankles and hands.

Celia followed her sister towards the front door. Thompson stood there, waiting for them, smiling. 'Come in, come in,' he said, taking their bags. Celia thought he didn't notice her stomach. She followed him up the stairs, dragging herself up, one by one. She touched the banister, feeling the dust on her fingers.

Her room was the same as it had always been, the desk laid out with her ornaments and books, the bed made up with lacy pillows and the green eiderdown. Her bookshelves were neatly arranged, largest book to the smallest, *The Water-Babies* to *Lorna Doone*. Her pictures of horses were hung on the walls. Someone – Verena, she supposed – had put in the two gold vases that had always been in the dining room. To make her feel welcome. She sat down heavily on the bed. The tears pricked at the back of her eyes.

'Celia!' Her mother was calling from downstairs. 'Come down to tea.'

She hauled herself off the bed and began walking downstairs.

Verena was serving tea in the sitting room. 'It is so nice to have everybody together again,' she was saying. A maid Celia didn't recognise was pouring tea into the cups. Jennie was away, looking after her children, and Smithson had found a new job in a factory in Winchester while Celia had been in London. He'd left a note for Celia saying he promised to come to see her.

If it hadn't been for her stomach, she could be at Smithson's cottage now, playing with Jennie's two little girls. Instead, she was watching the maid handing round cups of tea. The twins were playing on the floor with Albert's toy train. 'If you could play nicely without fighting for *one minute*,' Emmeline was saying.

'Celia!' Verena jumped up. 'My dear!'

Celia shied away and threw herself into the nearest armchair. She didn't want her mother hugging her, holding her close. Then she might know. Much better to be sitting down. She folded her shawl around her.

'Where is Father?' she said.

'Upstairs. We'll go after tea. He gets so tired these days.' Verena gestured at the maid to serve Celia. 'You must be exhausted after your journey, dear.'

Celia took the tea, held it out in her hand. Recently, she'd been balancing things on her bump as it was more comfortable. She put her head back against the chair, feeling its thick brocade on her hair. Verena was talking about the garden and whether they should have the hedges at the back replanted. 'Or maybe it just wouldn't be worth it. I have my suspicions, I'm not the only one you know, that the country's soil has been permanently weakened. Mrs Warrener was saying exactly the same thing to me. They put special substances in the soil in case the enemy invaded. They'd blow up and poison the wells. But now all those horrid things are in the soil and we can't grow a *thing*.'

'Are there any wells near here?' said Mr Janus.

'I should imagine that they're *everywhere*. But that's not the point. The point is whether I should replant the hedge. Or whether it is never going to get any better, and so our hedges are always going to be so very thin.'

Celia gazed out of the window. She couldn't really remember what the hedges had looked like before the war, but surely they hadn't looked so much better. They'd always been pretty sparse. She strained her eyes to see past them, to the spot at the back of the garden that was always hers, past the rose bushes and the hedges, the ornamental fountain and Verena's Versailles-style gardens, into the rackety old place at the end, where the willow tree almost touched the pond and she could edge under its leaves to sit on the rocks by the side of the water. She'd have a struggle to do it now, she supposed. 'I'll take you there,' she whispered to Michael. 'After you're born, we'll sit there together and think. You'll have a lot to think about. You're just starting life, after all.'

She had to admit, she hadn't thought much about what she'd do after Michael arrived. She supposed she'd spend some time at Stoneythorpe (after they'd all forgiven her) and then go back to London with Emmeline. They might even find a bigger flat for the three of them – six of them: Emmeline, Mr Janus, Celia, Michael, Albert and Lily. They'd share things between them and then she might get a job. Something in London where she could earn money, although what she wasn't sure.

'Celia?' Verena was holding up the cake. 'Are you paying attention? Would you like a slice?'

She shook her head. 'I was thinking about the garden.'

'A shadow,' said Verena, crossly, holding up her teaspoon. 'A poor shadow of its former self.'

When she tried to think of the future – *only a month away!* – she couldn't imagine it. Birth was the most baffling thing of all. 'You need to prepare,' Emmeline had said to her. 'Lie down and think about it. Imagine you're in pain and breathe through it. Not that I did much breathing. I mainly screamed, if you remember. But you should make the effort to learn. Then you might not have to be stitched back together like me.'

Celia meant to – remembering all the blood after the twins

were born. But every time she tried, she felt ridiculous, confused. 'What do you think, Michael?' she asked. After all, surely it would be hardest for him. She only had to wait, he was the one who had to *travel*. But he didn't answer. He spoke to her on lots of things, but on the subject of birth he was frustratingly silent. She supposed it would be new to both of them.

'Well, it won't last long,' she said. 'Then we can start being friends.'

'What was that, Celia?' Verena looked up. 'Did you say something?'

Celia shook her head. 'Sorry, Mama. Just mumbling.'

Verena shook her head. 'Dear Celia. Always the same.'

Celia looked at her mother. *No*, she wanted to say. *Not the same. Different.* She opened her mouth, started to speak.

Albert began wailing loudly as Lily snatched the train. 'Right, that's it,' said Emmeline. 'I'm putting the train away.'

Celia shook her head, looked down at the children. She couldn't say it. Not yet. Tonight, she thought. Tonight she would walk out, wander towards the back of the garden, touch the roses, try to edge her way under the willow. She'd sit there, on her favourite rock, and then she'd find the courage to speak, to say, 'Mama, something has happened.'

'Shall we all go upstairs now?' Verena stood up. 'Sarah, can you take the children? I don't think that Rudolf is quite up to seeing them.'

'He hasn't seen them for so long,' said Emmeline, from the floor where she was holding Albert. 'He'll ask after them. Especially Bertie.'

'Not tonight, Emmeline. He's tired.'

'Well, I'm not coming if they're not welcome. Or is it that you think they might catch something off him?'

'It's not that they're not welcome. Emmeline, please. Papa won't give them anything. He's just very weak. But they'll tire him.'

'I'll stay with them.'

Verena nodded, her shoulders slumping. 'Come on, then.'

'Alright, let's all go. Come on.' Emmeline stood up and hauled Bertie onto her hip.

'Could you take Lily, Celia?' Verena asked.

'No, no,' broke in Mr Janus. 'I can take her, or the maid can.'

Verena looked at Celia uncertainly, then shrugged. 'Off we go then.'

They set off up the stairs, Albert kicking at Emmeline and complaining. 'He wants to go outside,' she said, apologetically.

At the top of the stairs, they turned on to the landing, walked past the doors, until they arrived at Rudolf's room. A nurse was standing outside. Celia tried to remember when she had last seen her father in this room, perhaps when she had been twelve or so. While he'd been interned, during the war, she'd come sometimes, in her spare hours after the long afternoons of reading to Verena. She'd rested her head on his bed, touched his books on the shelf. She'd clenched her hand around the pile of small change on the bedside table – holding it because it broke her heart the most, the ten little coins, of which he'd thought nothing, barely regarded, thought he'd be using in the next day or so. Sometimes – she blushed at the imposition – she'd even lain in his bed, burrowing her head in the pillows, trying to find him, any part of him, still there in the fabric.

They walked in and two more nurses stood up, bobbed their heads. Rudolf was lying in the bed, hands resting on the cover. Celia clutched Emmeline's arm, shocked. His face was terribly pale. He looked half the size he had been, like a child. He opened his eyes and Albert let out a wail, hid his face in Emmeline's gown.

'Hello, children.' His voice was even weaker than he looked. 'I'm glad you came.' He held out a skeletal hand, riven with blue veins.

'Shall we sit you up?' said the nurse, a slender girl with reddish hair. The other dark-haired one darted forward, held Rudolf as she pushed up the pillows. He fell back against them, closed his eyes. Celia felt sick and pained, as if she had seen her father naked or he her. She couldn't believe he was so frail. He rested on the pillows for a second then opened his eyes. Albert was whimpering now.

'I'm so happy to see you.' His German accent was stronger than she recalled. 'Might you sit?' he asked. 'You'd be easier to look at.'

The nurse bustled around getting chairs. 'There's enough for two of you.'

'We'll take it in turns,' said Verena, perching herself on a far one. 'Celia, Samuel, you stand.'

Emmeline sat down, Albert wriggling in her arms, and Celia leant on her chair. As she did so, she was gripped by a flash of heat, a desire to collapse into the table next to her sister. She held tight to the chair, head spinning, limbs weak. *Don't fall*, she said to herself. *Don't fall.*

'You don't look well, Mr de Witt,' said Mr Janus, gravely. 'What has the doctor said?'

'It's my lungs,' said Rudolf. 'They're so weak. He says they can't withstand much.'

Verena shot an angry look at Mr Janus. 'But you'll be up and about in no time, won't you?'

'Perhaps, wife. But it is spring and I have pneumonia.'

'It's all the government, if you ask me,' said Mr Janus, his voice rising. 'What they did to you! You should demand compensation. Imprisoning an innocent man, ruining his health. Just to pander to the hysteria of the right, those *Mail* readers who wanted you all locked up.'

Rudolf turned his head, coughed. The nurse was beside him in a moment, held his head as he coughed again, dry and violent, retching hopelessly into her basin. Celia looked away, her eyes pricking.

'Water, sir?' the nurse was saying.

He nodded and the red-haired girl poured him a glass, passed it over. He sipped from it gratefully, like a child.

'Better out than in, that's what I say,' said Verena, smiling around the room. They sat, silent, staring at the bed, trying not to look at Rudolf's pained, hopeful face.

Emmeline broke the silence, holding up Albert. 'Look, Papa! Hasn't he grown?' She pushed the little boy to stand on her knee. 'Don't you think he's so much stronger?'

'Lillian's a fine girl too,' said Mr Janus from by the bed. 'Very quick.'

Emmeline gripped Albert under the arms. 'Let's go to shake

hands with Grandpapa,' she said to the little boy. He squirmed and shied away, but she rose, hauling him up and plopping him on the bed. 'Shake hands with Grandpapa,' she was saying. 'Be friendly.'

The child looked over, buried himself in his mother's bosom. Rudolf reached out a hand. 'Good boy,' he said. 'Good boy.'

I'm sorry! Celia wanted to cry. *I didn't mean to.* But she couldn't, for then the heat swept her again. Her head reeled. She gripped the chair, but without Emmeline's body it was weak and it tipped under her hands. She felt herself drop, scrabbled for the chair, missed it, felt herself falling to the floor. She aimed to catch herself with her hands, fell on her back, the chair flung to the side.

'Celia!' cried Verena. 'What is it?' She leapt up, started towards her daughter.

'Stop!' Emmeline cried. 'I'll go. You stay!' But it was too late, Verena was heading towards Celia. Celia tried to stand, fell back. The red-haired nurse was coming too. Her head throbbed and it felt like the whole of her was burning.

'My child!' Verena flung her arms around Celia, leaning across her. Celia saw her mother's face close to her, suddenly crossed with horror. 'Celia?' She pulled her hand down, just as Emmeline had. 'What is this?'

'Mama,' Emmeline started. Celia could see her giving Albert to Mr Janus.

Celia tried to look up, but Verena's hand was on her stomach, around her, lower. 'Are you ill? This is an illness, surely?'

'I—' She tried to speak, then the heat flooded through her again, and then a thunder, a rushing, battering at her head.

'Give her some air.' The red-haired nurse was standing over them now. 'Please, ma'am, step back.' Verena was gripping Celia now, holding her hands. 'What's happened to you? Tell me!'

Celia turned her head to the side, hoping that the floor might be cooler. *I feel so awful.* But the words wouldn't come out, just sat heavy in her head, burnt her eyes. *Am I dying?* she wanted to ask. *What's wrong with me? I must be dying. I must be.* She could hear Lily crying, somewhere far away.

Emmeline was pulling at Verena. 'Mother, she needs air. Let

me explain.' Celia could feel Verena pulling at her hands, shouting something.

Rudolf's voice was coming from the bed. 'What is it? What is happening? Is Celia ill?' The other nurse was trying to calm him.

Celia closed her eyes. Everything was red behind her eyelids, hot and burning. The voices were beginning to swim.

'How far along is she?' the red-haired nurse was saying to Emmeline. 'When's the date?'

'I don't know.' Celia could hear Emmeline panicking. 'I can't remember. Six weeks, maybe. Samuel, can you remember?'

'Ma'am, you need to give her some air,' the nurse was saying. 'Step back.' Albert and Lily were both crying now, wailing. Mr Janus was shouting something at Emmeline.

'Who did this to you?' Verena was crying out. 'Who? She was taken advantage of! We must get the police.'

'No need for the police,' said Mr Janus.

'So who was it?'

Celia turned her head. She felt a rush of nausea in her throat. 'Oh God,' she said, for no one to hear. 'God help me.'

Then the bed creaked. Rudolf's poor, weakened voice was crying out. 'Celia!' he said. 'My child.'

She tried to turn to him. 'Papa,' she tried. 'Forgive me.'

'Not really a child,' she could hear Mr Janus say. She shook him away. She wanted to reach out to her father, touch his hand. He, alone, would understand. He'd see, forgive her, love her. 'Papa,' she was saying, fighting with the red in her eyes and the sickness in her throat. 'Let me tell you.'

She heard him cry out. She tried again. 'I love you, Papa.' But there was Verena crying and the twins wailing and Mr Janus saying something she couldn't understand. She lifted her head. 'Listen to me.' He'd speak back, tell all of them to be quiet, say to forgive her, to care for her, that she was his Celia, still his favourite.

But before she could say it, Mr Janus stopped talking and a silence billowed up. Then the nausea rose and everything swelled black.

TWENTY-SEVEN

Stoneythorpe, April 1922

Celia

She couldn't tell if it were pain or not. Something swelled, rode her, took her back and forth, took her so far from her mind, her body, that she thought she would never return. But she wouldn't call it pain, not really. Pain was something she'd had before: headaches, a sprained ankle, toothache, the bout of measles at Winterbourne. This wasn't like that, was something else that rose with her, wasn't even her, not human. She'd imagined herself talking to Michael, telling him to stay calm, to keep breathing. Instead she was screaming, over and over, inside her mind because the thing was riding her too hard to allow the sound out. She begged it to stop.

'Keep going,' someone was saying, the red-haired nurse maybe. 'Pain is good. It shows things are progressing.'

'Good girl, not making a fuss,' said a man's voice. 'Only wastes time.'

But I want to, she tried to say. Then the pain came again, flung her hard against the wall.

They'd been there talking about her for hours, it seemed, talking *over* her. She'd woken up and found herself here, in this great bed she didn't recognise, a room she didn't recognise, must be somewhere at the top of the house. A new woman's voice was there, too, someone she hadn't heard before. They'd taken her clothes, put her in a nightgown, put covers around her. Jugs and bowls of hot water were constantly coming in and out – *what for?*

When she'd woken in this room, this bed, her first thought had been: *how am I still here? How am I not dead?*

She wanted to say: *I thought I was dead.* But they didn't want to talk to her. In fact, it was hardly as if she was in the room. They bustled around her, picking up water, towels, the doctor looking at things in his bag. *Who are you looking after? Who is the patient?* She felt like a spectator, soaring above them, looking down on herself from the ceiling, the twisted body bending from side to side, a weak tree in a storm.

In the moments between, when the thing set her down, let her think, all she could feel was thirst. But she couldn't ask for a drink, she tried but she couldn't make the words come out. It was too much, as if the huge effort that it would take to speak would give her completely over to the thing, the whole of her would fall into a hole, collapse into a hundred tiny pieces, tens of hundreds. She'd open her mouth and a fire would come out that would set her world aflame and burn the room, tear Stoneythorpe to the ground.

Perhaps they might see, she thought, perhaps they might say, *She'd like something to drink*, then hand her a glass, hold up her head so she could sip. But nothing came. She felt the pain come towards her, held on. Think of something else, she told herself. A boat on a lake, something that was still and calm. But the lake made her think only of the red-haired girl in Baden, scrambling to get into the boat, the others splashing her. She saw the girl laughing in her white gown, the men gazing at her.

'How long?' a voice was saying over her. The doctor. 'Nurse, time it.'

'I have done. Still three minutes. It's been like that for two hours.'

'Right.'

Celia felt him shake her shoulder. 'Come on, girl. You're getting behind. You need to put some effort in. Don't be lazy.'

I'm not being— she tried to say. Then the thing threw her against the wall again.

'Your sister had to be hurried up, didn't she?' said the doctor.

'She tells me you saw it all. You don't want the same happening to you. Time to get going, girl.'

'I'm not sure anyone can make it happen,' the nurse was saying.

'Not true. The way to do it is to get off the bed and start walking. It is my failsafe method. Nothing worse for getting a child going than lying around. Up you get, young lady.'

The thing let go of her and Celia lay back.

'Are you sure?' said the woman.

'Get her off the bed, please, Nurse.'

Celia felt the hands under her, grasping her and pulling her off the bed. She tried to fall back but they had their grip under her arms, were pulling her forwards.

'Start walking!' he said. 'Around the bedroom, standing straight as you can. Then let's see that child on its way.'

Celia felt the nurses pulling her around the room. She tried to speak, vomited on herself instead. She felt them sponging her nightdress. 'That's a good sign,' said the doctor. 'Excellent.'

Where's Emmeline? she wanted to say. Or her mother. Or any of them. Even Mr Janus would do. They'd all left her alone. Ashamed. Tears wanted to fall but they wouldn't come, the whole of her was too dry. *Drink*, she tried again, but the words still wouldn't come. The nurses dragged her on, pulling her around the room. 'Keep going,' the doctor said. 'It's working.'

Celia circled around the room, the nurses timing her breaths. 'Now,' said the doctor. 'Now it is time.'

Celia felt the nurse's hand on her shoulder. 'You need to do it, miss. Let's get the baby out.'

Celia felt sick. She knew her head was lolling. 'I can't.'

'You must. Your child is nearly born now.' She pushed hard on her shoulder. Celia bent over on to the bed, screamed. 'Let's get back on there,' said the doctor. 'I need to see.'

And then the thing was capturing her, throwing her around again. When it had taken her before, it had let her go, allowed her to rest for a moment. Now it didn't, it threw her against the wall again and again. Celia couldn't cry, she couldn't speak. 'Push!' the nurse was shouting. The other one jammed hard on her shoulder. 'Cord,' she heard the doctor say, and there was a spot of understanding in her heart, a small one, that said: the cord is probably around the neck.

The nurse angled a hand under her damp back. 'Again, miss.'

'I—'

'You must. Or we will have to cut the child out.'

'No!'

'Well, you know what you must do. Hold back now. Then you must push.' The nurse propped up Celia's head. 'You must stay straight, madam.'

'Water.' She heard herself beg.

'You must send the baby out now. Then you can have all the water you desire. Anything. Tea and scones.'

Celia felt a flash of breaking pain. The doctor's hands were in her, pulling her apart. 'I can't.'

'Come, miss. Now push until I say stop.'

Celia groaned. The doctor's hands were in further. The walls quivered, curtains slumped. The nurse looked up. 'Now!'

'Now, madam!' And Celia felt the nurse pushing too, hard on her shoulder. She cried out. 'Keep on!' said the nurse, holding her shoulder. 'Don't stop!'

'That's it!' cried the doctor. Celia fell back on the pillows as the child's head came into the doctor's pulling hands. 'That's it,' he said. 'Cord is free now.'

'Again, miss, one last time.'

The whole room seemed to throw back Celia's cries as the baby came into the doctor's hands. He brought it up. 'A boy!' Celia reached out. Her baby! He was grey, soundless.

'Stay still, miss,' the nurse soothed. 'Let the doctor take the child.'

The doctor dangled the baby upside down, slapped him on the back. No cry. He took up a blanket and rubbed hard on the child's stomach. Celia knew, the brief opening of sense in her mind let her know, that the doctor was about to start giving him air.

'Give him to me,' she said. The doctor was squeezing his chest. 'I want him.'

The doctor stared at her, then nodded. 'You can have him for two seconds,' he said. 'We'll ready the table. Give him warmth, it might help.'

Celia stared down at the baby, head bowed, sheened with blood. Legs, arms, head. Below her, the tangle of sheets, the blood, the evidence of the pain that had torn her body in two and yet had receded as soon as the child emerged. She touched the baby, its large grey head bent into her own skin. Behind her, she could hear the doctor bustling around, readying the table to pump his chest. She was aware, too, that there was sun breaking through the curtains, the white light of the early afternoon.

She put out her hand for the boy. 'Come', she said, hardly able to comprehend the sound of her own voice. Only a minute ago, it had been so low and guttural, so much screaming she could not think where it had come from. 'Come to me.' She touched the head, a little like stone. She picked up the child's hand, tiny and cold. Her son. 'You're Michael,' she said. 'Don't forget.'

'Put your hands on him, miss,' said the nurse. 'Bring him closer to you. You must try.' She lifted the child's great head so that the eyes, half shut, were near to her face.

'We'll take him now,' said the doctor, standing next to her.

'Look at me, little one,' Celia whispered. 'Little son.' Tom's arms around her when they met, his hands on her legs, touching her, whispering words she barely understood. His dark eyes and his words about what he'd done. She reached down to Michael, lifted him by the chest. As she did so, she felt the small body flutter in her hands. She held him close to her breast.

'Come on, now. Precious boy. Michael.' She patted his back. And with that, the boy made a cry. Only a weak one, like an infant foal, but a cry all the same. She held him tight, stared at him, amazed. 'You're mine!' she said. 'I made you.'

'Now, dear,' said the red-haired nurse. 'I'll take baby now. We need to wake him up.'

Celia held on to Michael. 'He needs me.'

The nurse reached down. 'He's still very weak. The doctor needs to look at him. You rest.'

'I can wash him. I'll do it. I want to feed him.'

'You can't!' said the nurse. 'The doctor needs to take him now. You want him well, don't you?'

'Come, Celia,' said Verena, who had appeared in the room – Celia hadn't noticed. 'The doctor needs to take him now. Think of him, not yourself.'

Her mother was right. She had to force herself. She held Michael up to the nurse. As she did so, the other nurse came to her side. 'Just something to help you sleep, dear. Later.' She pricked Celia's arm.

'You did very well,' a voice said. 'Very well indeed.' Celia heard her mother then, speaking about the doctor, how brave Celia had been, how quick, that Rudolf was quite well. Verena touched her forehead. When Celia had been a child and she couldn't sleep, her mother would sometimes come into her room, stroke her forehead until she fell asleep. Now, Verena was doing it again, smoothing her fingers over Celia's skin. 'Go to sleep,' she was saying. 'Sleep.'

Celia woke up and the sun was streaming through the windows. She was confused for a moment, disoriented. Why was she not in her bedroom? Why was her chest hurting? Then she realised. She was at Stoneythorpe and she had Michael! She sat up. Her body ached and her legs were weighted with exhaustion. Her throat was dry and her breasts were throbbing, hard with milk. Emmeline was in the corner, fully dressed, dozing on a chair.

'Emmeline!' she hissed. 'I need to feed Michael.' She gathered her nightdress around her and hobbled out of bed, pulling on a dressing gown by the door. Emmeline started, sat up.

'Oh, sister,' she said, holding out her hand. 'How are you?' A tear formed in her eye.

'I think I need to feed Michael!'

Emmeline sniffed. She was starting to cry in earnest now, tears pouring down her face. 'Wait, sister.'

'Where is he? It doesn't matter if he's asleep. Let's wake him up.' She seized the dressing gown, pulled open the door.

'Wait!' said Emmeline. 'Stop.'

Celia pushed past the door and out into the hall. She felt stiff, a hundred years old. She began to walk down the stairs.

'Listen, Celia,' Emmeline was saying behind her. 'I need you to sit down. Please.'

'I've been asleep all night,' she said, over her shoulder. 'Where's Michael?'

'You've been asleep for almost three days, sister. The doctor gave you something. Please, I need to tell you.'

'Two days? But what about Michael? Who has been feeding him? Did you get someone from the village? Why did you let me sleep for so long?'

'The doctor woke you up to give you some water, then gave you another injection. You weren't ready to be totally awake, that's what he said.'

Celia looked down and Verena was standing in the hall.

'You must be hungry, Celia.' She was clutching her cheek, her face white. Emmeline was weeping now, noisily behind her. 'I'll call for some tea.'

Celia gripped the banister. 'Where is Michael?'

Verena took a step forward. 'Celia. Come and sit down.'

She ushered her towards a chair. Celia's head was flashing, awful colours, black, purple, red. Tom's scarred face shot through her mind. 'Where's Michael? I want to find Michael.'

Emmeline was close behind her. 'Celia. Please.' She was weeping still, tears running down her face. She tried to catch her arm and Celia shook her off.

'Where's Michael? I want him.'

Verena looked at her.

'Now! Take me to him, now!'

Emmeline moved around to stand in front of her, put her hand on Celia's shoulder. Her face was wet with tears. 'He's dead, Celia. I'm sorry.'

'He died not long after he was born,' said Verena, her eyes ringed red. A tear fell down her cheek. 'You saw he was a little weak. We thought he was getting better. Then he went downhill.'

Celia stared at them, shook her head. 'Why didn't you wake me?'

'We couldn't,' said Verena. 'We tried but you were fast asleep.'

Emmeline was holding her now. 'I'm sorry, Celia. The doctors said they tried everything. But he just couldn't breathe. I'm sorry.'

'You're lying,' Celia said. 'You're lying.' And then she was falling on to the floor, the sobs coming up and smashing through the pictures on the wall, the marble vases, the sofa and chairs, and then the walls, and up and into her childhood bedroom, into the one in which she'd given birth, the sound echoing over and over, going out, coming back, every time weaker and quieter, empty noise.

PART FOUR

TWENTY-EIGHT

London, April 1923

Celia

Celia was walking. She knew she was walking. She put one foot forward, then the other, on to the pavement, and she was walking. But it didn't seem like walking, not in the way it had before. In those days, she had been going somewhere, moving *forward*. Now, she was just walking. She had never realised before how much it hurt to put her foot on the ground. But she had to walk, she had to. There was no other way she could get to where she was going. No buses went there, and taxis would only ask questions, in those dark roads near Oxford Street, houses with red lights in the windows, where a small old man would open the door and hurry her in, not smiling.

Every memory of Michael burnt her heart. *Why did I let him go?* she thought, over and over, begging. The moment when the nurse reached down came back; she reworked it, changed it, imagined her holding him back, refusing to let him go. *Why didn't I? Why?* When she heard about the funeral, all she'd wanted to do was throw herself on the coffin, pull it out, take his body for herself and *make him live again*. But she didn't, couldn't, he'd been buried before she woke and so she wept on Emmeline instead. And now here she was, begging these women in darkened rooms for help, words, anything.

Rudolf had recovered. He had grown stronger, was nearly back to his old self. This, Verena told Celia, was on the condition that she never talked about the baby – for that might send him straight back into the sickness.

She walked to dark rooms, glowing red lights in the corners, the only place she could be alive. There, holding hands with six, seven people, arms resting on the black tablecloth, the women in the centre, Eva or Claudia or Mrs Ern or Mrs Silver, dozens and dozens of names, faces. The others would give their stories first – Celia preferred it that way – talk of husbands lost at the Somme, Passchendaele or Mons, or battles you had never heard of, places you didn't even know there was fighting at all.

Sometimes she wondered about the women – their stories seemed so pat, like something you'd read in a magazine – and she thought, were you really engaged? Or did they meet briefly, a few tea outings and now it was a story, one to never forget, because that was your excuse for why you were single. Then she chastised herself for being cruel to them; thinking horrid, superior words about the girl in the pale suit next to her, hands twisting nervously, or the red-haired girl in green, the dark-haired one who'd smelt of lavender. For, after all, even if they'd only had two or three meetings over tea with a man who promised the moon but meant nothing – it was more than she'd had.

The girls, after all, you could say they were the lucky ones. They wept on to the table, said they'd never love again. Then they wept more when Mrs Silver or Eva or whoever it was said: 'Harry's talking to me. He says you must live your life. He says you must see friends on Saturday evenings, not spend them with his mother.' But you could tell, when they left, weeping into their handkerchiefs, that they'd listened and they would do something else on Saturday night, not see a man, perhaps, not yet, but at least meet other girls.

The mothers were the worst of them. They had the most, threw pounds and pounds into the purse at the centre of the table, money catching on money, silver, copper, wasted, useless money falling into the velvet. The mothers were the ones Celia could hardly bear to look at. The mothers couldn't go anywhere, they had to carry on sitting at the table, gazing at the pictures of the football squad, pretty much all of them dead.

And you are the same! Celia said to herself. You're not one of the girls, coming to ask if they should take off the engagement ring, put it in the box on her dressing table, take her naked hand out into the world (*Yes*, said Mrs Silver, solemnly. *I'm hearing Jimmy speak. Yes, you should. He said he will watch you happily from heaven*). You're a mother, like them. You can't replace a child. There's no ring to put in the box.

She could see that Mrs Silver preferred the girls to the mothers. Their grief was too much, too demanding. They wanted to know every detail, how he died, who was with him, where he was, *how much pain?* They remembered every word, totted them up, matched with one or another. *But you said he was in the left flank last time!*

'Oh yes,' said Mrs Silver. 'So I did. He gets confused with time. It's the morphine they gave him, you know.'

Nothing was ever enough for the mothers. It wasn't enough for Mrs Silver to say, 'He is happy where he is. He is content.' They wanted to know *why. Why* was he content? *Why* was he happy in such a place? And most of all, *why* did you have to die? Why *you*?

Celia looked at her hands when they started talking, tried to shield herself from their words. But she knew that she was like them, really. Except her child couldn't talk and hadn't chosen to die. *Why did you go away?* she said. *Why did you leave me?*

She knew that she shouldn't be here, that Verena would be horrified she had passed intimate details to *strangers*! But Celia told herself that it didn't matter, that the other women weren't listening anyway. They only cared about their own thoughts, they wanted to hear of the flowers, tumbling waterfalls, crystal lakes of the spirit world when it touched them.

'Michael,' she said, out loud in the room. 'Michael. I want to hear you.'

But the spiritualists couldn't get him for her. They often found the fiancés and the sons, but they couldn't grasp Michael and hold him. Eva said she couldn't hear him, patted Celia's hand, said surely he was happy, babies had pure souls and went straight to heaven. Claudia could hear him, said he was wonderfully happy, playing with other children, and would wait to see her when she arrived – although it would be some time before that happened.

Bridie said he was laughing although he did cry at the thought that he was no longer with her. Each one told her that was all they could hear – so Celia moved to try another.

Mrs Bright was her fourth, a slight woman living in an over-heated flat off Portman Square. She'd been to her every other day for two weeks. Mrs Bright, she was beginning to see, was growing weary of her, had had to rearrange her face to look enthusiastic when her maid showed Celia in.

'I'm not sure what else I can do for you, madam,' Mrs Bright said, at the end of the third week. 'I've tried, I've heard his voice, but he's a baby. He can't tell me why he died. If you ask me, you need a specialist.'

'Please,' Celia said. 'Tell me.'

'I wish I could. As I said, you need a specialist! I'll give you an address, dear. No guarantees, mind, but she is very experienced.'

'Couldn't you try one more time?'

Mrs Bright shook her head. 'I told you, dear. I can't help you any more. Mrs Stabatsky is the one. She's the best.' She pressed Celia's hand. 'Try her, dear.'

'If she can't help me, who can?'

'That I don't know, dear.' Mrs Bright squeezed her hands again, turned back to her room of women.

Michael would be a year old, if he'd lived. Celia stared at toddlers in the street and the park, trying to judge whether he would be so round or small or so fond of smiling. She tried to imagine him, the tiny baby on her breast grown into a bouncing child, almost too heavy to carry. She knew she shouldn't, but sometimes she found herself following small children with their mothers. There had been one little boy just yesterday, walking through Russell Square with his mother. She'd been carrying him in her arms and he'd smiled at Celia over her shoulder, a gap-toothed, cheery smile. Celia couldn't stop herself. She had to follow him. She waved at him, smiled. He flashed her his grin. And then – just as she was putting her hand on her nose to make him laugh – the mother turned around.

'He's very handsome,' Celia said, weakly.

'Thank you,' the woman said, but her tone was quick and sour. She whipped him up to the other side, put him facing forward. Celia supposed she'd feel the same. If you had such a handsome child, you'd want to keep him safe. There were always stories in the newspapers about desperate women stealing babies. 'I don't want to take him,' she said, under her breath, standing in the middle of Holborn. 'I just want to *touch* him.'

She went to parks in the mornings, when she knew that mothers would be there. She was careful, after the mother in Holborn, not to go to the same one too often. She sometimes went as far as Brook Green, near Miss Trammell's finishing school, where children ran around the flower beds and played catch by the trees. She stood close, pretending to take the air. Really, she listened to the other mothers complain about how tired they were, how their husbands left them alone to get on with it, and she wanted to slap them all. *Don't you know!*

Once, while at a playground in Belgravia, Celia saw a little girl fall and dirty her dress. Her mother, a big blonde woman, marched forward and pulled her out of the dirt. Then she smacked her, soundly. 'That's for ruining your dress!' she shouted. The other women nodded. 'Fanny is a careless child,' said one.

'I'll take her,' Celia said. The words were out before she knew it. 'I'll take her if she's careless.'

The women stared at her. Then, almost in unison, they stood and moved, silently, staring at her all the while, towards their children. They walked towards them, scooped them up into their arms, the children protesting about being torn from their games.

One, the tallest, stepped forward. 'I'd leave here now, if I were you. We'll call on the police.'

Celia turned and fled, stumbling, running to the Underground station. What had she been thinking? She flung herself into the carriage, her face on fire. *Idiot.* She put her head in her hands. Michael's tiny grave, the pitiful cross in the grounds of Stoney-thorpe. Rudolf had promised to buy him a proper headstone. His little body in the coffin, underground, that she'd never seen because they buried him before she awoke – had to, because the doctor said it would be better for her if she didn't see him. But she wanted to see him. Sometimes, when she couldn't sleep and the madness had taken hold of her mind, she imagined herself back at Stoneythorpe, going into the grounds, digging up his grave and taking his body from the coffin, so she could hold it tight, clasping him in her arms.

Celia had spent the first month after Michael died in bed. She had cried so much on that first night that Dr Grey had come and given her something, 'To help her sleep,' he said. Then she had to have that every night, and in the day too. She had Verena call him, beg him to come and give her the stuff. Dr Grey told her that she needed to try to lie awake without it, but she couldn't – and Verena and Emmeline agreed with her, told him so. He gave her injections of it, then they called in another doctor for the times he wouldn't come. She took the stuff all the time, wanted nothing else. Verena tried everything. She even said she'd written to Arthur, asked his advice – with no reply.

Emmeline came for her, a month or so after Michael died. 'You have to get up! I'm going back to London and you're coming with me. You need to take your mind off all this with a job. And you're certainly not having any more of that stuff.'

'I don't want a job.'

'I'm not listening to this. You have to have a job.'

'How can you be so cruel?'

'Well, I'm going back. My husband wants me back in London, and the children need their father. You'd better come back too. Otherwise, I will leave you here and you don't want that, do you?'

'Michael's here.'

'But he's dead, sister. Mama and Papa will stay with him. There's no point you staying here too.'

She was right, of course, Celia knew. There was nothing for her to do at home. And Michael had gone – really gone – and wasn't coming back. So she said to herself, rationally, objectively; she knew

Emmeline was right. But she couldn't go. She really couldn't. Michael needed her. He might want to speak to her.

Emmeline went without her and Celia remained. Verena said she could have only one visit from Dr Grey a week. The first would be on the following day. Two days later, after begging Verena to bring her Dr Grey and her mother refusing, Celia decided to go to London. There, she could get her hands on the stuff she needed. A hundred soldiers were probably selling it on the streets.

She returned to London, dreaming of morphine all the way on the train and then on the bus to Emmeline's. There, her bed was as they'd left it to run to Stoneythorpe. Celia threw herself on it, weeping. Lily crawled over to her and Celia clasped her in her arms.

The next day, she woke up sick, sweating, her head heavy, mouth dry. 'Flu,' said Emmeline, stroking her forehead. 'Trust you to get it a year later than anybody else. You probably weakened yourself with all that fuss with Dr Grey.' She brushed her hands. 'Try not to give it to the rest of us. Especially not the twins.'

'I'll try.' Celia fell back, her head hot. The bed felt close, swampy, thin. Her eyes were burning.

'No, Lily,' Emmeline called. 'Don't come and see Aunt Celia. She's made herself ill.'

'I'm thirsty,' Celia said.

'Well, I will try and find you a bottle. But don't expect me to wait on you hand and foot. I've got enough on my plate.'

Celia tried to press her head into her pillow. 'People die of Spanish flu.'

'Not any more. That was last year. You'll be fine. Probably only withdrawal from that horrible stuff anyway. And you might lose some weight.'

It was true, Celia thought, after Emmeline had closed the door and was telling Lily loudly to play properly with her toys. She had got fatter while she'd been carrying Michael. Of course, some of it had gone – the great bosom had reduced, once all the milk had gone down, lumpy and painful under the skin (the few times she'd come out of the morphine at all, it had been her bosoms that hurt the most). But still, even though they had no milk in them any more, they were now great swollen things. Her hips were heavy, her behind too, and her stomach was like a whale's. *Who cares?* she wanted to shout at Emmeline, loud at the door. *I don't want another man!*

But it wasn't that, not really. The great parts, heavy stomach, bosom, thighs bigger than they'd ever been, they'd been made for Michael. They were all she had of him. So they had to be kept.

She had the flu for nearly five weeks, long, miserable weeks in which all she could think of was morphine. She begged Mr Janus to buy it for her. 'You won't recover until you stop wanting that stuff,' said Emmeline. 'I promise. Think of something else.' Celia found herself thinking of food, sweet stuff, giant cakes full of cream and chocolate, pastry horns of custard, apple pies, biscuits. She thought of the kitchen in Stoneythorpe, herself as a child, gobbling up scraps of pastry, leftover biscuit mix from the bowl. The days of preparations for their annual children's parties. Those days in which she'd thought everything would be simple.

'That's it,' said Mr Janus, one day when she asked him to bring her a cake. 'Feed yourself up.' As she recovered, she ate more. For breakfast, she wanted six slices of bread, then sweets in the morning, four helpings at lunch. If you ate, she found, things didn't hurt. If your mouth was always moving, then you weren't thinking.

She'd soon run through the money that Rudolf had pressed in her hand. 'You'll have to get a job,' Emmeline said.

Celia supposed she needed an office job. She couldn't think of what else she could do.

'Yes, but you can't type,' said Emmeline, when Celia talked of an office. 'And Papa certainly hasn't got the money for you to do a course.'

Celia went to an employment bureau, trying to ignore the children on the way, promising herself a big cake when she'd finished. The woman there suggested a job in a small government office off Pall Mall, typing up compensation reports. She'd pursed her lips at Celia. 'It's perfect, Miss Witt. No – er – outward-facing work.

They only need someone for a week. But perhaps after that we can find you something further.'

On her first day, Celia arrived in a small dusty office, staffed by an elderly bespectacled man called Mr Penderstall and another youngish woman, a quiet girl called Miss Jeffs. There were piles of reports in brown card, scattered across the room. 'It's a mountain,' sighed Mr Penderstall. 'We need help. Are you quick?'

'Oh, very,' lied Celia. She had no idea how to type.

'Then we're away. Let's get to the end of the first week, give it a whirl, see how it goes.'

That first morning, Mr Penderstall had gone out for a long meeting at the Home Office and Miss Jeffs had shown Celia how to use the typewriter.

'I'm terribly slow,' said Celia, as she made another error. Every time she touched the 'M' it hurt her heart.

'Oh, don't worry. Mr Penderstall will never notice. We have so many piles of the things that I don't think we'll ever get through them. Once you've done ten, another load arrive. So you might as well go slow!'

By the time Mr Penderstall arrived back, Celia was typing out a list of one man's injuries, slowly but surely. 'Excellent work, Miss Witt. Excellent.'

At lunchtime, she went out and bought five cakes from the bakery around the corner, ate them all, in one quick go.

Four months later, they were still giving it a whirl and seeing how it went. At the end of each week, Mr Penderstall professed himself quite happy. 'I will write to Mrs Wilks's and tell her we'd like you for another week.' Celia had settled into a routine – four cakes on the way, a bag of sweets while working, lunch at Lyons's, then chocolate biscuits on the way home to Emmeline's. She had become great and round, whole rolls of flesh surrounding her belly. Her thighs rubbed together when she walked, grew sore. Emmeline laughed at her, made comments about not fitting through the door. Celia didn't care. Things didn't hurt her, not now.

Then Miss Jeffs invited her to tea with her mother, after work. 'Mama wanted to meet you,' she said. Celia supposed she should

KATE WILLIAMS

go, this was the sort of thing you should do to stay friendly with your workmates. Next day, she followed Miss Jeffs to the Lyons tea room, shook hands with a dowdy woman in a brown coat and hat. Celia and Miss Jeffs talked of work, she talked politely to Mrs Jeffs, who'd lost her sons in the war and her husband just after it. Miss Jeffs was all she had left. You could see, Celia thought painfully, that she wanted her daughter to have female friendship, saw it as the road to men. She saw Mrs Jeffs's eyes light up when Celia said she had one brother, still living. 'He's overseas,' she said hastily.

Then, as Celia rose to leave, saying she was needed back home, Mrs Jeffs reached up and clasped her hand. 'You seem sad, miss, if you don't mind me saying.'

'I miss my brother,' said Celia, furiously ashamed of herself for the lie. She did miss Michael, of course she did, but it wasn't him she yearned for, ate four custard cakes to stop herself thinking about.

'Of course you do. It's hard to lose a brother.'

Celia nodded, feeling wrong and fraudulent.

The woman pressed her hand. 'I have found some people a great help to me.'

'Mama!' Miss Jeffs drew herself up. 'Stop it!'

But Mrs Jeffs carried on, lowering her voice, whispering about the people she saw who found the spirits for her. 'She makes me hear them,' she said. 'Eric is swimming in the lakes, Stanley is with him, all of them quite happy, waiting for me.'

Miss Jeffs looked at Celia in agony. 'Please, Mama.'

But Celia was listening, watching the woman's eyes glitter as she talked.

Three days later, she took the tube to Marylebone to find the address marked out on the card Mrs Jeffs had pressed into her hand. That one was Mrs Ern. Then she went to Claudia and then Mrs Bright. With the spiritualists, she didn't need to eat cakes and sandwiches any more. The words filled her soul. She sometimes wouldn't eat at all, so no earthly thing touched her before she'd sit at the spiritualist's table, calling out for Michael.

'Glad you're getting thinner,' said Emmeline. Celia heard her talking with Mr Janus, deciding that Celia was losing weight and staying out late because she was in love. She was, it was true. She always had been. With Michael.

Mrs Stabatsky, the specialist, was in a tiny flat in a small alley off Oxford Street. She had the same clientele as everybody else, Celia thought, similar decor too – red curtains, black velvet, golden ornaments that looked as if they'd been stolen from the circus. She was small, dark-haired, hands covered in rings, and a thick accent (Russian, from Siberia, she claimed). Same as all the others. But there was *something* different. She asked Celia questions. Not about Michael – everyone had asked those. Celia fed her the usual line about losing her husband in the war. Unlike the others, Mrs Stabatsky asked her to come early, before the sessions, and questioned her about other people: Verena, Rudolf, Emmeline. She even asked about Winterbourne. Celia supposed she should find the questions intrusive, but really, she welcomed the chance to talk – and if it helped her find Michael, what did it matter?

But then, after three goes, Mrs Stabatsky told her that she couldn't really find anything without a belonging of the child.

'But he had nothing,' Celia told her, in front of the other women. 'You know. I saw him, he was taken away. Then he died. I asked for the blanket. They said they'd burnt it in case it was infectious.'

'They should have kept a lock of his hair for you.' The woman shook her head. 'What kind of nurse would do that, take away a child and never give you his hair?'

The other women shook their heads. 'Terrible!'

'I'm not sure I can help you, Mrs Witt, without a belonging. I just can't hear him.'

'But you have to,' said Celia. 'Please. Mrs Bright said you were the one who could help me. You were a specialist.'

'You know, Mrs Witt, I'm wondering something. This is just a possible thought. Forgive me. But are you really sure that Michael is dead?'

Celia felt the velvet table rock under her hands. 'What do you mean?'

'What I say. I just can't feel him, dear. More than that. The whole story sounds odd to me.'

'But babies *die*,' one of the grey-faced women sitting round the table said.

'Of course they do. Listen, Mrs Witt, forgive me. But I'd ask your family for more details.' She stood up abruptly. 'Let me show you out. Ladies, I will be back in two minutes. Hold your beloved's belonging, if you would.'

Celia followed her outside, her heart pounding. She was being told to leave. 'What do you mean?' she said, furiously. 'He's dead.'

'Your story doesn't ring true to me,' said Mrs Stabatsky, flatly. Her accent was slipping, Celia realised, more East London than Russia. 'I tell you, Mrs Witt, I hear a million stories and there's something not right about yours. Someone's lying. At first I thought it was you – and of course you are about that husband business – but now I think someone else is lying too.'

'The husband business?'

'That's a poor lie, *Mrs* Witt. I wouldn't try it on anyone of importance. No one seems less like a married woman than you.'

Celia stopped. Her whole body felt as if was being shaken. She started to speak.

'Listen, we don't have time. Think about it. You were unmarried – right? Goodness knows who the father is. Do you know?'

Celia nodded.

'Well, that's a start. But what a disgrace for your family. Yes, don't think that scruffy hat fools anyone. Obvious you're from a good family. And the touch of German in your speech.'

'What?'

'Oh, don't worry, *miss*.' She dropped her voice, moved closer. The smell of violets was suffocating. 'Only the most sensitive would spot it. That's what I am, you know, sensitive. I pick up on things. That's how I find out so much about those who come to me.'

'But—'

'Oh, smoke and mirrors, all that stuff. People tell you everything the minute they open their mouths. But listen, you're rich – from that *de Witt de Witt, keeps you fit* canned meat lot, are you? Yes, thought so, I have a researcher who looks into that kind of thing. Anyway, you were pregnant. Yes, that I could tell. Whatever else you were lying about, you've definitely had a child. But that child, it's a disgrace for the family. They tell you the baby's dead. Maybe it is. Maybe it isn't.'

'Maybe it isn't?'

'I've had a thousand women in here who've lost babies. Even the poorest keep something of the child, a scrap of rag it wore, hair. You have nothing. Your family kept nothing – at all? Funny. The nurses didn't take pity on you and slip you something? Impossible.'

'So he's *alive?*'

'I don't know. Not saying anything. All I think is that it's time for you to stop seeing people like me and Mrs Bright and start asking some questions.'

Celia stood in the hall, stared.

'Get along with you, miss. You've got something over the women I see. You've got money. Real money. You don't need me. You can find things out. And you might have something over everyone else in here. The person you seek might still be alive.'

'I don't understand.' Celia pulled up her purse, was fumbling for money. She found a note, held it out.

Mrs Stabatsky folded it into her sleeve. 'Well, try to. Anyway, I have my clients. I must return. Good day, *Miss* Witt.'

She pulled open the door. Celia stumbled out into the chill, pale air. Around her, people flowed. A man bustled past, two newspaper boys were shouting. She clutched the wall. *Still alive.*

TWENTY-NINE

———

London, April 1923

Celia

Celia opened the door into Emmeline's flat. The twins were shouting, Lily, she thought, complaining the loudest. Emmeline was telling them crossly that she was exhausted and they needed to stop shrieking, immediately, right this minute. Celia slammed the door behind her, hard.

'Is that you, Samuel?'

'It's me,' said Celia, walking into the bedroom. Lily was rolling on the bed, her small face screwed up red. Emmeline was trying to rub her stomach, holding Albert in the other arm. 'What's happened?'

'Oh, you know. They're always cross. Where've you been? You must have finished work ages ago. You can make yourself useful and take them out.'

'I've been thinking.'

'You think too much. Take Lily for me, will you?'

Celia bent down, hauled the child on to her hip. 'You're getting too heavy to carry, now you're almost four!' She bounced her but Lily only screamed more. 'I think they're hungry.'

'Of course they're hungry. They're always hungry.'

'I'll get them some bread and milk.'

'The milk's off.'

'I'll see what I can find.' Celia took Lily with her, still howling, and walked to the kitchen. She tore a crust off the loaf of bread on the side and stuffed it into Lily's mouth. 'Here you go, little one.'

Lily coughed, hiccuped and started chewing. 'Good girl,' said

Celia, patting her as she hunted for the milk. She pulled down a bowl, tipped in milk and tore up bread.

'Come on, Lily, let's take this to your brother.' She carried the bowl out, balancing the child on her hip.

'She was hungry,' she said, pushing open the door. 'I brought some for Albert.'

'You're ruining their routine. They're supposed to stick to meal times. No snacks.'

'Yes, but they're hungry.' Celia set down the bread and milk on the floor by Albert. He threw aside the spoon and started gobbling it up by hand. Lily was still chewing.

'As I said, Emmy, I've been thinking. About Michael. Baby Michael.'

Emmeline looked at her. 'What about Michael?'

'I wanted to know if he's dead.'

'Dead? What do you mean?' She dropped her voice. 'Please, Celia. I know it is hard. But you have to accept it. He's gone.'

'But you weren't there. You said you were asleep.'

Emmeline patted Lily. 'I was. It happened in the middle of the night. When I came down, Mama said he was gone. But you know, Celia, it happens. Babies die. All the time. I'm sorry he did, but he did.'

'You wanted me to get rid of him!'

Emmeline turned away. 'Don't be cruel. I did at the beginning, I admit it. But I didn't want him to die. He was so weak, sister. Don't you remember? He couldn't even cry and he wouldn't feed.'

'Why didn't you keep anything of his? Why didn't you keep any hair or a blanket?'

'A blanket!' Albert shouted. He splashed a hand in his bowl and then climbed on to the sofa.

'No jumping,' said Emmeline. 'I'm trying to talk. Celia, Mama decided not to. That's the way they did it in her day. She thought it would be better that way. A clean break, that's what she said. She wanted to make life easier for you.'

'One single piece of hair?'

'Stop that!' Emmeline hauled Albert on to the bed. She tugged a clump of rug from his fingers. 'I'm sorry, sister. I know it hurts. And coming so soon after Louisa too, you were still so sad about her, and brother Michael before that. We all were so sad. But time will heal. One day you'll have more children. I promise.'

Emmeline hauled the twins up to stand. 'Come along,' she said. 'Out we go.'

Celia followed her. 'What were the names of the nurses?'

'What nurses?'

'Father's nurses, Nurse Brown and Nurse Black. Or whatever their names were. The ones who attended me. What were they called?'

Emmeline patted the sofa for the twins to get up onto, put a book in front of Lily, gave Arthur a wooden carriage. She turned for the kitchen. 'I can't remember.' Albert stood up and started bouncing.

Celia put her arms around Lily. 'The nurses would know the truth,' she said, quietly. 'I could ask them.'

'The truth is that he died.' Emmeline ruffled Lily's hair. 'I'm sorry, Celia, but he did. You could ask Mama about the nurses but she probably won't know.'

Lily began to sniff. 'Died,' she said, experimentally. Albert was still bouncing.

Celia patted Lily, absently. 'Someone is lying to me.'

Emmeline threw the towel she was holding to the floor. 'Why can't you accept it?'

Just then, the door slammed. 'I'm back.' Mr Janus sounded weary. He walked into the sitting room.

Emmeline marched up to meet him. 'Celia's upsetting everyone.'

He sat down heavily on his chair and opened his arms to Lily. 'The committee are arguing too. Can't decide what kind of action to take. Whether a full strike would be too far. They say I want to hide the truth about the real figures of poverty and starvation. They say I don't want the men to strike. Griffiths says that he could snap his fingers and five million men would be on the streets, demonstrating. I say to him, I know you could. But what would happen if they did? The government might kill us all. Remember West Riding a hundred years ago? They were all hung for treason.'

'Are you listening to me, Samuel?'

'It would be another war.'

Lily began to cry again.

'You're holding her too tightly! Give her to me.' Emmeline pulled the child from his arms. 'You're not listening to a word we say.' She jogged Lily on her hip but the child only cried more.

Samuel put his head in his hands. 'Tell me again.'

'Celia can't accept her child is dead. She needs to. Tell her!'

He shook his head. 'But Emmeline, how should I know? I wasn't there.'

'Don't be ridiculous.'

Celia stood up. 'So you know something?' she asked, walking towards him. 'You know that he wasn't dead, after all?'

He stood up. 'I'm ignorant on this. I really don't know anything.'

'You do! Otherwise you'd back her up.'

He held up his hand. 'I've had enough. I'm going to our room. I don't know anything about any of this. You can both leave me out of it.' He flung off to their room, the door shut behind him.

Albert was screaming now, both children wailing. Emmeline dropped Lily back on the couch.

'Now look what you've done! Celia, I'm sorry for you, really I am, but you must understand it. Poor Michael was never healthy. He died.'

Celia held Lily to her. 'I want to hear the truth. That's all.'

'You have heard it. You just don't believe it.'

Celia gazed up at the ceiling, holding the child tightly. She rocked her, staring at the cracks in the ceiling, thousands of them snaking through the grimy paint.

That night, Emmeline slammed off to her room, told Celia it was her job to get the children to sleep. Celia sat with Lily, rocking her in her arms, while Albert dozed leaning against her, head propped on her shoulder, in his favourite position. She could be doing the same for Michael now, singing 'Twinkle Twinkle' to him, reciting his favourite story. Her heart lurched, flipped. The words were out before she knew it, so loud that Albert started. 'Michael!' she cried. 'Come back!'

In the following days, it was like she was two people, sometimes three. One of them was Celia, the girl everybody knew, doing the things she should, going to work, tidying the flat, taking Albert and Lily out for walks, occasionally exchanging words with Emmeline, about practical things, not conversation. She read to Lily, fed her, tried to encourage her to talk, played trains with Albert.

And then there was the other girl, who thought only of Michael. She wrote to Verena and Rudolf demanding the names of the nurses, then again when they didn't answer. She tried to recall what had happened, over and over. *Who* had taken Michael first, Verena or the nurse? She cried, alone in her room, not caring if Emmeline could hear.

Then there was another voice that intervened, told her it wasn't really true. That she was believing a medium over her own sister. Mrs Stabatsky was a charlatan, of course she was, her fake bracelets, the swathes of red velvet, the cloudy crystal ball. Normal, rational people would tell Celia that she was simply wrong and Mrs Stabatsky was just another one who made money out of vulnerable women (*The Times* was currently getting rather exercised on the subject). And why would her kindly family lie to her? They loved her. Michael would be their own flesh and blood, after all. Celia listened to the voice. *I see your point*, she said. *I agree with you, why believe a charlatan like Mrs Stabatsky?* But still. The voice was weak. Michael might be alive. Someone was lying.

PART FIVE

THIRTY

———

Paris, July 1924

Celia

Celia stood on the platform, hot and exhausted. Arthur wasn't there. She hadn't seen him for four years and he'd promised he'd be there. She looked around the bustle of French people hurrying around, men in suits, women carrying children, two old people hunting for their friends. He wasn't anywhere. She waved the porter forward. 'I'll just wait there,' she said, pointing to the edge of the platform.

He shook his head. 'You can't wait there. Not a lady.'

'My brother will be here in a minute. He's been held up. He won't be long.'

He shook his head. 'You can't wait there. Impossible. You must go to the Ladies' Waiting Room.'

'But my brother won't know where I am.'

He looked incredulous. 'Everyone knows to come to the Ladies' Waiting Room at the Gare du Nord. No one would meet a lady in the station.'

People were beginning to stare. She shrugged. 'Very well. Let's go there.' She followed him through the crowds – mostly French, she supposed, but some people looked so *English* – off to the Ladies' Waiting Room.

He deposited her trunk unceremoniously in the room. She stood against the wall. Arthur would never think of looking here. She glanced over at the ladies, knitting, fiddling with their carpet bags. Her trunk was safe with them. She walked to the door and peered out, looking for Arthur. She could see nothing but

287

throngs of people. She walked out further, towards the platform. He wasn't there.

Something cool was creeping around her heart. *What if he wasn't coming?* It would be easy enough, she assured herself, she could just find a hotel, go back to London tomorrow. She'd stayed alone in the Somme and in Dover on the way back. Paris would be no different. But still, this was a huge city. It made her afraid. The whole idea of coming here had been to get away from things. Or so Verena had said.

Celia had tried her hardest to forget about what Mrs Stabatsky had said. She had spent whole months doing her best not to think about Michael, or any of it. She threw herself into her work, into looking after the children. But no matter what she did, she kept on coming back to her son. On a visit to Stoneythorpe with Emmeline, Celia had demanded the truth from Verena and Rudolf. They'd told her she was wrong, said they wouldn't hear another word about it. Verena and Emmeline had told her they'd decided Celia was overworn, that her mind had gone wild and she had too much strain.

Then Verena said there was a letter to her from Paris, two weeks old, they'd forgotten to send it on. Celia didn't recognise the handwriting on the envelope. She opened it – and it was Arthur, his familiar scrawl spreading over the page. He said he'd asked a friend to send it for him. He said he wondered how she was. *I'm in Paris now,* he wrote. *Come and see me, if you like.*

'Arthur's in Paris,' she said to Verena. 'He said I can go and see him.'

Verena and Rudolf were in shock. Emmeline jumped in. 'You should go. Take your mind off all this. Father, give her the money to go. You can persuade Arthur to come home. Papa needs the help with the business.'

'But why has he changed his mind?' said Verena. 'Why suddenly say where he is?'

'I suppose he grew tired of hiding,' said Emmeline. 'Not that there's any need for it. I wrote to him at his old address in Paris. When the agency said they thought he'd gone abroad, I wondered if he might go back there. I told him that Celia had lost her baby and she was unhappy. So he's thinking of her, I'd say, although it's taken him a while to do anything.'

'He always was a good boy,' said Verena.

Emmeline snorted. 'Sometimes.'

'Tell him to come home,' said Rudolf. Celia thought she would. It had all died down now. The papers stopped mentioning the scandal long ago and the police hadn't been in further contact. None of the sewing ladies made comments to Verena now. They still hadn't given back Louisa's belongings, but Rudolf said maybe they shouldn't ask, didn't do to be too difficult.

'Why don't you go to Paris?' said Emmeline. 'Talk some sense into our idiot brother. There's nothing to run away from, and if it's grief, he should get over it.'

'I will have to check with Mr Penderstall.'

But Mr Penderstall was quite happy about it all – said Celia deserved a holiday – he'd save all the work up for when she returned. She packed her bag, bought new books, set off for Paris, firmly resolved to tell Arthur to come back home. She'd tell him about Michael. If he came back and asked Verena the truth, perhaps she'd tell him.

But that all relied upon him turning up. She stared at the platform, willing Arthur to appear. He didn't. People were beginning to assemble for the next train coming in. She felt her heart start to pound. She would have to find her way on her own. He wasn't coming. Her breath was rising, choking her throat. The porter would laugh at her, say – *I knew you didn't have a brother.* What if someone took her for a courtesan? She was really choking now, breath high. A woman looked at her concerned, asked if she was well.

Celia nodded, couldn't summon up the French to reply. The heat of the place was rising. A child next to her was eating a sandwich, she smelt the sourness of cheese and felt sick. She needed air. It didn't matter about her trunk, the thing would be fine. She needed fresh air, to clear her head. Over to the side was a door. She hurried towards it, ignoring people, pushing past, desperate to get outside. She broke out into the air, saw what looked like a hundred cab drivers waiting, groups of men. She closed her eyes, leant against the wall.

'Hello, sister,' said a voice. 'Didn't you bring anything with you?'

She opened her eyes, her heart still cartwheeling. Arthur stood in front of her. A cigarette was burning down in his fingers.

'You really don't have anything,' he said, wonderingly. 'And where have you been? I've been waiting for you.' He looked well, she thought, better than any of them at home. You might even say he looked a little younger, his brow less furrowed, his eyes bright. He'd had his hair cut, it was further off his forehead, looked smarter. He was wearing a neat three-piece suit, as if he'd come straight from a business meeting.

The words wouldn't come out. She gestured behind her. 'I've been inside.'

He brought the cigarette to his mouth and puffed. 'I thought you were never coming. I was beginning to think about giving up and going.'

'I've been inside all the time.'

'What were you doing there?'

'You said you'd meet me at the station.'

He shook his head. 'Everyone knows to meet here! Anyone would have said if you'd asked. No wonder you took so long to find the right place.'

'Look, I did!' Then she thought better of arguing. What was the point? 'Well, I'm here now. My trunk is in the Ladies' Waiting Room. Well, that's if it's still there. Will you come with me to find it?'

'Is there not a porter?' He looked around him.

'I found one before. He said I had to go to the Ladies' Waiting Room.'

'You left your bag behind? Someone could take it, you know.'

'I know.' She felt suddenly tired, couldn't face any more of this. After the trains and the boat and the train again, she just wanted to sit down in a car, get taken to wherever Arthur lived, lie down on his sofa. 'I'll go and get it. Can I borrow some French money?'

'Of course.' He took a wallet from his pocket, pulled it open. It was full of notes. He handed her two.

'I'll wait for you here.'

She shrugged, walked back in, through the throng, found a porter, collected her trunk (the other passengers were looking askance at it). Then they returned, piled it into a car and Arthur directed it to set off into Paris.

His flat was off a square, a few banks and a small market flourishing at the corner. 'This is the Place Maubert,' he said. 'The Seine is just behind us.'

He unlocked a big gate in the wall and ushered her through to a great building around a courtyard.

'This is pretty,' she said. Arthur picked up her trunk, unlocked the door and moved into the courtyard. They walked up the stairs to a flat, Arthur puffing as he dragged the trunk. He unlocked the door and went through to a hall.

'This is my humble abode,' he said, waving his hand. 'Welcome!' He ushered her through, showed her two parlours and a kitchen. She followed him around. It was neat, had paintings of Paris on the walls. She couldn't see any pictures of Louisa or the family. He talked on and on about how difficult it was to find good places to rent in Paris, how actually life was much more expensive than you might think, and contacts didn't get you anywhere. The words were flooding her head.

'I'm so tired,' she said. 'Could I lie down? Just for a little while.'

'Why of course,' he said. 'You should have asked earlier.' He ushered her into a room. It was the spare room, unloved; there was a small single bed, a table, a chair. The wallpaper was ugly green flowers. He stood in the doorway, awkwardly. 'Do you need anything?'

She shook her head. 'I'll just rest. I'll only need an hour or so.' He closed the door and she pulled off her boots, fell on the bed. The sleep came quickly, washing fast over her body.

*

She awoke and the flat was dark. There were the lights of the odd car passing in the street below, the sound of people talking outside, shouts. She walked to the door. 'Arthur?' There was no reply. She edged into the hallway, holding the walls. Still no one answered. The parlour was deserted. He must have gone out. She found her way to the kitchen, took a glass of water, then used her hands to move back to her room. She undressed in the dark, fumbled in her trunk for her nightdress, pulled it on, lay in bed, feeling cold and unwashed. The blanket was thin and the sheets were rough. The lights passed across her ceiling. She put her pillow over her head to block out the sound.

Next morning, the light was flooding on to her face and there was the smell of cooking. She pulled herself out of bed, and wrapped the blanket around herself. Arthur was talking to someone. She stepped through to the kitchen and saw there was a dark-haired woman there, back turned as she cooked at the stove.

'Morning, Celia.' Arthur jumped up from the table. He was wearing a thick red dressing gown that pooled around his feet. 'Did you sleep well?'

'Not bad.' She gazed at the woman.

'This is Marie-Rose.' The woman turned and smiled. She had a very beautiful face, great grey eyes like pale pools, cream skin. 'Marie-Rose, meet my sister.'

She smiled, nodded, turned back to the pan.

'What would you like for breakfast? I've taught Marie-Rose how to make an excellent breakfast. She really has learnt fast. Would you like bacon?'

Celia stared at Marie-Rose's slender back. Was this his maid? Or his cook? She looked at Arthur, uncertain.

Arthur gestured around the kitchen. 'Doesn't Marie-Rose keep everything ship-shape? She's a marvellous cook and housekeeper.' Marie-Rose turned, smiled again. 'She comes in every day.' The woman lowered her eyes, went back to the stove.

Celia nodded. 'It is beautifully clean.'

After a while, Arthur got up from the table, said he was going to dress. Celia followed him out of the kitchen and Marie-Rose brought some water to her room.

She met him again in the parlour. 'Matthew is dead, Arthur,' said Celia. 'I don't know if you knew.'

Arthur nodded. 'I did know. One of Mama's letters. I kept it from Louisa. It would have been too much for her.'

I tried to tell her when I saw her in London, she was about to say – then thought better of it.

'I'm so sorry about what happened to Louisa, Arthur. It must have been terrible. I – can't imagine.'

Arthur nodded. 'It was awful. But let's not talk about it now. Too many sad things.'

'But you know, brother, there's no need to stay here. No one thinks you did anything wrong. You could come home. Papa and Mama miss you so much.'

'I aimed to look after her,' he said. 'I tried. I failed.' He shook his head, as if to throw away the thought. 'Now, little sister. What would you like to do? You've never seen Paris?'

She shook her head.

'Well, I have so much to show you.'

She gazed around him at Marie-Rose, sweeping the corridor. 'Will Marie-Rose come too?'

He shrugged. 'No, no. She's quite happy here. Now come along, get ready. I shall show you Paris.'

And so he did. They spent the day wandering the city, playing at being tourists. They walked to the Eiffel Tower (such a blight on the landscape, Arthur said), took a boat down the Seine. Arthur talked the whole time, pointing out things of interest, landmarks, people. Everything, he said, had been more beautiful before the war. He pointed out places he had eaten, where he drank with friends. They ate lunch in a restaurant near the Town Hall, Arthur taking out his wallet, bulging with notes. She tried to think how it must have been for Louisa, listening to his jokes, laughing with him.

He was charming, she had to admit, different even to the day before.

This was a whole new Arthur, one she'd never seen before, or one she'd never noticed, at least. He was nothing like her big brother, not the one she'd known. This was the man Louisa must have loved.

He talked, made things easy, so you didn't have to think or worry because he was always talking, his voice springing lightly between subjects, never resting on anything for long. He made her laugh about a duck floating on the Seine, a waiter staring at a fly in a glass of water, a dog chasing a bone. She fought down her desire to wonder – how many women has he practised this on? But despite all the charm, she was always trying to ignore the question: *what happened with Louisa?*

'Did you and she go to lots of parties before she died?' Celia said. They were walking along by the Seine. The water was dark, you couldn't see into it, not even a foot under the surface.

'Who?'

'You and Louisa.'

'Oh. Yes, I suppose we did. She loved parties. She had a lot of nice dresses. You know.'

'But then you had to run away. The papers said there were some threats, something ridiculous about a fish. And her cat died.'

'Yes. I wanted to take her away from all that. But it was always in her mind, you know. I told her to stop thinking about it. But I could tell she always was. Even in Margate, when we were away from London, she was still thinking about it. She loved that cat so much.'

'Poor Louisa.'

'I think it really affected her. I don't think she forgot about the cat. That's when she started talking about death, how she might join her mother and father.'

Celia gasped. 'About death?'

'She talked about it all the time in Margate. How life would be easier if she died. She'd be with her mother, wouldn't be a burden. I told her that she wasn't a burden. But she wouldn't listen to me.'

'You mean she tried to kill *herself*?'

Arthur stopped. Around them, people wandered, gentlemen and ladies arm in arm, nursemaids with prams.

'I know she did.'

'What do you mean?'

'She wanted to die. That's what she talked about. I kept telling her how much there was to live for, but she wouldn't listen. She didn't *want* to listen.'

'But—' Celia stopped. 'Why didn't you tell us?'

'This is a secret! You mustn't tell anyone. Imagine what it will do to our parents. Mama would be devastated. It has to be kept secret.'

'But if you'd told the police—'

'What good would it have done? Nothing.' He was starting to walk again.

'So you think she ... she threw herself off the cliff?'

'We were already close. Then I felt her – I felt her move. I tried to catch her. I shouted *no*, but she was gone.'

'She jumped?' Celia could hardly say the word.

Arthur nodded.

'Oh no. I can't—' She couldn't speak. A man pushed past her. Her mind swayed, she began to fall. Arthur caught her arm. 'I'm sorry, Celia. I shouldn't have told you.'

She shook her head. 'No, I'm fine.' Was she? She tried to steady her mind but it was flooded with the view from the hotel room in Margate. The view of the cliffs.

'But I thought she was happy!' Had that been what it was? All the times that Louisa and Arthur had been whispering together in Stoneythorpe. Had it been because she was telling him how sad she was? She shook her head.

'I know it's hard to take in.'

'I can't believe it. She was always laughing with you!'

'I was trying to take her mind off it. But she was often sad.'

'I could have helped her,' Celia said. But as soon as the words were out, she knew she couldn't have, not really. Louisa hadn't wanted her help. She only wanted Arthur's. But in the end, that wasn't enough. 'This is awful.'

'Come, Celia, I'll take you to a cafe. I really shouldn't have told you.' He gripped her arm. 'You see now why I stayed away. I couldn't tell Mama. I couldn't tell any of you.'

'You didn't want to tell us.'

He shook his head.

So that was why he'd refused to come back. He hadn't wanted them to know.

He pressed his arm in hers. 'Come on, sister. Let's get you a drink.'

In the small cafe, surrounded by the noise of drinks, glasses being served up, bustling waiters, she held tight to his hand. 'I can't believe it,' she said. 'I'm so sorry.' How could she ever have doubted him? At first, she'd wondered why the police suspected him, hoped and prayed they'd got it wrong – then she'd come to agree with Emmeline. He'd stayed away because he liked the drama.

'It was hard. She hid her sadness from the rest of the family so well. I felt as if I was the only one she could tell it to.'

What an awful secret he'd had to bear. He was like her, keeping the secret of Michael's death from the family. She was flooded with a desire to tell him, then thought better. He was bowed down enough by Louisa. She couldn't add to it, not now.

'I tried everything to make her happy,' he said. 'Took her to the parties and dances. Bought her dresses.'

'You did your best.' She fingered the sugar by her cup of coffee, dry, scrapy stuff.

'But it didn't make things any better. She was still sad. She got afraid that someone was following her. There were those odd incidents at the Merlings'. I tried to help her.'

'Someone was following her?'

'So she said.'

'Who?'

'A man. Someone who hated her. She said she saw him in Margate.'

'She saw him in Margate?' She felt the dryness of the sugar in her hand. The crystals were hard. 'Did you tell the police?'

He shook his head. 'Why would I do that?'

'Because it's important. It might be important. You don't know.'

He shook his head. 'It doesn't matter now.' He stood up. 'Come on, Celia, let's go back.'

She clutched his arm as they walked. She tried to talk about Louisa, but he brushed it off. Next morning, he didn't want to talk about it either. She'd have to wait. And she would, she thought. She'd wait until he was ready to talk to her again. Then, perhaps, her thoughts would be clear. She'd understand more about Louisa wanting to die – and this man. Surely, she thought, surely it was connected, that Louisa received odd parcels, then she was followed. It had to be.

Over the next few days, they wandered the streets, or sometimes she remained in the rooms, reading three new novels Arthur had bought her, while he went out on business. She longed to wander the flat alone, search for any things of Louisa's. But Marie-Rose was always there, washing the floor or tidying the parlour, preparing lunch or dinner, and Arthur didn't mention it again. In the evening, he took Celia out for dinner. He sat there, handsome and upright. Other people stared at him, admiring, and she swelled with pride. When they came back to the rooms, she readied herself for bed – and heard him pad gently past her room, opening the front door, going out, locking it behind him.

On the fourth evening they ate at a pretty restaurant near the river. Arthur was talking about the local politics. She listened to him, watched him pour more wine into her glass. Behind him a family were eating, the children playing with their food while the father spoke intently to the mother.

She looked at Arthur, talking. 'You know I had a baby,' she said, when he broke for breath. 'A little boy.'

He nodded, held his glass. 'I heard. Mama and Emmeline wrote to me. Our sister's letter made more sense, I have to say. She said you were unhappy, wanted to forget about it.'

'I can't, though.'

He poured more wine into his glass. Hers was still full. 'You have to. Those of us who are left have to try and live.'

She leant forward. 'Emmeline means well. I know she does. But she won't listen to me. Because I don't think he's dead. I think he's alive.'

Arthur looked at the glass. 'Yes, Emmeline said that.'

'And it's true.' The mother in the family behind Arthur had started talking now. The children were still fiddling with their food.

'But you buried him, Celia. That's what Emmeline said. I know it's painful – I know it is – but you have to try to forget. Or at least live. You know, babies die, so many of them. He was weak when he was born, Mama said. That happens.'

'They're lying.'

'Emmeline said you suddenly decided that, out of the blue. She thinks you're overtired. She's right, isn't she? There's no reason behind it.'

'I just know.'

'So why change your mind, over a year on?' The waiter came, offering dessert. Arthur shook his head.

She bowed her head. 'Someone told me. They said that if Mama hadn't kept anything of his, then that was strange. They said they knew he was alive.'

'Who said that?'

She blushed. 'Just someone.'

'One of the women at the birth? They were fooling you, Celia, trying to get money out of the family. Don't listen.'

She shook her head again. 'It was a woman I . . . met.'

Arthur rolled his eyes. 'Well then, whoever that was, they were definitely trying to get money out of you. If they weren't even there! Look, Celia, it's written all over your face. Anyone can see you're desperate for something, you're seeking a miracle. Even a rather stupid person could see that and try to get money out of you. How much money did you give this woman?'

She shook her head. 'I didn't.'

'I don't believe that.' He poured more wine into his glass.

'Anyway, even if you didn't, she'll come for it. Oh, Celia, how could you have been so naïve? You lose someone, they're lost for good.'

She felt a rush of shame. He could never get Louisa back. He'd seen her, probably, dead at the bottom of the cliff. 'I'm so sorry about Louisa, Arthur.'

He looked at her, seemed about to speak, then turned to his wine. He drank the rest of it, quickly. 'Let's go. You must be tired.' He called over the waiter, asked for the bill. 'Let's take the short way home.'

Had she been naïve? She wondered, that night, lying in bed attempting sleep. Arthur was still in his room, preparing to go out, she supposed. Had Mrs Stabatsky (or whatever her name really was) been lying to her? But if she had, Celia didn't know why. Nothing was in it for her. Indeed, Mrs Stabatsky had sent her away. Perhaps she would come back and ask for more. Or maybe, Celia thought, hearing Arthur pad past her room and close the front door, sending him out into the city, maybe Mrs Stabatsky had just been playing with her. Experimenting for the fun of it. She stared at the ceiling, afraid, eyes wide.

Next day, Arthur was gone. She wandered around her room and the parlour, toying with opening her books. He didn't come back at lunchtime. She lay on the bed, thought of Michael, Mrs Stabatsky.

At five o'clock, Arthur arrived back. 'Hello!' he shouted. She called back, opened her door. He was smart in a grey coat she hadn't seen before. He leant against the wall. 'Long day,' he said. 'Very long day. I'm not sure I can face going out tonight. Why don't we just eat here?'

'Of course!' After last night, she was tired of restaurants too, wanted not to sit opposite her brother at a table while other women sneaked glances at him, having to try not to cry while she talked about Michael.

'Well, good. Marie-Rose shall make us something. I'll ask her. Sevenish?'

She nodded as he sauntered past her towards the kitchen.

Two hours later, she was waiting in the kitchen doorway. Marie-Rose had gone and Arthur was standing by the oven, peering into a saucepan.

'Let me serve it to you,' she said. 'You sit down.'

Marie-Rose had set out plates. Celia spooned casserole on to each one, then potatoes and beans from the other pans.

'I'll take them through,' he said. 'Marie-Rose has laid the table next door.'

She followed him into the parlour. There was a white tablecloth over the table and heavy cutlery. 'Mama would be pleased with you!' she said. 'This is all very fine.'

'I try,' he said, shrugging. She sat down at the table, wondering: had Louisa sat opposite Arthur in the same way? Did she pick up a glass of wine, smile over the rim at Arthur? Did he pass her casserole, put out the fine tablecloth for her? She longed to ask.

Arthur started asking more questions about Mr Janus and Emmeline, the twins.

She began to speak. She ate the casserole, drank the wine, talked about Albert and Lily, how he still liked trains and running about, how Mr Janus had been worried about Lily not talking but Celia had always known she was just a listener and now she was fine, completely fine. She talked about how Mr Janus had been in prison, his plans for revolution, and how the government were taking money from the workers so that the only answer was to strike.

Arthur brought through a cake, a great pile of cream and strawberries with sugar dusted over the top. He had two bowls balanced on his arm. She felt so full of food she could barely eat more, but more wine in her glass helped, and before she knew it, she'd eaten the whole slice. She could even eat another, she thought. Pure greed, of course.

Arthur pushed his bowl away, sat back, wine glass in hand. 'What a pleasant evening, dear Celia. It is such a pleasure talking to you.'

'I'm sorry I never came to visit you in London,' she said. 'I wanted to.' And then wine and boldness flooded her and she spoke the words that had been buzzing in her head. 'I could have seen you and Louisa.'

He swilled the wine in his glass, gazing at it. She waited, feeling as if time was standing still. Then he leapt to his feet. 'Come on!' he said. 'There's still time. Let's go out!'

'Out? But it's late!'

'Not so late! Come on, sister! You're in Paris, after all! Come along. Let's get our coats.' He rushed out of the room. 'Come on!' he called.

She scrambled to put on her coat and then followed him as he hurried out of the door. 'I know just the place,' he was saying as they ran down the stairs. 'You'll love it.' Outside, the street was quiet. He seized her arm and pulled her forward. 'It's a really fun place. The real Paris.'

They walked along the streets, turning right, left, then around a corner, past a church. He tugged her into a dark alleyway and then through a door guarded by two men in suits. Arthur spoke to them in quick French – and they were waved through. She followed him down a dark stairway to a room decorated in red, low chairs dotted around tables. People were everywhere, tall men, handsome women. There was a woman in a purple gown singing in the corner. The noise drove into her mind. She smiled, resisted the urge to clutch Arthur's arm. He ushered her through to a small table in the corner.

'Wait there. I'll go and get some more wine.'

'I'm not sure I need any more,' she was saying, but her voice was drowned by the noise and Arthur was off to the bar. She waited for him, staring at the couples around her. She supposed they'd think she was Arthur's lady friend, his lover. The man next to them was fondling the woman's leg. She was pretty, a little like Marie-Rose, and didn't seem to mind. Celia watched the singing woman, admired her piled-up yellow hair, red lips. In comparison, Celia felt lanky and dowdy. No one would pay her money to sing in the corner of a bar.

Questions about Louisa were coursing through her mind. Arthur sat down, a waiter following behind him with bottles and glasses. She watched the dark wine splash into the glass, pulled her mind free. She'd ask something else. 'What were all these people doing during the war?' she asked.

He raised an eyebrow. 'Same as now, I imagine.'

'But the Germans were here.'

He lifted the glass to his mouth. 'Sometimes they were. They were everywhere in Paris.'

'It must have been awful.'

He shrugged. 'But we are German too, remember. They weren't so bad. I sold them things. Have some wine.'

'I always thought you did.'

'So did everyone. Nothing wrong in it. They were the only ones with money. Anyway, you don't need Mr Janus, your old tutor, or whatever you call him, to remind you that the whole war was a lie. The British were just spoiling for a fight, wanted to make themselves look like heroes and keep their empire. And now look how they have succeeded. Paris is in ruins.'

'It's not that bad.' Her mind was dizzying with the Empire, trying to make the separation between how Arthur talked about the war and the rich and Mr Janus talked about the war and the poor.

'Well, you should have seen it before.'

'I wish I had.'

He looked at her, turned away. 'It would have been different.'

She grasped his hand. The voice of the woman pounded into her head. 'I'm sure you can come home now. I'll keep the secret about how she died. No one will know.'

'The police tried to arrest me. I hate them.'

'Yes, but that was ages ago. You can come home now. That is, if you want to.' Why would he, she thought, when he had Marie-Rose and rooms and the city of Paris to explore – and whatever he was doing for his business?

'I like it here. As you can see. But even if I wanted to, I couldn't. They still suspect me. The minute I arrived at Dover, they'd haul me in again and then I'd be in their hands. They'll ask so many questions and muddle me and tell me I'm a liar.'

The woman was still singing, the high notes carving into Celia's mind. 'Well, Arthur, they might for just a few days. But then you'll be free. They haven't got any proof of anything. And if they really ask you, you can tell the truth about the suicide.'

'I'd never do that. It would break Mama's heart.'

'You could ask the police to keep it secret.'

He shook his head. 'Why would they do that? No, Celia, it would be a mistake.'

She nodded. 'The truth is that you looked after her.'

He shook his head. 'I did.'

She sat back, sipped her drink, gazed past him at a woman swaying as she danced, the men who were staring at her, the couple at a table at the front who were arguing. The drink was going to her head, she could feel it. She sat back, heart thumping. She drank again and the stuff was hot in her throat.

'They'd only have to see you to understand how kind you were to her. They'd only have to hear you talk.'

He shrugged. 'That may be. But I need to keep something secret from them.'

'From who?' she said, gazing past him still.

'The police.'

'What would you need to keep secret from them?' She was watching the woman, not really listening to Arthur. She was so beautiful, bright red lips, short hair. The sparkles on her dress caught the light. She wondered what her home was like; surely, she thought, someone so beautiful wouldn't live in a normal apartment, with a kitchen, a bathroom. She smiled at her, but the woman didn't see. The music danced in her mind, shone at her eyes.

Arthur coughed. 'Because we were married.'

The music stopped. The place stopped. All the talking and laughing, words, shouts, all froze. She stared at him. 'You were married?'

He nodded. 'Louisa and I.'

She stared at him. 'You married her?' The room was still, as if a thousand spells had been thrown over it. The people were silent.

He nodded. 'I thought that would make her happy. Make her feel safe.'

Her head throbbed. *Married*. 'I thought you were looking after her. I thought you were—' *Friends*, she wanted to say.

'I was looking after her. It seemed to be the best way.'

She gripped the seat, her heart flooded with pain. 'When did you get married? How?'

'We did it quickly in London, before we left. Louisa wanted it that way. Not a huge wedding with a gown and bridesmaids and a banquet.'

'She didn't want us there?' *Louisa wanted it that way.*

He shrugged. 'I don't know.' He was only being kind. Louisa hadn't wanted them there, she had wanted to marry without them.

'She had a wedding dress?'

'She had a blue dress she liked, she wore that. She didn't want a fuss. She just wanted to feel safe.' He put his head in his hands. 'And I couldn't even give her that. I tried so hard.'

She felt as if she was spinning. When had Arthur *really* married her? When had he taken her to his bed, used her as a wife?

'But you were cousins—' Then she stopped. Tom and she were cousins too. She bowed her head.

'So you see why the police would suspect me.'

'Why?' The things she was meant to think had been lost to her. 'You know.'

'No.' But then she did, she heard Emmeline and Verena speaking, talking about Mr Pemberton trying to understand Louisa's accounts, talking about the police and words about Arthur's motives.

'Celia. I'm sure they've talked about it at home.' Arthur spoke slowly, as if explaining things to a child. She nodded, hearing the words.

The piano was swooping. She gazed at him. 'Because you have rights to her money, if you were married.'

'That's it. I never touched it. It wasn't about that. But you know how they'd think.'

'You kept it secret.' The woman had stopped singing now, the pianist speeding over the keys.

'We were going to tell you, but after Louisa... After she died, I had to leave. You must see that.'

'Yes.' And he was right, of course he was right; she thought of the police, talking to them about the accounts and marriage and motive. How much money Louisa had. All the questions they asked about his debts. She wanted to cry. A small, swollen spot of doubt formed in her heart, small as the last few drops of water in a glass.

The words burst out of her. '*Did* you want her money?'

He looked at her in shock. 'What are you talking about? Of course I didn't! Celia, how can you ask such a thing? Don't you know your own brother?'

And she was immediately ashamed. Of course. He was her brother. She was wrong and sinful asking him such questions. She felt filled with shame.

'That's why I have to stay here. Even you suspect me.'

'I'm sorry. I don't know what came over me.' She took it all in. 'What if they find out you were married?'

'No one knows. Except you.'

'Except me?'

'You're the only one.'

She reached out and clutched his hand then, tight, pressing his fingers, squeezing them so that the ring he wore on his little finger was crushing into hers, the whorls on his knuckles imprinting on her palms, as though she could send back the burden he had just passed her. But it was no good, the words were part of her now, burrowed deep in her heart.

THIRTY-ONE

London, August 1924

Celia

'Celia!' the voice shouted. 'Over here.'

She looked but couldn't see anyone. It was probably some man shouting for someone else. The station was full of shouting, after all. The noise echoed up to the steel girders in the roof. Or perhaps it was just that she was so tired, so weary of words, she didn't want to speak any more. It was only two weeks since she'd been wandering around the Paris station, looking for Arthur. She felt years older. Her brother had hugged her goodbye, told her to come and visit again. He talked of how much of a relief it had been to share things. *But you weighed me down*, she thought now, the train coming in from somewhere or other. *You weighed me down with your secret and now it's heavy on me.*

She looked around Waterloo station. All the way on the train she'd been saying to herself: *don't tell them, you mustn't tell them.* Arthur would stay in Paris, for how long she didn't know. For ever, maybe. And every time her family puzzled over why he wouldn't come home, she'd have to shrug.

'Celia!' the voice shouted again. 'Here!' The voice sounded closer. Now, she thought, she didn't even want to turn round, to see some friend of her family or maybe even a brother or friend of someone from school. She looked forward.

'Celia.' There was a hand on her shoulder. The voice was Tom's. She turned around and gazed at his face. His eye was still faintly scarred, his face red with the exertion of rushing to her. He was wearing a smart suit and brown coat, cane tipped with silver. He looked like a man from a newspaper advertisement – some sort of happy life.

'Long time,' he said. 'How are you, Celia?'

She gazed into his face, couldn't speak. Surely, she thought, surely he must notice. He must see how different she was, how her face, her body, her whole soul had changed. She held out her hand. It was moving towards his, slowly. She wanted to pull it back. In spite of herself, she felt a warm flash of vanity, wishing she'd taken more time with her hair this morning, wasn't so worn after so many late nights with Arthur. *Treachery*, she told her heart, catching it fretting about her unkempt hair. Michael had been killed in France, didn't have the chance to worry about his hair.

'How are you?'

She couldn't speak. Some words were in her throat, thickened and afraid. A tear – tears were swelling. She shook her head.

'How are you here?' Her head filled with thoughts of their baby. Michael holding her hand, his little palm wrapped in hers. She clasping him close to her, promising to keep him safe for ever. Tom was talking about the weather and his journey. She stared at him as people billowed around them.

What if, she thought, what if she stood there and said, *I had your child. I gave birth to your son and it tore my body and then they took him away. I cried over him and walked all over London to spiritualists and mesmerists and palm readers – and then one said he was actually alive. Could you help me find him? Please.*

He was still talking. 'I wanted to see you. I found out you were arriving today in London. I asked your mother. I wasn't expecting her to tell me but I think she thinks you need cheering up.'

Celia stared at him. *Cheering up? By the man who killed her brother?* Then she thought again. Perhaps a man like Tom could help her find Michael, think of ways she hadn't, find documents or talk to people. Or perhaps he couldn't. She could give Tom her hand now and at least he would listen to her. Or, then, perhaps not. Maybe he might say the child couldn't have lived, he was weak, as they said. Or maybe even he might not want their child to have lived. A smart man like him. A child would only weigh him down. She stared at him, miserably, couldn't speak.

'How was Paris? Did you see Arthur? How is he?' Tom was talking fast now, spewing out words. He didn't dare say, *let us find somewhere to sit down*, because that's when she'd realise that she shouldn't be there, she'd break away and his chance would be ended.

A man with a case bumped at her back and finally she roused herself. 'Yes, I've been staying with Arthur. We talked a lot. He's changed from how he used to be. Or maybe I just couldn't see what a good person he was when I was younger.'

'I expect it's easier to be good if you didn't go to war. He stayed in Paris and had a nice time.'

She started. Her voice was high in her throat. She forced herself to lower it. 'Well, at least he was out of the killing. Perhaps that's better.'

He flushed, a bright, painful red. They couldn't talk about it, she saw. They couldn't mention it. Otherwise the world would fall down around them. It was the bargain you made to live every day – you couldn't show what was really going on in your mind because if you did, everyone in this station would be screaming and shouting against the blackness, not rushing for trains, staring at announcement boards, picking up children, nibbling biscuits pulled out from their suitcases. But the deal she had with Tom was even greater. If she mentioned any word about Michael, the fighting, the betrayal, then everything would fall in on them, and perhaps she might kill him. She might kill the father of her child.

'Arthur was very upset about Louisa. He was looking after her, you see.'

'I understood that,' he said, strangled, face still burning. 'I understood from the newspapers.'

'He thinks people suspect him. So he has to stay away.'

He nodded, leant on his cane. 'I went to your house. Stoneythorpe is in a bad way. I've almost forgotten how it used to be.'

She shook her head and changed the subject. 'How are your family?'

'My sister's a nurse now.'

'That's good.'

'She likes to keep busy.' He smiled, looking past her. 'Do you remember when you put on that play of *Cinderella*? You were Cinderella. You were only twelve or so. You invited me and my sisters to watch, Mother too. Do you remember?'

She nodded. The question flamed in her heart. *Who played Buttons?* she wanted to say. *Can you remember? It was Michael, Michael in the golden-edged jacket, laughing at all the jokes, waving at you and your sisters. Michael who you shot, you lifted up your gun and fired at him.* She tried to push away the thoughts, smiled.

And then he did it. He saw her smile, put his hand out, said, 'Shall we go to get something to drink?'

She looked up at him. They could, she thought, although it wasn't long until her train. But then what if he was passing her the milk for tea or offering her a sandwich and the words came out from her? What if she said them, hissed them, whispered them. *I had a baby.*

'What did you say?'

She had said it out loud. She had. She stared at him, mouth open.

'What did you just say, Celia?' He was bending towards her, looking at her. The station stopped still. The people around them were frozen. She looked at his eyes, the eyelashes around them, the face that had been so close to hers. *Michael's face.* 'Did you say you had a baby?'

She couldn't answer.

'You had a child? What?' And then his face opened, a burst of shock. 'When? Where is it? Whose is it?' The last question was a whisper.

And that, the whisper, the dropped voice, threw her back into herself. There was shock, pity in his eyes. She wanted to send it away, along with every feeling for him in her treacherous heart. 'It was a soldier I met. The December after I came back from Germany, I met a soldier in a hotel. And it happened there.'

He was shaking his head, slightly, very slightly. He was silent a long while. She stared at him under the clock. His face both flushed and pale. 'This is ... well – I can't believe this. Is this true, Celia?'

'Very true. The baby's dead now. It died just after it was born.'

'I'm sorry.' He held out his hand to her. 'Poor you. It must have been very hard.'

She nodded, her head on fire with Michael playing Buttons, the baby in her arms, her words that had jumped out in spite of her.

'Well ...' he said, and paused. He opened his mouth to say something further – but she drew back. She knew what the words were.

'Were you going to say it? That it *perhaps was just as well*? I can't tell you how many times I see people thinking it. The girls at the—' She stopped, not wanting to mention seances. 'The girls. And my family. How dare you? How can you say it?'

'I think,' he said, dazed, 'people are only trying to be kind. It's hard being on your own—'

She stepped away again. 'I hate you. I really hate you. You dare speak to me about death *when you murdered my brother*.' He was saying something, reaching out to her, but her mind was whirling and her body was flaming. 'Leave me alone!' she shouted, too loud, so loud everyone in the station might hear. 'Leave me alone for good!' And she turned and ran, her bag bumping against her legs, headlong through the station, not knowing where she was running to, just that she was moving forward, barrelling through people, even though she could hear them protesting. People were shouting *miss*, and Tom was calling *Celia*, but she kept running, wanting to do it until the words weren't in her head any more, until the image of Michael playing Buttons was gone, along with the baby and Tom thinking perhaps it was just as well.

Three days later, there was a letter at the Post Office address she'd given to Verena. It was from Tom, forwarded from Stoneythorpe – saying he was sorry, asking to meet. She tore it up, threw it into the fire.

THIRTY-TWO

London, February 1925

Celia

VAD dances were the rage. Even more so if you actually had *been* a VAD. Almost ten years on and it was all about nostalgia, girls who were eighteen, nineteen, only children during the war, dressed up as nurses.

Ellen, one of the girls in the office, had spotted an advertisement for a party near Oxford Street – and when Celia told them she'd been an ambulance driver, well, then they were quite delighted. 'You must come!' they said. 'You can tell us exactly what to do as well!'

'Check our outfits!' said Mary.

Celia had only been out with them once before. When she'd got the job a few weeks after returning to London, Mr Ellerton had told her that she should hold herself apart from them, since she was the one who was supposed to be in charge. 'You need to maintain a little distance,' he said. 'Tempting as it may be to accept their offer of friendship.'

Celia had agreed, immediately. While she'd been away, Mr Penderstall had taken on another girl to do her work – and liked her so much he kept her. Celia had to admit it was probably fair – she'd never really been excellent at the job. So she wished goodbye to Miss Jeffs and set off to the employment bureau. They sent her to Mr Ellerton – who said he was in urgent need and asked if she could start that day.

She would be in charge of an office of three girls, and their job would be typing up scripts sent in by writers for possible radio plays. Celia would be there to check over them before they went forth to production. It seemed rather marvellous, really, being paid to read plays.

'If you could mark out the plays about war,' said Mr Ellerton. 'We don't want those, thank you. We want new material.'

Every morning she took the tube to Oxford Street, walked with the crowds to Regent Street and on to the tiny typist office on the lower-ground floor and set about reading the scripts. At lunchtime, she went to the canteen, sometimes with the other girls, sometimes sitting alone to read. It wasn't too hard, really, to stay away from them as Mr Ellerton had suggested. They seemed so young, only nineteen or so – Mary was the oldest at twenty. Celia felt a million years older than them, not five. They spent their money on cakes from Lyons's, lipsticks from the Smith's pharmacy nearby, saved up to buy short gowns, went to the hairdresser every week for a permanent wave, every three weeks for a trim. They met up in the evenings, went dancing, free, unencumbered.

'You're always so serious, Miss Witt,' said Ellen once, when they were having their tea break together. Celia nodded. Of course. They had everything in front of them, men, husbands, babies, a house. She'd done it, but all wrong, so she had nothing, no wedding, no child, no home.

She still knew nothing about Michael, not even if he was alive. He could be anywhere, she told herself. If Verena had taken him, it would have made most sense for him to be sent off to be adopted into a family – but how would she find him then? Just another war baby, born to an unmarried mother who'd given him up. *What if he really is dead after all?*

She shook the words off. On the way back from France, she'd been thinking, and after meeting Tom, she'd decided: she wouldn't speak to her family. It was the only way. The thoughts circled in her head, gathered together then swooped apart, a flock of birds flying to settle at night. She'd wait her family out, until they cracked and told her the truth.

That first night back in London, in the cheap hotel where the walls seemed to magnify every noise, she wrote to Emmeline. *I have found a place to live,* she wrote. *I am going to stay here and get a job. I won't come to you. I won't, not until one of you tells me where Michael is.* Her pen shook around the words.

She folded up the letter, trying not to think of Lily and Albert. If she didn't see Emmeline for six months, no matter, her sister would hardly change. But Lily and Albert might be entirely different – talking even more, making up little stories. Well perhaps Emmeline would give in fast and tell her all. She picked up her pen and began writing the same letter to her mother, folded it and sealed it, put both letters on the bedside table for posting the next day. She lay back on her bed, hands behind her head. The sounds of dozens of people welled up around her room, talking, washing, putting things away, arguing, closing their doors.

Celia took a room with two other girls off Marylebone Street and gave her mother a Post Office address for mail. A few days later, Emmeline had written saying she should reconsider, Verena had sent a letter saying she was heartbroken. Celia wept over both, forced herself not to write back. If they knew where Michael was, they could tell her.

She had to force herself not to care about them, not to look at children in the street and wonder how much bigger Albert and Lily were, not to read about the discussion of a strike and wonder what part Mr Janus was taking, to ignore newspaper articles about how servants preferred to be in factories or shops nowadays, rather than be locked up in the middle of nowhere, and so the middling country houses were falling into ruin. Every time one of her family came into her head, she tried to conjure up something else. It didn't always work.

She had become like all the other girls. She wore her hair short now – how strange it had been to sit there while it was cut away – small heels, shorter gowns. Anyone would look at her on the bus and say, 'Just another one of those modern girls!' The newspapers had plenty of articles about them, how they had too much money, spent it on whatever they liked, went out every night, had no idea how to run a household. The others in the office brought in women's magazines. Every one you picked up exhorted them,

'Not to give up! There might be a man just around the corner!' Women should try harder, they said, be always ready, never go out without make-up, be eager to smile softly even when it was raining and you had missed the bus. For you never knew where he might be! And you might have only once chance – if you weren't pretty or smiling or had a run in your stockings, he could find plenty of other girls who were ready for the moment.

Mary, Ellen and Sarah paid attention to the advice, tried to put it into action, carried lipstick, touched it up on the journey home and even when popping out of the basement to the WC (not that any men ever came near them except the ones from the post room or Mr Ellerton, all of whom were married). Celia didn't join in. Who would marry her? She had only one thought: Michael. He was always there when she talked about work to the other girls, answered Mr Ellerton, deciphered the illegible writing in a script, exchanged pleasantries with the bus driver or in a shop, talking briefly while she boiled an egg or heated soup with Milly or Grace, the two girls in her shared flat. If she spoke to a man or even went for tea with one, she knew she'd sit in the tea room or even the supper club, thinking about Michael. She looked every day for the letter from her parents which would tell her the truth. Nothing came – from anyone, not even Arthur. She'd told herself that if Tom sent a letter to Stoneythorpe and it was forwarded to her, she'd throw it away.

This is your life now. This is what you have. You read the scripts, talk to the others, make yourself sleep well at night. She would go to a party dressed as a VAD and pretend the whole thing was marvellous fun.

For the next two weeks, they talked about VAD outfits in every spare moment. Ellen brought in possible things they could make into nurses' gowns, Mary bought red ribbons to sew the red cross. Sarah even found a photograph in a small junk shop near Warren Street of some VADS with their patients and Mary pored over it, trying to work out the exact position of the crosses. The scripts mounted up in the trays behind them. Celia picked up her post at the Post Office. Verena wrote to say that they were having problems with the business. She said she was really worried, had begged Arthur to help. Then there was another letter saying Arthur might even come back to England to help. Celia knew he never would. She folded up the letter, put it in the box where she kept them all.

'Do you think this way would look correct, Miss Witt?' Mary asked, white material draped over her head. 'Or is it more Queen Alexandra than VAD?'

'I think so,' said Celia. 'I'm sure the exact details don't matter anyway.'

'But of course they matter!' Mary said, anguished. 'How can you say that? We have to get it right.'

Sarah was adjusting her headdress next to them. She didn't need to spend too much time worrying. She was so pretty, with pale blonde hair and great blue eyes, that she could get away with a few faults in the costume.

'Well then, I think they are very good.' Celia was wondering about what the men would be dressed as at this party. Were they all going to be orderlies? Or patients? Perhaps there wouldn't be any there at all, it would be the same as her dancing lessons at school, girls dancing with girls.

'What do you think the men are going to be?' she ventured, next day, at lunch. 'Did the advertisement say?'

All three stared at her. 'They will be soldiers, of course,' said Mary. 'Fine, brave soldiers.'

'Even though most of them never fought,' said Celia.

'Oh, but they would have done!'

Celia picked up her sandwich. 'Of course.'

The men would be perfect soldiers, she thought, upright, honourable. Mary and the rest wouldn't see any relation between them and the ones they passed in the streets, turned away from because they were holding out saucers for money, standing up and rattling tins on the Underground.

'Why can't they look after themselves?' she'd heard Mary say yesterday. 'The rest of us have to.'

The Times talked about soldiers who couldn't work when their wives could, so these men took the children, but left them tied to the posts outside the pub.

'Miss Witt!' Mary was waving in front of her face. 'We've lost you, Miss Witt.'

Celia smiled, shook her head. 'I'm sorry! I was deep in thought.

'We should go upstairs, ladies. Resume.' They gathered up their bags, Mary piled up the trays and took them to the canteen desk. Ellen started talking about a writer they had nicknamed Mr Squiggle. His handwriting was probably the worst Celia had ever seen and yet the higher-ups commissioned him to write an inordinate amount of plays. Yesterday, they'd all spent an hour poring over one word alone, eventually deciding it said 'firework'.

'No one thinks of us,' said Sarah. 'They think we can read anything so they send us Mr Squiggle.' She brushed back her blonde hair. It looked soft in her hands, Celia thought enviously.

'I shall meet him one day,' said Ellen. 'And I shall tell him he needs to change his ways. Didn't his first teachers teach him how to hold his pencil properly?'

Ten days later it was Saturday, and Celia and the others were at the party in a large townhouse in Portman Place.

'I suppose it was an aristocratic house once,' Celia said to Mary. She imagined a rather grand family using it as their London home. Now the place was dark, decorated with khaki flags, war souvenirs everywhere. There were VAD uniforms draped over the banisters – where had they got them from? – and war medals pinned over the wall. Around them were dozens of girls in uniforms (not as good as theirs, Celia thought) and some men dressed as soldiers. Outside there were even more waiting, queuing up to pay ten shillings each to get in. Two of the rooms were playing loud music, wartime songs. She recognised the song about the flying machine that all the men had liked. The last time Celia heard it was in her ambulance. One of the men had been singing it to the others, his voice cracked, stumbling over the high notes. 'Keep going,' they had shouted. 'Don't stop.'

'Let's go and dance!' shouted Mary. Ellen nodded and they followed after her. They passed through the door and there were twenty or so couples – some double girls – twirling and hopping to the flying machine song. Now it was loud – so loud it would burst your ears – a chorus of voices joining in. No one would be interested, Celia thought, if she told them about the man singing it to the others (he'd died not long after arriving in hospital, a nurse had said). She shook her head when Ellen held out her hand for dancing, stood by the side against the slightly damp wall. She watched Mary and Ellen twirling and laughing. Sarah was already talking to one of the men dressed as soldiers, one hand touching her long hair.

Celia waved, smiled, as they whirled past her, still dancing. The VAD uniforms were so terribly uncomfortable, she was almost surprised that any of them managed to dance at all. She leant against the wall. Probably ten years ago or so, some man might have come up to her to talk. Now, they were in such short supply you had to go up to them.

A new song came on. She didn't recognise it. The girls kept dancing. She thought she might go to get them all a drink – although perhaps not Sarah, because she looked deep in conversation. Against her instinct, she was rather enjoying herself. Everybody looked so happy you could almost believe they were. She was wondering where the drinks were sold and how much they might cost. Then she felt a hand on her shoulder.

'Celia.'

She turned and Emmeline was standing there, Mr Janus a few steps behind her.

'They said you were here,' Emmeline shouted over the music.

Celia gazed at her, baffled. 'Who?'

'That girl you live with. Whatever her name is.'

'But how did you have my address?'

'Your work. Samuel saw you going into the building a month or two ago. Your man in charge, Mr Ellerton, is it? Well, he gave us your address. We said we were your family.'

'Right. And now you're here.' Just over Emmeline's shoulder,

Mary and Ellen were looking at her quizzically. She grinned at them, and they turned back to the dance.

'We have to tell you something.'

'Is it about Michael? I'm not interested if it's not.' Celia felt cruel even saying the words. In a room of young, happy, dancing people, they looked painfully tired and old. Samuel looked even greyer than ever, his face gaunt, the rest of him so thin that his jacket looked like he'd borrowed it for the evening. Emmeline had got thin too and her eyes were sunken, cheeks so pale she almost looked like she'd painted them white.

'It's about Louisa. And Arthur.'

Celia looked away. The music turned, resounded. Another song. Sarah was dancing with the soldier, twirling around the room in some sort of Scottish dance. 'I saw him in Paris. He told me about it.'

Mr Janus shook his head. 'Could you come outside with us, Celia?'

'Never! I told you. I won't speak to you until you tell me the truth about Michael.'

'Please,' Emmeline said. She put out her hand. 'Please, sister.'

'I won't. I should go back to my friends.' She turned away, looked back. 'How is Lily? And Albert?'

Emmeline nodded. A tear was glittering on her pale cheek. 'They are well.'

'Give them a kiss from me. But I have to go. I'm sorry, but until you tell me about Michael, we can't talk.'

'Tell her,' Samuel said. 'Now.'

'They went to Paris to arrest Arthur. They said they had new evidence. They've ... they've arrested him on suspicion of killing Louisa.'

Celia looked at her, mind reeling. '*Killing* her.' The music was slowing around her, the notes lengthening, sagging, as if someone was pulling on the record.

'We don't know much,' said Emmeline. 'The police came to Stoneythorpe. They told Mama. She's suffering.'

'It was an accident,' Celia said. 'Death by misadventure. The coroner said so.' The bright faces of the others were sickly now, lipstick greasy, eyes slathered in garish, vulgar colour. The heat rose up from their sweaty, dirty bodies and swamped her. She gripped the wall.

'It looks like the police have changed their minds.'

'But – why?' *Stop!* she wanted to cry to the awful, endless circling music. *Stop it!*

Emmeline shook her head. 'We don't know. We don't know much.'

Celia swayed. Mr Janus reached out and gripped her shoulders. 'Hold still, now,' he said. 'Breathe.'

'Arthur wouldn't have killed her.' A VAD uniform was pinned up over Emmeline's head. Celia wanted to tear it down, the ridiculous, stupid thing. 'It was suicide, that's what it was. Arthur didn't want to say, but it was.'

'Will you come with us?' said Mr Janus. 'We need to think about what we do next.'

Celia nodded. She shook his hands off her shoulders. 'Thank you. I think I can breathe now.' She walked up to Ellen and Mary, who were standing watching at the near side of the dance floor.

'I should go,' she said. 'Something's come up. I might not be at work on Monday. Tell Mr Ellerton.'

Mary caught her hand. 'Who are those people? They look odd.'

'I don't think you should go with them,' said Ellen.

'Don't worry. That's my sister. Please tell Mr Ellerton. I'll come back when I can.'

She followed them out, past the pictures of VADS and Land Girls, a draped uniform over the banister. Emmeline walked ahead, dodging around the couples, a laughing group of women dressed as orderlies. There was still a long queue of guests outside.

'Come,' Emmeline said, turning back to Celia, just outside the door. Celia stepped out of the heat of the house, into the darkness. All she could think of was Louisa.

THIRTY-THREE

Paris, 1911

Arthur

When he'd first arrived in Paris, back before the war, he'd been afraid. He'd spent the first night alone in the small flat off the Place Maubert, fearful of the noises. It sounded nothing like home. There were shouts from outside and some sort of animal scratching at the door. Every time he forced his eyelids closed, the pipes banged again – such a bang – and they sprang open once more and he stared at the ceiling in terror. Why had he come? But he knew, of course, why he'd come. He'd had no choice. 'Overseas or I report you,' Rudolf had said.

That night in France reminded him of his first night at school. He'd been five. No one had told him he was going to school. His father had said he was going on a drive with Thompson. Verena dressed him up in his best coat, Emmeline, a fat toddler, hiding behind her legs. He tried to imagine, looking back, that she'd been crying. But he didn't think she had been.

'When are we stopping?' he had asked Thompson. Then, when he grew more afraid, he began to ask more questions. 'When are we going home?'

'We'll be there soon,' Thompson said.

He had wanted to go to the WC, but Thompson wouldn't stop and so he had to cross his legs. 'Please,' he said. 'I need to go.'

'Your father told me not to stop. This road isn't safe,' said Thompson. 'Won't be long now.'

Arthur wanted his mother to take him into her arms, say it didn't matter. But she hadn't, she wouldn't, she'd been too busy with Emmeline. Ever since she'd been born, no one had wanted Arthur. He remembered when Verena had gone away. Nurses had come to the house and they wouldn't let him into his mother's room. They'd said the room was locked and his mother was sleeping. She wouldn't see him. He banged on the door, shouting for her. The nurse slapped his legs, said he was a naughty little boy when his mother was suffering like this! The nanny he hated, Muriel, pulled him away, slapped his legs again. That night, in the nursery, he heard his mother crying out. He shouted for her, tried to get out of bed, but the door was locked. Then he heard Muriel come for him and ran back into his bed. Still, she stood over him, called him a bad little boy and said he deserved to lose his mother, behaving like that! He spent all night staring at the ceiling, because every time he closed his eyes, great monsters came and ate his mother.

'You can see her now,' said Muriel, next morning.

He went down with her. His mother was asleep and the nurses said not to wake her. 'You can see your new sister instead,' they said. There was a strange basket on legs next to his mother's bed. 'There she is!' said the nurse. 'What a pretty little girl. Emmy. Very good.'

He looked at her and knew Mama would prefer him, of course she would. Not this thing that had made her scream like she was being bitten.

But that wasn't what happened at all. Mama loved Emmy. Everyone loved Emmy. Every day, new people came to the house. They didn't want to see Arthur, they only wanted to hold the baby, look in the blankets, coo over the thing. He sat in the room and nobody wanted to talk to him or play with him.

They all knew what to do with Emmy straight away. He kept making mistakes. He asked Mama if he could play with Emmy but as soon as he held the baby she screwed up her bright-red face and started crying.

'What have you done to her?' said Muriel. Emmy hated him, he could tell.

Everything he did was wrong. Mama was always with the baby and Papa was tired and seemed angry with him.

Now, two years later, he didn't know why the drive was taking so long – and Thompson wouldn't stop. He crossed his legs.

He tried thinking of something else, trees or a boat. But the need inside him built, fast and hard. 'Please,' he said. 'I need to go.'

Finally, Thompson slowed at a verge. But just as Arthur was climbing down, he felt it all let through and there was a terrible gushing. He couldn't stop it. He never could, once it started. The stuff soaked through his trousers, down the side, over the wheels.

'Sorry,' he said, hopelessly, to Thompson, feeling the sickly heat on his legs. He was standing on the verge, weak, a baby. The people passing could see as well, all of them laughing at the baby who wet himself!

'We're nearly there,' said Thompson, distractedly. 'I don't know. Maybe we could get some clothes from the trunk. But probably best to wait, have a bath when you get there.'

'Have a bath?' Arthur didn't understand. Why would he have a bath at wherever they were going? He had baths at *home*.

'Yes,' said Thompson. 'That's the answer.' He patted Arthur on the shoulder. 'Poor little chap. Don't worry. These things happen. Once we get there, they can get you nice and clean again.'

And then he knew. He knew he wasn't going to see a friend or go out for a picnic. So when Thompson turned up the great drive of a giant house, knocked on the door and a bent old man answered, Arthur knew what was coming next. The old man sent them to a waiting room and a tall man with spectacles arrived.

'Oh no,' he said, looking at Arthur in disgust. 'I shall have to call for Matron.'

A thin woman with a bun arrived and looked at Arthur in horror. 'Already. Mr Eccles, we are going to have trouble with this one.'

He knew he was stuck there, at the place called Winchester Hall, with Mr Eccles and Matron and a thin bed he wet every night so that all the other boys laughed at him, called him baby, threw pencils at him in the classroom, hit him in the playground. The teachers shrugged him off, said he shouldn't be so weak. Matron wrote his first letters and he traced over them. She said he was telling his mama how happy he was, because of course he was. He tried to put what he was really feeling into the words, sure she would see and understand. But she wrote back telling him how pleased she was that he had settled in and they would see him at Christmas. That was when he realised he had weeks and weeks of it yet.

And then when he did go home, he thought they'd welcome him like a hero. Instead, Mama was always thinking about Emmy and Papa was still cross with everyone. They talked of how *lucky* he was to have so much money spent on him, those expensive fees at Winchester Hall. Papa went on about how no one had cared so much about *his* education. But still, Arthur thought, he had endured it and now he would get his reward. Then after Christmas, he saw that the maids were packing up his trunk. In January, when they sent him back again, he cried for the first nights. But after a while he decided – if his family hated him enough to send him here, then he would hate them back. He would find a way.

If they hated him when he was good, kind, gentle to Emmy – well, now he would give them real reason. If they had no love for him, who cared? He didn't. Well, he couldn't lie to himself, he did care, but he would try not to, and if he kept pretending, it would become the truth.

Later, when he was at Harrow, he told himself that they'd set him free. The other boys were always trying to please, worrying about how their families would receive their reports. Not him. He didn't worry about what they thought. He'd just narrowly avoided being expelled at school – escaped only thanks to the three large payments from Rudolf to the new arts building – then he failed his entrance exams for Cambridge (or did not even try, as the headmaster put it). He laughed at his family. He didn't need them. They *owed* him – money, experiences, position.

He took a job in the office of Mr Christopher, Rudolf's supplier. He looked down on the other men there, the greyest things in the world. He resented Rudolf for forcing him to work, it was unfair. Other fathers wouldn't have done it. He arrived late, left early and, when that didn't work, kept turning up so drunk he could barely see. Still, Mr Christopher was so indulgent that even that didn't get the response that he wanted. He had to grasp one of the secretaries and drag her into the back room for a kiss before Mr Christopher declared that wasn't the sort of behaviour he'd ever thought he'd see in a family firm – and Arthur was free. Rudolf had stormed up to town and shouted at him in some collection of German syllables. *Just speak English, why can't you?* Arthur had said, laughing. That had made Rudolf even angrier. But who cared? Rudolf had paid the rent in advance so Arthur had the flat in Berkeley Square for another six months. He was going to enjoy it. So he did. He borrowed money and every night he found a party to go to – easy enough if you were a rich, handsome young man. He went to balls, dinners, dances, pleased pretty girls, nodded at mamas – smiling inside, because he was never getting married until he was at least forty.

After a few months, the parties grew not stale, but a little the same. Similar music, dress, decoration – and always the same people. It became like school, seeing the same chaps day in and day out. And no matter how much you drank, it still didn't help to make anything seem different. He was sitting on a bench one night, watching pretty, virtuous girls dance with upstanding men, feeling as if he'd rather be anywhere else – and Ernest Wyerling came to sit by him.

'You look like I feel,' Arthur said.

'It's all so dull.'

'Life is dull.'

'Why don't you come and make money with me?'

'Are you making money? How?'

'Well, that, I will have to tell you.'

An hour later, they were in *such* a place, boxes of tea and coffee smuggled in without paying duty. It was a warehouse in the East End. They could box up the imports, sell them on.

The idea was flawless. Arthur emptied his accounts, borrowed more from Rudolf. Wyerling busied himself putting it all into the business. One night he took Arthur to an opium parlour in East London, where all the girls looked like they were for sale.

Wyerling said they needed to store the stuff at Arthur's. And he needed more money. Arthur borrowed yet more from Rudolf, saying he was looking at properties. Wyerling wrote to him, saying they'd do well, really they would, just wait a little longer. Arthur began to ask him about the money, but Wyerling said to just wait a little longer, 'Then we will have success!'

When Wyerling stopped replying, Arthur went to his rooms and his landlady said he'd gone. Arthur was left with piles of boxes. Perhaps, he thought, all the buyers that Wyerling had mentioned would contact him.

That's how Rudolf found him, sitting on one of the boxes of hopeless tea.

'So this is what you've been doing with all the money?' He'd pushed his way in, along with the solicitor, Mr Pemberton. They were pulling open the boxes. Arthur watched them, feeling again like the tiny child his father had always ignored. He'd been about to do something useful. He'd been about to make his family *money*.

'That's it,' said Rudolf, sitting up, his hands full of tea. 'I've done everything for you. And still you throw it in our faces. This is a crime, you know.'

You've done nothing, he wanted to say. *Not a thing.*

'I'm sending you abroad before you cause more trouble. You can cool your heels there.'

Three days later he was on the boat to Paris. And in the horrible small room Rudolf had reserved for him, he became afraid of the noises. He knew nobody. The city banged and squealed around him. He was in the cart again, going to Winchester Hall, his legs hot and wet with urine.

He slept late next day and went out for a walk in the afternoon. *This is your new life*, he said to himself. *You must enjoy it.*

He was alone.

That night, he walked out again. He took the bridge over the river, past Notre-Dame. Everyone was in groups; giggling families, a couple with their arms around each other, a group of German schoolgirls deep in conversation. They all had each other. What was wrong with him? Why could no one love *him*?

'*Psst*,' came a voice. '*Vous cherchez une amie?*'

He looked around, could see no one.

'*Psst!*' came the voice.

He moved closer to the wall of a house. Was the noise coming from there?

'*Une amie?*'

He moved closer, saw the shine of two bright eyes, a white face. A girl stepped out, small, dark-haired, wearing a thick coat.

'Monsieur?'

'*Oui*,' he ventured, wishing for the first time that he'd paid more attention in French. '*Une amie.*'

'You look for friend?'

He nodded. She put her arm in his. '*Avec moi?*' she said. '*Suivez-moi.*'

He did. He followed her and he talked to her. She was his friend. She smiled, said *oui* here and there, so he supposed she understood. Maybe she didn't. But he couldn't stop. He talked and talked. He told her about his family and his father and how he tried to make them proud but he couldn't. How his mother didn't love him, had always preferred his sister. 'Why did they love me at all?' he said. 'Because they did. Before Emmy came along.' They had loved him. Verena had held him close, rocked him, told him stories. He might have said that parents could only love one child at a time – but Michael and Celia had come along and his parents seemed to love them alright.

'There is always one in a *famille*,' said the girl. 'One that everyone blames for everything that goes – how do I say – *mal?*'

'Bad.'

'Everything that goes bad. It is the fault of one. That was you.'

'That was me.'

'It makes everyone else good. If you are the bad one. All families have to have the bad egg.'

'Are things that simple?'

'Yes, sir.'

Of course they were. There had to be one bad egg.

'*Suivez-moi,*' she said, holding her hand out next to a dark-looking door. '*C'est bien.*'

Looking back, he pinpointed this as the moment he felt free. He was not just away from it all, with the girl, but he realised that she'd given him the truth about his family, made him see how it wasn't his fault, there was nothing he could have done to change it. He never forgot the lightness, the expansion he felt with her. In the months, years that followed in Paris, and then back in England, he kept it at the forefront of his mind. Sometimes he would be doing something and he would say to himself – what would the girl from Paris do? When he wanted to be free, what would she do? He would think of her, holding out her hand, that first night, and the liberty would enter his bloodstream – and so he would do the thing and then he was free.

THIRTY-FOUR

London, March 1925

Celia

Emmeline clutched Celia as they walked forward. 'Stop it!' hissed Celia. 'You're hurting me. It's only a prison.' You'd think, she wanted to say, that you'd be used to this. But this prison wasn't the same one as Mr Janus's, a place where a hundred men were locked up together for demonstrating for votes or miners' pensions or inflation or whatever else. They were going to see Arthur and he was being held on suspicion of murder.

'Come through, ladies,' said the officer. 'This way.'

They stepped into a grey corridor. The floor was so filthy you could almost feel it through your shoes. Celia pulled free of Emmeline's hand. She knew she was being cruel, but she couldn't stop herself. I'm afraid too, she wanted to say.

'This way, ladies. Keep up, please.' The officer led them through another corridor and then to a heavy blue door. 'Here's our man.' He tugged out a heavy set of keys, opened the door. 'Just a moment, please.' The door slammed after him.

'Don't lean on the wall,' Celia said. 'That's probably as dirty as the floor.'

Emmeline nodded, eyes wide.

Now that Arthur had been arrested, the newspapers had started up again with their coverage. The papers were covered with pictures of Arthur, discussions about the family – Arthur and his evil, Celia a 'war spinster', the rest of the family decadent, decayed. Some of the papers had just reprinted the old pieces they'd used years before.

The men were outside Stoneythorpe, taking pictures, Emmeline was being followed with the twins. *Murderous Germans!* the words shouted.

Celia clipped out the relevant articles, stuffed them into a box, hid it under her bed. She didn't see, couldn't see with it all in front of her, how anyone could come to a trial and think anything good of Arthur at all.

Every moment, the reporters were in the square under the flat. She looked out at midnight, two a.m., five, eight, and they were always there. Waiting.

Celia tried to sound braver than she felt. 'Listen, Emmy, we have to be calm with him. We can't help him otherwise.'

Emmeline turned her head. 'I always used to make him angry.'

'So did I. So did everyone. But we're helping him now. Anyway, I told you how different he was in Paris.'

Arthur had been intending to come back. But at the last minute, he changed his mind. And then the police came for him, found him in France by tracing his letters. They had new evidence, that's what the detective had told the family.

'What?' asked Verena. 'What new evidence?'

'We can't say. All that we can say is it's new.'

Celia had moved out of the rooms with the other girls on the night Emmeline had come to find her.

'Can we see him?' She asked Mr Janus as soon as they came out of the dance.

'In a week or two.'

She'd begged to go. She'd said that she should go alone, since she'd seen Arthur so recently. But Emmeline insisted on coming. Mr Janus didn't want to get too close to the policemen.

A tear was gleaming in Emmeline's eye. 'But what if we're wrong?' she said. She lowered her voice, but Celia saw her mouth make the sounds. 'He might *hang*.'

'He's innocent, Emmeline, no doubt about that. Let's hear what he says.'

'The papers say he did it.'

'Well, we know he didn't. They can't prove it either.' She was going to have to tell them about Louisa committing suicide. Even if Arthur said not to. He couldn't protect Louisa for ever. Not if the cost was years in prison – or even, as Emmeline said, his life. She tried to throw Paris from her mind. *Married. I wanted to keep her safe.* She spoke to the police detective, up high, somewhere in an office in Scotland Yard. *Don't discover the marriage.*

'Come on in, ladies,' said the officer. 'The prisoner will see you now.'

Emmeline hung back. Celia pushed forward, past the officer, into a large room, just as dirty as the rest. Arthur was sitting at one end, behind a yellowing table, wearing a grey prisoner's suit. Two other men were talking to visitors on other tables. Three officers were standing apart, watching over the scene.

'He's over there,' said the policeman, pointing unnecessarily. 'Very grateful for his family to visit him at all, I'd say.'

Celia smiled at him. She supposed he didn't read the papers that said Arthur's family were evil Germans, or perhaps he did and was so used to heated words that he forgot them the minute he'd read them.

'Thank you.' She and Emmeline walked towards Arthur. He looked up as they approached. Celia wanted to stop when she saw him. He looked nothing like he had in Paris, less than nine months ago. His handsome face was thin, lined and there were grey streaks in his thick brown hair.

'Hello, brother.'

Celia sat down on the chair opposite him, sweeping her skirt under herself. She didn't know if she was allowed to touch his arm. Emmeline sat down next to her and immediately put her head in her hands.

The officer to the side was watching them.

'He probably can't hear,' said Arthur, catching Celia's eye. 'You can say what you like.' His voice was heavy with misery. It was almost a shock to hear him. Looking at him, his face ashen, eyes sunken, she knew that he was innocent. Louisa had thrown herself over – and it was up to Celia to say so.

'How are you, brother?' She clenched her hand, over Louisa's ring, but he wasn't looking.

He shook his head. 'I suppose I need a barrister. Are the newspapers full of it? The guards here say so.'

'A little. They'll find something else soon.'

'I expect so. Are you looking for a lawyer? I'll need someone good. Expensive.'

'We'll find someone. Papa is looking.' That was a lie. Emmeline had said that Rudolf was too ill to speak. 'He fell into bed on the first day,' she said. 'Shock.'

Celia leant over the table, grasped his hand. 'In Paris, you told me Louisa meant to fall. I haven't told Emmeline. Or anyone. But I have to now.' She looked sideways at her sister. Emmeline was shocked but Celia thought – cruelly, she knew – they didn't have time for it.

He nodded. 'It's true. She wanted to die. But I've told them this now. I said I felt her fall. But they won't believe me. They say they have new evidence.'

'What new evidence can there be?' She dipped her voice. 'I'll tell Emmeline the thing you told me. But even if they have that on you, it's not enough.'

'What?' she heard Emmeline saying. Celia shook her off.

'You loved her. You wanted to look after her. That's the truth, like I said in Paris.'

'Well,' said Emmeline. 'We have to convince the court of that now.'

'We can just tell the truth,' Celia said. 'It's what happened.'

'They won't believe me. I've heard about some of the newspaper reports, sister. Evil Germans and all that. People have made up their minds. But there's something they don't know. I told you, sister. About the man Louisa thought was following her.'

'What's that?' Emmeline was whispering now.

'I told Celia in Paris. Louisa said that a man had been following her in Margate. She told me that she'd seen him outside her window, tracking her to the shops. She said she was sure he'd been in London too.' He bowed his head. 'I didn't really pay as much attention as I should have to it.'

Celia looked up at the officer, gazing into space. She lowered her voice. 'I think he was the same person who sent Louisa all those horrible things in London, the dead fish. Don't you?'

'Who did she tell about this?' said Emmeline. 'Apart from you.'

'I don't know. Maybe no one. She didn't have many friends.'

'Surely, she must have told someone,' said Emmeline. 'Your hotel owner. Someone. If I thought there was a man following me, I'd *ask* people.'

He cocked his head slightly and half smiled. Then, for the first time, he almost looked handsome again. 'You and Louisa are quite different.'

'Still, though.'

'But why would someone be so cruel to her?' said Celia. 'Did she have any ideas?'

Arthur splayed his fingers on the table. The nails on his two middle fingers were bitten down, the cuticles almost bleeding. 'When we had to leave the Merlings', she said she was in danger, but I didn't really believe it. I thought she was overreacting. I don't know. Louisa was very rich. People were envious of her. Or perhaps it was some ex-soldier who read about her in the newspaper and thought she was an example of everything that was wrong with the world. Young, pretty, wealthy.'

'So you think this strange man had some effect on her?' asked Celia.

'He followed us to Margate. I saw someone who looked a little odd, hanging around. I'm sure – I feel sure – that he was there at the cliffs. Maybe he made her jump. There was something about him.'

'How awful,' whispered Emmeline.

'Why didn't you tell me this in Paris?' asked Celia. 'You said you thought it might be that she killed herself. You didn't say it might be this man too.'

'I didn't want to talk much about it. But like we said, the cat dying, this man, she wasn't in her right mind. She was always talking about her mother, how she wanted to join her.'

'But this is terrible,' said Emmeline. 'I can't think.'

Arthur put his head in his hands. 'I wish I'd listened to her properly. I wish I'd done something.'

Celia leant forwards. 'We have to tell them,' she said. 'We have to tell them and we have to find him. We must.' She looked quickly at the other police officer, still gazing into space. 'Would anyone else have seen this man?'

Arthur shook his head. 'I don't think so. There was an older pair there, walking, some sellers of ice cream, a few families. But they were probably too far away to see anything.'

'That was the older pair that called the police?' Celia had read about them. They had seen the fall. The woman had fainted and the man had been so terrified that he'd left her to run into the town and call for help.

'Yes, that's them. They didn't see anything. I doubt they even looked our way until Louisa screamed.'

Louisa crying out, falling on to the rocks. How much would you have seen? Celia wondered. What did you know? She'd heard that people confronted by a horse rearing saw everything slow down. Not her. It went faster, so fast that she couldn't see a thing. Hopefully, it had been the same for Louisa. Black, cold shame flung itself across Celia's mind. Louisa had arrived at Stoneythorpe lonely, orphaned. She had wanted friendship. Celia had been too selfish, too wrapped up in herself. She had been cruel, wrong. And what was the point of vowing to change? The damage had been done.

'If only you'd never taken her away, brother,' she said.

Arthur shrugged. 'She was lonely at Stoneythorpe.'

Celia dropped her eyes in shame.

Emmeline sighed. 'I wish Samuel was here. He would know exactly what to do. Maybe they'll let him bring us next time.'

'Can you tell us what this man looked like?' asked Celia. 'You said you thought he might be a former soldier.'

'I can't really. I think he changed his appearance sometimes, wore different things. I think he was smallish, short hair, probably forty or so. Nothing special. I don't know.'

'After Louisa fell, what did he do? Did he just run away?'

He nodded.

'Well, then we have to find him.'

Emmeline roused herself. 'And he was the same one who frightened her in London?'

Arthur shrugged. 'Probably. He wanted to frighten her, that's for sure.'

Celia shook her head. 'But why? I don't understand why.'

Emmeline sighed. 'But you know, Celia, even if we do find him, so what? He didn't push her off. He just frightened her.'

'It shows so much about her state of *mind*, don't you see? That she threw herself off. This man was after her. He killed her cat. Then he turns up in Margate. It's important. She thought there was no escape.'

She looked up and saw the guard moving forward. He was looking at them, waving his hand.

She seized the chance. 'Brother,' she hissed. 'Do the police know you're married?' She heard Emmeline gasp.

He nodded. 'They found the certificate.'

She stared at him. 'Is *that* the new evidence?'

He shook his head. 'I asked that. They said not.'

The man was coming closer.

'I think our time's up,' Celia said, straightening up, talking loudly now.

He held her hand. 'Will you come back tomorrow?'

'I can't,' said Emmeline. 'I'll be with the twins. Samuel has them today. Celia could.'

'I don't think we're allowed to come here every day.' The guard was nearing them. 'But listen, Arthur, is there anything else you can tell us? Anything at all. I will speak to the solicitor.'

Arthur shook his head. 'Just find him,' he whispered. 'I need us to find him. And—'

'What?'

'I need money. A lot of it. I need a defence. But I've also run up a lot of debts.'

'How much?'

'Probably three thousand pounds.'

Celia heard the words, didn't quite understand. 'That's a lot,' said Emmeline. 'How did you manage that?'

Arthur shook his head. 'It just happened.'

'But what about Louisa's money?' Celia burst in.

'I can't have any of her accounts. Her solicitors asked for that. The estate wants it back, they say, whatever happens. Even though Matthew is dead.'

'What do you mean, whatever happens?' said Emmeline.

'If they find me guilty or not. Tell Papa I need money. A good solicitor. One from London. I need the best.'

'I'll tell him. I'll go and see them.' Celia felt ashamed for even thinking about Louisa's money.

'*Now* you agree to visit our parents,' said Emmeline. Celia ignored her.

The guard was there. Celia nodded to him. 'We're going now.'

'You have to find him.' Arthur said.

'Visit's up, ladies,' said the guard. 'Time to go.'

Celia picked up her skirt. Then she turned back to Arthur. 'This man. Can you remember when she started to say he was following her?'

Arthur pondered. 'It had to be London. But I don't know when. Perhaps not long after we arrived.'

'Off we go, please, ladies.'

Celia strode ahead. They hurried to the door, where the guard let them out. Another was waiting for them on the other side. Celia expected to see the same man who had taken them there, jumped a little when it was not him.

'Afternoon, ladies,' he said. 'Find what you were looking for?'

'We found our brother, yes,' said Emmeline, haughtily. 'Now we wish to leave. I need to get back to my children.'

As soon as they were out, in a cab, finally safe, Emmeline

turned, gripped Celia's hand. 'What are we going to do?' she said, eyes wet. 'What on earth are we going to do?'

'We'll find him,' said Celia. 'We'll find that man. The solicitor will be able to help us.' She clutched her sister's arm. 'Don't worry, Emmy. We'll get him out.'

They rolled on towards Bloomsbury. Celia knew she should have been thinking about future plans, decisions, the solicitor. Or the man. But her thoughts were swooping, tangling. She could think of nothing but Louisa's funeral, nearly five years ago. The freezing church, the tiny grave, Celia's ridiculous gift of orange blossoms propped over the coffin. There was only Celia, Emmeline, Mr Janus, Verena and an old governess of Louisa's, Miss Griffin. Rudolf was too ill. Lily and Albert clung to Emmeline, shy and not understanding. The whole thing looked, Celia thought, like a funeral for an old person, all their friends dead. The vicar threw soil over the coffin and Verena wept. Celia wanted to throw herself on the coffin, tell Louisa to wake up, to stop the game. She thought of Louisa at Michael's funeral, quiet in the parlour afterwards. She looked up, past the church, grief clawing at her heart.

THIRTY-FIVE

London, March 1925

Celia

'This is marginally interesting information, Miss de Witt,' said the detective in charge of the investigation. 'But I hardly see it changing the case that we have in front of us. Your brother tells you another man was following him and Mrs de Witt. But we have no evidence, no sightings. We have nothing but Mr de Witt's word.'

Inspector Haines was small and rather round, bald-headed, a turned-up mouth. If you saw him on the train, you might think he was an ordinary sort of shopman. Perhaps, Celia thought, that was his strength, people underestimated him. It shocked her to hear Louisa called Mrs de Witt. She tried not to start at it.

It was three days after Celia had seen Arthur in prison. She was at her interview with the inspector, trying to explain the truth. He'd reluctantly agreed to see her. Now they were talking, but he wasn't taking any notes.

She thought she wasn't making sense, she was too tired. On the previous day, she and Emmeline had gone down to Stoneythorpe to report back to Rudolf and Verena. Celia hadn't been able to believe the house. It was even more dilapidated than it ever had been. She asked Rudolf to see the books – and all he could show her was a muddle of figures. 'We don't have anything,' she said.

She had had to push Rudolf into mortgaging the land. Verena had refused to sign on his behalf and he had protested. Celia only persuaded him after screaming that he had to, that otherwise Arthur would die, conjuring terrible scenarios of him hanging in a prison cell. Verena shrieked and Rudolf wept but Celia kept going with cruel words, until finally Rudolf relented and signed the papers to agree. She hated herself for it, felt sickened by not only how she had done it, but the enthusiasm, the relish that she had felt. At one point, it had not been about Arthur, but about her own rhetoric. She felt like an actor might when a speech was going particularly well. She'd felt drunk on herself, thrown more words at her ill and elderly parents. She tried to block the memory from her mind, but it kept bubbling up again, like a spring of water when you cleared back the leaves: the cruel beat of her own words.

'Louisa saw him too. He was following her too.' She couldn't say Mrs de Witt. It wouldn't come out straight.

Inspector Haines looked down at his notes. 'As you say. But we only have your brother's word for that too, do we not?'

'Why would he lie? Look, as I said, Louisa jumped. She was unhappy, distressed. He didn't want to say anything. He wanted to save her reputation and protect the family.'

'And yet the witnesses we have – the married couple – they are quite adamant they saw him push Mrs de Witt off the cliff.'

She stared at him. 'Who?'

'That is right, Miss de Witt. More people have come forward. They tell us that they saw Mr de Witt push his wife.'

She gazed at him, his smooth face, dark eyes like currants in a gingerbread man. 'That's your new evidence?'

'If I may speak frankly, miss. And between us?'

'Of course.'

'The whole thing seemed suspicious from the start. But we could never prove anything. Nobody seemed to see anything. But then we found that he had been married to Miss Deerhurst – Mrs de Witt, I should say. Yet he told the officers on the scene that he was not married. Why didn't he come forward sooner to say they were married? And why did he run away?'

'He thought you'd suspect him if you knew that.'

The inspector tapped his desk with his pen. 'He should have been honest in the first place.'

'Please don't dismiss this. I honestly think it's important.'

He stood up. 'Let us decide what is important, Miss de Witt. I assure you, we have our best men on this.' It was her cue to leave.

As she walked out into the hard winter sun, Celia felt her heart weighing down in her chest. The police weren't interested in the man who had followed Louisa, Arthur didn't know anything about him. And who else could find him? An odd question struck her heart – did he even exist? Perhaps Louisa had thought she saw him – and then Arthur had believed her, become obsessed by it as a way to explain what had happened. After all, he'd pretty much discounted him in Paris. Now, he thought he was true. She shook her head. Arthur must be right. She walked past a newsboy shouting about Arthur and Louisa, hurried on.

Next day, she and Emmeline went to see the barrister, a Mr Bird, with chambers in Doughty Street. Mr Pemberton had been quick in giving the recommendation. Mr Bird's office was even grander than Mr Pemberton's, decorated in paintings of country landscapes that almost looked as if they should be in the National Gallery.

Mr Bird was tall and thin, with small eyeglasses and a tiny moustache. He looked the perfectionist type, Celia thought, the sort of man to sit up all night anxiously looking at papers. That could only benefit them. 'I can't see, Miss de Witt and Mrs Janus, that there is much of a case here at all,' he said. 'I've reviewed all the papers and it is rather flimsy. You really don't need to worry about your brother. The only evidence that he even pushed Mrs de Witt comes from this couple and there is already disagreement in the statements as to how near they were to the cliffs. Certainly, they were not right beside Arthur. It is not enough. Juries are cautious when they confront the – er...'

Celia cleared her throat. 'Hanging of a man, you mean, Mr Bird.'

'Quite so.'

'But what are we going to say?' said Emmeline.

'I would advise us to say it was a tragic accident. That Mr and Mrs de Witt were just admiring the sea, a little too closely, but they were young, enjoying themselves. And Mrs de Witt lost her footing, Mr de Witt only narrowly avoiding a fatal end too. What the couple saw – if they saw anything at all - was Arthur attempting to save his wife, not a scuffle to push her over. He was trying to hold her, not push her. You can see how they would look the same from afar.'

'That sounds sensible to me,' said Emmeline, adjusting her hat.

'It's not the truth, though,' said Celia. 'She jumped off. And probably because she was afraid of that man.'

'We can't prove that though. You know this. It could all sound like pie in the sky. And we need to counter this evidence that says they saw him push her. She fell and he was trying to catch her.'

'No one will believe that. The newspapers didn't – and everyone's read them.'

'We will suggest that the newspapers were unfair because of the German connection. And that will not stand up in a proper court of law.'

'Well, they *were* unfair because of the German connection.'

Celia tore her gaze from the picture of a hay barn. 'I think we should tell the truth. Arthur said someone was following Louisa – a man. At least from when they were in London, and into Margate as well. He said the man did something to frighten her, make Louisa fall. Surely if we could find that man, we have the answer.'

'As I said, Miss Witt, I think this is all rather tenuous. There is no evidence about this man, we have no sightings of him.'

'But surely someone else on the cliffs saw him. Is there any way we could try to find him?'

Mr Bird put his fingers into a steeple. 'I don't say that we couldn't try. It would add to the cost, of course. But it is my strong belief that the approach of saying it was a tragic accident is the best. It is much simpler, easier for the jury to grasp.'

'I agree,' said Emmeline. 'Let's not go on another wild goose chase.'

'I think we should try and find this man,' said Celia. 'I really do. How long to the trial, would you say, Mr Bird?'

'That is impossible to say for sure, Miss de Witt. I would suggest at least a year. Since the war, the courts have moved slower than ever.'

Emmeline sat forward. 'A year? Our brother will be in prison for a year?'

'If you are fortunate, Mrs Janus. It might be longer. I am afraid that what are deemed big cases – liable to attract attention and scrutiny, as this one surely will – tend to take even longer. The courts want to make entirely sure the papers are quite correct.'

'He will be stuck in that place for a year,' said Celia, dully.

'A year is nothing in the longer run, Miss Witt. He will be given his freedom and he will recover. There are some positive benefits of the period of time. We can assemble all our evidence with due care. Perhaps we can investigate the question of this mysterious man.'

'Thank you, Mr Bird.'

'What if... we don't have quite enough money?' asked Celia.

'I know the sum we have, Miss Witt. Mr Pemberton told me all about it. I can guarantee that our services will remain quite within it. Do not worry on that account.'

'Thank you.'

'Now, ladies. I must ask you one thing. The period before the trial is of critical importance. As you know, there has been much attention drawn to your family in the newspapers. We must ensure that there is no more. I feel quite at odds telling this to two such respectable ladies. But the family must be entirely, entirely untouched by any sort of – er – scandal. Nothing.'

'Of course,' said Celia quickly.

'Mrs Janus?'

Emmeline nodded. 'Yes, sir.'

'There must be no mention of any of you in the newspapers. I insist. These things are critical. As we all know, your brother's life is in the balance. Everything counts. The – er – heritage weighs against you. So you need to do everything you can to balance it.'

Celia nodded, trying to push the heated words of the newspapers from her mind.

'I hesitate to speak of such delicate matters. Just as negative acts can undermine, so positive acts can only help. It is always to a lady's advantage if she – well – expands her family.' He steepled his fingers again. 'Such things are of course up to the individuals. But if the bounteous act were to occur in the next year or so, it would indubitably add to your sympathy.'

'Goodness,' said Celia. She could sense that Emmeline was blushing beside her.

'As I say, these are delicate matters and ones that I indeed doubted to bring up. But I just feel that if it were to occur, Mrs Janus, do not feel that such joyous news should be hidden. On the contrary. The world should know.'

Celia couldn't look at him.

'I apologise, ladies. I spoke out of turn. Forget that I said such things. What is most important is to ensure that there is no untoward attention brought to your family. You really must pay very great care.' He brought his hands down on the dark leather of his desk, smiled up at them, showing his teeth.

'He meant Mr Janus,' Celia said to Emmeline, once they were safely in the throngs heading out of Bloomsbury.

'Not necessarily. Can't you get married or something? Find an aristocrat?'

'I'm not listening to that. You need to tell Samuel. He can't be arrested. Not for the next year or so. Really, he can't.' They stumbled around two nursemaids pushing prams. 'Tell him he can do whatever he wants after Arthur is free. But he needs to stop.'

'I can't say that to him. The revolution is important, that's what he says. Anyway, what does it matter what he does? Mr Bird meant our family. That means us, the de Witts.'

'No, it means all of us. You have to tell him, Emmy, please.'

'He can't go back on his beliefs, though. He can't just *stop*.'

'I'll tell him.'

'He'll be angry with you. And he won't listen.'

'I don't care,' said Celia, striding ahead. 'I'll tell him. I will. If you're too afraid.'

But, as it happened, Celia was afraid as well. Mr Janus refused to listen, shouted at her, told her she was an idiot, didn't understand. He shouted so much that the twins woke up screaming and the people above and below came to bang on the door. He swung his fist at the door. Celia found herself apologising, begging him not to, saying she didn't mean it. He marched to the bedroom, slammed the door. She stayed on her bed in the sitting room, staring into the darkness, eyes wide with anger and fear.

PART SIX

THIRTY-SIX

London, February 1926

Celia

Arthur's trial was set for February. On the third of the month, Celia and Emmeline put on their best coats and hats and took a taxi to the Old Bailey. They passed queues of people on the street. 'They've all come for us,' said Emmeline. 'Haven't they?'

'Maybe another trial,' Celia lied.

The time had dragged by so slowly. Celia had remained living with Emmeline. She'd visited Arthur every month, the only visits they were allowed. They weren't supposed to tell the twins, but they'd picked up on it anyway. Lily listened to everything, Celia could see, and Albert was always asking what was happening with Uncle Arthur. Celia had been avoiding her parents – for every time she saw them, they said they were bowed down by the mortgage, could never pay it. *What choice did we have?* she said angrily to herself. *It was the only way.*

The newspapers had been worse than ever, pages and pages on Arthur and the evil of the family. When the police gave them the information about the marriage, they splashed it all over their pages. Most of it scandalous, but in ones with a reputation, she read lengthy articles about cousin marriage – once the ballast of the Victorians, now a source of decay.

Celia told herself to get used to it, that they'd find another new target, the minute the trial was over. Then they found pages of stuff about Louisa in London, speaking to all the people she went to parties with. They said she'd made an exhibition of herself over some man, annoyed all the other women.

'Look!' Celia said to Emmeline. 'Maybe that's why she was followed. Someone was angry or jealous of her.'

Emmeline shook her head. 'Why don't you stop this, Celia? Even Mr Bird says there's no point in it.'

With the trial, she'd had letters. Tom, Waterton and two other girls from her ambulance days, two from Jonathan in New York (the news had reached America, then). They all said the same thing: you must be strong. Don't listen to what others say. We're thinking of you. She knew how kind it was of them to write when others were shunning them. But she couldn't reply, just couldn't find the words to say anything to any of them. Her life was on hold – all of their lives were on hold – until after the trial, when they could all be free again.

Emmeline had given birth to a little boy, Euan.

'I'm not doing it because Mr Bird *said* so,' she said crossly, when Celia had asked about her expanding stomach a few months after their meeting with the solicitor. 'It just happened. We were always planning it. Nothing to do with what he said.'

Celia had worried that he would be a child tinged with sadness, difficult and angry, since he was being born into a house in which someone was always crying, or arguing. But he was a bonny child, content to sit and watch, reaching for light in the sky, learning to smile.

Euan's birth – Celia was ashamed to admit it – had been of help. Mr Bird had been right. There had been recent articles about Arthur's 'respectable family', words about Emmeline's children and even some notes about Celia's ambulance days. When she wheeled Euan out in the pram, she blushed with guilt at how a child of such innocence could have become part of a thing so dreadful.

Mr Janus was looking after all three of the children that day – his mother had agreed to come to help, which surprised Celia. She'd barely even remembered that Mr Janus had a mother, since she never visited – and she hadn't been at the wedding. 'We don't get on,' he said darkly. 'But she said she's going to stay until the end of the trial. Three is too much for me!' Anyway, he had hardly been in this last year, absent even more than ever. He said that there was a big revolution coming – so, he said, Celia and Emmeline could stop telling him to stay at home. As important as the trial was, this was more so. If they let the ruling classes get away with it, everyone would be dead and destitute in a year. He locked up papers in the cupboard, hurried out late at night. Celia held Euan tight trying not to think where he might be.

Rudolf and Verena were not coming. Verena said the trial would be too much for them. Celia had supposed they were right. Her father was old now, shook, looked confused. He might shout something out, get too upset. Though now, just the two of them, huddled together, she wished that their parents were there.

The court was a dusty cavern of wood, more crammed than she could possibly imagine. They were ushered into the area reserved for families. The officer had said that, because it was only them, the court would have to open it up to others. Not members of the public, of course, he said. Court officials.

'With all the public interest, we can't have any empty seats,' he said. 'People won't like it.'

There were throngs of people above them, men, women, some who looked like children, dozens of hats and coats, pairs of gloves, newspapers, cardigans, shawls. Celia craned up. The women had packed up their handbags this morning, put in fresh tissues (because you're sure to cry), throat sweets to stop the cough, lipstick, even a pencil and paper, thinking they might want to take notes. The men had picked up their umbrellas, checked the money in their wallets and then all of them had come, on trains, autobuses, taxis, on a day when they could have been doing any number of things: earning money, caring for their children, walking in the park. Instead, they were crammed into the Old Bailey, craning for a glimpse of Arthur de Witt, predicting whether or not he would hang.

'Don't look at them. Don't let them see you know they're there,' Emmeline said. Celia gazed ahead at a clerk shuffling papers on a wooden bench. 'Nothing would please them more than to see us cry. So we won't.'

They stared ahead. Celia supposed somewhere there must be some of the more distant relations of Lord Deerhurst, perhaps even the Coventry ones, if they would deign to come into a public court. Her mind whirled around the new couple – the pair who had come forth and said that Arthur pushed Louisa. Were they in the queue? Celia had built him up, this main witness, the man who held Arthur's future in his hand. At night, unable to sleep, she had conjured him in her mind, a tall man, sharp and angry, well dressed, forceful. The type of man who would always say – no, I'm sure, it was *this* way. Who would always be certain, never discouraged, like the most determined type of teacher.

'Remember,' Celia hissed to Emmeline. 'We don't need to worry. Mr Bird said.' Over the last months, Mr Bird had been even more confident of a win. He'd told them that he'd barely have to do a thing – the case would simply win itself. 'And, after all, we have the most splendid news of all,' he said.

Celia squeezed Emmeline's hand. Her sister was still feeding the baby. She'd strapped down her bosoms that morning, filled her clothes with tissues, said she was going to have to squeeze the stuff out in the WC at break time. 'I can't simply keep my coat on,' she said. 'That won't look dignified.'

'I'm sure people will understand,' said Celia.

'You heard what Mr Bird said. Every appearance matters.'

'I suppose so, sister.'

The hubbub of the room had reached something of a crescendo. Celia looked down and saw that Mr Bird and his clerk were in place. Across from them was a thin-looking man in a suit, the prosecution, she supposed. He was rather colourless, pale hair, pale eyes, spindly-looking hands. Her heart rose again. Someone of such an unprepossessing appearance couldn't possibly win against Mr Bird.

Then there was a ripple of noise in the room. Arthur had come through the door, escorted by a police officer. He was looking resolutely at his hands. The police officer beside him was as upright as the Tower of Westminster. Every month Celia had seen him, Arthur had looked worse. Now, he looked slightly better, more spirited. It was the waiting, Celia supposed. That had been the worst.

'Poor Arthur,' murmured Emmeline.

'He'll be fine.' Mr Bird had lined up a good set of witnesses – character testimonials from the minister at Stoneythorpe, a few schoolmasters, some business partners of de Witt Meats. The only problem, Mr Bird had said, was that Arthur hadn't actually *fought* in the war. But they were going to get round that by saying he'd been in Paris and hadn't been allowed to leave – which Celia supposed was more or less true.

The clerk banged his hammer on the wood. In filed the jury, ten men, two women, one short in a grey suit and the other tall in brown, schoolmistress types.

'They shouldn't have women!' hissed Emmeline.

'Stop that!' Celia squeezed her hand. She'd read an article about how women were more sympathetic.

The clerk banged his hammer again. In came the judge looking almost like a child's picture of one, red gown, large wig, gold chains. Celia could hardly see his face. He seated himself on his chair, rather like a king on a throne.

'Mr Cedric. If you could begin?'

The colourless man stepped forward. People above them hushed. Celia thought they'd surely be disappointed, for he was hardly going to put on much of a show. He started droning in a dull-sounding voice about the events of that terrible afternoon, all the evidence everyone had read about before. Celia clasped Emmeline's hand. Arthur continued to stand, head bowed. The policeman beside him was scratching his wrist. Celia watched the jury. Both women were taking notes more intently than the men.

She looked at her hand, found it was shaking. She pushed it into her sleeve. *Why are you doing that?* she wanted to say. *You're not the one being judged.*

There was a ripple of movement and gasps as the first witness came in. She was a stolid-looking woman of about fifty or so, dressed in dark blue. She gazed around the room, uncertain. She stated her name for the clerk and said she was Mrs Betts, housekeeper of the White Cliffs Hotel. Mr Cedric rose to interview her. In response to his questions, she said that it was a medium-sized hotel, thirty bedrooms, respectable. Mr and Mrs de Witt had taken the second most expensive room – at the front with a balcony and a sea view. She said they were very respectable, quiet. Mr de Witt sometimes walked alone, Mrs de Witt stayed in the hotel alone. She didn't talk much.

'Would you say that Mr de Witt was kind to his wife?' said Mr Cedric.

'I wouldn't have any reason to think otherwise. They seemed happy enough. I didn't see much of them.'

'But going out alone and leaving her – that was hardly *very* kind, was it?'

'Plenty of couples seem to work that way and rather like it,' she said. 'I don't make it my business to enquire.'

On and on they went, Mr Cedric pushing her to say that Arthur was cruel, she refusing to say. He gave her up to Mr Bird, who asked her another set of questions. She remembered that Arthur had even bought Louisa a large bunch of flowers.

'Well, that was hardly the act of a cruel husband, was it, Mrs Betts?'

'No, sir. I wouldn't have said he was cruel, sir. Not at all. Seemed fonder of her than most husbands.' He questioned her further and she said she'd seen him squeeze her arm on many occasions, guide her to the breakfast room. 'They seemed fond enough.'

'So he bought flowers, held her arm, helped her to her seat.'

'Yes, sir.'

'He escorted her out, waited for her, spoke gently to her.'

'Yes, sir.'

'Not the act of someone wishing to murder his wife.'

'Not at all, sir.'

'Thank you, Mrs Betts. No further questions.'

The morning progressed. Mrs Betts was followed by three maids from the hotel who said variously that they'd thought Arthur a respectable husband, kinder than most, hadn't seen anything amiss, thought him rather a pleasant, good-looking fellow and her a happy wife. The court then adjourned for lunch. Celia and Emmeline sat on the family bench, next to a pack of journalists scribbling. 'They should be somewhere else,' said Celia, miserably. 'We can't talk here.'

'Nothing to talk about,' said Emmeline. 'You were right in everything you said before.' She squeezed her sister's hand. 'No need to worry! Mr Bird is excellent.'

They hadn't thought to bring lunch. One of the reporters was eating a ham sandwich and Celia suddenly felt dreadfully hungry. *Well, you will have to wait!* she told herself. 'We'll bring food tomorrow, Emmy.'

'We can't eat it *here*. Not with all these people around.'

'Oh, don't be so silly. You're feeding a baby. You should eat. I'll ask that man if you can have a sandwich.'

'You'll do no such thing!' Emmeline slapped down her hand. 'If you do, it will be a story in the papers by tomorrow. The minute we get out of here, we'll eat.'

'We have to at least bring something to drink tomorrow.'

Emmeline inclined her head. 'That we can do. Now, I'm going to the bathroom. You'll have to wait.'

Half an hour later, they filed back into the court room. It felt even stuffier than before. Celia was wedged in next to a fat man, who didn't look much like a court official to her. She stared straight ahead.

It was Arthur's turn to take the stand. Emmeline clutched her hand as Celia looked forward. He was dressed in his pale suit, hands folded. Mr Cedric stepped forward first, asked Arthur his name and home address. Arthur spoke in a low voice, looking outward. The entire court breathed in, gazing at him.

Mr Cedric began asking him about Louisa.

'I loved her,' he said. 'I loved her from the first moment I saw her. Well, no, not the first moment, because that was probably when she was three. But when she came to live at our home after the death of her mother in 1919. Then I fell in love. I didn't realise it until later, but that was the moment.'

'So in love that you had to kidnap her.'

'She wanted to go to London.'

'But you forced her.'

'No. It was her idea.'

On and on they talked, Arthur saying over and over that he loved her, that he longed to marry her, that her death had plunged him into despair.

'But if you were so in love with her, why did you keep your wedding secret? Surely your family would have desired to come.'

He nodded. 'They would. But we thought we would have a celebration later. Louisa wanted it to be quiet.'

'Was it not that the terms of her family's will demanded that she did not marry under the age of twenty-one? And your father was in charge of ensuring that didn't happen.'

Arthur nodded.

'And yet she then took out all the money that she could from her accounts? It is my understanding that she was to have an allowance from her interest. And yet somehow she managed to access the actual capital – and removed a full quarter of it. How did she do this?'

He shook his head. 'I didn't know she did that. I didn't know she could get at her money.'

Mr Cedric raised an eyebrow. 'And how did you travel, stay in fine hotels, holiday in Margate?'

'My money. My parents had given me money. We lived off that.'

'And yet, Mrs de Witt's accounts are much depleted.'

'Not by me. She must have taken it out. I don't know why. She liked nice dresses and jewellery. I told her I would buy them for her, but sometimes she had clothes I didn't recognise. It could have been that, I suppose.'

Celia gripped Emmeline's hand. 'That man who was following Louisa,' she whispered. 'What if he was blackmailing her?'

Emmeline nodded.

Mr Cedric paced around the box. 'What a mystery. Mrs de Witt and her missing money. So, sir. You fell in love with this lady. Married her in secret. Then she died. And now, by the terms of her will, I believe, you would have been entitled to her share of the Deerhurst estate on the date when she would have reached the age of twenty-one – if it were not for these circumstances.' He turned to the jury. 'An odd provision, I think you will agree, but that is the provision. Possibly the Deerhursts thought it the way to dissuade fortune hunters. It seems to me that it would be the best way to encourage them!'

He got the laugh. Men in the gallery snorted.

Arthur lifted his head. 'I loved Louisa. And I didn't just lose her when she died.'

'What do you mean, sir?' probed Mr Cedric.

'A week before her death, she told me she was carrying our child.'

There was a terrible intake of breath from the gallery. Celia gripped Emmeline's hand. Mr Cedric looked as surprised as she felt. He looked around, blankly. 'Carrying a child?'

'She told me she was. I was so pleased. She was so happy. But maybe she made a mistake. The doctors found – nothing.' He broke into tears. He put his hands on the witness box. A clerk passed him a handkerchief. The judge looked at Mr Bird.

'Questions, Mr Bird?'

Both barristers were deep in conversation with their clerks. The taller man was writing notes. Celia looked at Arthur, seated behind the box, head in his hands. *Why hadn't he told them?*

She couldn't stop herself. 'It must have been so early that she muddled the dates,' she whispered into Emmeline's ear.

'Or she lied.'

Celia stared at Emmeline, was about to answer.

'Look forward, sister. We'll talk later.'

Mr Bird stepped up, asked Arthur about Louisa. He talked about love and the idealism of the young.

'There may be many of us here who were so overwhelmed by love that they – with the exception of the Honourable Gentleman, of course – have thought of keeping such love affairs secret from their family and friends. A quite understandable impulse, especially when one is young. One thinks that love is so special that one wants to keep it secret. Quite understandable.'

He talked on. Everyone, Celia thought – the people in the gallery, the jury, even Mr Cedric – was only seeing Arthur weeping over the child that wasn't there.

The days rolled on. The judge called forth more witnesses. An ice-cream seller from near the cliffs said the pair had looked contented, a woman who sold roses said she'd seen Louisa lean her head on his shoulder. A guest at the hotel said the pair had seemed very happy and a woman who'd been staying at the hotel with her children said she'd struck up a conversation with Louisa in the grounds and Louisa had said that she and her husband were looking forward to having children.

Then, on the fourth day, when it was four and Celia could see even the reporters fighting not to yawn, the judge called for a Mr Werth. Celia watched as a small man shuffled to the witness box. He gave his name to Mr Cedric and answered a few inconsequential questions.

Mr Cedric walked calmly towards the box. 'So, Mr Werth. You were out walking by the cliffs on the afternoon of 14 August 1920.' That was *him*! Celia realised. He was the new evidence. The small man in a too large suit was the proof that Arthur had pushed Louisa.

'Yes, sir.' He looked up at the roof of the Old Bailey, somewhat cowed by its grandeur, perhaps. His accent was London. He was a clerk in a railway office, Mr Bird had said, an intelligent man. This wasn't the man she'd imagined, tall and angry, a furious teacher sort. Who would always be certain, never discouraged. She hadn't thought he would look like this, a slight man whose suit fell off his frame. She watched his eyes swivel around the court, taking in the crowds. He looked at Arthur, then dropped his head.

'Mr Werth, I presume that there were other couples also walking. Taking the air.'

'Yes, sir.'

'Did you notice anyone in particular?'

'Yes, sir. That gentleman over there, sir.' He gestured his head towards Arthur, looked away. *You could at least look at him in the eye,* Celia thought. If you're going to send him down, if *you're* the one who's going to hang him. She knew she was being unfair, that the man was only meaning to tell the truth. Still, he had mistaken what he had seen happen and now they were all in front of the court.

'The one in the defendant box? Mr de Witt?'

'That's him.'

'Are you quite sure, Mr Werth? You are entirely sure that the gentleman was him?'

'Yes, sir.'

'And why did you notice him, Mr Werth?'

'My wife and I noticed him in the first place because he was rather handsome. He seemed a better type of man than I'd normally seen around there. And his wife was such a good-looking woman. She seemed fond too, leaning on his arm a lot, looking into his face.'

'Love's young dream?'

'Not exactly. Her, maybe. She was very fond, as I say. Him not so much. My wife thought he looked bored.'

'Now, Mr Werth, we will speak to your wife later. We'd like to know what you think. Did *you* think he looked *bored*, as you put it?'

'I rather think I did. She'd speak and he didn't look interested. I remember thinking that if I had a wife quite that pretty, I would pay attention to what she said. Or at least her face while she said it.'

There was a ripple of laughter through the upper gallery. Mr Werth looked up, smiled. Celia's heart sank. He knew they liked him! He was playing to the gallery now. For those up there, the first lot of witnesses, praising Arthur and saying he didn't mistreat Louisa, had been terribly disappointing. Now they had what they really wanted: the man who showed him as a villain. They were settling back in their seats, opening up tins of cough sweets, getting ready for the show.

Mr Cedric began asking more questions about the day, Arthur's appearance, how Louisa had seemed. Mr Werth answered every one, smiling, even looking up to the gallery after one joke about Arthur's smart dress making him look a bit like a chap out of a music hall. Celia could feel the warmth of the room swelling towards him. Even one of the men on the jury let out a smile and then suppressed it.

'So, we see Mr de Witt on the cliff with Mrs de Witt,' said Mr Cedric. 'They were walking towards it, you say.'

'That's right. I didn't spend too long looking at them. I was with my wife, of course!' The court laughed again. 'But I did notice that they were walking closer to the edge. I said to my wife, as a joke, "The fancy man is going to jump in!" Then we looked away.'

'But you looked back.'

'We were still walking. And when I looked back I saw that they were so *very* close to the cliff. I told my wife to look. It reminded me, sir, of when I was a little boy, playing chicken, you know that game?'

'I do, Mr Werth. But I shall explain for the benefit of anyone who does not. Children dare each other to run close to the edge, run back, is that correct?'

'Yes, sir.'

'And so it seemed to you that Mr de Witt was playing chicken. With himself or Mrs de Witt. But they were not racing to the cliff, that is correct?'

Celia looked over at the jury. Everyone was scribbling notes. Now they were listening.

'Yes, sir. They weren't running. She was in front, he was holding her. They were edging, that's what they were doing. They were edging further towards the cliff. Getting closer.'

'And why do you think they were doing that, Mr Werth?'

'I really can't say, sir. Admiring the view?' There was another laugh from the gallery at that.

'You really can't say?'

'I suppose I think they were being daring. I'm not sure. She liked it less than him.'

'Ah.' Mr Cedric gave a long pause. Every second scraped on

Celia's nerves. She couldn't bear to look at Arthur. And she mustn't, of course, she mustn't. The newspapers would see her doing it, think it meant something. Or even worse, the *jury* would see her doing it. 'You say the young lady had less enthusiasm for this game of chicken than Mr de Witt.'

'I'd say so. I heard her give a little shriek.' There was an intake of breath. 'I heard her say "No!"' There was another gasp and a hubbub of voices. *Oh, the satisfaction*, Celia thought angrily. This was the kind of thing that everybody came to hear. Scandal. She felt Emmeline tense beside her.

The clerk banged his hammer. 'Silence!' The voices quietened.

Mr Cedric walked closer. 'Mr Werth. If you could repeat this for me. You said you heard a shriek? That you heard the lady say – "no"?'

'I did, sir. I was shocked. I thought perhaps I should go forward and see.'

'And you are quite sure you heard this shriek? You are quite sure that the lady said "no"?'

'Couldn't be surer, sir.' Celia tried not to stare at the jury. They were scribbling hard, one of the women bent so low over her paper that her hair was falling out of its style. She looked across at Mr Bird. He was watching impassively, face calm. *Don't you care?* she wanted to cry. *Haven't you noticed?* Perhaps they had been entirely deluded by his words in the oak-panelled office, his confident smile, promises that it would be quickly over and it wasn't a thing to worry about. It had all been a lie. *Pay attention!* she wanted to scream. *Arthur is going to hang!* Mr Bird looked down at his paper and made a mark with his pen. It probably wasn't even a word. It was probably just a doodle. There was no possibility that his 'tragic accident' plan was going to work. They should have followed after the man Arthur had seen. But it was too late now. She clutched at Emmeline's hand.

Mr Cedric was still talking. 'So. You're quite sure that the lady gave a shriek and said no. And then what did you do?'

'I wasn't sure what to do. And it all happened so fast. She was falling and she really screamed. Then I shouted, ran forward.

My wife fell on to the ground, she was so shocked. Someone else must have heard me shouting because they started running too.'

'So you hurried towards Mr de Witt?'

'I did.'

'And what did you see?'

'I didn't go exactly very close. I didn't know, you see. Thought he might push me off next.'

The judge leant forward. 'If the witness could refrain from speculation, please.'

'Of course, Your Honour. We apologise. So, Mr Werth. You hurried forward. You saw Mr de Witt. And Mrs de Witt?'

'Oh no, sir. She was gone. Gone over the edge!' There was a low, strangled scream from the gallery and someone shouted for air. There was a flurry of doors and voices. The judge looked up, his face impassive. 'One moment, please, before we continue, Mr Werth. An onlooker requires some air.'

There were further voices, men's. 'This way, madam,' one said. The judge touched his papers.

The doors closed and the hall was silent once more.

'Thank you, Your Honour,' said Mr Cedric. 'Now, Mr Werth, if you could go through this for me, one more time. The young lady was not standing on the cliff?'

'No, sir. She had fallen over the cliff. I didn't look, sir. It wasn't my opinion that she'd be hanging on somewhere. I didn't think. I just knew – she's *gone over*!' There was another shriek from the back of the court, more shuffling and an opening of the door. The clerk demanded quiet once more.

'The young lady was not there,' said Mr Cedric, raising an eyebrow. 'Dear me. How was Mr de Witt behaving at this point?'

'He was standing with his back to me, looking out. I couldn't say what his expression was.'

'Did he look upset? As if he were screaming out or crying?'

'No, sir. He was just standing there, quite upright. I think he was talking to himself.'

'And he wasn't flinging himself down to the ground, trying to see over in the safest way. I believe that *is* the safest way, to spread your body over the ground, lean out. And he wasn't doing that?'

'No, sir.' Celia looked up and realised that two of the journalists in the front row of the press box were not scribbling like the rest but looking directly at her and Emmeline. She realised they were looking for a reaction. She wanted to shake her head at them. Instead she looked away from them, towards the judge. *I won't cry for you*, she wanted to say. *You can find a story from somewhere else.*

'He was just standing there?'

'Yes, sir.'

'Dear me. You would think that a man who had just seen his wife go over the edge would be distraught, would you not?'

'Yes, sir.'

'You would think he'd be tearing his hair out, screaming. Some men might even be so upset that they'd try to get down after her and have to be restrained. But he was doing none of those things?'

'He was just standing there, sir.'

'Well. And then what happened?'

'People came then. I think they heard my wife screaming. There was an officer too. I stood there for a bit longer. Mr de Witt didn't move. Then the officer approached him and took his arm. He took him away.'

'He took him away. Surely Mr de Witt must have protested? Surely no man could bear to leave his beloved wife at the bottom of a cliff? You would scream, beg, say you needed to be with her, beg them to save her. Wouldn't you?'

The judge cleared his throat. 'Mr Cedric.'

'I'm sorry, Your Honour. But I am simply surprised. Mr de Witt was not possessed by madness at what he had seen, shock and terror, like anyone here might be. He was very calm. Mr Werth?'

'He was very calm, sir, you are quite right.'

'And did you catch a look at his face as they led him away?'

'I did, sir. His face was still. He didn't even seem to see me.'

'Goodness me. And then what happened? Did you see him again after that?'

'No, sir. I waited for a minute, but more police officers came then and I thought I should rejoin my wife. We returned to the town. She was very shaken up, sir.'

'Quite understandable. Anyone would be upset after witnessing such an event. And did you see Mr de Witt again?'

'No, sir. I never saw him again.'

'Not until today.'

Mr Cedric wandered around the witness box. His face was stern with concentration. 'Now, sir, I have one more question. Why, exactly, did you not come forward with this evidence at the time? You were not ill, Mr Werth?'

'I was not, sir.'

'And yet you waited for almost five years to give it. There is a reason for that?'

Mr Werth hung his head. 'I'd rather not say, sir.'

'I am afraid you have to, Mr Werth.' Mr Cedric looked sorrowful, almost comically so.

Mr Werth looked up. 'Yes, sir. I am sorry for it. But at the time, the lady was not my wife. She was the wife of another. A violent man, sir. I could not have it known that we were keeping company. He died last year in a fight and she and I were married. Then I went to the police.'

'So you understandably kept quiet because you thought her husband would be angry with the lady who is now your wife? You wanted to protect her.'

'Yes, sir.'

'An honourable impulse, of course, but a wrong one. You accept that now.'

'Yes, sir. I – and Matilda – we are very sorry for it, sir.'

'Well, I am sure everyone here would understand. Thank you, Mr Werth. You have been most helpful. We are very grateful for your time and your account. Your witness, Mr Bird.' He returned to his seat, nodded to his clerk.

'This is terrible,' whispered Emmeline.

'Don't let them see,' Celia whispered back. 'We'll talk about it later.' She gazed ahead, looking at the judge. She saw nothing but a slight exasperation with the upper gallery, who were talking loudly. Arthur was sitting, looking paler than ever. *Why didn't we listen to you?* she wanted to say. *Why didn't we find the man who was following Louisa?* She wanted to cry and forced herself to look away before the newspapers saw. She stared at the policeman to the right of Arthur, who appeared to be sucking something out of his tooth.

'Silence!' called the clerk, once more.

Mr Bird sauntered forward. So relaxed! Why had they thought he would be a good idea? They'd been so stupid. So completely and utterly stupid. Celia watched Mr Bird ask inconsequential questions of Mr Werth about what he could and couldn't see. None of it made any impression. The people in the gallery above were shuffling, the jury were gazing vacantly. Everyone had had the story – that *the young lady had gone over the cliff* – and they weren't listening to anything else. Celia wanted to put her head in her hands. She clenched Emmy's arm, holding it hard under the cover of their shawls.

Then Mrs Werth came forward, a respectable little woman in a dark suit and hat, looking as far from an adulteress as you could be. Celia's heart sank. Mr Cedric interviewed her and she backed up every word of her husband's story.

'I heard the cry,' she said. 'I heard the poor lady cry out. My husband rushed forward and I was too shocked. I fell to the ground. I saw him run forward. I was afraid he might be pushed over too, I was so afraid. I was weeping.'

'I'm sure you were,' said Mr Cedric sympathetically. 'I'm sure you were terrified. You were so afraid for your husband's safety. As any wife would be!'

At this, Mrs Werth burst into pitiful tears. 'I was so afraid!' she said, through hiccuping sobs. Celia heard her sobs echo around the hall and saw nods of sympathy in the gallery. It was hopeless, she thought, hopeless. Arthur was going to be hanged by Mrs Werth's tears. She looked at the woman crying, shoulders shaking, holding a handkerchief to her streaming eyes.

THIRTY-SEVEN

London, February 1926

Celia

'It has been a little more difficult than I expected,' said Mr Bird. 'But, still, dear Miss de Witt, it is all without weight and certainty.' Celia had gone straight to the chambers after the end of that day in a taxi. Mr Bird had not yet arrived. She told the clerks that she'd wait for him, and after an hour, he arrived. While she'd been waiting, a dark-haired, very pretty girl in blue had introduced herself as his assistant secretary, Miss Sillen. Celia supposed she was twenty, no more.

'Thank you, Miss Sillen,' Mr Bird said when he arrived. He closed the door behind Celia. 'She is an excellent secretary. First-rate brain. Shame that she is of the fairer sex. I could do a lot with her if she were a man. Now,' he said, settling down in his chair behind his desk. 'What is it I can do for you?'

'I'm worried about the trial,' she said.

'Oh, do not worry, Miss de Witt. The first week is always the most arduous. That man is all that the prosecution has. When the jury is weighing everything up, they will ask themselves – is this sufficient to convict? All without weight and certainty.'

He'd said the same after the first day.

'And I am pleased to say it is surely not sufficient to convict. In this country, we need to prove beyond reasonable doubt. And one man's word on a windy cliff is not sufficient. As all the others have told us, Arthur was fond of his wife. The point about the baby was a master stroke.'

'Louisa must have been mistaken. If the doctor found nothing.'

'Well, whatever. Or maybe he misheard.'

'Do you think he lied? Made it up?'

'Some men on the stand do. Anyway, it has been established: there was absolutely no reason to kill his wife.'

'But they were trying to say that he killed her for her money.'

'Pure speculation. We have a set of character witnesses today and tomorrow. It is hardly Arthur's fault that he was married to a wealthy woman. He cannot be blamed for that. It was, as we will prove, a tragic accident.'

'He should have come forward sooner, told the truth that he was married.'

'He should have done. But you cannot be hanged for avoiding the truth.'

'What about Mrs Werth? They were all moved by her.'

'Now, Miss de Witt, I often have clients who say this kind of thing. But it doesn't matter what the gallery thinks. Only the jury matters, and His Honour. He, I can assure you, has seen many women cry. He cares only for the facts.'

'He was watching more carefully when Mr Cedric was speaking. He really was.'

'But of course, Miss de Witt. It is the job of the prosecution to prove the case. I've had dealings with Judge Grayson-Land before. He's a fair man, very cautious. No judge wants a wrongful death on his conscience and he is one of the most thoughtful of all.' He smiled, gently. 'Come now, Miss de Witt. I have never lost a man yet. I am not about to start at my advanced age. Why don't you get on home? The best way you can help me is by allowing my clerks and I to go over the papers once more. And you should ensure you sleep well. If you or your sister look tired or unhappy tomorrow, the newspapers will be sure to comment. You need to be fresh-faced, calm.'

She nodded. He was right, she could see that. The best way to help him was by letting him read his papers. It was unreasonable for her to expect him to see the case with the same urgency as she did. This was work for him, a job. She bade him good evening and set off for home. She ignored the newspapers on the way, but she heard the newspaper boy shouting 'He Pushed Her Off!' That night Celia slept with Lily in her bed, curling herself around the child, trying to push the thoughts from her mind.

The next morning, the courtroom was even more crammed than it had been before. Celia looked up at the gallery, saw them shuffling and jostling. They'd never all get in, she thought, they'd never manage it. She and Emmeline had the fat man beside them again. He wished her good morning and she didn't respond. Despite what Mr Bird had said, she'd slept badly, fidgeting, her head full of terrible thoughts. Not even Lily, her childish body warm, her breathing innocent, regular, could lull Celia's mind into rest. By five a.m., she'd given up, went to lie in her own bed, staring at the cracks snaking through the ceiling in the dirty half light.

She felt sick, tired, as if everything was at one remove from her, words slower, faces broken down into their parts, nothing whole. She watched the jury file in once more, then the judge. She stared down at Arthur. He didn't look like he'd slept either. He looked worse today, his back stooped, staring at the floor. *Don't let them see!* she wanted to say. *Don't let them!* If only she could tell him what Mr Bird had told her – the only word was Mr Werth's and you couldn't send a man to hang based on *that*.

The morning was for character witnesses, Mr Bird had said. People vouching for Arthur's probity and kindness. First was the headmaster of Arthur's old school. Celia watched as a rake-thin old man was helped to the witness box. He looked frail – but he was sharp when he spoke. Mr Cedric tried but could not distract him from his point. Arthur, he said, was an upstanding, kindly pupil. Yes, he was not a prefect or head boy, but what did that matter? Some people are leaders, some are not. He had cared for others and it had been obvious to him and everyone that Arthur had loved his family.

Then came Reverend Campson, their vicar when Arthur had been younger. He talked of how Arthur had come to Sunday school, been a godly boy, liked to help at church events. Celia couldn't remember Arthur ever helping at a church event or going to Sunday school very much. But she was sure he'd *meant* to. Anyway, as Mr Bird had said, it was all just a game they had to play. You needed these external proofs of goodness, the internal ones weren't enough.

Celia watched men from Winter Meats talk of how kind Arthur had been and clients of the company discuss his honesty, how you could always rely on him, how he'd done so much to get the business running after all the failures of the war. Mr Cedric tried and failed to find gaps in what they said, look for inconsistencies, but they were all quite sure. Arthur was a good man! He would never do such a thing to his wife. Celia watched the judge taking notes, the jury paying attention, felt ashamed of herself for judging Mr Bird. She had jumped to conclusions, just as he'd said. Mr Cedric tried to ask about Arthur's failure to go to university and pressed again and again on the point that Arthur didn't fight. A client of the company blinked in confusion. 'But he was stuck in Paris. He wanted to. He couldn't get out. I know that his heart was broken when he couldn't fight.' Earlier, the vicar had said that Arthur had returned to the church and prayed about how he'd been denied the chance to do his duty. He said he'd wept over the loss of so many of his schoolfriends.

'It cut him to the heart,' said the vicar. 'Really it did.'

At one o'clock, the court adjourned for lunch. That day Celia and Emmeline had brought a flask of tea and a bag of chocolate sweets. 'They will give us spirit, if nothing else,' said Emmeline. 'Eat them so no one can see.' The night before, she had got back to the flat and her chest had been hard with milk. 'It's the worry, I suppose,' she'd said, letting Euan clear it by feeding, crying a little as she did.

'You need to go to the bathroom now,' Celia said. 'Try and get some of it out.'

'I can't in there. It's too horrible. I'll wait. Things will be back to normal soon.'

'Yes.' Celia put a chocolate sweet in her mouth. She'd picked a mint one, never her favourite flavour. It exploded into her teeth, sharp, sour, unpleasant.

*

The next day the gallery was a little reduced. *So there was no scandal for you yesterday,* Celia thought, looking up at the ladies in hats, passing sweets. *Serves you right!* They were like vultures, these people, leaping on misfortune, hungry for more. She took a chocolate from the new bag – strawberry this time, much better – waited for things to begin.

'Call Mrs McElwell,' said the clerk. Celia looked up. Was that another schoolteacher? A large woman in a cheap dark-blue gown came through, thin mousy hair curled weakly over her head.

'Could you tell us how you met the defendant, Mrs McElwell?' Mr Cedric asked.

'He and – well, she wasn't his wife then, was she? – came to stay at my guest house in Weymouth.'

'And this was?'

She gave the dates. Celia calculated them in her mind. Just after Arthur and Louisa had left London.

'And just to be sure, can you verify if this man is in the room?'

She looked over at Arthur. 'It's him,' she said. 'That one.'

'Thank you, Mrs McElwell. Now, if you could tell us how long they were with you?'

'They came to stay for a month. He took a room not good enough for a gentleman like him, if you ask me. She had one a door or so along.'

'And what kind of guests were they?'

'Quiet, I suppose. He paid on time.'

'But they told you that they were married?'

'Yes, sir. I didn't suspect they weren't. He said he had to sleep separately to take the air, needed the window wide open and all that. I've had a few couples who were doing that. I didn't think they were lying. I was shocked when I heard. I don't keep that type of house!'

'I'm sure you don't, Mrs McElwell. So you thought that Mr de Witt was married to the then Miss Deerhurst. What kind of husband did he appear to be? Not that he was a husband. He lied to you about that.' He was standing close to her, smiling.

Celia would have almost said that, with his gentle, insinuating tone of voice, he was flirting with her. She wanted to push him away, tell him to stop.

Mrs McElwell coughed. 'He didn't seem to be much of a husband. I suppose that's why I didn't mistrust that they were married. In my experience, I can tell people who aren't married because they won't stop looking at each other. You can tell they want to – well – touch each other. That's when I turn them away.'

'So you thought these two were married, Mrs McElwell, because they *could* stop looking at each other?'

'Him definitely. She was always looking at him. He never wanted to look at her. I was surprised.'

'Why were you surprised, Mrs McElwell?'

'She was such a pretty girl. And they weren't that old. It usually takes couples much longer to be so weary of each other. That's what I expect when they've been married a good ten years or so. I thought she was so young, they couldn't have been married more than a year.'

'Dear me. So it seemed to you that she was fond of him, but not the other way round?'

'That's right.'

'Did they spend much of their time together?'

'Never. I hardly ever saw them together. He went out every day into town, left early, didn't come back until late.'

'Dear me. That must have been hard for a young girl on her own?' Celia had begun to hate it when Mr Cedric said 'dear me'.

'Without a doubt, sir. I've seen the same happen with wives, but they often have things to do. Embroidery, sewing, letters to write. She seemed to have nothing to occupy herself. Too young, I suppose.'

'Do you think, Mrs McElwell, that she expected to be spending her days with her husband? Or her companion, we should say.'

'I do think she expected it, yes, sir. It was heartbreaking in the morning, sometimes. She'd come down, all dressed up in one of her white dresses, hair curled, looking so pretty it would melt your soul. And then I'd have to tell her that he'd gone out for the day, no idea when he'd be back. She'd look crushed then, you know, really crushed.'

'Poor girl. So he kept breaking her heart.'

'I'd say so, sir, yes. I thought at the time, she wants to be a proper wife to him and he won't let her. I wondered what it was that had made him so unhappy with her.'

'I'm sure you did, Mrs McElwell. So Miss Deerhurst was keen to be with Mr de Witt, but he kept her at arm's length. Would you say he left very early in the morning in order to escape her?'

'I expect he probably did, sir.'

'Would you even say that he might have told her to come to breakfast at a particular time – only for him to have already gone?'

The judge cleared his throat again. Mr Cedric nodded to him. 'Perhaps I put that a little too baldly. What I meant was, perhaps he tried to avoid his wife?'

Mrs McElwell pondered. 'I hadn't thought of that, sir. But now that I do, I think you're right.'

'How cruel,' said Mr Cedric, shaking his head. 'How cruel. As we all know now, Miss Deerhurst and Mr de Witt had just fled London. She had felt under threat, as if she were at risk of actual violence, if not worse. You would think that a young lady in such a vulnerable situation would need more friendship, more kindness, would you not, Mrs McElwell?'

'You would, sir.'

'Yes, you would expect this older, wiser man to comfort her and support her. But instead, as you say, he was never there. No! Worse than that. He *actively* tried to avoid her.'

Mrs McElwell looked rather dazed, bowled over, Celia supposed, by the wild force of Mr Cedric's argument. She was gripping the side of the box.

'Yes, sir.'

Mr Cedric shook his head. 'This is all such a *very* sad picture. So very sad. First this in Weymouth, then goodness knows what, and finally she falls from the cliff in Margate and Mr de Witt flees the country. Not the actions of a loving husband.'

'I don't think so, sir. I tried to give her ideas of things to do myself. I sent her off to do a few errands. I once asked her to buy some medals for me from the antiques market in town. I collect medals from Passchendaele, you know. It was where I lost my husband.' She brought her handkerchief up and dabbed her eye.

'Commiserations, madam. Your husband fought to give us our freedom now. He fought bravely, accepted his fate.' *Unlike Arthur*, Celia knew he wanted people to think.

Mrs McElwell gave a large sniff. 'Yes, sir.' She wiped her eyes again.

'And do you have any idea where Mr de Witt was during the day? Where he went to so early in the morning and stayed until late at night?'

'No, sir. But he often came home smelling of alcohol, I can tell you that much. So I would say that at least *some* of it was spent in the public house!'

'Goodness me. But surely, public houses don't open all day in Weymouth?'

'No, sir, not since the war.'

'I have verified this matter for myself and I believe that the public houses open at eleven in the morning, close at two-thirty after the lunchtime rush and reopen at five until the end of the night. So he cannot have been there all day.'

'No, sir.'

Mr Cedric looked up at the gallery. 'Well, I wonder where else he might have been?' There was gruff, embarrassed laughter.

'I really can't say, sir. I don't think I'd like to know.'

'You are quite right, Mrs McElwell. There are some things that it is best for a lady not to know. Still, we have established important ground, have we not. Mr de Witt seemed to have no fondness for Mrs de Witt—'

'Yes, sir!' Mrs McElwell broke in. 'So much so, sir, that...'

'Yes?'

Mrs McElwell dropped her voice to a whisper. 'She tried to make herself thin, sir.'

'What did you say, Mrs McElwell? I didn't quite understand.'

'She tried to make herself thin, sir. I saw it after a week or two.

In the first week she was with me, she ate what you'd expect a young girl to eat, taste for the sweet stuff, you know. Then, she started buying these magazines.'

'What sort of magazines, Mrs McElwell?'

'Oh, you know, magazines for women. I never touch them myself. But she had them. And she always left them open at articles about slenderising. Diets that said you should only have two potatoes all day long and an apple. Terrible things. And that's what she started doing. She'd ringed that diet with a pen. Two potatoes and an apple.'

'Eating two potatoes and an apple for an entire day?' Celia could hear shuffling in the gallery.

'That's right, sir. I saw her eat nothing else. It was terrible to watch. I'd put her dinner in front of her and she'd find a way of hiding it. She'd put it in her skirts, take it upstairs, then try and throw it down the lavatory. I had to call in the plumber to unblock the pipes more than once. She'd say she'd eaten dinner out and didn't want anything or avoid the breakfast by saying she didn't feel well.'

'That must have been very hard to see.'

'It was, sir. In the first week, I suppose, I wondered if she was in the family way. You often lose your appetite.'

'So I understand. Then you realised it was something else. That she was not eating in order to become thinner.'

'Yes, sir. She simply grew thinner and thinner. She grew terribly thin! You wouldn't think anyone could get like that in just a few weeks.'

'Indeed. Well, if one is eating nothing but two potatoes and an apple, one would get very thin. And what was the reaction of Mr de Witt to this? Surely he could not have failed to notice?'

'I'm sure he did notice, sir. But it didn't make him like her more. In fact, I think he got more offhand with her.'

'So he became crueller to her?'

The judge leant forward, about to say something. He stopped.

'You could put it that way.'

'Crueller. You know, Mrs McElwell, I rather wonder something. Given that Miss Deerhurst was so under the thumb of Mr de

Witt – wouldn't you agree? Well, given this, I even wonder if this slenderising idea might have come from him?'

Celia saw Mr Bird gesture to the judge. The judge nodded.

'Mr Cedric. Is this line of questioning leading anywhere?'

'It is, Your Honour. I am establishing the relationship.'

'Proceed then. But not for too long.'

Mr Cedric resumed. 'So. My suggestion is that perhaps Mr de Witt himself put the idea into our lady's head. He told her that she might do well to slenderise. Perhaps it was an offhand comment. But it hit home.'

'I suppose so, sir.'

Mr Cedric looked up at the court. 'I have looked into these matters. There is much talk that young ladies are introduced into this sort of behaviour by magazines. And yet there are hundreds of ladies who read magazines who never decide to do such things. Why some and not others?' He waved his hand. 'The answer is that someone that the young lady loves puts it into her head. A little word: "Have you got larger?" "Are you sure you should take another piece of cake?" "Your gown is too tight, you know." For a sensitive young lady this could create much distress. Would you agree that Mrs de Witt was a sensitive young lady, Mrs McElwell?'

'I would very much so, sir.'

'The person who often sets a lady off on this trajectory is the mother. But, of course, we have no mother in this case. Miss Deerhurst was sadly orphaned. And the only person she sees is Mr de Witt. So if anyone planted the seed in her head, it was *him*.' He flourished his hand.

'Oh dear, sir.' Mrs McElwell looked shocked, her face pale. 'I can't imagine.'

'Yes, Mrs McElwell. Mr de Witt put the idea in her head. He said it to her, offhand, uncaring, because he had no affection for her. He probably was just trying to stop her from talking, he was lashing out because he disliked her. And instead, the poor girl began to starve herself. She convinced herself that Mr de Witt would admire her if she consumed nothing! She was faint, sick and ill. Her bones, Mrs McElwell, if you will forgive me, her bones would have begun to crumble fast for lack of food. Her body was in a desperate state. And this was all to please Mr de Witt!'

'Oh.' Mrs McElwell looked faintly at him. She swayed a little. A clerk passed her a glass of water. She closed her eyes, opened them again.

'I am sorry, Mrs McElwell. If only we could avoid these painful subjects. But the fact of the matter is that the defendant there detested Miss Deerhurst. To please him, she tried to starve herself. But he simply ignored her. What a tragedy!'

'Yes, sir.'

'And yet, this is a tragedy that could have been avoided. He didn't have to marry her. He didn't even have to keep company with her. But he ran away with her from Stoneythorpe, the home where she was safe with her aunt and uncle. He took her away – but not because he loved her. This is no modern-day Romeo and Juliet. Oh no. He wanted only one thing from her.'

Mr Cedric paused. He looked around the courtroom. There was no need. The entire room was hanging on every word of his thunderous rhetoric. Celia held Emmeline's hand, miserably. She couldn't bear to look at Arthur.

'And what was that one thing Mr de Witt wanted?' Mr Cedric said, loud enough, Celia thought, for everyone in the next court to hear. 'What was it?'

Mrs McElwell shook her head, although everybody knew he wasn't talking to her.

'He wanted her money. Plain and simple, he wanted her money. And he was willing to do anything to get it.'

He looked around the court room, dipped his voice. 'Thank you, Your Honour.'

Celia could almost feel the gallery burst into applause above her. A bravura performance, you could say. The journalists were scrawling wildly, about to dash from the room, she wouldn't wonder. The jury sat staring. Even the judge was paying attention. She looked down at Arthur. She saw two trails of tears glittering on his face.

*

The judge finally called for a break. Mrs McElwell looked about to faint and Celia supposed he wanted to allow the journalists a chance to call in the story in time to catch the afternoon editions. She and Emmeline sat on the bench outside.

'Don't talk,' she said to Emmeline. 'We'll only make it worse.' She took a sweet from the bag. This time she picked out a mint one on purpose, claiming the harsh, sour, nasty taste to match her own misery.

After the break, Mr Bird addressed Mrs McElwell. But the woman's story was straight now and there was nothing he could find, no hole to break into. Celia rather longed for Mr Bird to stop trying. The woman seemed so stunned by the whole thing that she could barely answer, and his questioning looked unfair, ungallant.

After Mrs McElwell came Albert Greeson, the pub landlord of the Bear in Weymouth. He testified that he had seen Arthur on most days, but that he believed that he spent his time elsewhere. He agreed with Mr Cedric that there were many illegal gambling dens in Weymouth. He said that he knew little about them himself, but knew by reputation that they had sprung up in the war after Lloyd George's changes to the drinking laws. Now, he said darkly, you couldn't get rid of them. Mr Cedric asked if he had heard what went on in such places. Mr Greeson said he did not but had heard of men losing thousands of pounds.

'Were these all-male establishments?' asked Mr Cedric.

'No, sir. I have heard of women waitresses. And there were also other ladies there in – er – other occupations.'

'What sort of occupations?'

The man looked in confusion at the judge.

'You may go on, Mr Greeson,' said the judge. 'Anyone in the gallery who wishes to should stop their ears at this point.'

'Ladies of the night, sir,' said Greeson, emboldened. 'Who met men for money. There were plenty of those.' He looked at the jury. 'Or – er – so I heard.'

'Thank you, Mr Greeson,' said Mr Cedric. 'What a picture. The young lady starves herself in her room, attempting to create love in a man who feels nothing for her. He goes to public houses and gambling dens. He spends money – that surely is hers – on the card table and he is surrounded by ladies of the night. Dear me. Dear, dear me.'

Celia longed for the judge to call another break, but instead, they were to plough on after the jury had had a moment to complete any notes. Who next? she thought. A gambling friend? A lady of the night, in a short skirt with a feather on her wrist? She hoped that Reverend Campson had left, not stayed to hear such awful things.

'Call Mrs Eglantine Merling,' declared the court official. The door opened and the woman came through.

THIRTY-EIGHT

London, February 1926

Celia

Mrs Merling walked into the room, settled herself at the witness box. Celia felt heartened. She'd been fond of Arthur, that had been clear when Celia had met her. She looked plumper now, her face wide and puffy. She'd dressed her hair carefully, piling it on top of her head in an elaborate Edwardian style. She looked intelligent, trustworthy. The sort of woman they'd used after the war as an example of a lady who deserved the vote: a good citizen and mother, thoughtful and utterly respectable.

She gave her name to the court, her voice ringing clearly. Mr Cedric asked her how she had first met Arthur. She said he had taken rooms in her home for Miss Deerhurst and he had taken the rooms upstairs for himself. No, they had never said they were married. He'd told her that Louisa was his cousin and he was bringing her to town for the season. No, she'd never seen any impropriety. In fact, she thought, quite the opposite, Mr de Witt had been quite punctilious about visiting her home in correct hours. She had found him a very respectable man, almost too much so; sometimes it had seemed to her that Miss Deerhurst had wished he might visit more.

'So Miss Deerhurst felt neglected that Mr de Witt did not come to visit her?' Celia gazed down at Arthur but he looked ahead, impassive. This courtroom was a disaster! Because Mr Cedric went first, he could plant all these terrible ideas in the minds of the jury. Mr Bird was always running to catch up. It wasn't fair.

Mrs Merling shook her head. 'I don't think he neglected her. I feel that she wished to see him more than he knew. Then, after he started to take her to more parties, she seemed happier.' Celia squeezed Emmeline's hand. One dared not to hope too much, but finally, it seemed, there was a witness who was fair, saw things on their own merits, judged Arthur on the fact that he was a good man. Mrs Merling wasn't the sort of woman to read those awful newspapers. And the people in the gallery were paying her atten-tion. They liked her. It was as if they were saying – here, finally, after a parade of people who lied, here is someone we can *trust*.

Mr Cedric asked her about the nature of the parties and Mrs Merling said she knew little about them but that Louisa had seemed to enjoy the evenings and they'd taken her to the dressmaker's to buy gowns and twice for the material to make fancy-dress costumes.

'Did she tell you about the parties?'

'I didn't ask much, sir. I thought she and Mr de Witt were very respectable. But I didn't want my daughters to think about visiting such establishments or mixing with those sets when they were older.'

'Why would you not wish for that, Mrs Merling?'

'I prefer that my daughters will go to small gatherings of family and friends.'

'So the parties that Mrs de Witt attended were not small gatherings of family and friends?'

'No. I know little, sir, only what I have read in the newspapers, so you probably know more than me. But I understood that they were celebrations of hundreds of young people who barely knew each other, in large hotels such as the Savoy. This may be the fashion nowadays, but that is not where I expect my daughters to go.'

'So, Mrs Merling, Mr de Witt was taking the then Miss Deer-hurst to parties that you don't consider respectable? That was hardly fair on her, was it?'

'I believe that Miss Deerhurst wished to go. She had come to London to visit such parties. She talked so much to my daughters about how she liked them that I had to request that she talked a little less. I believe that Mr de Witt had brought her to London at her request. But I thought that they might go to a few less parties and he could have suggested to her that she could mute the celebrations a little. He was her guardian, after all.'

'So you thought that Mr de Witt was remiss in his duties by not taking her to other places? Museums, for example?'

'Not remiss, sir. Just a little too indulgent, I would say.' *That's it!* thought Celia. *He was indulgent, he loved her! Go on, Mr Cedric, make something of that. Surely you can't.*

'So the parties were very well attended?' Celia wanted to smile. He'd changed tack, couldn't do a thing with a picture of Arthur as an indulgent guardian.

'I believe so, sir. As I said, I know little more than what I read in the newspapers.'

'Did she mention much about a gentleman called Mr Edward Munsden?'

'I did hear the name, sir. She told us to expect a visit from him.'

'Did you see him?'

'No, sir. He never visited.'

'So, Miss Deerhurst expected a visit but she never saw him?'

'Yes.'

'He was a gentleman she'd met at the parties.'

'So I understand, sir.'

'And do you know what Mr de Witt thought about him?'

'I believe he never mentioned him.'

'But he was jealous of him, wasn't he?'

'I didn't see any of that, sir.' Mrs Merling was clearly growing impatient, Celia thought. Mr Cedric could get nothing from her.

'Wouldn't you have thought that Mr de Witt would be jealous about Mr Munsden? That he'd hate the idea of Louisa liking him, inviting him to visit, and tell her not to.'

'I don't know anything about that.'

The judge leant forward. 'Might we keep matters to the realm of fact, Mr Cedric?'

'Yes, Your Honour. But, Mrs Merling, he'd get angry, wouldn't he?

Furious with Louisa. Try to force her to stay away from Mr Munsden.'

Mr Bird was waving frantically at the judge.

'As I said, sir, I saw nothing of that.' *Oh, just you try*, said Celia in her head. *Just you try! You can't get her with your ways. She won't listen.*

'Surely you saw him shout at Louisa about Mr Munsden?'

'Never, sir.'

The judge tapped his bench. 'The realm of fact, please, Mr Cedric.'

Cedric nodded. 'But what about Miss Jennifer Redesdale? She was a lady who was close friends with Mr Munsden. They were then engaged, now married, I believe. She and Miss Deerhurst did not see eye to eye. In fact, Miss Deerhurst was far too close to Mr Munsden. Mr de Witt was furious with Miss Deerhurst about her friendship with Mr Munsden.' All the hateful words about Arthur and Louisa's time in London that Celia had read about in the papers. Now here they were, announced to everybody.

'I know nothing about that either, sir.'

'Oh just stop!' Celia whispered. 'Mrs Merling won't say the hateful words you want.'

Mr Cedric paused. 'Let us return to the subject of fancy dress. How did Miss Deerhurst dress for fancy dress?'

'I barely remember, sir.'

'Are you sure you cannot remember?'

'I feel quite sure, sir.'

'I believe that she dressed as a shepherdess for one. And then I think that she dressed as a mermaid.'

'Yes, indeed, sir, I do recall the mermaid one, now you mention it.'

'Did you see the mermaid costume?'

'No, sir.'

'Did you hear anything about the evening when Louisa dressed up as a mermaid?'

'She told my elder daughter that she enjoyed it.'

'Indeed? Did she tell you anything else?'

'No, sir.'

'It is our proposal that Miss Deerhurst made a great social *splash* dressed as a mermaid. She captured the attention of the ball. She captured the attention of Mr Munsden. Other people were jealous.'

'I really don't know about it, sir.'

'She didn't mention it?'

'I recall she was unusually tired after it. And it was after that ball that she told us to expect a visit from Mr Munsden.'

'This would suggest she had made a particular impression on him.'

'Perhaps, sir. As you know, I was not there.'

Celia's mind drifted a little. When she returned, Mr Cedric was asking Mrs Merling about the cat. He seemed to be asking rather irrelevant questions about Petra and why she'd been bought, about Louisa loving her so much. Celia listened, wondered why he was asking all this. It was surely pointless – and actually, it only backed up their argument (well, the truth) that there was someone odd following Louisa, scaring her.

'Someone purposefully killed the cat, did they not? They took Miss Deerhurst's poor beloved Petra and put it on the railings so that it was impaled. Rather like some kind of medieval torture. They murdered the innocent thing in the most cold and cruel way possible!'

There was a general intake of breath. Mr Cedric played to it. He looked up at the court, opened out his hands. 'What a terrible act of barbarism.'

The people in the court shuffled, tutted, whispered.

'What an awful act of cruelty towards Miss Deerhurst,' he said. 'She adored the cat. It was like *killing her baby*.'

There was a gasp from the court. Emmeline was clutching Celia's hand. 'I feel sick,' she whispered.

Celia gripped her other hand, crossing it over her chest. 'Don't be. You really can't be. Hold it in. Remember, this is good for us.' Because it was. This only proved that someone was after Louisa.

Mr Cedric nodded at the gallery. 'I shall repeat it. It was like *killing her newborn baby.*'

There was another sigh and then a startled shriek and shuffling. Celia looked up at the gallery. Two women on different benches had fainted and the rest of the people were standing up to let them be carried out. She could only see one of the women, plump with a purple hat drooping off her head, bringing down the pinned hair with it. She looked back at Mr Cedric, his face satisfied, enjoying the effect.

He turned back to Mrs Merling. 'Miss Deerhurst was devastated, of course.'

'She was. She left soon after. Mr de Witt told me she did not feel safe with me.'

'That is when they went to Weymouth?'

'I believe so, sir.'

'Well, it was all rather convenient for Mr de Witt, was it not? We have hazarded that he was growing weary of Miss Deerhurst's passion for the nightlife of London and certain individuals within it. He was maybe even a little jealous. And then here is the perfect excuse. She is not safe in London, so she must be whisked away to Weymouth, where there is little opportunity for amusement.'

The judge sighed. 'Mr Cedric. Please. Must I warn you again? This is a court room. We deal in fact.'

Mr Cedric nodded. 'Do you have any suspicion as to who killed the cat, Mrs Merling?'

Mrs Merling held out her hand. The clerk passed her a glass of water. She shook her head, touched her hand to her face.

'Do tell us, Mrs Merling.'

She gripped the side of the witness box, stared out. 'My daughter told me that she was on her way out after Miss Deerhurst. In front of her, going down the stairs, was Mr de Witt. He was carrying a brown sack, with something in it. At the bottom of the stairs, he gave the sack to a man she didn't know. Then he left the house. She waited until he had gone, then walked to the front door herself. She returned upstairs and told me. I dressed and came outside. Miss Deerhurst was weeping by the railings,

Mr de Witt comforting her. Then my daughter noted that the brown sack had been tossed into the public rubbish bin just next to the gardens. She retrieved it.'

'And what did you do with it?'

'I am afraid that my daughter forgot about it. We were caught up in the drama of Miss Deerhurst leaving and then my husband fell ill. But then when we heard of Mr de Witt's arrest, I came forward and I brought the bag.'

Mr Cedric walked over to his clerk. He seized a brown bag. 'This one?' he said. He held it up. 'There is a red stain on the bottom.'

'Yes, sir.'

'It looks like blood to me. Our police scientist believes it is blood.' He gazed around the court, but they were silent, watching him speak. 'No doubt of an animal, but who knows? So, unless Mr de Witt had caught an unusually large rat, he had in fact killed the cat, put it in here and given it to some henchman to prop on the railings outside.'

Mrs Merling held her hands, twisting them.

'Mr de Witt killed Miss Deerhurst's cat in order to frighten her. He also sent the letter, I feel we can be sure of that.' He looked up at the gallery, spread his hands. 'If he was so quick to kill a cat out of simple jealousy – wishing to have Miss Deerhurst to himself – then he was capable of killing Miss Deerhurst herself, pushing her over the cliff.' He turned, pointed his finger at Arthur in the dock. 'This man, ladies and gentlemen, is a murderer!'

Celia was about to stand, but then the room began to switch and jolt. She turned around. Tom was behind her, looking at her. He smiled. He looked *pleased*. The people beside him loomed large and bulged. She was about to shout, *Stop!* But the words wouldn't come. The court went dark.

THIRTY-NINE

London, February 1926

Celia

Celia was staring at an unfamiliar ceiling. It was dark brown, the wood old and peeling.

'Ah,' said Emmeline's voice. 'You're awake.'

Celia looked around.

'Drink some water. If you can sit up.'

Celia struggled up and Emmeline passed her a glass. 'I thought you were stirring. I've sent the lady out for some tea. Although goodness knows what it will be like. I've had some and it was worse than school cocoa.'

'I fainted.'

'You did. That's what I was planning to do. So you really stole my thunder. Mind you, so did about four other ladies. And Arthur looked as if he wasn't far off doing the same.'

'How is Arthur?'

Emmeline shrugged. 'Still standing.'

Celia gazed up at the clock. It was a quarter past three. 'What have I missed?'

'Not much. Mr Bird talked to Mrs Merling, didn't get anywhere really. Then some man who said Arthur gave the bag to a friend and told him to stick the cat on the railings. The friend has since died in a street fight, which is rather convenient for Mr Cedric, if you ask me. Anyway, the court seemed to believe him. Everyone seemed to believe that Arthur killed the cat.

'I was so stupid,' said Celia. 'I thought he was giving us help with talking about the cat. Of course he knew something we didn't.'

'It looks bad.'

'We should have done what I said from the beginning. We should have talked about that man following Louisa. Mr Bird wouldn't.'

Emmeline shrugged. 'Well, after the chap talking about Arthur, we had Edward Munsden, who is nothing but a pretty face, frankly.'

'What did he say?'

'Said Louisa seemed to want to escape. It was obvious that Munsden led her on, if you ask me. He was a sheepish kind of chap. Wedding ring now.'

'Not much good for Arthur?'

'Not really.'

A policeman and a woman in a pink suit came with two cups of tea. Celia thanked them, drank hers. The milk was off.

'Tom was there. Behind us. I'm sure it was him.'

'Who?'

'Tom Cotton.'

Emmeline gaped. 'Impossible! Anyway, you probably don't recognise him. It's been years. He'd be entirely different. You're imagining things, Celia, you really are.'

'I saw him when I got back from Paris. I'm sure it was him. And he wrote after he heard the news. I didn't write back. I suppose it was kind of him to come.'

Emmeline shrugged. 'I suppose. Who knows? I think we're the best entertainment in London this week.'

Celia put down the cup. 'Now what's happening?'

'A short break for the judge to assemble his papers. Then we have to go back for the final witness of the day.'

Celia dropped her head back. 'Another one.'

Emmeline patted her hand. 'But this time it's one of ours! It's Smithson!'

'Smithson? I thought we had had all the character witnesses.'

'Well, then, they have allowed us one more. Come along, Celia, drink up that tea. They start again in ten minutes.'

*

In ten minutes, they were settled back on the bench. Celia could feel people staring at her and she looked straight ahead. The court moved around, settled, the judge readied himself. The women on the jury looked sick and pale. Celia wondered if they'd be expected to cook for their husbands after this. Surely, she thought, they'd be allowed to sit at home, think. They needed to. This was too important for them to spend their evening fussing about potatoes. Arthur was going to be convicted!

The clerk called Smithson. Celia's heart leapt as he came out. He looked thinner, older. But his voice sounded the same. She heard him speak out and her heart flooded, expanding across her body. It was Smithson. He would tell them the truth, about who Arthur really was.

He began to speak, answering questions about his name and address, how long he had worked at Stoneythorpe. She meant to listen, really she did. But she found her attention wandering, her mind taking itself back to when they had all been in the house together. She thought of the party before the war had begun, how Thompson and Smithson had laid out the tables for the children, decorated the house for the celebrations that nobody but Tom and his sister, Missy, had come to. Smithson travelling off to Gallipoli, Jennie crying when she thought no one could see. Their wedding in the village when Celia wasn't joyous, as she would have been, for she thought only of her brother, Michael, and how he hadn't come home from the war. She looked down at Smithson, smart in his suit, answering the questions. He looked rather like one of the solicitors' clerks, even a solicitor himself. He looked back at Mr Bird, not at Arthur or up at the gallery. And then a thought bolted through her, fast and sharp. What if he had hated being their servant? He hated having to smile, give them things, be cheerful, respond when they rang the bell. He'd come back after the war, but only because there was no other job elsewhere. And now he hated them even more, kept in tiny, shambolic Stoneythorpe with nothing but the occasional visit from the vicar. Why, she thought, why hadn't they even called him Mr Smithson? She leant forward.

Mr Cedric was questioning him. He was asking about Arthur's behaviour after Paris. Smithson was quiet, his answers short.

'Now, Mr Smithson. I'm sure you feel very loyal to the family who employed you for so long. But I must stress to you that this is a trial for a very serious offence. You must overcome your scruples and tell me everything you know.'

Smithson nodded.

'Let's recommence. Could you please describe your relationship with Mr Arthur de Witt.'

Smithson cleared his throat. 'Well, sir. I was his servant. After he came back from Paris and I was returned from the army. He had tasks he asked me to do, look after his clothes, attend to his room, order this or that. He was used to being obeyed. Occasionally he'd ask me to buy him alcohol. Stuff we didn't keep in the house day to day.'

'I'm sure. But he paid you?'

Smithson paused. 'Not always. And then I asked him for money towards my wedding. He said he didn't have any money and I was well paid enough.'

'Indeed. Not the most desirable of employers, I think we can say. Tell me of his attitude towards Miss Deerhurst?'

'We all knew he was following her around. Almost as soon as she arrived he was off trying to get to her. Obvious why.'

'Why, Mr Smithson?'

'All her money. Who wouldn't want to get close to a woman with that much money?'

'Well, indeed. But then, they left quickly, did they not?'

'They did, sir, all thanks to me.'

Emmeline coughed. Celia wanted to lean her head on her shoulder. She wished she'd stayed in the room, gazing at the ceiling, the peeled paint, drinking lukewarm tea.

'Why do you say that it was all thanks to you, Mr Smithson?'

'Because he wanted me to scare her. He made me make strange noises outside her room, odd bangs. He knew she was the nervous type. He wanted to make her run to him. Not that he ever paid me, of course, sir. Said he would, but never did. I asked again about money for the wedding, but he still said no. Arthur made a lot of plans, you know. He was going to persuade Miss Deerhurst to run away with him and marry him. If that didn't work, he was going to say that his parents would lock her up. All sorts of lies. I was going to help. If she didn't agree by her own will, I was to pretend that people were coming for her, Rudolf's men, coming to seize her.'

Mr Cedric raised an eyebrow. 'How dramatic.'

'He was determined, you see. He thought she might be unwilling. Being so young.'

'And did you agree?'

'I did, sir. We needed the money. I got the carriage from the village, sent a man for it, brought it outside. But in the end, we didn't need it as he persuaded her well enough himself. We took the cart, then I dropped them at the inn, where they took a car. And I never saw them again.'

'So Miss Deerhurst was to be tricked, frightened – and then abducted if all that failed?'

'Yes, sir,' said Smithson.

Mr Cedric summarised it, nodding and smiling. 'Thank you, Mr Smithson. You have been most helpful.'

The clerk banged his hammer. The day was over.

'We're lost,' Celia was saying. 'We're completely lost.'

'I thought Smithson would help,' Emmeline added.

'I knew halfway through. I knew it. Arthur's completely damned. We might as well give up now. If he says he's guilty, will he get more mercy?' They were sitting in Mr Bird's offices. They'd had to push through the crowd to get to the car. At the end of the day, the judge had said they would be adjourning for a week. Another week for them all to suffer, Celia thought.

'Maybe he should say that,' said Emmeline. 'Say he did it and it was a mistake or something. It might be better for him.'

Celia thought of how she'd meant to go and see Smithson and Jennie, but never had done. She hadn't even sent them a present, she'd been so caught up in herself, Louisa, Tom, Arthur.

'I wish I'd gone to see them,' she said.

'Don't be ridiculous,' snapped Emmeline. 'One tea visit isn't going to change anything. Smithson was asked to tell the truth and he did.'

Mr Bird held up his hand. 'Ladies, please. Do not be alarmed. Things look worse than they are. Remember, Mr de Witt must be proved guilty beyond all reasonable doubt. And no proof has been given. All Mr Cedric's conversations with the witnesses have shown us is that Mr de Witt had an odd way of winning his wife and was not always kind to her when he did win her. True of half of the men in England, I expect. And there has been the suggestion that he wanted her money. Again, most of those with money are not loved for their charm alone. All of this might be a little unsavoury, but it is not a crime.'

'But Mrs Merling. And Smithson.'

'Yes, Arthur wanted to frighten her. But the judge sees hundreds of husbands here who have actually beaten their wives. Banging about to imitate angry men is hardly a crime. No one has said, remember, that Mr de Witt exposed Miss Deerhurst to violence. He may have been odd and neglectful. But that is hardly enough to see him hang.'

That word. Hang. Arthur, legs dangling as he kicked for air.

'He killed the cat. That's what they think.' Celia didn't know what to believe. It looked true, as if Arthur really had done it. But she couldn't believe it. 'Surely—'

'Oh, don't start on about that mystery man again,' said Emmeline. 'Even if he did exist, we'll never find him.'

Celia sat back in her chair. The pretty dark-haired girl came in with some papers for Mr Bird.

'Thank you, Miss Sillen.' She smiled at Celia as she left. Celia envied her. Her life must be so simple, working for Mr Bird in the day, returning to flatmates, washing her hair, thinking about how to find a fiancé. She surely had a gentleman, such a pretty girl. Celia wondered if she were ever cast down, reading about all the awful cases Mr Bird had. Then she told herself, *Of course not.*

Miss Sillen was young, she thought these things would never come to her, she was like Celia had been once.

'It was all so terrible today,' said Celia.

Mr Bird shrugged. 'A man cannot be hanged for killing a cat. Luckily for us. Still, I think I may have to do a little further investigation. Just to make sure our case is absolutely watertight.'

'But you said it was.'

'Then I shall make it more so.'

They took a cab from Mr Bird's. It was a terrible extravagance, Emmeline said as they waited for it, but they deserved it. Today had been too much. They needed to relax. Celia agreed, imagined them leaning back in the plush interior. But instead, something else came over them when they climbed into the cab. They began arguing, the day's anger buzzing from their mouths like furious flies. Emmeline berated Celia for fainting, Celia argued back. By Holborn, Celia had had enough. 'I'm getting out here,' she said. 'Then I am walking. I need the air.'

'Oh, you're so *dramatic*.'

'I don't care what you think. I'm going to walk. If I come to yours at all.'

Celia slammed out of the carriage, jumped down to the wet ground. She began to walk, the anger pounding in her brain. She knew, objectively, that she and Emmeline were just lashing out, throwing around their fear that Arthur would be hanged. And yet, still, she hated her sister at that moment, wanted her to beg forgiveness. Weeping, she stamped hard on the cobbles as if beating down all the failures of their stupid, deluded, hateful de Witt family. The rain was spotting around her. She didn't care. She hoped it poured down on her and everyone else for the rest of their lives.

FORTY

London, February 1926

Celia

How do you pass a week when everyone thinks your brother is going to be sentenced to death? Celia meant not to read the newspapers, but every time she went out, there were sellers shouting out about Arthur and every stall was covered with the stories. She saw them even in the shops that didn't sell papers: chemists, dress shops, toy shops, all of them full of people carrying papers screaming out *Brutal Murder!* She walked out and she could sometimes hardly believe that the city continued as it did, that people were driving or eating, working in factories, looking after children, clerks assessing legal documents, teachers marking work, that not every one of them was caught up in the same trial, the forthcoming days which would decide if Arthur lived or died.

The reporters weren't in Bedford Square any more – they'd all moved to the court – but still they might be waiting anywhere. The pictures of her and Emmeline in the paper were so grainy that she thought no one would recognise her. Still, you never knew, people might. They tried to stay inside as much as they could. But the children had to play and there were things to buy. She walked out with her hat pulled low, chose different shops each time. Still, they knew, she thought. They saw her. She scurried back, fast as she could, clutching the bag of bread, eggs and the rest.

Tom wrote to her, asked to meet. She agreed to go to the British Museum to meet him, hoping no reporters would see.

'Hello, Celia,' he said. They were standing in the great hall,

tourists wandering past with maps. They'd probably read the
newspapers too, pored over the articles about Arthur.

'How are you?'

She shook her head, couldn't speak. The last time she'd seen
him, in Waterloo, she'd been so furious at his unspoken *it's just
as well* it had sent her dashing across the station desperate to
escape him.

'I'm sorry about what's happened,' he said. She stared past him
at a vase, right in the middle of the room.

'You were in there,' she said. 'You were watching. I thought I
saw you.'

'I had to come, when I read about it.'

She nodded. 'Everyone's read about it. They've probably read
about it in Timbuctoo.'

'I've been writing. You never answer my letters.' She wanted to
stand away from him, far, didn't want their clothes to touch. Their
skin had touched, the two of them nothing but bodies, their arms
around each other.

She shook her head. 'I don't. Sorry.'

'Because of what I did. You hate me. I understand.'

She shook her head. 'I don't.' And the words were true, she
didn't. Not any more. Not hate. But not *like* either. She'd told him,
let the words out in the station: *I had a baby*.

'Shall we walk?' he said. She nodded. They could look at things,
so they didn't have to look at each other. She followed him towards
the Egyptian section. They stood in front of a mummy.

'Sorry that you fainted the other day,' he said. 'It must all be
a shock.'

'He's innocent. I know he is. They're just twisting the words.'

'They do that, I suppose.'

She looked at him. She could tell him, here in the middle of the
museum. *Michael's still alive. I can't find him. Help me.* The words
flew in her mind. But then what if Michael could never be found?
She felt her face wrinkle in pain.

'Poor Celia,' he said. 'I'm sorry.'

A tourist pushed past her for a better view of the mummy.

'I can't bear to read the newspapers. I know what they'll say, German family fallen low. How did they ever let us in? We're poor criminals who everyone hates. People call Arthur a murderer, want him to hang.'

'It doesn't matter what they think.'

'It does! Even if they do find him innocent, people will never forget. They'll always think he was a murderer.'

'The truth will prevail, I'm sure,' he said. 'I'm sure.'

'I hate all the people watching. It's like it's a play for them.'

'It must be hard.'

She gazed at the mummy. Surely the colours weren't so bright, years later. They'd repainted it, they had to have done. 'I hate it that it's free entertainment. I know what it must seem like. I can see it. The rich family brought low, a parade of ordinary people telling the truth about them. Even you probably think he's guilty.'

'No, Celia. But it's up to the jury, isn't it? Listen, shall we go and get some tea?'

'I really can't, I should go back soon. Emmeline needs me.'

'Well, I will say it now. Do you think you should – Celia – should you ... you know ... prepare yourself for the worst?'

And even though she knew he was sympathetic, that he meant well, all the frustration, the anger and the misery rose. 'No! You're just like all the rest! He's innocent. They're all lying.' She tried to fight her voice down.

He gazed straight ahead. 'Why would they lie?'

'I don't know.' She looked at him, thought of the boy she'd played with in the grounds of Stoneythorpe, the young man holding Missy's hand at her parents' party. She thought of Heinrich telling him to leave. But it wouldn't work. The awful words, the worst words, were rising in her and they had to come.

'Well, you'd know about being a murderer,' she said. 'Wouldn't you?'

She watched his face crash, the angry man turn into the boy, crumpled, fallen. He opened his mouth, closed it again. Then she couldn't watch any more. She turned on her heel, ran away, pushing through the crowds, down the steps and out of the museum.

That night she was sharp with the twins, she couldn't help it. Lily wanted to practise reading her book and Celia couldn't read it – didn't want to. Albert was jumping on the cushions, playing with his trains. 'What's got into you, Celia?' said Emmeline.

She needed distraction, she decided, the next day. She needed something else to think about. She'd received a letter from Jonathan Corrigan and shoved it in the drawer. Jonathan, Michael's friend from university, who'd been so kind to her when he'd visited Stoneythorpe before the war. The man she'd been with years later when she'd learnt the truth about Michael's death. The man she'd offered herself to.

He said he was in London, was there anything she needed? She wrote to him, gave him her address. *It would be good to see you*, she said. She sent it off, before she could regret it. Who cared if he thought she was forward. Her brother was about to hang.

Three days later, she got back from shopping and he was outside the building.

'Celia! I've been looking for you! I rang the bell up there but there was no answer.'

He looked older than he had, but not the nine years it had been. His hair was thinning and his skin was wrinklier, tight around the eyes. But it was still him, handsome, brash, confident, American Jonathan.

She gazed at him.

'Thanks for your letter. So our fame has reached America?'

He nodded. 'Sorry.'

'Are they covering it a lot over there?' The bag of shopping was hurting her hand.

'A little.'

'You came all the way here. You're staying in a hotel?' But he was rich, she supposed, doing these things didn't matter to him.

'Your family was kind to me. I'm sorry for what's happened.' She blushed a little to think how he must see her, dowdy in Emmeline's brown coat, ugly shoes, no make-up and a bag of shopping. She hadn't even bothered to do her hair that morning, had pulled it back into a bun. 'I am. I've been at the trial but I didn't want to disturb you.' She nodded. He looked up. 'Is this your flat?'

'My sister's. Emmeline, you remember? I live with her.'

'I didn't see your parents at the trial?'

She shook her head. 'They can't face it. It's just me and Emmeline.'

'Arthur must be pleased that you're there. Listen, let me help you with your bag,' he said, leaning towards the shopping. She let him pick it up.

'Emmeline – there are three children now.'

'Well, that's a piece of nice news. Do you have any more shops to visit?'

She shook her head. 'I've finished now.' She smiled. 'You could come with me,' she said. 'You could come with me and see Emmeline.'

He nodded. 'Why not? She might be surprised seeing me, for the first time in – what – nearly thirteen years?'

'She might be. She's usually very busy with the children. But you could come and say hello.'

'If it wouldn't be an intrusion?' His American accent was so much lighter now. Or perhaps she'd become more used to American accents, hearing them around London, sometimes on the radio.

She shook her head and they set off up to the flat. He asked her other questions, pretending, she supposed, not to have read every detail about them in the newspapers. She told him about Stoneythorpe as a hospital, Emmeline's twins and Euan. Not the other things – Louisa, Arthur, how Tom had been one of the men who'd killed Michael. He told her a little about New York and his family there, his sisters and their children. She tried to pay attention.

Almost as soon as she arrived back at the flat, she realised that the visit had been a mistake. She could hear Euan screaming and Lily making a fuss about something or other. She stood outside the door, hearing the shouts and knowing Emmeline would be harried and cross, not wanting a visit.

'Perhaps it isn't a good time,' said Jonathan. 'I'm sure the children are tired.'

'No, no,' she replied, against herself. 'Come on in.' She pulled open the door and Lily was on the floor, kicking at the sofa. Emmeline was jogging Euan, trying to get him to take some milk from a bottle. Albert was sitting apart from them all, playing with a toy car.

Emmeline looked up. 'Celia! I've been waiting for you.' She gazed at Jonathan. 'Who are you?'

'It's Jonathan, Emmy, Michael's friend. Don't you remember?'

She was staring at him, the milk bottle in her hand. 'It's like seeing a ghost. I haven't seen you for years.'

'Not since before the war. So much has changed.' He reached out to shake her hand. 'We all miss Michael so much.' Euan started screaming again. Emmeline looked back at her baby, tried to jog him again.

Celia held out her arms to Emmeline. 'I'll take Euan. You're exhausted.' She sat on the sofa with him, red and bawling, patting his forehead. She felt a little ashamed, but she didn't think she loved him as much as she had Albert and Lily when they were born. Perhaps it was because she'd been there at the time, but still, she found Euan cross and more difficult to soothe. She patted his forehead again.

Jonathan had found a wooden clothes peg on the side. He'd taken out a pen and he was drawing a face on it. 'See,' he said to Lily. 'I'll make you a doll.'

Even Albert was looking, watching Jonathan draw on a face. 'Do you have a piece of material?' he said. 'I could make it a dress.' Emmeline looked around and found a red scrap.

'See,' said Jonathan. 'You shall go to the ball.' He pulled out a piece of string from his pocket, and a knife, and cut a small piece, tied it around the peg and in a bow. 'The finest gown.'

Lily picked up the doll, smiling.

'Does she have a name?' said Jonathan.

'Princess,' she pondered. 'Princess London.'

'Princess London it is. Do you think she would like to drive around in your brother's car?'

She nodded. 'I think so, very much.'

Celia watched as he charmed the children, made Lily talk, made Albert share his toy. Emmeline took Euan off to settle him. 'What do they usually have for supper?'

'Chicken, maybe.'

'Let's have a look.' He hauled Lily up into his arms and they set off to the kitchen.

'Where did you learn this?' Celia asked, following him with Euan.

'What?' he said, perching Lily on the side and peering into the cupboard.

'This. Children.' He looked so incongruous in the kitchen, like a giant.

He shrugged, pulled out some eggs, broke them in a bowl. 'I help my sisters sometimes.' He held the bowl out to Lily. 'Want to beat the eggs?'

She took it from him.

Two hours later, the children were settled in bed and Emmeline was asleep on the sofa. 'Incredible,' said Celia, looking around. 'I've never seen it so quiet here. It takes us hours to get Albert into bed. You're a magician.'

He laughed. 'They're cute kids.'

'You really came all the way over from New York to put the children to bed?'

'Why not?'

She laughed.

'I think Emmeline will sleep properly now. Poor thing, she's exhausted.'

'She's fast asleep.' He paused. 'So why don't we go out?'

She gazed at him. 'Well.' She wasn't doing anything else. She normally went to bed with Emmeline, in case one of the children woke in the night. But they looked sound asleep. 'I don't know. I never go out.' She had with Tom in Baden Baden, with Arthur. The VAD dance didn't count, not really. 'I don't think I should. What if I'm seen?'

'Well, I could find somewhere quiet. And if you put on your hat, no one will see.'

'I should go to sleep.'

'Just for a little while. There must be places around here. And you haven't eaten. Nor me.'

She shook her head. She hadn't, that was true. She didn't normally, usually ate some bread and cheese after the children were in bed.

'Come on, it won't be long. Let's go out. Just for a little while.' She nodded. He'd come so far. And part of her thought that if she went with him, they could be like they were, young again, how she had been before she found out how her brother died – and everything that followed. She went to the bathroom, plumped her hair. They left quietly. She closed the door softly behind her.

They went to a small restaurant he knew, near his hotel. It was run by a jolly Italian man who called Jonathan *signor*, Celia *signorina*. They ate the fish and sauce, and a pudding of pastry and cream. She drank wine. 'I don't want to talk,' she said. 'Not really. You talk to me. Tell me about America. What it looks like.'

So he did. He talked about New York and skyscrapers and places where people danced to fast music, dark doorways, shops full of things, the museums and the art. She listened, let his voice flow. She thought of when she offered herself to him at the Ritz, after seeing the pretty girls like butterflies. He said no, you're not like them, and she supposed she wasn't, but she had wanted to be like them for a moment, happy, free.

'What are you thinking?' he said.

She blushed, looked down at her coffee. 'About the Ritz.'

His face flushed too. She saw his eyes change.

'I remember it,' he said. 'Everything.'

She met his eyes.

The sky was lowering when they came out of the restaurant. 'It's about to rain,' he said.

She shrugged. 'I like the rain.'

They set off towards Bedford Square. At a corner, he clasped her hands. 'Come back with me?' he said. 'Please.'

And she did. She couldn't stop herself from going into the hotel room with him, hurrying past the man on the desk, up the dingy stairs and into a shabby-looking bedroom, probably how they all were in Bloomsbury. 'Come,' he said. 'Sit here.' And she did, next to him on the bed. If she did it, put out her arms to him, then she'd forget the others, forget everything. Be new.

After a week, they were back in the Old Bailey. Mr Bird had asked to interview Mr Werth once more. He was called and went through his story again, just as he had the first time. Mr Werth's declaration that Arthur had pushed Louisa was even more cataclysmic for the gallery now. Someone shouted, 'Shame!' and another, 'Murderer!' The policeman signalled up at his colleague in the gallery and the clerk banged his hammer for silence.

Celia tried to concentrate. She flushed miserably. How could she have gone back with Jonathan to his hotel? When her brother was close to being hanged. What if a newspaper had heard of it? Then they would have written about her: decadent, disgraceful. She felt sickened by herself. He'd come to call twice after that night, played with the children. But it was strange, awkward, and she felt even more that she had been in bed with ghosts. He was in the gallery. He'd asked to accompany her, but she'd said it was better not to. She fixed her gaze on Arthur, not looking up. She supposed Tom was sitting up there too, shook the thought away.

Then Mr Bird came forward. He looked at the jury. The clerk banged again. Mr Bird cleared his throat.

'So, Mr Werth, you have given us – well – quite a story.'

Werth didn't reply.

'Quite a story, have you not?'

'It is all true, sir.'

'Well, I wonder at that. You know, we all remember matters differently. Last week I said to my wife that we had walked home past two friends. But we hadn't. There'd only been one. But I could have sworn it was two. These things happen, do they not, Mr Werth?'

'Not on this occasion, no, sir. I remember what I saw.'

'But do you remember exactly? Can you tell me – say, using this courtroom – exactly where in relation to you were Mr de Witt and Mrs de Witt when you first saw them walking near the cliff? For example, were they as near to you as I am?'

Mr Werth shook his head. 'No.'

'Where, then? The distance of Mr Cedric and his esteemed friend?'

He shook his head again. 'A little further.'

'Then perhaps the officer at the back of the room?' Mr Bird pointed towards a constable leaning against the panel. The man stood up, looking surprised. Celia could see the people above them craning to get a glimpse of the constable, trying to work out the distances.

'I suppose so. Yes. That's probably about right.'

'But we cannot deal in suppositions here. We need certainty. We could adjust and alter the distance all afternoon and indeed tomorrow, if it is necessary. We all have plenty of time.' The constable was blushing with the attention focused on him.

Celia saw a flicker in the judge's eye, a grimace. As a spectator, she supposed, she would have found it vaguely amusing. Now it made her angry. *You can watch until we get the facts right.* It was alright for him. No one was going to hang *him*.

Mr Werth was silent. 'No, sir. I think that is correct. The distance of the constable.'

'Very well. The distance of the constable it is. Certainly, you are indeed close enough to see some – facial expressions. And probably close enough to hear some sort of cry.'

'Yes, sir.' Celia could see that Mr Cedric was gesturing at the judge, trying to catch his attention.

Mr Bird forged on. 'Could you oblige us, Constable? A small cry if you would?'

The judge leant forward. 'I take it that this spectacle has a point, Mr Bird?'

'Of course, my lord. I assure you.'

'I will allow it to continue then. For the moment.'

The constable was staring at Mr Bird in consternation. Celia felt for him.

'Come now, officer. I am sure you can oblige us with a slight cry.'

The man nodded, dumbly.

'Do go ahead. We await it.'

The constable, red-faced, made a small, strangled noise. It sounded more as if he was choking on a piece of fruit than blind panic, Celia supposed, her heart sinking at the horridness of it all, the fact that some strange man was pretending to be Louisa. *Boy my greatness.* Hadn't Shakespeare's Cleopatra said that? It was all horrible.

'Well, I could hear that rather well,' said Mr Bird. 'And I am only a little nearer the constable than you, and considerably older than you. My wife tells me I never hear her.'

There was an appreciative chuckle from the gallery. They liked the joke, Celia thought, defusing with its ordinariness the strange horror of asking a stranger to cry out as if falling over a cliff.

'So we can conclude that you could hear Mrs de Witt perfectly well.'

'I said I could,' replied Mr Werth. He looked annoyed already. Mr Bird was getting to him.

'Now. Could you hear it over wind, Mr Werth? For my understanding is that the day was very windy. And by the cliffs, it must have been awfully so.'

'It was a little windy, yes. Not by me.'

'Not by you?'

'No, sir. It was windy beside Mr de Witt. But not me.'

'Really? For surely if you were on the same cliff, you must be subject to the same weather conditions?'

'We were not on the same spot of land.' Mr Werth was exasperated now, spat out the words. The jury members were writing fast.

'Oh. You were not on the same spot of land? I see. But would we not say, if this were grass under my feet, that our constable and

I were on the same patch of grass? I feel sure that if he was to sense wind in his hair, then so should I.' Mr Bird patted his head. 'Of course I have very little hair these days.' The gallery laughed again. They were siding with him and his little jokes, leaving Mr Werth and his cross replies.

'There is still a distance,' Mr Werth said, almost sulkily.

'Well, you know, I am confused, Mr Werth. On one hand, you tell me you are so close to our constable that we can see his facial expressions. But then you say you don't feel the same wind. To me, I have to say, that is a mystery. Something – something does not add up.' He tapped his pen on the wood. Celia cringed a little. Surely this was too obvious. But the gallery above were enjoying it – and the jury were watching intently.

'You see, Mr Werth, I suggest that you were much further from Mr de Witt than you remember. It is my proposal that you were at least twice the distance that you are now from the constable. And in that case, since it was so terribly windy, I propose that it would have been almost impossible to hear anything. And I also suggest that you could have barely seen the faces of either Mr de Witt or Mrs de Witt. When the wind gets in my eyes, I squint and can't always see. I expect the same is true for you.'

'I saw them.'

'Are you sure?'

'Yes.'

Mr Bird paused, walked a little to the side. 'But, you know, Mr Werth … when one reads the police reports of the afternoon, they are terribly clear. Now, we can assert that before you ran forward, you were standing more or less in the spot where the police officer found your wife sitting?'

'Yes, sir.'

'But the police officer asserts that she was at a distance of almost a hundred feet. That is much further than you are now from our constable at the back of the room. More than twice as far.' There was coughing and rustling from the gallery. Mr Bird looked around the room.

'That would make a distance of about the length – well, from the constable perhaps to that other officer over there. Much, much further, would you agree?'

Mr Werth looked down. 'Yes, sir. I suppose so. I am not so good at judging distances by eye.'

'So are you saying that you were mistaken in our initial discussion of distance? That Mr and Mrs de Witt were actually a hundred feet away from you?'

'I don't know. It didn't feel that way. Maybe the officer was wrong.'

'The officer was wrong? When he measured where your wife was sitting? This may be the case, of course. But we are benefited by the fact that the officer was a local man. He knew the cliffs so well that he didn't have to measure distance. In fact, he noted your wife's position by saying that she was sitting a foot to the left of a prominent stone which he knew well. The stone had apparently been a favourite spot for his own children. Do you remember the stone?'

'Possibly.'

'Well, I quite understand the officer. I am sure all of us who are parents here remember the certain places that our offspring wished to visit over and over during their childhood. But I wanted to be sure. So I went to the stone myself, accompanied by my clerk, Mr Honeywell. We took some photographs of the place itself.' He walked back to his seat and Mr Honeywell passed him a bundle of photographs. 'If I have permission to hand these to Mr Werth?'

The judge held out his hand. 'If I might look at them first, Mr Bird.'

'Of course, Your Honour.' Mr Bird handed the photographs to the clerk.

The judge regarded them, slowly. 'There are ten photographs here of the cliff and the area around it. There are photographs of the stone that has been discussed. Allowed. Mr Werth may peruse them, then they should be handed to the jury. The jury may ask to see these again. As may I.'

'Yes, sir.' Mr Bird took the photographs from the clerk and handed them to Mr Werth.

'Do you see the stone on these photographs, Mr Werth? I believe it is photograph four?'

'I do.' Mr Werth's voice was quiet.

'And could you say that this was where your wife was sitting?'

'She might have been. You could say she might have been.'

'And would you agree with our measurement that this is about a hundred feet away from the side of the cliff?'

'If you say so, sir.'

'Indeed. I think it is actually a little more than a hundred. Mr Honeywell and I put it at one hundred and two feet and one inch. And, if I recall correctly from my geography lessons as a schoolboy, we lose a little of a cliff every year, and so, nearly five years ago, you might have been separated from Mr Witt by a distance of one hundred and two feet and another half foot or so.'

Mr Werth dropped his head. 'Perhaps.'

'As I said earlier, Mr Werth, we cannot deal in probabilities. We must have certainties. As I do not need to remind anyone in the room, a man's life is at stake. We must be absolutely sure, sure beyond reasonable doubt, that Mr de Witt purposely pushed his wife over the cliff. And I don't need to remind you, sir, that your evidence is key here. So we must be entirely sure. Can you definitely say you were at a distance of fifty feet from Mr de Witt?'

Mr Werth paused, shook his head. He said something, very slight.

'Could you repeat that, Mr Werth? I am not sure everyone here quite heard.'

'No,' said Mr Werth, more loudly. 'No, I can't.'

'You were closer? Or further?'

'Further.'

'How much further? I suggest you were not fifty, but over one hundred feet away from Mr de Witt. And that, as we all know, is a most significant distance. Many of us cannot see well over the length of a hundred feet, Mr Werth. I myself could not without my spectacles. Do you, sir, use spectacles?'

There was a silence. Mr Werth looked down.

'Do you use spectacles, Mr Werth?'

The judge leant forward. 'Answer the question, please, Mr Werth.'

'Yes, sir.'

'For short sight or long sight?'

'Short sight.'

'Which means you cannot see clearly things far away?'

'Yes, sir.'

'And were you wearing them when Mrs de Witt fell over the cliff?'

'No, sir.'

There was a gasp from the gallery. The judge frowned at his papers. Mr Werth looked down.

'If His Honour will permit me, I have an experiment. I would say that the back of the gallery is about a hundred feet away. Would His Honour agree?'

'About that, Mr Bird.'

'Thank you, Your Honour. Now, at the back of the court is a lady who will now stand up.' He waved up at the gallery and the lady stood. 'That, Mr Werth, is Miss Sillen, who occasionally does some extra typing for me. An excellent secretary, and a very attractive young lady, as you can see, perhaps. Or perhaps not. Could you tell me the style of her hair, Mr Werth?'

Mr Werth looked down. 'No, sir.'

'Or the colour of her eyes?'

'No.'

'Could you tell me if she is smiling or frowning?'

'I cannot.'

'And what is the cut of her coat?'

'I cannot say, sir.'

'Can you see her at all, Mr Werth?'

'I confess I cannot really see her, sir.'

Mr Bird waved up. 'I shall not ask Miss Sillen to say "no", for this is a courtroom that is quite silent. But I have been to the rock in question and the wind is very high. I propose that no one a hundred feet away, in conditions of wind, could hear a shout of anything. I would be very happy to take His Honour to the spot to show him quite how windy it is.'

'I don't think that will be necessary,' said the judge. 'Thank you.'

Mr Bird waved up again. 'Thank you, Miss Sillen. Most kind.' He turned back to Mr Werth.

'Are you sure, Mr Werth, that you heard the word "no"?'

Mr Werth's head was drooping low.

'Are you quite sure? Might it not just have been a trick of the wind? The wind tricks us, after all. It could have been any sound. Perhaps even a child crying out when he had lost his balloon. Anything. Are you quite sure it was Mrs de Witt? Remember, sir, a man is on trial for his life.'

Mr Werth raised his eyes. He shook his head.

'Are you saying you cannot be sure?'

'I cannot be sure.' Mr Werth sat back, his face crushed. Celia stared at him. He'd misremembered, captured in the glamour of it like everybody in the gallery, all those people writing in the newspapers.

'Thank you.' Mr Bird turned to the judge. 'Your Honour, I propose that Mr Werth did not see anything of use at all. Few of us could, unless we had quite marvellous eyesight. And Mr Werth's eyesight is not strong. He may have thought he saw something. He may have been caught up in the excitement of the story. But he did actually see nothing and so his evidence that he saw Mr de Witt push Mrs de Witt over the cliff must be entirely discounted.

'It happens, when one is part of great trials, that one makes mistakes, one is caught up in the excitement, but actually what one recalls is not correct. And without that evidence, we have nothing but some hearsay about an unhappy marriage, in which, as I have proved, there has been no suggestion of violence.

'Mr de Witt may not have been the most attentive husband. Or they may have been very happy. We have had nothing but a succession of circumstantial accounts. As I said I suspect, with the exception of His Honour, many of us gentlemen here have given way to the occasional shabby impulse when it comes to the treatment of our dearest wives. Mr de Witt was indeed guilty of keeping his marriage a secret, but that is hardly a sin, and I might remind you all that Mrs de Witt also chose to keep it a secret.

'Mr de Witt and Mrs de Witt were very unwise to go near the edge. That is the foolishness of the young. They have indeed paid the highest price for their foolishness. She is dead, he is on trial. But, Your Honour, ladies and gentlemen of the jury, he is no murderer and there has clearly been no crime.'

There was the sound of a mass rush as the journalists in the gallery ran out, pushing past everyone, stamping on feet, flinging themselves forward, seized by immediacy, every face looking forwards, quick and directed to file the story.

FORTY-ONE

London, March 1926

Celia

'To us!' Arthur said, holding up his glass of champagne. 'To the family!'

It was three weeks after the trial. Already Celia had forgotten the day when she and Emmeline had walked out of the court – and Arthur had followed behind them. It was a blur, a painfully bright blur.

'Don't speak to the papers,' Mr Bird advised, as they were bundling out of the building. 'However much money they offer you.' So they didn't. Arthur came back with Celia and Emmeline and stayed a few nights, then took his own flat.

After two days of coverage on the trial, the newspapers moved to a different story and the pages were full of discussion about arguments in the House of Lords.

'Thank you, ladies,' Mr Bird had said, shaking hands after court. It was all over. And yet Celia couldn't believe it. 'You'll be in shock for a while,' Mr Bird had said. She woke up every morning, thinking about the trial – then realising it was over. Everyone knew Arthur was innocent. He was a free man.

'To the family!' Emmeline raised a glass, her hand shaky. They were in the Ritz, supposedly to celebrate Arthur's freedom. Celia thought how strange it was. During the trial, she would have done anything to see Arthur free, to be sitting next to him in a restaurant. Now, there was something strange and dissatisfying about it. The words they said didn't work, came out clumsy and wrong. Rudolf was ill and confused, drooped silently over his plate, eating slowly. He and Verena had taken a car up from Stoneythorpe, but still the journey had been difficult and too slow – and now Verena was fretting about the expense. Arthur was taking them out. 'Have anything you like!' he said, waving his hand across the menu. Rudolf and Verena couldn't, though, they looked at the thing miserably, made sure, Celia noted, to choose the most inexpensive dishes. Emmeline looked sick and pale and Mr Janus stared into space, distracted – occasionally coming out to shake his head at the excess of it all. 'This cost a whole year's wages,' he said to Celia, pointing to a bottle of wine. 'Don't they understand it's disgraceful?'

He coughed loudly every time a waiter walked by. 'How much do you think they get paid? A pittance, I imagine, to smile and serve us like lackeys. We need a world in which there are no servants. No restaurants. These places make us into infants, sitting here waiting to be fed. No one fought for more *restaurants*, did they?'

The Ritz didn't look like it was closing any time soon. The chandelier glittered over the cream marble tables and ornate wallpaper. Every table was occupied with men and women eating and drinking together, young and old, all rich. The women wore beautifully embroidered short gowns in a variety of colours – blush peach, pale yellow, mint. Celia and Emmeline looked dowdy.

Celia's mind was full of the last time she'd been in the Ritz, drinking with Jonathan during the war. Then the room had whirled and glittered around her. Now it looked much bigger and even a little dreary, the curtains too short, and none of the women she saw had the beauty of those girls from back then. Perhaps she had invented it all, she thought. Jonathan had gone off to Edinburgh, some sort of business. He'd come to say goodbye to the children before he left. 'Please write,' he'd said. 'Even if it's only short.'

And none of them fitted in, either. Arthur might have, before prison, but now he looked thin and old, trying too hard, a bad actor pretending to laugh. It had touched him, Celia thought, those months in prison, stuck in that place with all those guards and goodness knows who. She wondered again what they'd done to him there, if the other men had hit him, attacked him because he was rich or, even worse, because he was a man who hadn't fought. She'd tried to ask him, the day of the verdict.

'It was fine, little sister,' he said, shrugging. 'Glad to be out, that's all.'

She'd asked him about the other men, the food, were there *rats*? But he batted her away. 'I'm a new man now. That's all in the past. I don't want to dwell on it.'

She tried to go over the trial, the horror of it, how they'd been so worried, but he shook his head again. 'I'll think about all that on my death bed. Right now, it is time to look to the future. I have a new life now.'

And he did, she supposed it was true. He was rich now. It was almost awful to think it but he was rich, very much so. The Deerhurst estate had released half of Louisa's money, were trying to hold on to the other half because the marriage had been 'irregular'. But Mr Pemberton said it was not going to work. Arthur and Louisa had been married and so the money was his. There was no one else for it to go to, really, except some sort of distant cousin on Louisa's father's side, who Mr Pemberton thought wouldn't put up too much of a fight.

Celia knew it was fair for Arthur to have Louisa's money, that any husband deserved his wife's estate. And yet it was dreadful to hear about it, think that now, in the Ritz, they were eating lamb and fish bought with Deerhurst money, that they wouldn't have had it at all if she hadn't fallen.

In the days after the trial, she'd woken up every night, sweating in the dark. Mr Werth's voice – 'She shouted *no!*' – had been in her head. In the daytime, doing her usual round of activities – looking after the twins, soothing Euan, going to the shops – if ever the normal train of thought stopped or she was left alone, she heard a woman screaming in her mind and she knew it was Louisa.

She looked at Arthur over the table, drinking champagne, offering Rudolf his lobster. She supposed, knew even, that he must hear the screams too and that was why he was so keen to eat, drink, tell jokes and make them all smile; he was like everyone had been after the war ended, throwing those violent parties, twirling in feathers and shiny gowns, so desperate to forget.

'Are you listening, Celia?' Emmeline nudged her. 'Arthur was telling us his plans.'

'Oh.' Celia looked at her brother, his eyes shining. It must have been the champagne or the food or perhaps just the reflection of the chandelier, but he'd become the old Arthur again, the lines of his face filled out, his body greater. He had a plan, she realised. He'd invited them here to tell them it.

'I want to talk about America,' he said. 'That's where everything is. America! There is no point staying here any more. Britain is a joke. We are over, done. There is nothing now. We can't make any money here. Winter Meats is over, Father. You have to see that.'

Rudolf nodded, gazing at his plate. Celia wasn't sure he was hearing any of it.

Arthur wasn't stopping, he was still talking, waving his hands. 'I'm going to take the company to America. We still have our reputation, our name is known. We'll change the name back to de Witt Meats. That's the answer. We're going to borrow against what's left of the company and put it in American shares. They're going up so quickly, they rise like you wouldn't believe. So that's what we'll do. We can have enough to start building a new empire there. Just think of them, millions and millions of Americans, who all need to eat meat. They all love meat! They will love our produce.'

'Stock markets are fool's gold,' said Mr Janus. 'Why don't you start by actually doing something there, then investing? You could build a shop in New York.'

Arthur waved his hand impatiently. 'Yes, yes, that as well. But the stock market is the way to go. I'm going to set up meetings. No time to lose! We have to strike now! Otherwise our chance will be gone. In just a few months, it will be over. Now is our moment to make money!'

But you have money, Celia wanted to say. *Louisa's money. Isn't that enough?* And yet she imagined those great shining towers of

New York she'd seen in pictures, all of them advertising de Witt Meats. American radio stations talking about the company.

'I've read about this stock market business in *The Times*,' she said. 'They did say it was the time to invest now. But they also said that you need a lot.'

'Well, of course you need a lot. That's what I'm talking about. We can't just stick in a little capital. We have to play big. Fortune favours the brave, isn't that right?'

'Brave or foolish?' said Mr Janus.

Arthur ignored him. 'This is for the future of the family. Mama, wouldn't you like to see Stoneythorpe improved? You could have the money to do the roof.'

Verena inclined her head. 'That would be nice.'

'Well, it's more than nice. Some might say that we'd be lost without it. You could get Stoneythorpe back to how it once was. Grand again. Otherwise, it's just collapsing, really, isn't it? You'd have to sell it.'

Rudolf straightened up. 'I'll never sell it,' he said, voice thin and weak.

Arthur slapped the table. 'There you go! America is the answer.'

Rudolf looked at Celia. 'America,' he said, shaking his head. Verena touched his shoulder. 'You go to America.'

'Husband,' Verena was saying. 'Quiet.'

'I agree,' said Arthur. 'Make a new start. No one would know me there.'

'Not you.' Rudolf pointed his finger. 'Her.'

'What do you mean, Papa?' asked Celia. 'Why America?'

'You have to go to America. That's where he is.'

'That's where *who* is?'

Emmeline was gazing at him. 'Papa? What do you mean?'

'It's where he is. As I said. He's in America.'

'No!' Verena grasped his hand. 'Husband, be quiet.'

Celia plucked at Emmeline's sleeve. 'What does he mean?' Her sister looked back, her face confused.

'America!' Rudolf said. He was looking past them, at the

chandelier hanging above the next table, throwing its pools of light over the four men sitting there. 'Go to America!'

Verena was holding his hand, gripping hard.

Celia looked around the table. 'What is he talking about?'

Mr Janus raised an eyebrow. 'Yes indeed. What are you talking about?'

'It is time to tell me!' said Celia. 'I'm not leaving here until one of you tells me what you're going on about. Any one of you will do.'

Emmeline shrugged. 'I don't know.'

Rudolf stood up. 'You need to go to America.'

Celia stood too. 'Why? Why do I need to go there?'

Verena was trying to pull Rudolf down. 'Husband. Let's enjoy our dinner. This is all just talk.' She looked at her children, round-eyed at the table. 'It's nothing. He doesn't know what he's saying.'

'What are you saying, Papa?' asked Celia.

'Yes,' said Arthur. 'What is all this cryptic stuff? I'm trying to enjoy myself. Why does dear Celia need to go to America?'

Rudolf smiled and it spread across his face, beatific. 'She must! Because Michael is there.'

Verena screamed and jumped up, far too late. Rudolf was staring across at Celia, smiling.

Celia stared at her father. 'Michael is dead, Father. He was killed in the war.'

'Not that Michael. Your son. Didn't you know?'

The table was silent. 'Well,' said Arthur. 'Well.'

Emmeline turned in her chair and stared at Celia. Verena was covering her face with her hands.

Celia shook her head. 'No. I didn't know,' she whispered. 'You all told me he was dead.' She was still standing, the world turning around her. 'Where in America?'

She could hear, just behind her, that Emmeline had begun to sob. Arthur was drinking fast from his glass.

Rudolf smiled across at her, dumbly. She stared at Verena. 'Where in America?'

'I don't know.'

Arthur rolled his eyes. 'Why don't you tell, Mother? If this is true. Otherwise we'll be here all night.' He shook his head. 'Put Celia out of her misery, can't you?'

'I can't remember,' Verena whispered, gazing at the table. 'Emmeline?'

'I don't know anything.' She looked horrified, and Celia believed her.

Rudolf looked ahead, past all of them. 'The baby was taken and given to a religious agency. We said it had been a maid's and she wanted him to have a better life in America. They sent him on the boat.'

Celia was still standing, staring at her father. 'On his *own?*'

'I believe they took them over in batches. Accompanied by nurses. Anyway, that's where he was sent.'

'And then what? He was just to sit in New York by himself?'

'He was sent to a kind family north of New York,' Verena said, stiffly. 'A farming family. He's their child now. He's happy.'

'You've received letters from them?'

'Not exactly letters. We received a report from the agency last year. They said he was helping on the farm, growing up strong.'

'Or cheap labour,' said Mr Janus, but quietly.

'I want to see that report. And then I will go and find him. You're right, Papa. I have to go to America.'

Verena shook her head. 'He's their child now, Celia. Not yours. They've brought him up. He calls them mother and father. You can't go and interrupt their lives.'

'He's mine.'

'The agency won't give you the address, anyway,' said Emmeline. 'One of Mr Sparks's friends did the same. She's changed her mind now. But they said she signed away all her rights and can't see him.'

'I didn't sign anything.'

'We did for you,' said Verena. 'Look, Celia, what's done is done. It was for the best, can't you see? He has a better life there. He's happy. He has a mother and a father.'

'He already had a mother.'

'Children need a father too.'

And in that minute, Celia's blood rose. She was bigger, angrier, furious, her heart beating, her mind moving her forward, her face on fire. She was walking towards her mother. There was someone else, another voice in her mind. Her mother shrank back. Celia reached up her hand. She could bring it down on Verena's face and everything would be better, over, clear once more. Then two arms wrapped around her from behind. She was up off the ground and she was screaming. 'Stop it!' Arthur shouted. Men were coming towards them from all across the restaurant. She looked down, saw her mother, face all fear. 'Let me go,' she said to Mr Janus, who was holding her. 'You can let me go now.'

Arthur waved at the men. 'We're quite alright, thank you. Actually, two more bottles of champagne.' The tables alongside stared again then turned back to their dinner.

Emmeline was round by her mother, coaxing her back on to the chair. Rudolf sat, eyes closed, clutching himself. Celia leant against Mr Janus, let him take her back to her chair. She put her head in her hands.

'Come now, everyone,' said Arthur. 'This is too much drama. We are disgracing ourselves in public. Celia, you wanted to know where your son was. Now you do. And I am decided. I shall be going to New York in the summer to make us rich. If you wish to come with me and try to find the boy, you can. You could always enlist the help of that friend of Michael's who used to write to you. What was his name?'

'Jonathan Corrigan,' said Emmeline. 'He was rich. We saw him recently, didn't we, Celia?' Her look was pointed.

'Exactly. He can only direct us to further and better investment. America is the place to put our money.'

'I am not sure about the investment—' Mr Janus began. Arthur shouted over him.

'It is time to celebrate. We shall celebrate America.'

The men came with the bottles of champagne and the glasses, started laying them on the table. Celia heard the stuff being poured into hers.

'Come!' said Arthur. 'Let us all be upstanding. To America and our marvellous future there!'

And Celia looked up at Arthur, the bright chandelier behind him, the reflection from the edges of the glass, the candles flickering, and even though the shock in her heart was heavy, the thought of the boat arriving in New York, Michael waiting, rose up in her; hope unfurling, reaching for the light. She held her glass high. 'To America!' she said.

EPILOGUE

He started playing truth or dare at Winchester Hall. It was the only way he could get through that first term. He'd dare himself to hold the water in his mouth for longer at lunch, until his eyes were watering and he was nearly sick. Or he'd see how long he could push the nail under his desk into his knee before the pain was too much. He made bargains – he'd hold his breath for this long, and then the next teacher wouldn't mock him for not knowing the answer. Or when he was on his own, he'd hold his arm out until it wobbled with pain and then the other boys would leave him alone at lunchtime, not hit him when he walked past or throw stones at his back. Sometimes it worked. Sometimes it did not. But he did it over and over, banking on those few times when it worked and he managed to hold his breath for two minutes and then Lethbridge and the rest didn't come over to hit him while they walked down to the cricket field. He felt flooded with relief and lightness, knew that the game had worked.

By Harrow, for the most part, nobody was hitting him at break time and because he'd grown tall, he was decent at cricket, which helped. Everyone picked on Petherlet, a skinny, small boy whose father had saved every penny to send him to Harrow and had no money for anything else. Sometimes, when they were pushing him around after lunch, hitting him or chasing him down the corridor, Arthur would walk past. Petherlet would look at him, eyes begging for help. It made Arthur uneasy. He started to wonder whether he could see that Arthur had once been the one that everyone hated. Maybe Petherlet *sensed* the weakness. Arthur felt sick at the thought. If Petherlet could, then maybe the others would too, and so perhaps they'd move away from Petherlet and he'd be back where he started, attacked, the weak chick in the bunch, pecked at by the others.

So he started to play the game again. Just in case. He wasn't going back to where he had been! But this time, he played it harder. He said – *how close can I get to death?* Because if you got to touch it, really touch it, and then pulled yourself back, you'd have luck that would keep you alive for ever.

So, that first time, he held his breath for longer than he ever had, nearly three minutes. He could feel his eyes popping out, his face turning blue. And he still did it! Then he strode past Petherlet, trying to hide at the back of the dining room, knowing that he wouldn't be caught any more! He did something new every day – held his breath, put his hand over his nose, tried to sneeze with his eyes open (Mr Bills had said you immediately died if you did that). Sometimes, when he felt safe, he did easier things, like pull out whole clumps of hair or try to tease up as much of a fingernail as he could. Really, though, all that could grow dull. He wanted more, something that would be truly exciting. But the school area was tediously safe. No river to throw himself in or, which would be even better, a bridge he could suspend himself from, feel the wind pull through his hair before he scrambled up again, still alive.

So he had to do it at Stoneythorpe. There was a deep pond at the back of the house, under an overhanging willow. It was a spot that Celia liked to sit in, so he had to be careful to go there when she was occupied in the house. He would hang out on the tree, over the pond, his pockets full of stones, weighted down so that if he fell in, he'd truly drown. He did it every morning, when Celia was off riding horses with Tom or whatever it was she did. He lay on the thin branch, crept further, felt it bend, made his bargain that no one would hit him again. Funny, how he'd met Louisa when he'd been doing precisely that.

And yet, he knew, it only really mattered if he was at school at the *time*. He had the chance only once – on a school geography trip to a great bridge near Bristol. Then, while all the rest had been sketching out the struts, with Mr Wilton shouting against the wind, he'd crept away, to the cliffs themselves. Mr Wilton hadn't noticed, nor the other master and the teacher-pleasers like Lucas, the type to say, 'Look, sir, de Witt is up there!' – they were deep in drawing. He walked up on to the bridge, stared down at the swirling river below. He crawled out between the gaps in the iron railings, sat on the side, dangled his feet over the edge. If he pitched himself forward just an inch, then he'd nearly be in. Two inches and he'd fall. And he doubted he could live, not if he fell from such a height. He shuffled forwards a quarter inch or so. He felt the air slash against his face. He looked down. *Come to me!* said the water. *Come!* He was close to death, closer than he'd ever been. And then he heard Mr Wilton shouting.

'De Witt! What the hell are you doing? Get here immediately.' The teacher was standing at the edge of the bridge. 'Now!' He was shouting commands but Arthur heard the fear in his voice. He turned, put out a hand to the water.

'Don't do that!' Wilton shouted. 'Get back.'

The other boys were watching now. Petherlet looked the sickest of all. *Don't you care for me, you weakling*, Arthur wanted to shout. Instead he waved at Mr Wilton. He looked down at the water, how close to it he was. Just a tiny movement forwards would be all it took. He would *really* know. He held his body, paused for a second, then moved back. He pulled himself under the iron railings, on to the bridge. Then, behind Mr Wilton, the boys began to clap, the applause rolling up around them. He knew that they were doing it because they were relieved, they'd really thought he might die, it was the release of panic. But in his mind, it was something else – it was that hanging so far out on the bridge, nearly touching the force of the water, had made him see something they would never see. He'd seen God.

He stopped playing the game after he finished school. No need. In the adult world, no one put you in a corner, chased you down the corridor. You could find another corridor to walk down, another place to be. If he ever saw the look in another man's eyes of *I know you are weak* he would leave the place as quick as he could. The old game was for children.

But then it began again. With Louisa.

When the men he knew talked about marriage, they said the younger the better. Then they'll listen to you. Louisa was perfect. And even more so when it came to his family. Through her, he'd get their respect. His parents and Celia had spent so much time flurrying around, preparing for her, and then when she arrived they ignored her. She came to them, but she fell in love with him. She needed him, more than anyone else. It was typical of his parents, he thought, to fuss over someone when you didn't actually know them, then leave them alone when you met them. *I was doing her a favour!* he wanted to say. *Didn't you see?*

They never saw. You would have thought, he reflected, that when he came home from Paris after the war ended, having lost Michael, they might treasure him, Arthur. No. He would always be the wrong one. He could tell by the way his mother looked at him. He'd done well in Paris, made money with his business importing goods for shops. But they didn't care. Michael had given himself for his country, which was all that mattered. They let Arthur live at Stoneythorpe, gave him his room. But they didn't love him.

He'd go back to Paris, he thought at the time, after a year. Once things had calmed down over there and he could do business again. It was a shame to have had to rush back to England, leaving everything behind. But discretion was the better part of valour, really it was. Arthur just thought he'd wait. Then he'd met Louisa.

No one but him saw what he did for her. But they would, he thought, once he took her away and they came back married. They'd be pleased with him, keeping her money in the family. Of course, as it turned out, they weren't pleased with him taking Louisa away, not at all, they sent letters demanding he bring her back, calling him all sorts of names. So then he knew that he had to keep her with him – he had to make her marry him. They didn't love him – but they might if he was with her.

And yet, he hadn't done things right for her. He'd meant to, really he had. But he found her annoying, he was ashamed to say, irritating, like a child. Those people who said *the younger the better* were wrong. In Paris, he'd been used to sophisticated women, or at least grown ones who could choose their own gown, hold a conversation, even make themselves a cup of tea in his cold rooms. Louisa could do nothing. She wanted his advice on the tiniest thing – she needed him, always needed him. He couldn't count the times he'd had to come down to help her search in her room for a ribbon or a pencil or some other trivial thing. She fussed over what she ate, what she wore, even what she said. She made friends with the most idiotic of people. The infatuation with Munsden had been the last straw – and that cretinous mermaid costume … that's when he knew she wasn't *like* other people. He'd have to get her away.

He was in over his head, he knew that. It was too late to go back, say he'd made a mistake, here is Louisa, let's return to how we were before. They married the day they were leaving London, two men from the club as witnesses, and he paid the minister too much money for the convenience. He took her for lunch afterwards and he felt the roof closing in. He was in a corridor, being chased, and he couldn't get out and find a different one. So he began to play the game again. If he got close to death, then he'd find an answer. Something would come and make things clear. He'd be free.

In Weymouth, in the gambling house he'd found near the station, he'd started holding his breath again. He wasn't as good at it as he'd been at school – too much smoking, he supposed. Sometimes he could only manage two minutes before he felt like his whole face was blue. He tried walking down by the cliffs, but they were not high. And drinking didn't help, nor did smoking. To play the game, you had to almost die, running out of breath or falling. Not just because you'd smoked too much.

He liked Louisa less and less. The very sound of her breathing annoyed him. Still she couldn't do a thing for herself, and he found himself saying, 'I'm not your father!'

He couldn't get away from her. He'd hoped that leaving London might help, give both of them a new life. Instead, it only reminded him of the liberty he'd had before, the ease.

He wandered around Weymouth, hearing the calls of the prostitutes.

But it wasn't the same as in Paris, they were all money-grubbing, cared only about exactly how much, what you wanted to do, how long – you'd never get a full hour. His own girl from back then was probably some Normandy housewife now, with children, married to a farmer. He tried to see her in his mind, couldn't, not her face, not even her eyes.

No matter how many times he balanced himself on the edge of the port, dangling his legs over the side, nothing changed. He would go back and there would be Louisa in his rooms, sleeping with her mouth open. The game wasn't working.

Then, walking through Weymouth in the second week they were there, he saw a young girl take the arm of a man. He turned to her, about to shake her off. Then the man saw her face. He paused, nodded, let her take him forward. Arthur supposed she must be beautiful. What was it Stendhal had said, about beauty being the promise of happiness? The man must have seen freedom in her, liberty like Arthur had found that first time in Paris.

And then he understood. He would have to play the game with Louisa. Both of them were stuck, stranded in the same corner. If he wanted to be free, it was a case of freeing them both. He had to play it with *her*.

He explained it to her – taking her out to dinner, which always softened her up a bit – telling her that it was something he did to feel spiritual. Of course he didn't say it was to get out of being trapped.

'I don't understand,' she said. 'Shouldn't we pray to feel closer to God?'

'You'll understand once we do it,' he said. 'I promise.'

Still she didn't agree. So he had to find a new way to phrase it. If she loved him, she would do it with him. It would bring them closer! And telling her then, he really believed that it would, that somehow, if they both felt it, he would love her more, give her the affection she deserved. So that night he helped her up on to the harbour edge, and they balanced, looking down.

'I can't bear it!' she said. 'I'm cold!'

'I'll hold you,' he said. 'I will.'

She was weeping when he brought her down, clutching him. 'It's too dreadful!' she said. 'Promise me you won't do this again.'

He agreed, he had to of course. She was a stubborn girl. He understood that he'd have to make a longer campaign, do one or two risks, less frequently. Then he'd succeed. He did it himself, standing on the bridges, jumping in front of the traffic. But still, nothing changed. When they'd married, they had been bound together for life. She threw her arms around him, telling him how much she loved him. It took everything in him not to shrink back. He told himself to smile. Instead his eyes filled with poor bullied Petherlet and his tiny, fearful face. Even he was probably happier than Arthur now. Perhaps the game would help.

And then she told him the news. She put her hands on his, her face glowing. 'Are you not pleased, husband? It is a new start for us.'

He felt her hands. 'Of course. Of course I am pleased.'

'We will keep it just for us, at the moment. As it is so early. In a few months we can tell everyone. Your family will be pleased.'

'Oh, of course. They will.'

'Are you not proud of me, husband?'

He put his arm around her, held her close. His heart spread with clouds. They travelled to London and passed a week together, then took a place by the sea in Margate. Every day, the storm in him mounted. He knew he had to play the game, get closer to God. He decided he would make the day perfect. He told her he loved her, took her out for an expensive dinner, put his arm around her. He gave her flowers. Then the next day he took her to the cliffs. 'You will never see anywhere so beautiful,' he said. 'Never.'

He took her out to the cliff edge. 'Look down,' he said. 'Isn't it beautiful? Don't worry. I'll hold you.'

She was afraid, he knew it. He could feel her trembling. 'You can trust me,' he said. 'I'll look after you.'

'I want to go back,' she said.

He pretended not to hear her.

'Darling,' she began. But she couldn't finish. She was trembling so much.

'See,' he said in her ear, his voice low. 'Regard the beauties of nature.'

'But—'

'The world is ours,' he said, as muffled as the sound of a shell held against her ear. 'We could hold it in our hands.'

He felt her body, the flesh and blood of her through her ugly woollen gown. He looked down at the sea, churning, the drop of the cliffs. It was bigger than them, greater than anyone. It overwhelmed everything, everyone. It had its own rules.

He threw back his head, closed his eyes. And then, for the first time in years, the girl in Paris came truly into his head. It was her, really her, not the half versions of her he'd found before. This time, she spoke, looked at him, her eyes danced. She was truly there! She whispered, close in his ear, '*Qu'est ce que tu cherches?*'

'I don't know,' he whispered back. '*Liberté*. Freedom.'

'Well, then,' she said, a laugh in her voice. 'Be free.' He was young again, she was holding his hand on that first night in Paris. 'Do the thing that makes you free.'

'I can't,' he said. 'I can't.'

'Do it!' Her accent was entrancing, her eyelashes brushing softly on her cheek. 'But quickly. You only have one chance to live.'

She was right. He'd done it before. He did the thing and then he was free.

In one quick moment, he moved his body forward to the edge of the cliff. He pushed hard with his torso, his whole being, using all his might. Louisa didn't scream, she was too shocked to scream. He shoved hard with his hands. He felt her cling to him, try to clutch, and then her grip faded. She shrieked, an awful, desperate cry.

He lifted his head, whispered to the sky. 'I've done it,' he said. 'I have!'

There was no answer. The girl had gone.